SHANNIVAR

Book Two of
The Seven-Petaled Shield

Deborah J. Ross

DAW BOOKS, INC.

DONALD A. WOLLHEIM, FOUNDER

375 Hudson Street, New York, NY 10014

ELIZABETH R. WOLLHEIM
SHEILA E. GILBERT
PUBLISHERS

www.dawbooks.com

First Printing, December 2013
1 2 3 4 5 6 7 8 9

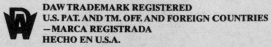

DAW TRADEMARK REGISTERED
U.S. PAT. AND TM. OFF. AND FOREIGN COUNTRIES
—MARCA REGISTRADA
HECHO EN U.S.A.

PRINTED IN THE U.S.A

**Shannivar could no longer hear the chanting
or feel the bone-deep shivers of her body.**

Winds bore her up as if she were no more than a downy feather from her clan's totem eagle. Overhead, storm clouds collided, and in their turbulent depths, colors writhed and coalesced. Shapes moved, no—one single shape, man-like and erect, but distorted. She made out a heavy-jawed skull, arms, and legs that reached down into the very marrow of the land. It blotted out half the sky.

The figure was moving now, emerging from the clouds to stride across a wide green field. A corona of fire surrounded it. Whatever it touched burst into flames and left cinders of frost. Its shadow spawned smaller creatures—stone-drakes, winged snakes, things that might have been wolves except for their many-forked tails and firelit eyes, and many others too dim and misshapen to recognize.

The mountains glowed, belching molten rock and ash. Shannivar became aware that she was not alone. Rising up behind her, as if she had floated on a banner in their forefront, stood a company of men. One man in particular stood out. Although she could not see his face and his armor and weapons were foreign to her, she knew him. The soldiers chanted in unison, but she paid them no heed. Her attention was drawn to the object the man now raised overhead, a rainbow of colored crystals, shimmering with power. At their heart lay a clear faceted gem, forged for a single purpose—to focus that power. Golden light streamed through it and suffused the face of the man. It glimmered under his skin.

"Khored! Khored!" the men shouted. Their voices filled the wind . . .

Also by Deborah J. Ross:

*Coming soon from DAW Books

To Bonnie Stockman
May the Mother of Horses hold you ever in her heart

PART I:

Zevaron's War

Chapter 1

DREAMING, Zevaron clutched his chest, kneading muscle and skin to ease the ache within. He heard the whispers of his mother's words. She was trying to tell him something, but there was no time. She was dying already.

I will come back, he'd sworn. *I will save you.*

And she had answered him as she lay in her filthy prison cell. *You have already saved what is most dear to me.*

Gone, she was gone.

Gone as Maharrad his father was gone, and Shorennon his brother, and Meklavar his country.

Cinath had done these things. She was dead, and Cinath, may-he-rot-forever, had killed her.

Her life was worth a thousand Ar-Kings. Ten thousand.

Cinath will pay—

His empire would pay. Gelon would burn. By all the gods of Gelon and Denariya, where he'd sailed as a pirate for four long years, by the ancient powers of his own people, he would bring down this accursed land and everyone in it. If he had to make a treaty with his bitterest enemy, if he had to march into the pit of hell itself, he would do it. He would do whatever he had to, for the power to accomplish his revenge.

Gelon will pay.

Zevaron had not meant to sleep the night through, only to rest for a time, once his first frenzy of grief had subsided. When he opened his eyes and smeared away the gummy residue of tears, pale yellow dawn light was sifting through the tower windows. He washed, packed away his mother's few possessions, and went downstairs.

Voices reached him from the garden atrium, Jaxar's hoarse rumble in counterpoint to Danar's clear tenor. He should take his leave of them properly, he thought, to honor what they had done for his mother, Tsorreh. At least Jaxar's wife, Lycian, did not seem to be in attendance. He would not have to witness her gloating.

In the garden, a freshness hung on the leaves. A hidden bird chirped and then fell silent. It was an oasis, this place. Zevaron hoped his mother had found a refuge here.

Danar sat across from Jaxar, his father. Sun glinted on his red-gold hair, but his face looked pale, even for a Gelon. Jaxar gestured for Zevaron to take the empty chair, just as if he were a guest invited to break his fast with the family.

Zevaron chewed a piece of bread, still warm from the oven, and sipped the lightly fermented fruit juice. The bread was surprisingly good, with a thin, crisp crust.

Jaxar waited until Zevaron had finished eating and then spoke, clearly having prepared his thoughts. "Zevaron, I know you wish to leave Aidon. The city must hold nothing but painful memories for you, after all that has happened. I would offer you a place in this household if it would ease your grief, but I fear that any place in Gelon will quickly become too dangerous for one of your race."

Zevaron nodded, thinking Jaxar had never spoken truer words. "I thank you for everything you have done, but I would not impose on you a single night longer."

"Have you thought where you might go?" Jaxar asked. "Back to Denariya?"

Anywhere I can find help.

"Perhaps," Zevaron said carelessly. "Yet the way is long, and the passage through the Firelands can be treacherous."

"You have made the journey many times?" Danar asked with a touch of eagerness.

"Often enough."

"What about Isarre?" Jaxar said. "Would you not have a place there, as Tsorreh's son?"

Zevaron sat back, studying the older man. "You are not interested in my travel plans. Tell me straight out what you want, and have done with it."

Danar and Jaxar exchanged uncomfortable

glances. Danar's expression turned rebellious, the muscles of his jaw standing out as he clenched his teeth.

"I wish Tsorreh were still alive, so that I might admit to her face that she was right about Cinath." Jaxar sighed. "I thought, I foolishly believed, that the devotion he and I once shared as brothers, as well as my own position, would protect those I love."

He paused, his eyes desolate. "The only thing I can say in my own defense, and his, is that he was not always so ruthless, so bent on power. He had always been ambitious, yes, but he was reasonable, too. Now he will listen to no one, and any dissident voice—even mine—only provokes him further."

Jaxar fears the Ar-King's retaliation for having defended Tsorreh. "I am sorry," Zevaron said, aware there was no hint of sympathy in his tone, "but this no longer has anything to do with me." *And it changes nothing.*

"Perhaps, perhaps not." Jaxar sat back, drumming his fingers on the table. "Sad times have befallen my country. I do not know precisely when or how the change came about. Certainly, the loss of a beloved son and heir is enough to break the mind of any father, even a king. But I think Cinath must have been, if not mad, then gravely mistaken, to send Thessar to Azkhantia in the first place— Azkhantia, the rock on which armies shatter and fall!"

Isarre was weak, Zevaron reflected, barely able to defend its borders, or he and his mother would not have been taken prisoner at the fall of the port city of Gatacinne. On the other hand, the nomadic horse peoples of the Azkhantian steppe had repulsed wave after wave of Gelonian incursions. Cinath's own son had met his death at their hands. The possibility of an alliance with the Azkhantians merited further consideration. If he were to have any chance of avenging himself on Gelon, he would need such a force.

"Perhaps it all started to go wrong when we invaded Meklavar," Jaxar mused. "Nothing but sorrow has come of that. As happy as I have been to have Tsorreh in my house, to study with me and discuss my work, to teach Danar and become his friend, I would that she had stayed at home in peace."

Zevaron had not expected such graciousness. He looked away.

After a breath, Jaxar went on. "He will come for Danar next."

"But not for you?"

"My life has never been very secure, as you can see." Jaxar gave a slight, self-deprecating gesture at his swollen body and twisted foot. "The priest-physicians have been telling me I was going to die since before Danar was born. If Cinath comes for me tomorrow, or if this weary heart gives out at last, then I will have had more time than I ever expected. These last four years have truly been a gift."

Danar, who might well challenge Cinath's younger son for the throne—yes, Cinath would see him as a threat, one he cannot permit to live.

"Father, you must not speak this way." Danar got up and began pacing. "You cannot ask me to leave you."

Jaxar waved him to silence. "Zevaron, I have no right to ask anything of you. We are already deeply in your debt. You saved the life of my son once. Now I beg you to do so again. You yourself must leave Aidon. For the sake of Tsorreh, who loved him too, take Danar with you. Take him to Isarre, beyond Cinath's grasp. Keep him safe. Keep both of you safe."

"Father—"

"Danar, no more foolish talk! I do not wish to mourn my only son, and that is what will happen if you stay here."

"Then you must come, too! I will find a way— Zevaron, help me to convince him! We cannot leave him here!"

Madness, Zevaron thought. It was bad enough to consider taking a city boy out on the seas, assuming they could make it to the coast, but not an old man, an invalid, someone easily recognized. They would not find a haven in Isarre, and he would not find the allies he needed. It would be sheerest folly.

"The elder generation must pass away," Jaxar said, his voice shifting from stern to gentle. "Sooner or later, in the rightness of things, you will lose me. I want to lay down this life knowing that you are free."

Danar turned his face away.

"Someday, if the gods are kind," Jaxar said, "you will return to Gelon and make it a better place, the place it ought to be. Then the sun will truly shine upon our Golden Land. Perhaps you will be the one to make things right. A free Meklavar and a re-awakened Gelon will live at peace, as brothers, even as you and Zevaron will."

Zevaron's heart caught in his throat. Of all the things he had expected Jaxar to say, this was wildest and yet the most true. He had never thought that Danar might have the power to restore Meklavar, that this might be the result of saving his life. It was the one argument Zevaron had no defense against, and it was not even being addressed to him. These words were spoken as a prayer, a father's hopes for his son, and not as a bribe.

Jaxar turned to him. "Zevaron, you are the only one I can trust who has the fighting skills and cunning to get Danar to safety. I cannot ask Jonath or Haslar to become outlaws, not even for my sake. Will you help us?"

Madness, Zevaron thought again. And then: *This is what Tsorreh would have done.* Tsorreh had trusted these people and had looked to them for protection, but in the end, they had not been able to protect her from Cinath. Jaxar's pledges of aid for Meklavar might well amount to nothing.

But, Zevaron thought, Jaxar's scheme offered a practical way out of the city and a better chance than he would have alone. If he were to find allies—Azkhantian, Isarran, or otherwise—he must search beyond Gelon's borders.

"Give me a good sword, some food, and money for passage," he said. "And both of us shall reach Isarre alive, or neither of us will."

Chapter 2

IT was not much of a disguise, Zevaron thought as he followed Danar along a circuitous path through the aristocratic hill district, angling down to the river. A battered, creased, broad-brimmed straw hat from the gardener's shed shadowed his face, but his dark hair and honey-gold skin revealed him to be a foreigner, Denariyan or Meklavaran. Danar wore the clothing of a free laborer, but his pale skin and uncalloused hands could not be hidden. If they were stopped and questioned, their escape would be short-lived.

The plan was to make for the river harbor, where they would take passage to the port of Verenzza, and from there to Gelon-held Gatacinne on the shores of Isarre. Jaxar had supplied them with Isarran as well as Gelonian currency and a small pouch of fine-quality rubies that Zevaron carried in the folds of his belt, along with his mother's Arandel token. Their packs contained food of the sort that would keep a man going for a long while: nuts, compressed seed bread, dried fruit, and parched barley. Jaxar's steward had evidently been planning for this escape for some time.

As they crossed the southern border of the hill district, Zevaron began to feel more confident. They had been keeping to smaller streets, but here they must cross the main avenue, a paved expanse filled with pedestrians, wagons, and old-style carts with solid wheels, drawn by yoked oxen instead of onagers. At least, they would be less noticeable here, among the workmen and servants, many of whom carried panniers or satchels.

Zevaron nudged Danar, reminding him to slouch, as they merged into the flow of traffic. Despite the number of people, animals, and vehicles, they made good speed. They were not the only ones who wanted to get somewhere in a hurry this morning. Several times, a servant would shove past them, crying, "Make way! Make way!"

Zevaron had passed this way before, on his way to the harbor in search of men and a boat to take him and his mother out of Aidon, down the river, and then past the boundaries of Gelon. Ahead lay a plaza and the Avenue of the Gulls, a straight route south. His skin prickled the instant before he spied a disturbance in the crowd. That swirl that could only mean trouble, and it was coming toward them.

Zevaron pulled Danar into the nearest open shop doorway, not caring what it sold so long as it got them off the street. Shelves lined the inside walls, displaying small pottery idols—laughing, round-bellied men on donkeys, women slender as willows or hugely pregnant, men with bulging muscles and enlarged genitals, rabbits and frogs, other things he did not recognize. A thin layer of dust gave the merchandise a tattered, neglected air.

A moment later, a group of armed soldiers marched past, in the direction of Jaxar's compound. If they had delayed their departure for even a quarter of an hour, Zevaron thought, it might have been too late. For Jaxar, it mostly likely already was. Zevaron did not know what to say to Danar. They had not discussed what Cinath might do when his men found Danar gone. Could Jaxar, as weak and ill as he was, survive another stay in prison? Or would Cinath execute him right away?

"Good day to you, fine sirs!" A wizened little man in a clay-smeared apron bustled out from the back of the shop. His smile fell as he took in their laborers' garb. From the look of the shop, business had been poor of late, undoubtedly due to the recent surge in the popularity of Qr, the scorpion god.

"I wish to buy an offering to The Lady of Mercy," Danar said, deliberately slurring his words. He added in a low voice to Zevaron, "She is the special protector of invalids. Surely she will watch over him."

Zevaron said nothing. He knew that gods—or something very like them—were real. He had spoken to one such, a supernatural king of the sea, and had heard a prophecy from that god. But he did not think a statuette would protect Jaxar, any more than Tsorreh's prayers had saved her.

The shopkeeper began taking down one clay idol

after another, explaining the provenance and special meaning of each.

Zevaron glanced uneasily at the street. The commotion had passed, and it was dangerous to linger so close to Jaxar's residence. "Danar, we don't have time for this."

"Danar?" The shopkeeper's voice rose in pitch. "Danar, the son of Lord Jaxar?"

"Please, don't—" Danar began.

Zevaron did not like the sudden leap of interest in the shopkeeper's eyes. This was not the pleasure of serving a member of a royal house, it was something more, a flare of suspicion perhaps, or avarice—

"Let's go!" He grabbed Danar's arm, spun him around, and shoved him out the door. The shopkeeper barely managed to catch the idol Danar had been holding before it shattered on the floor.

Outside, Danar started to protest. "We've got a little time. You don't have to—"

"Who's the bodyguard?" Zevaron snapped. "You or me? Down here!" He darted into a side street and broke into a run.

Danar followed, his pack slapping against his spine. "But the soldiers were going—in the opposite direction—and that's a dead end. All right, this way!"

Panting, Danar took the lead down a narrow street overhung with sagging lines of laundry. The buildings here were cramped, often a single block pierced by an occasional common entrance, very different from the spacious and private walled gardens of the hill district.

A naked child, not more than two or three years old, gawked at them while a young woman poured a jug of water over him. A couple of dogs, so thin their ribs stared from their dull coats, nosed in the piles of refuse. They scattered, tails between their hind legs, as Zevaron and Danar approached.

Out of sight from the main boulevard, they slowed to a walk. "There was no need to bolt like that," Danar protested. "We had—a little more time. Now we'll be remembered for certain—for such suspicious behavior. We acted like fugitives."

Zevaron bit back a retort. He'd been the one who'd blurted out Danar's name. He could not undo that mistake now. They had to keep moving, but in such a way as to not draw any more attention to themselves. "You're right about not behaving like fugitives," he admitted. "But that shopkeeper was on the alert for you, so word has already gone out, maybe a reward offered. Our best hope is still to find a riverboat captain who has reasons of his own to avoid notice. Preferably one just pulling away from the dock, if you take my meaning."

They went west, then south, paralleling the main thoroughfare. For a time, they made good progress. The streets were not entirely empty, but the people they passed seemed incurious, bent on their own business. It was, Zevaron realized, a district of working men, poor shops, and barely decent living quarters.

The orderly arrangement of streets and alleys gave way to unpaved lanes, haphazard and twisting. They passed street shrines, set among the open-air cook shops, stalls of clothing and battered leather shoes, women selling apples from baskets slung over their backs, and clusters of old men hunkered down on tattered rugs. A half-grown boy sold water from a cart pulled by a huge reptilian beast, its hide peeling away in scaly yellow patches. A dancer performed on one corner of the square, accompanied by a drum beaten by a blind, bald-headed Xian and her own finger-cymbals. Women in fluttering veils that barely covered their skimpy wraparound gowns called out to passing men. Danar looked embarrassed, but Zevaron turned away, the sight abhorrent to him. He'd seen courtesans aplenty in Denariya, women of culture and influence who often amassed great wealth. It seemed to him that Gelon degraded everyone who lived within its borders.

"We are safe here," Zevaron said. "If Cinath's men approach, the market will disperse, and we with it. No one will have seen anything."

Danar looked thoughtful. "I don't suppose everything that happens here is legal."

Zevaron tilted his head to the half-grown boy who was expertly picking the pockets of anyone who lingered to watch the dancer. In the shadowed doorways, more was bought and sold than the favors of the women in their garish costumes: hemp resin, dreamberries, elixir of poppies, and more. Chalil, the Denariyan pirate he'd sailed with, had sometimes carried such things, small items that brought high prices in the right markets.

Zevaron's hand closed around the urchin's wrist

just as the boy reached for the strap that held Danar's pack closed. "Not this time, my lad. Off you go to seek richer prey."

The boy jerked free, flashed a defiant grin, and melted into the crowd. The dancing drew to a climax, the drumming faster and louder, like the beat of a racing heart, and the girl let out a series of ululating cries like those of the Sand Lands people.

As suddenly, Zevaron's ears filled with the clash of steel on steel and something more, like the sound made by shattering obsidian or ice, but sharper and louder. His vision fractured. He still stood in the market square, but looked out on a very different landscape.

Before him stretched a plain and from it rose a wall of white, glittering and burning like ice on fire. A fissure cracked the fuming surface in a jagged hairline. It grew rapidly wider, big enough to engulf a horse, then a dozen horses, then a ship the size of his old *Wave Dancer*. Its depths exhaled a mist that curled and eddied in strange patterns, as if it had an intelligence of its own. Something moved within that miasma, clambering up from the pit. Rising into the day, it lifted cragged, impossibly deformed hands. Its head was still hidden, and Zevaron both longed to see it and shrank away, certain that . . . that *what?* He could not remember.

Dimly, he felt his own body take a step, one hand raised to shield his eyes, and tasted the sudden rush of acid in his mouth.

"Zevaron! Zev! Are you all right?" Danar grasped his arm, peering urgently into his face.

Zevaron's vision leapt into focus. Before him lay the market, the dancer now bowing to her admirers, the old men on their carpets, the sellers and buyers in the shadows. He was sweating and shivering at the same time.

"I'm all right," he lied. "Let's go."

As they drew closer to the river, the air changed and a fitful breeze sprang up. Zevaron tasted moisture, not the clean salt tang of the ocean but a dank, weedy smell. Slow broad barges, like the one that had brought him upriver to Aidon, were moored beside fleeter vessels, passenger craft and fishing boats. With Danar at his heels, Zevaron strolled from one drinking stall to the next, looking bored but in truth searching for the men he had spoken to before.

A thought hovered at the edge of his senses, a keening wail: *I meant to take Tsorreh to safety in just this way.* He thrust it from him, lest his grief overwhelm him.

He must have had a touch of sun-poisoning or bad food, for waves of queasiness spread outward from his belly. That would explain the vision he'd seen in the dancer's square. Something sat like a lump of lead below his diaphragm, so that he could not quite catch his breath. Could a broken heart, broken hopes, hurt this much? Despite his efforts at concentration, at not thinking about Tsorreh, it was getting harder to keep his mind on what he was doing. They needed to get indoors, someplace dark and quiet where he could sit down.

"How about that place?" Danar pointed to a tavern on a corner. Colored streamers fluttered from its eaves.

"Ah, this looks more like it." Zevaron indicated a ramshackle, weathered building.

Danar stared at the unpainted walls and the banner hanging in tatters above the warped door. "Here?"

Zevaron pushed the door open. He'd never been in this particular tavern before, but it felt as familiar as the *Wave Dancer*'s deck. In a blink or two, his eyes adapted to the dimmer light. He studied the shelves of pottery jugs and wooden kegs, and the men standing over their drinks or lounging around the collection of much-mended tables. At the counter, a barrel-chested riverman, one side of his mouth twisted by whitened, criss-crossing scars, took out a curved knife and laid it on the surface.

"Zev, are you sure this is a good idea?"

"Keep close and keep quiet, like a lamb in a den of jackals."

Zevaron sauntered to the far corner, where he had recognized one of the Denariyan pirates he'd spoken to before. He slid onto the single free chair, leaving Danar to stand behind him.

After a few preliminary remarks and the offer of a round of ale, accepted with a grunt and a nod, the Denariyan looked pointedly at Danar, "Thought it was a woman you wanted passage for."

Zevaron shrugged. "Things change."

"Not my business."

"Right. It's not."

The barkeep set a pitcher with a cracked lip down on the table. The Denariyan refilled his tankard, lifted it in salute, and for a time, there was little conversation. With a sigh, the pirate lowered his cup. "You drinking?"

Zevaron's mouth had watered at the smell of the ale, rough and sour though it would be. But his head had still not stopped spinning, and he dared not unsettle his stomach any further. "No, just buying."

"In the market for a boat?"

"Passage. For two."

The Denariyan's eyebrows lifted, and he glanced from Zevaron to Danar and back again. "Special rates?"

Zevaron nodded. Chalil had used a similar phrase to indicate that discretion and speed were an essential part of the deal. They haggled a little over the price, and Zevaron paid him a third, with the second portion to come with the finding of the boat and the last, once they were safely aboard.

After the Denariyan slid out of the bar, Zevaron ordered another round of ale and pretended to drink, huddled over his dented tin cup. After a sip, Danar did the same.

Time passed. Men drifted through the bar, drank, carried on conversations in hushed tones, glanced incuriously at Zevaron and Danar, and walked away. The barkeep came over, looked into the pitcher, found it still half-full, and asked if they wanted to eat. Zevaron wasn't hungry, but Danar looked too nervous to be sitting with only a mug of untouched ale. The barkeep brought wooden bowls of barley and fish, still wrapped in the leaves it had been steamed in.

"It's taking too long," Danar said, pushing away his half-empty bowl. "Something's gone wrong."

"Relax. These things take time to arrange."

"I don't like it. We're just *sitting* here, waiting for the Elite Guard to catch up with us."

"Best not to speak that name where it can be overheard." Zevaron rubbed his eyes. He felt sick and unexpectedly weary, and his heart ached. He should be here with Tsorreh, talking about the freedom that lay before them. "There's a time to run and a time to wait. And the time to wait is when the men we've employed are doing their work to get us out of here in the only way possible. Slowly. Carefully. Quietly."

"But can we trust that man?"

"Look at it this way. If he gives us away, it's his execution as well."

Danar's mouth fell open. He closed it and went back to pretending to sip his warm ale and pick at the remains of his fish.

After a time, the Denariyan came back, closely followed by a Mearan in the clothing of a barge captain. It took only a few minutes, using the coded phrases Zevaron had learned from Chalil, to establish the man was accustomed to "special cargo," meaning smuggling both goods and passengers. Despite his uneasy stomach, Zevaron's spirits rose. It was exactly the kind of arrangement he'd hoped for. The only drawback was that the barge, the *Mud*

Puppy, would not be ready to depart until first light tomorrow. Danar looked as if he were about to burst out in objections, but Zevaron said, "Done!"

He paid the Denariyan the second part of his fee, and a portion to the captain, and then another, smaller amount to the Denariyan for the location of the worst brothel in the district.

Danar looked scandalized until Zevaron explained that, should the hunt for them reach the river district, that would be the last place the patrols would look. "Not because they wouldn't raid a whorehouse, because they would, but because they'd be sure we would not dare take the time."

They hired a room and a woman, went up a creaky flight of stairs, and paid an exorbitant price for another pitcher of sour ale. Zevaron handed the pitcher to the woman and stretched out on the floor. Even in his weariness, the inevitable bed-lice were not worth the dubious comfort of a lumpy mattress. Danar propped himself against the corner and rested his forehead against his folded arms. When Zevaron opened his eyes again, the woman was curled up on the bed, the empty jug at her side. She was snoring gently. Asleep, she looked even younger.

Zevaron blinked, trying to clear his head. He could not shake the uneasy sensation of having dreamed something intense and meaningful but without any specific memory of it. He felt a twinge of pity for the girl, but there was nothing he could do for her.

He pulled aside the greasy curtain and looked

out over the lane. A gust of air brought the smells of human waste and rot. Across the narrow gap, an old woman emptied a bucket on top of a refuse heap. He could not make out her features, only the lighter color of her head scarf. Only a trace of brightness remained in the western sky.

It was time to find a place for the night. The tavern looked as if it had rooms for rent on the second floor, but it would not be prudent to return to the same establishment, in the event their presence had been remarked. Where there was one such place, he told himself, there would be others. He felt less tired now, although still groggy. He should be able to stay on guard most of the night.

I'll sleep once we're safely under way, trading watches with Danar. Let him do his share of the work when fewer things can go wrong.

Rubbing the sore place in his chest, he woke Danar. The girl roused at the same time. To Zevaron's inquiry, she replied that her mother rented out rooms for a few coppers a night.

Outside, the street was no emptier than before but filled with a different sort of crowd. Most of the women, the smaller children, and laborers were gone. Lights winked on in drinking and eating establishments.

Outside the corner tavern, the one Danar had first pointed to, lanterns of colored paper had been hung on strings. The enticing aroma of fried pastries mingled with the curling smoke. A table had been set up outside the door, and a woman in a greasy apron was fishing bits of crisp dough from a kettle, dusting them with powder, crystallized honey most likely, and handing them out as fast as her customers could offer their coins.

Danar glanced at Zevaron, mutely pleading. Zevaron's stomach gurgled, reminding him that they had not eaten since the fish at the tavern. Maybe hunger was what was wrong with him.

"Get us some," he said, "and I'll keep watch out here."

With a grin, Danar waded into the little crowd. Zevaron turned slowly, trying to look casual as he scanned the intersection. All seemed as normal and undisturbed as things ever were in a place like this. Two seedy-looking men, obviously drunk, started a fight. A pickpocket, perhaps the boy from earlier, had chosen the wrong victim and was sent sprawling.

Zevaron relaxed, but only for an instant. A pair of armed Gelon, whether soldiers or ordinary patrol or royal guards he could not tell, entered the intersection. One of them carried a torch. They ignored the brawling drunks and moved across the square, stopping to peer into the faces of the younger men. They questioned one ragged fellow, who looked too terrified to give a coherent account of himself.

Zevaron turned toward the pastry seller, putting his back to the soldiers. As he did so, he glanced about for the quickest way out of the square. Not back the way they'd come. Too many onlookers, and too much could go wrong—

"Got them!" Danar's clear tenor voice, with its

unmistakable aristocratic accent, rang out. He emerged from the throng, and the light from the nearest soldier's torch lit his face.

"You there!" The harsh-edged voice carried above the noise of the crowd.

Zevaron reached for his sword. His head whirled sickeningly, and his muscles felt as if they had turned to clay.

The soldiers now had a clear path to Danar. Danar stared at them, holding a pair of crullers by their thin wooden skewers. His eyes widened as they rushed toward him.

No battle reflexes! Cursing silently, Zevaron yanked the sword free and lunged between Danar and the patrol.

"Run!" he yelled at Danar.

The first Gelon reached him, sword swinging. The heavy steel slashed down, with all the soldier's larger mass behind it. Zevaron reacted without thinking. His early training, enhanced by years of practice on a pirate ship, took command. He caught the blow on the flat of his own sword, deflecting and blunting its full force. Steel whined and then hummed as, for an instant, blades joined and swept through the air in a single spiraling pathway. Now to end the dance with a flick that sent the other sword spinning free—

Zevaron's stomach lurched and his skin went cold. He wavered, his balance broken. The swords jerked apart. Voices swept over him, people crying out, shouting, some of them almost upon him—

"Never mind that one! Get the boy! Jaxar's cub!"

—and others dim and distant, the surging roar of a great army—

"Khored! Khored!"

The Gelon recovered with a grunt of surprise and raised his sword again. Overlaid on that image, Zevaron saw a thousand other swords, flashing in the sun.

He stood on a hilltop, looking down on the massed armies, knowing they waited only for his command. Snow-crystal clouds glowed across the horizon. Wind whipped his cheeks, tasting of ashes and ice.

Retching, half-blind, Zevaron lifted his hand to the gathering storm. Almost too late, he saw the hilt of the sword clenched between his fingers. Instinct and training took over again. Quicker than thought, he scrambled to his feet. He parried and fell back, fighting for balance.

The voices rose about him, a whirlwind—

"Khored! Khored!"

—and somehow, beyond all hope and reason, his mother's voice sang in his blood, rising and falling in ancient rhythm.

> *May the light of Khored shine ever upon*
>   *you;*
> *May his wisdom guide you,*
> *May his Shield protect you . . .*

The sky went dark, as if the shadow of something vast and terrible stretched across the living world. At the very margin of Zevaron's vision, light gleamed on steel. A face loomed over him.

He staggered backward. Slow, too slow.

The storm reached down to him with fingers as cold as ice. Burning white and beautiful, they plunged into his side. For an instant, he felt no pain, only wonder.

In the distance, someone screamed his name. The world slipped sideways.

He raised one hand to the place where the ice had branded him. His fingers came away hot and sticky.

Pain shocked through him. Laced his breath. Sent him to his knees, sword loose in his grasp.

He looked up, forced his bleared vision to clear. *Get up*, he screamed, but no sound came. He hauled himself to one foot, then the other.

Someone appeared in front of him, beating back the Gelonian soldier, not the one he himself had fought, but another man.

He could not breathe. The wound in his chest burned, molten. His fingers were going numb, and yet he managed to lift his sword again, bracing one hand over the other. Darkness lapped at him.

"Zev! Let's go!"

At the sound of Danar's frantic shout, a mist fell away from Zevaron's vision. He was standing, but just barely, on a darkened street, lit only by a guttering torch and a string of garish paper lanterns. The knot of people had scattered. The one remaining Gelonian soldier sat in an awkward jumble, clutching the front of his shoulder. Blood streamed through his fingers.

"Zev?" Danar sheathed his own sword and reached out his free hand to Zevaron. "Can you walk?"

Zevaron's injured side throbbed with each pulsation of his heart. He struggled for air, managed to wheeze out, "Got to—" and then toppled into Danar's outstretched arms.

Danar cursed in earnest now, phrases in Gelone Zevaron had never heard, not even in all his time with Chalil. Zevaron didn't care what the words meant. He had to stay on his feet and keep moving. Grunting with the effort, he straightened up and managed a shambling run.

"Hold on, Zev. I've got you. Just stay with me. A little further and then you can rest."

Air rasped through Zevaron's chest. From the pain and his shortness of breath, he thought his lung had been punctured and collapsed. Once in Tomarziya Varya, he'd seen a wound like this.

He couldn't think what to do. His muscles had turned to powder. Grayness, like a surging tide, washed in waves across his vision.

Hold on, the voice had said.

He held on.

Chapter 3

STREETS blurred, lights smearing together into a wash of agony. Zevaron heard Danar's voice, asking directions.

Which way to the river barges? Do you know where the Mud Puppy *is? Down this way?*

His hand pressed over the still-bleeding wound, Zevaron leaned heavily on Danar. Somehow he managed to stay on his feet, one lurching step after another. Now they had no hope of disguising their flight. He must be leaving a path of blood that even a blind man could follow. Once or twice, he came close to fainting.

Eventually Zevaron realized he was no longer staggering across cobbled paving stones or hard-packed dirt, but over planks of wood. River-tang filled his head. He heard the creak of timbers, of ropes stretching against their moorings. Before him, in the shadowed dark, lay a boat. He heard a distant wail, the sound of pain too great to bear.

"... we've got to ... right now, do you hear me ..." Danar pleaded.

Zevaron shook his head and stared at the flat, clumsy outlines of a river-barge. He did not know the man who stood before Danar, anger and fear in his every gesture.

There was more discussion in hushed and urgent voices. Then hands slipped beneath his armpits and lifted him as if he were a baby. He felt a bed under him, a thin straw pallet, and then the rocking movement of a vessel over water. Paddles splashed. A voice called out orders. The boat settled as the current took it.

Light soared and swooped above him, an osprey hovering over its prey. It stung his eyes.

"Seen somewhat like this before," a man said with quiet authority. Zevaron felt a touch on his side, over the center of red pain. "Sword musta slipped between the ribs, maybe nicked a rib, I can't say."

"But what do we do for him? There must be something." Danar's voice was laced with desperation. "He can hardly breathe."

"Nothin' to be done. If the fever don't get him, if the wound don't go bad, then he'll mend."

Movement, a stir of the air, and then he was alone. And not alone.

Voices spoke to him, at times a woman's—his mother's? *No, she was lost forever, dead!* Laid over her words like a ghostly echo, he heard the deep bass of a man's.

"*Gelon is not the enemy,*" Tsorreh whispered. "*Qr . . . and its progenitor . . . Forgive me, I did not have enough time to prepare you . . .*"

Qr? Gelon? What was she talking about? The fever must have affected his brain. Yet as he heard the word *progenitor*, another phrase resonated through his thoughts: *"Shadows that cast themselves upon the souls of men . . ."*

The words hung before him, as if written in fire. He had read them a hundred times in the *te-Ketav*, the holy book of his people. He could trace every line and loop of the letters that formed them. Almost, he could feel the texture of the age-worn pages between his fingers.

Shadows. And darkness, and fire. Fire and Ice.

Khored and his brothers and the magical Shield, the Shield of seven crystals . . .

"Rivers boiled, mountains crumbled . . . fields became peaks of hardened ash."

Swords sang beneath a sky torn with light and thunder. *"And it came to pass that Khored and his brothers defeated Fire and Ice and exiled it to the mountains of the north."*

Once again, he sat with his mother in Jaxar's laboratory and climbed the ladder to the tower observatory. In hushed, urgent tones, she spoke of a comet sweeping through the northern sky. He stood alone now on a platform, surrounded on every side with night. Above stretched a band of stars. The air was cold, the points of brilliance edged in ice.

"There," Tsorreh whispered, *"look there."* And he lifted his eyes.

At first, he saw only a smudge of dimness, a thread stretching to the north. As he watched, it grew brighter and larger. Its light shimmered, an iridescent corona that filled the heavens. Moment by moment, it drew him. He soared with it, higher and faster than any bird, than any arrow.

Around him and through him, the firmament glowed, cold and burning like moonlight on ice-clouds. Its music sang in his veins.

High and wide, sweeping, arching, he sped faster. Faster. Ahead lay high desert plains of grass, silver in the moonlight. Beyond them, hills rose into mountains, massive and ancient, forming range upon snow-whitened range. Zevaron watched as the flaming ice plunged to earth beyond the peaks.

The ground shuddered as it struck. Sheets of glacial ice broke apart and tumbled free down the sides of the mountains. Rock shattered, setting off more avalanches.

The Shield is scattered, the mountain prison breached.

Was it Tsorreh's voice, or some other's, deep and ancient?

The vision was shredding now, the mountains tattering into mist, into bits of flying whiteness. Behind the images, he sensed a stirring, as if a vast, incomprehensible force roused itself from slumber. He had no sense of its nature, hidden as it was behind the thickening mist, the vapors that froze and burned. He only knew, in the shivering marrow of his bones, in the innermost chamber of his heart, that something terrible had happened.

Zevaron woke again from a dream of sailing past the Firelands, with gray-blue icebergs to either side. He had been standing at the *Wave Dancer*'s prow when a chunk of ice clipped him on the side. Melting, it trickled down his skin.

No, he lay on his back, naked to the waist and shivering, and the slow chill touch was the sponge Danar used to wipe him. Light streamed in from above. The cabin was narrow and low-ceilinged, and the vessel beneath them rocked gently.

Danar lifted a metal cup to Zevaron's lips, but Zevaron pushed it away and struggled to sit up. His head barely missed the sloping ceiling. The effort left him gasping, and he realized that he was now able to draw air into both lungs. Gratefully, he accepted the cup. The drink in the cup was watered wine, thin but pleasantly fruity.

"How long until we reach Verenzza?" He slid his feet off the edge of the built-in bed and craned his neck to look at his wound. It had closed, although a ring of fiery red bordered the scabbed area.

"Two days, but as soon as it's dark, Aratchy will put us ashore."

Zevaron frowned, trying to think. Going ashore in midpassage wasn't part of the plan. They'd have to find another boat, and that might not be easy.

"Word on the river is the ports are being watched," Danar went on. "Nothing gets on or off a boat without Cinath's men searching. They'll be waiting for us at Verenzza. This is as far as we dare take the river. We must go overland instead."

"Overland? To where?"

"Isarre, of course. Our captain says there's a trading post inland where we can buy horses without too many questions. Um . . . can you ride?"

"Isarre? Are you crazy?" Immediately, Zevaron wished he hadn't spoken so loudly. Bolts of pain jagged through his skull. He lowered his voice. "We can't get there by land."

"I think we can. Remember, I brought maps from Father's library. I've been studying them while you were asleep. It *is* possible. But that's not the problem. Our route will take us along the borders of Azkhantia. That will be the most dangerous part, but it's also the safest. The steppe is the one place Cinath will never think to look for us. We can do it if we don't lose our nerve. We *will* do it." Zevaron heard a stubborn note in Danar's voice and remembered how fiercely he had worked to free both his father and Tsorreh. "We have to. There's no other way."

"Where's my shirt? I've got to talk to the captain."

"You're wasting your breath." Danar crossed his arms over his chest. "I've already paid him, and he wants us off the boat before he reaches Verenzza. Do you think he's going to risk his skin by keeping us aboard? Or do you propose throwing him to the fishes and piloting this thing yourself?"

Danar was undoubtedly right. If Cinath's men were searching all boats on the water, they had to get off the river as soon as possible. This Aratchy, this barge captain, had already stretched his own agreement to take them this far, and then probably only because Zevaron had not been fit to travel in any other way.

Danar had saved his life back at the Aidon river district. He'd been unconscious for longer than he realized, wounded and ill, seeing visions.

He had promised Jaxar to see Danar to safety in Isarre. At the time, it had been the logical choice, for Tsorreh was of that royal lineage. As her son, Zevaron could claim the bonds of kinship. Jaxar had thought it a suitable sanctuary for his son. But Isarre was barely capable of holding Gelon at bay.

Azkhantia, on the other hand, was home to bloodthirsty savages, horse-nomads who obeyed no law and knew no restraint, or so the stories said. They'd thrown back Gelonian invasions time and again, not just in Cinath's time, but in his father's, and his grandfather's before him.

Perhaps it was not in Isarre but in the wind-swept steppe that he would find the allies he needed to free Meklavar and avenge his mother's death. The route Danar had described would take them close to the borders of Azkhantia.

"In that case," he said, "I can ride." *And then* . . .

Zevaron's fingers curled, claws tightening into fists. In his mind, fire raged across the hills of Aidon, as hot as the blood pounding through his temples, and the ashes of the conquerors blew away in the wind.

He would return with an Azkhantian horde at his back, bring down the towers and palaces, and set all the seven hills ablaze. The Golden Land would crumble into salt, and no man would remember those who once lived here.

By the Shield of Khored, by the memory of my mother, by everything holy, and by all that is unholy if need be, I swear that Gelon will pay.

PART II:

Shannivar's Hope

Chapter 4

ON the Azkhantian steppe, the Moon of Mares had given birth to the Moon of Golden Grass. Now, on a bright summer day, Shannivar daughter of Ardellis rode laughing through the feathergrass. Grasshoppers scattered beneath the hooves of her horse. The scent of the ripening seeds rose up around her. Surely, she thought, the goddess Tabilit must have been drunk on *k'th* when she created the steppe and covered it with such a sky as this, such rolling hills, such a sweep of gold and green. What more could anyone desire in life but a fine horse, a hunting bow, and the wind on her face?

Like all her people, Shannivar was small and bronze-skinned, her body sculpted by long days in the saddle. Her hands were broad and strong, her dark eyes hooded like a falcon's. A single braid of glossy black hair hung down her back from beneath her peaked felt cap. Feathers from the totem animal of her clan, the Golden Eagle, fluttered from the point of the cap. She wore no jacket, only a shirt and felt vest, embellished with stylized eagles and symbols of good fortune, loose camel's-wool trousers, a wide woven sash in bright colors, and buttersoft boots laced to the knee.

Shannivar's dun mare, Radu, skimmed the earth with her soft-foot gait. The pack pony trotted placidly behind them, the legs of the dead gazelle flopping against his sides.

The sun dipped toward the ridge, beyond which lay the river valley where Shannivar's clan had set up their *dharlak*, their summering-place. Ribbons of brightness spread across the western horizon. The grass rippled in the lengthening shadows. The sky was clear of any trace of the strange white star, so much more brilliant than its fellows. Surrounded by a peculiar misty halo, it had swept across the northern rim last summer and then disappeared. Now the heavens seemed untroubled, as serene as if the star had never existed.

There would be light enough, and time enough, to do all that was meant to be done. That had been her father's favorite saying, and she wondered if he were smiling down on her from the Sky Kingdom, urging her to patience as he had so many times in her childhood. She sighed, for the memory was both a blessing and a shadow on her heart. It was yet another reason to hate the Gelon, whose raids into Azkhantia had increased in recent years. Shannivar's bond with her father had been unusually strong; daughters bore the names of their mothers, as sons did their fathers, each following in the traditional path of their same-sex parent.

Shannivar passed the lake and the outlying pastures where the wealth of the clan, the cream-and-russet sheep and the shaggy two-humped camels, grazed. In the *dharlak* encampment itself, felt-sided *jorts* stood in concentric circles around a common area. Beyond the crumbling walls of an ancient fortress, a mews housed hunting falcons, but they were only for men.

One of Shannivar's younger cousins led a string of horses to drink at the lake's edge. He spotted her and waved, giving a whistling cry. A covey of children ran out to meet her.

"Shannivar the hunter!" the children cried. "May your arrows fly true! We will feast tonight!"

"Yes, little ones," she said, laughing. Giggling, they clustered around her. "May your words always be sweet! Here, carry the gazelle to Grandmother."

She slipped the carcass of the gazelle from the back of the pony and laid it across their joined hands. Even the youngest had learned the ways of working together. Separately, none of them could have managed its weight.

The Sky People, Tabilit and her consort Onjhol, made us one. We praise them by our oneness in work, in love, in war, went an ancient saying.

Not one in all things, Shannivar reflected somberly. There came a time when men and women went apart, a time she had been dreading.

She set aside her tack, the saddle of use-softened leather with its high cantle for support over long distances, the girth and breastplate, the thick blanket, the bridle ornamented with beads of silver and turquoise. She began rubbing down Radu with a plait of dried feathergrass, one long stroke after another. Layers of dried sweat came away, motes of dust billowing in the slanting light. The mare leaned into the rhythmic pressure, eyes half closed in contentment.

The dun mare was not nearly as fast as Shannivar's other horse, Eriu, a black with fire in his eye, but few horses could match him. Radu was getting old and had not borne a foal this last spring. She was one of two horses left to Shannivar by Ardellis, the mother who had died at her birth, and was a treasure indeed, one of the fabled soft-gaited horses, said to be Tabilit's favored children. The other, a washed-out gray mare of indifferent quality, had given birth to Eriu, a mount worthy of any warrior.

When Shannivar finished, giving the muscled rump a pat, Radu turned to look at her with an aggrieved expression. *More?* the mare seemed to say.

Shannivar tugged the long forelock. "You would stand here all night to be groomed, but I have other duties."

Radu blew out a resigned sigh. She followed docilely as Shannivar took a handful of mane and led her to the horse field.

Eriu pricked his small, inwardly curved ears and flared his nostrils as Shannivar approached. Like most Azkhantian horses, he was compactly built, with a short, strong back and dense hooves. Unlike the others, however, he had not been turned out to run wild for the first two years of his life. Shannivar, guarding her small treasure of horses, had kept him close and fed him by hand. She'd sung to him through the long winter nights. He had never needed spurs or whip, for he answered to her voice, the shift of her weight, and the pressure of her knees.

"Soon," she murmured, stroking his neck. "We will run, you and I."

Small fires, many of them fueled with dried camel dung, burned brightly in the encampment. Shannivar's friends and cousins waited beside the largest, where the gazelle was roasting. The younger married women had already brought out the rest of the evening meal, cheeses made from the milk of sheep and camels, flatbread, summer greens cooked with herbs, and boiled wild barley.

Shannivar nodded to her friends before presenting herself to Grandmother. She could not remember a time when Grandmother had not been the oldest living person in the family, perhaps in the entire sept of her clan, and terrifying. It was said she had outlived three husbands and four sons, including Shannivar's own father. Although her eldest son was chief in name and in war, everyone deferred to Grandmother.

Grandmother's *jort* dominated the center of the *dharlak*, always the first to be set up and the last to be taken down. Age had darkened the framework of birch and willow, although the brightly dyed felt was thick and new. Inside, layers of carpet, some of them from Grandmother's own grandmother, covered the floor. The door flap had been tied back to admit the night breeze, framing the small upright figure on her hassock of stitched camel hide.

Grandmother wore the traditional dress of a married woman of importance, a long robe of Denariyan silk of a green so dark it looked black, its sleeves brightened by embroidered eagles, the totem of the Golden Eagle clan. Instead of the usual felt cap, she wore a headdress, a silver band in which were set pale-red corals. Chains of jade beads and silver good-luck charms hung from the band on either side, chiming softly with her movements.

Shannivar approached and bowed respectfully. She kept her eyes lowered and her voice gentle. "May your hearth fire always burn brightly."

"May good sense grace your *jort*," Grandmother answered dryly. The old woman's voice had once been strong, like the cry of a hawk, but the last few winters had left her with a lingering hoarseness. "Sit beside me, Granddaughter."

Shannivar lowered herself at her grandmother's feet. They sat for a moment in silence. A fragrance arose from within the *jort*, old wool and cedar, a touch of cleansing incense.

Sounds filled Shannivar's ears, men singing, children shrieking at their games, and iron pots clanging. At the far edge of the encampment, the smith was still at his work in the ancient stone hut. She could hear the tapping of his hammers. Only his apprentice knew the secrets of the smith's craft, another mystery she would never learn.

"The other young women have set aside their

bows for husbands, all but you." The old woman paused. "Shannivar daughter of Ardellis, it is time."

Time? Shannivar thought irritably, although she had been expecting and dreading this moment. *Why now? Was the white star an omen?* With an effort, she remained silent. How could it be her time when something wild and thirsty, like the totem of her clan, sang in her blood? She still dreamed of battles to come, of loosing her arrows at the enemy over the back of her horse.

Once she had asked the clan *enaree* what these dreams meant, whether they were memories of past battles with the Gelon or a prophecy of deeds to come. The shaman had only shaken his head and retreated into his smoke-filled *jort*.

"I do not yet see the clear way," Shannivar said. In her voice, trembling mixed in equal measure with truth.

"Do you think you are the first woman to find the chase more pleasing than the cookpot? You are a skilled hunter, and I have never seen a woman who rides more boldly. Already you have seen more battle than most. You have killed your enemy, and thereby brought honor to yourself and your lineage. No one can challenge your fitness to marry."

"Until my people are safe, until the Gelon no longer come to our land, how can I put aside my bow and my sword? How can I sit at my ease while my cousins fight and die in my stead? No one suggests that any of *them* set aside their bows. I am as good an archer, and I am a better rider!"

This was not entirely true, for although Shannivar could certainly ride as well as any of the young men, neither she nor anyone else of the clan could equal their best men archers with the recurved, laminated bow.

Grandmother turned to Shannivar, black eyes glittering. The beads and silver ornaments clashed lightly on their chains. Shannivar lowered her gaze. It was unseemly to have spoken so to an elder, in particular this formidable ancestor.

"There will always be an enemy to fight," Grandmother said, but not harshly, "if not Gelon, then some other. That is the way of things, and it is not a valid reason to refuse your obligations. Granddaughter, I care for your happiness, but I am also responsible for the welfare of the clan. If every young woman thought as you do, then who would bear sons and daughters to carry on after us? Who would tend the flocks and milk the she-camels, prepare the *k'th*, and keep the traditional songs alive? In my day, women proved themselves in battle the same way they do now, but then we settled down decently, with our husbands and babies. That is the way of things."

Shannivar wanted to answer that times had changed, that since the coming of the new Ar-King, Gelon pressed them harder than ever before. A year or so ago, the Ar-King's heir had led an expedition into the territory of the Antelope clan. Everyone had heard the story at the last gathering, how the Gelon had been driven back and the Ar-King's son had been slain, but at a terrible cost, for many fine steppe warriors met their deaths as well.

Since then, the Gelonian monarch had sent even more soldiers. Azkhantia needed all her defenders now, daughters as well as sons. Those very songs Grandmother spoke of, did they not tell of women winning glory with their courage and skill? Shannivar had grown up on tales of Aimellina daughter of Oomara, of her own namesake, the first Shannivar, and of Saramark daughter of Julisse, perhaps the greatest heroine of them all.

Every child of the steppe knew the legend of Saramark. Three generations ago, when her chieftain husband was severely wounded and unable to lead the men into battle, her entire clan had faced annihilation. Saramark took up her husband's sword. At midnight, she led her band of women warriors against the enemy. Heartened, the men of her clan followed her, and disaster turned into triumph. It was Shannivar's favorite story, one she never tired of hearing.

Do you presume to follow in Saramark's footsteps? her uncle, Esdarash son of Akhisarak, who was chief of their clan, would say whenever he heard her humming the tune. *Those times are long gone.*

The night wind must have blown smoke from the cooking fire in her direction, for Shannivar's eyes stung. A lump thickened her throat.

Grandmother was trying to help, to warn Shannivar that she had run out of time, and to offer a chance to gracefully bend to what was expected of her without suffering the humiliation of a public confrontation. Shannivar knew that if she refused outright, that would not be the end of it. Her uncle would pressure her to marry. He could not compel her to take a husband, but he could make it impossible for her to remain with the clan. Even as the fledgling golden eagle must fly from the nest of its parents, so too she must leave.

"In a short time," Grandmother said, "you will travel to the *khural*."

The annual gathering of the clans was a month-long festival, with contests of archery and horsemanship, feasting, dancing and drinking *k'th* into the night, buying and selling livestock, and the inevitable courtships. Her older cousins had either stayed with the clans of their new husbands or brought home strange wives. Always before, she had returned as she had gone, unpromised, her heart untouched. At the *khural*, there would be eligible young men from distant clans, men who had not known her when they were children together and she had outraced so many of them.

Outraced . . .

A plan took shape in Shannivar's mind. She would go to the *khural* under the guise of obedience, but once there, she would put off any suitors until she had won the Long Ride. Of all the races, the Long Ride was the most grueling and carried the greatest honor. Then, with triumph upon her shoulders, she would accept a husband of her own choosing and on her own terms, one who would permit her to ride and hunt as she always had, and, when the Gelon returned, as they surely would, she would fight.

"Grandmother, I will obey."

Shannivar's thoughts raced ahead, making plans. She would bring Radu and Eriu with her, for they were her own property, and her bow and sword. In the chest of cypress wood lay the dowry she would place at the feet of her future mother-in-law.

"You have ever been a dutiful daughter of the Golden Eagle," Grandmother said, patting Shannivar's shoulder with a gnarled hand. "May Tabilit look with favor upon your husband, and may you bear him many strong sons. May Olash-giyn-Olash, the Shadow of Shadows, never darken your tent." The old woman recited the traditional blessing upon a bride. "May her grace shine upon your bed, your flocks, your *jort*."

With the exception of the tribe's *enaree*, who was regarded as neither male nor female, only married women might own a *jort*. Men lived in the dwellings of their mothers or wives, or, if they were bachelors, with a sister or aunt. A bride proved herself by both her prowess in battle and her skill at shaping the flexible framework and felt walls. It was said that a true daughter of the steppe could ride out with nothing but her knife and an axe, and return three days later with the completed lattice. Shannivar had helped several women friends in this task. Now it would be her turn.

Shannivar awoke the next morning in a subdued mood. Her temples ached as if she had drunken too much *k'th* the night before, although she had hardly

sipped the fermented mare's milk. She lay quietly,
letting her eyes adjust to the light that filtered
through the central roof opening, listening to the
sound of Grandmother snoring and the softer
sounds of the woman who shared her *jort* and
helped to tend her, a young cousin, unmarried and
likely to remain so, for as an infant she had been so
badly burned her features were distorted into a
permanent grimace. Everyone called her Scarface,
as if her real name had been charred away with her
skin. It was said as a kindness, for while the customary wishes of good fortune could no longer protect
her, the evil spirits would not know her true name.

It was still early, barely dawn. Even in the dim
light, Shannivar knew every chest, every article of
furniture—the folding wooden bed, the carpets and
cushions, the chests for clothing and bedding, the
smaller caskets for ornaments of silver and copper,
beads of turquoise, jade, coral and pearl, packets of
spices and powdered cedar. At the bottom of her
own personal chest lay the little wooden horse her
father had carved for her when she was a child.
What would it be like to live in a place where nothing smelled of memories, of family, of home?

Shannivar folded her blanket and laid it in its
accustomed place. Lifting the door flap, she slipped
outside. Pale eastern light softened the contours of
the other *jorts*.

At the old well, she cleaned her teeth with a
blackroot stick, rinsed her mouth of the lingering
bitter taste, and scrubbed her face with a paste of
cedar and frankincense.

Already the younger wives were stirring the fires to life and preparing a breakfast of boiled barley and shredded gazelle meat from the night before. The smell of the porridge made Shannivar's mouth water. After eating, she drank a cup of strong tea laced with butter and went down to the horse field. A ride on Eriu would banish whatever gnawed at her nerves.

"Heyo, Shannivar! May your morning be bright. You're up early." Grinning, her cousin Alsanobal son of Esdarash led his copper-red stallion away to be saddled. The horse was big for the Azkhantian breed and ill-tempered. He laid back his ears and bared his teeth at his rider. Alsanobal cuffed him lightly on the side of the head. The horse gave an aggrieved snort.

"That horse will kill you someday," Shannivar said cheerfully. Red horses were said to be holy. In ancient times, they were consecrated to Onjhol, the consort of the goddess Tabilit. No woman was allowed to mount them. Any coward who came into contact with such a horse would immediately fall ill. Alsanobal delighted in these stories, boasting that his continued good health demonstrated the excellence of his own valor.

The red horse carried no special merit in Shannivar's eyes, only a malicious disposition. Then, because she liked her cousin even if he was a hothead braggart, she wished him a bright day.

Alsanobal lingered as Shannivar slipped a lead line over Eriu's neck. "Race?"

Shannivar hesitated, although she had never

shrunk from such a challenge before. There was not another horse in all the Golden Eagle clans, and very few in Azkhantia, that could match Eriu's speed. No, this was something else. Perhaps she was already mourning this place and its people. Perhaps this might be her last race with her cousin.

"What's the matter?" he jibed. "Lost your nerve? Don't think you can beat me?"

"All right, then."

Shannivar settled her saddle over the thick blanket, tracing the patterned weave with her fingertips. Red and yellow threads highlighted the stylized Tree of Life, symbol of the goddess who had given horses to men. It had been her father's, woven by her mother.

Eriu dipped his head, taking the bit easily. Shannivar swung up on his back and adjusted her bow case beside her left knee. Alsanobal also went armed, as did every rider in these uncertain times.

They turned west, up the slopes and away from the river valley. Shannivar felt Eriu's stride lengthen, the flex and arch of his spine as his muscles warmed up. His head stayed low, one ear cocked back toward her. From the spring in his step, however, he was eager to run.

They had almost arrived at the flat stretch of grass, the usual starting point for a friendly race, when Shannivar heard the noise of a galloping mount. They halted, the red horse prancing and fighting the bit, wringing his tail in frustration.

One of the ponies kept for the youngest children, round-bodied and puffing with exertion, scrambled ıp the hill. Alsanobal's youngest brother, a boy of ıx, clung to the pony's back, beating her sides with ıis heels.

"Come quickly, elder brother!" the child called ıut. As soon as he stopped kicking the pony, she ıropped to a walk. "Strangers have come!"

"Gelon?" Alsanobal wheeled his horse. Shanni-var did the same as she reached for her bow.

"Not a war party, Father says. He says for you to come now."

Alsanobal gave the red his head, and the horse raced back the way they had come. Shannivar tapped Eriu with her heels. The black gathered his hindquarters under him, then burst into a full-out gallop. The coarse hairs of his mane whipped across Shannivar's face. She leaned over his forequarters, secretly pleased that they would have their race after all.

Eriu's speed was like fire, like silk, as intoxicating as *k'th*. Even on the rough downhill footing, he never missed a step. The air itself sustained him.

By day, you are my wings, the poet sang to his favorite steed. *By night, you never fail me.*

They plunged downhill, caught Alsanobal on his red, and passed them. Shannivar whooped in triumph.

The *dharlak* came into sight, the familiar arrangement of *jorts*, the ancient crumbling walls, the horses in their field. There was no sign of Esdarash, the chief, although most of the adult members of the clan had gathered in the central area. Two unfamiliar horses of poor quality stood beside a laden donkey. Their saddles were strange and flat, hardly fit for the rough terrain of the steppe. All three beasts showed signs of hard usage and privation.

As Shannivar slowed her mount, Alsanobal caught up with her. They exchanged glances.

"Go on," Shannivar told Alsanobal, as she reached over to grasp the reins of his horse. Nodding, Alsanobal jumped from the saddle and slipped inside his mother's *jort*, where Esdarash was meeting with the strangers.

Shannivar spoke soothingly to the red horse. With a snort and a skeptical glare, he lowered his head. A few moments later, he had quieted enough to follow her without protest. She left the horses in the care of one of the bright-eyed youngsters who ran to greet her.

She approached a group of clansmen as they squatted in a rough circle. Like her, they wore full-cut trousers tucked into soft boots, quilted vests, and felt caps adorned with feathers and strings of beads.

"May your day be lucky and your horses swift," she said, settling beside them. "Who are these strangers? Gelonian spies?"

"They say not," replied white-haired Taraghay, who had ridden against the invaders with Shannivar's father. Shannivar liked him, for he had always treated her fairly. His only daughter, Mirrimal, was Shannivar's closest friend.

"Who can tell with these lowland devils?" Taraghay went on. "Their names are Leanthos—he is the old one, and—what was the other? Pharrus?

No, Phannus, that is it. Outland names if I ever heard them. They speak trade-dialect with a terrible accent! They *say* they have come to make common purpose with us against the Gelon. But who can tell, with names like that?"

"They must be half-witted or struck mad from living in their stone houses, to think *we* need allies!" joked his brother, who was still young enough to fight.

"Or drunk on more *k'th* than they can stomach!" someone else added. At that, Shannivar laughed along with the men.

The Azkhantian clans had never needed the help of any other people. They moved where the winds took them, seeking pasture for their herds, water for the hot, lazy summer days, and shelter against the bitter winter cold. They looked to the Sky People, Tabilit and her consort Onjhol, their totem animals, and their own strength, never to other races.

As old Taraghay rose, the joints of his knees popped loudly. He rubbed the hilt of the knife tucked into his sash. "We'll learn their purpose in good time. There were but two of them, and neither looks to be a warrior."

"You cannot tell with outlanders," another of the men said with a frown. "They were asleep when the gods gave out sense. They wear no trousers, they cannot hold their drink, and their women are all blind in one eye."

"And a good thing that is, too, or none would take these for husbands."

"They'll be a week deciding anything." His friend sounded glum. "Meanwhile, work will not wait." He meant the preparations for the *khural*, the gathering, as well as ongoing care of the herds, milking the mares and she-goats, making cheese and fermenting *k'th*, mending harness, and reaping the summer's bounty of wild barley to see them through the winter.

The group broke up and the older men went about their business. One of the younger men remained behind with Shannivar. She knew Rhuzenjin son of Semador only slightly. They had not grown up together, for he had come lately to the clan when his mother, a widow of the Rabbit totem, married one of the older men. Rhuzenjin was a good archer and an even better wrestler, sturdily built, with powerful shoulders and quiet hands on the reins.

"Shannivar daughter of Ardellis, I would speak with you," he said, gaze lowered.

A moment of heightened awareness swept over Shannivar. She had never before noticed how smooth his skin was, how his thin moustache bracketed his sensitive mouth, the arch of his cheekbones, or his glossy dark eyes.

Before Shannivar could respond, Kendira daughter of Zomarre approached them. "Rhuzenjin, Shannivar, may Tabilit bless your horses with speed. Will you want any more tea?" As the wife of Alsanobal, Kendira carried a certain status, but she had been awake since before dawn, cooking breakfast with the other young married women. Now her face flushed beneath her white headscarf and she moved awkwardly, her belly thickened with pregnancy. She wore a knee-length robe of camel's hair, embroidered with symbols of fertility and the emblems of her own birth clan, Black Marmot.

When Kendira had married Alsanobal a little over a year ago, her speech and manners had seemed strange, although she'd behaved properly in all things. She was respectful to the men of the Golden Eagle clan and even more so to her husband's mother. Now that her advancing pregnancy gave her a topic of conversation with the other women, they were gradually beginning to accept her into their circles.

Kendira sighed, glancing at the fading embers of the cook fire. Shannivar would have liked more tea, strong, pleasantly bitter, and swimming with butter. Any man would have thought nothing of telling Kendira to build the fire up again, even if it meant collecting more camel dung as fuel. Her cousin's wife, however, looked so weary, perhaps still homesick, that Shannivar could not ask it.

"Will you not sit and gossip with us?" Shannivar gestured for Kendira to rest. "Did you see the strangers as they came into camp? What are they like? Is it true they are not Gelon?"

"I know no more of these strangers than you do." Kendira lowered herself with another sigh. She rubbed her lower back with one hand. "I can stay only for a moment. My mother-in-law will scold if I am late."

"Surely, once your child is born, you need not

work so hard," Shannivar said. "Your mother-in-law will dote upon her first grandson, and so will all the other aunties."

"No, no, it must never be said that I shirked a wife's duties." Kendira glanced speculatively at Rhuzenjin, who blushed and turned away. "We must not complain of the responsibilities of marriage or our husbands will think we are not eager."

Shannivar bit her lip. Kendira was said to have killed three Gelon before her marriage. Alsanobal had bragged about her prowess, what a fine warrior wife he had. Now she moved like an old woman and thought of nothing more than marriages and babies! She would not be going to the gathering this year, to drink *k'th* and dance until sunrise.

"As for the strangers, I myself know little of them," Rhuzenjin said. "Only that they are not Azkhantian."

"Surely they cannot be Gelon," Kendira said, making a face of disdain. "Or if they are, they must be cursed by Onjhol, to be so lacking in sense as to walk freely among their enemies, like the rabbit that hops of its own will into the cookpot."

Rhuzenjin, whose birth clan flourished under the totem of the Rabbit, crafty and agile, made a noise like an aborted snort.

"They could be outlaws among their own people," Shannivar mused aloud. "Or spies pretending to be traitors in order to gain our confidence."

"Do they think to discover our weaknesses?" Rhuzenjin shook his head. "Then they are fools indeed."

"What they are is none of our concern," Kendira said tartly. "It is for the chieftain and the elders to decide. If necessary, the *enaree* will use his magic to separate out the truth."

There was no denying any of this, so neither Shannivar nor Rhuzenjin said anything.

Kendira clambered to her feet. "I must get back to work. Grandmother has ordered wool to be beaten and soaked for felt."

Shannivar looked away. Kendira's tone shifted, friendly now. "Come and join us, Shannivar. We must become better cousins to one another. There will be work aplenty."

"I will come in a little while."

After Kendira left, Shannivar and Rhuzenjin sat in silence, alone. "Shannivar," he said, clearly ill at ease, "is it true that you intend to find a husband at the *khural*?"

"I intend to ride Eriu in the Long Ride."

"It is the time for young men to choose wives. Strong wives, to bear them many sons."

"And daughters, too, or there will be none for the sons to marry!" Shannivar said, laughing to cover her discomfort. "I wonder what the strangers want. They are taking a long time in there."

"It is said you are to build your *jort*. And that means you will not be returning to us."

Only last night she had spoken with Grandmother. Tabilit's golden fingers, did everyone in the entire *dharlak* know of that conversation?

She reminded herself that men gossiped just as much as women did. But men also lived their whole lives with one another, with their brothers and comrades. They had no need to leave their families to marry. Or to marry at all.

"If—if there were a man here among your own people, one who—who pleased you," Rhuzenjin stammered, "then would you stay?"

"I have never wished to leave my clan," Shannivar admitted. "Many things can happen at a gathering. The man who seeks to—to *please me*," she repeated Rhuzenjin's words, "must first *catch me.*"

She meant the comment as a joke, but it fell flat. Unsaid words hung like smoke between them.

Bidding Rhuzenjin a bright morning, Shannivar went to retrieve Eriu and see to the care of Alsanobal's wretched horse. She had half a mind to swing up on the red's back and ride through the encampment just to defy the old legends and create as much outrage as possible.

Chapter 5

AFTER the horses were tended, Shannivar joined the other women on the grassy field as they pounded the piles of sheep's wool, a process that took several hours. Afterward, the wool would be folded with an old felt, too thin and ragged for further use, and soaked with water. Then came the grueling work of dragging and rolling the sodden mass until the fibers meshed together. Once that was done, they would make offerings to Tabilit, milk and incense to bless the new felt before it was spread to dry in the sun.

The older women sat a little apart, casting sidelong glances at the younger ones. They were scheming, Shannivar thought, about who would be the next to marry. Kendira, sitting with the other young wives, grinned and waved. Shannivar smiled back, but found a place with her closest friend, Mirrimal daughter of Sayyiqan.

After one look at her friend's expression, Shannivar made no attempt at light conversation. Mirrimal bent over the wool, her face set in concentration. Exertion flushed her cheeks, high and broad, with the stamp of her Antelope clan mother. She had shoved her shirt sleeves above her elbows, so that the muscles of her forearms stood out like ropes. Sweating, she pounded the mat of fibers as if it were an enemy who refused to die.

Because Mirrimal was two years older than Shannivar, they had not been close as children. As they grew to womanhood and watched their age mates set aside bows for marriage, a bond of wordless understanding had grown between them. Shannivar wondered if Grandmother had spoken to Mirrimal, and that was why her friend was angry. *Perhaps we will both find husbands at the* khural. *Maybe brothers, so we will not be parted.*

"A song!" one of the young women cried. "Shannivar, a song!"

"Sing to us of Saramark," another urged, "so that her strength may pass into the felt!"

"'May the strong bones of my body rest in the earth,'" Shannivar sang, and the other women answered, beating in rhythm, *"Ayay, ayay!"*

"'May the black hair on my head turn to meadow-grass.'"

"Ayay, ayay!"

"'May my bright eyes become springs that never fail.'"

"Ayay, ayay!"

"'May the hungry camels come and eat. May the thirsty horses come and drink.'"

"Ayay, ayay! Ayay, ayay!"

Kendira's mother-in-law circled the work party, inspecting the heaped wool. She bent over Mirrimal's work and scowled. "You'll never get a husband that way!"

Mirrimal tossed her head. "I do not want a husband who thinks a woman is good only for pounding wool."

"Oh, husbands are interested in far more than that, I can tell you!" Kendira patted her swollen belly. "At least, mine is!"

"Yours is young and strong," one of the older women cackled. "Just wait until he's old and shriveled!"

"Oh, no," her sister, long since widowed, answered. "What they lack in stamina, they make up for in experience!"

The other women laughed and someone began the old courting song about the blind woman and the radish. Only Shannivar and Mirrimal did not laugh.

Shannivar looked away from her friend's reddened cheeks and unhappy expression. Like Shannivar, Mirrimal loved her present life. In addition to prowess with the bow, she was skilled with handling livestock of all sorts. For a time, Shannivar heard whispers that her cousin Alsanobal had asked for Mirrimal, and that there had been several meetings between Mirrimal's father and Grandmother. Old heads had wagged, winks and nods had been exchanged, and Mirrimal had prepared for the next round of raids against the Gelon as if for her own funeral. The night of their victorious return, Mirrimal would not speak to Shannivar, but sat beside the fire and downed skin after skin of potent *k'th*. Shannivar glimpsed her friend and Alsanobal stagger from the firelit circles together. After that, there was no more talk of marriage. Mirrimal refused to say what had happened. Alsanobal returned from the next gathering with his new wife, Kendira.

Shannivar's brows tightened. There was not much hope for any Azkhantian woman to remain unmarried, not unless she was deformed like Scarface or too old to bear children. A widow had control of her own *jort*, as well as her husband's horses and his share of the sheep and camels; she could not be forced to remarry unless she wished it, but to refuse was considered improper, even scandalous. There were many ways of pressuring a young, fertile woman to take another husband.

"I am glad you will be riding to the *khural*," Shannivar said, low enough so that only Mirrimal could hear her under the new song, a traditional courting chant. "We will have one more adventure together."

"I did not think *you* would bow so easily to custom." Mirrimal scowled as she surveyed the felt.

Not custom alone, Shannivar thought. *You have never shared Grandmother's* jort. "I do not wish to delay until all my choices are gone," she tried to sound gentle. "Perhaps—if you competed in the Long Ride with me, then you too would have a choice of husbands. You could—"

"You know me better than that!" Mirrimal's voice was tight with anger and the accusation of betrayal.

"I am sorry to have offended you. But the Gelon

will never relent, at least not this Ar-King. Perhaps if we lived in a time of peace. Since we do not, is it not better to exercise what choice we still have?"

"Not you, Shannu—I cannot believe that of you. Have you given up your dreams of glory?"

Shannivar set her lips together. "Now it is *you* who mistake *me*, dear friend. I have not forgotten, I am trying to be practical. What about your own hopes? What do you wish for?"

"I wish a woman could become an *enaree*!" Mirrimal sighed. "Then I might have an honest place in the world! Why is it that a man can tread the boundaries of dreams and a woman cannot? When he dons the garments of a woman, he becomes neither one nor the other, ripe for visions. Why can't a woman take on the trappings of a man and do the same?"

"Yet it is the custom. Only men may become shamans. Perhaps it is easier to give up the hope of siring a child than of bearing one."

"I refuse to believe that Tabilit ordered such a thing!" Mirrimal renewed her attack on the felt. "This is one more stupid rule. Made up by *men*!"

After a long moment, Shannivar said, "Do you despise me, then, because I will make my *jort* and seek a husband?"

"No, no." Mirrimal put down her pounding stick. She sounded weary, all her vehemence spent. She leaned over and kissed Shannivar with surprising tenderness. "You will always be my true friend. I am afraid, that is all."

"You, who are not afraid of anything." Shannivar forced a laugh. "How can that be?"

Mirrimal gave her a sideways glance. "There are worse things than cloud leopards or Gelonian armies. Even than death."

A life confined, drained of honor, without hope of glory. Shannivar shuddered.

"It is not death I fear," Mirrimal whispered.

Shannivar touched her friend's hand. "We are of the race of great women warriors. Think of Saramark and Aimellina daughter of Oomara, of the first Shannivar! Tabilit will not turn away from our prayers. Are we not women, as she is? Does she not bestow special care on those who fight in her name?"

"Oh, Shannu," Mirrimal cried, using the childhood familiar name. "I wish I had your faith! We give our loyalty to the goddess, but more times than not, she leaves our fate in the hands of *men*. Is it a wonder that sometimes I wish I were dead?"

"She leaves our fate in our *own* hands. You must believe that! You are not helpless, any more than I am! Why not appeal to the Council of elders at the *khural*—or the *enarees* themselves?"

"For what? What would you have me ask that they have within their power to grant?"

No words rose to Shannivar's mouth. Her heart was too full of what Mirrimal had said: *It is not death I fear.*

When one of the younger boys brought word that Esdarash and the strangers had emerged, all but the oldest women set aside their pounding sticks and an to the center of the camp. Shannivar and Mirimal quickly outdistanced the others.

Most of the adult population of the encampment, as well as the older children, had gathered around Grandmother's *jort*. Everyone was talking at once, pointing and gesturing. Some made protective signs against evil influences.

Esdarash's wife elbowed her way to the front of the crowd. "Get out of my way! Let me through!"

Esdarash himself stood in front of the *jort*, flanked by his son and the *enaree*. Alsanobal thrust his chest out, clearly pleased with his position of responsibility. As for the shaman, Shannivar had never been able to read the expression on his moon-round face, and she could not do so now. Like all of his kind, he wore a long deerskin robe over his trousers. Layers of faded symbols covered the yoke and shoulders of the robe. Strings of beads knotted with tiny bones and feathers dangled from his dream stick. His gaze seemed fixed, turned inward to some vision that only he could see. Whether he was terrified, entranced, or simply attending to his magical duties, Shannivar could not say.

Her uncle was another matter. He was the firstborn of Grandmother's sons, older than Shannivar's father by ten years, and now he looked his age. Lines of worry marked his weathered face. White frosted his moustache as well as the hair partly hidden beneath his peaked cap with its chieftain's feathers. Yet his voice was strong and firm as he commanded the assembly to order.

Everyone settled into their places, and Shannivar

got her first look at the two strangers. Instead of sensible trousers, boots, and jackets cut close to the body, they wore belted knee-length gowns, short cloaks, and sandals, utterly impractical for riding. At first glance, she thought they must surely be Gelon. Their skins were pale, except where the sun had darkened them. Both had unbound dark red curls, the head of one shot with gray. That must be the one called Leanthos.

Shannivar peered at him, trying to decide if he were very brave or simply very foolish to venture into clan territory. Certainly, he was no match for any Azkhantian child, with his thin arms and knobby knees. Yet as he glanced at the waiting crowd and back to Esdarash, his expression was confident and calculating. Weak he might be, and unskilled at arms, but not a fool.

The younger man, with his slab-like jaw and beaked nose, clearly deferred to the gray-hair, and he carried himself with the subtle alertness of a fighter. He might be trying to pass himself off as a mere assistant, but no one with sense could mistake him for anything but a man of action.

Esdarash explained that the strangers had ridden freely into the *dharlak*, their weapons undrawn, bearing gifts.

Gifts? A murmur spread through the assembly.

Two of the younger warriors, Rhuzenjin and another, came forward at Esdarash's signal and placed the gifts on a blanket. They laid out strings of beads in brilliant colors, jewelry of silver and copper, and several small daggers of Denariyan steel. The craftsmanship of the jewelry and dagger hilts was good, although not as fine as the best Azkhantian work, but the stones—amber, turquoise, coral, and others Shannivar did not know—were of excellent quality.

Around her, people exclaimed in delight, but suspicion roused in Shannivar's mind. What was the purpose of such rich offerings? What did these men want in return?

She turned her attention back to her uncle, who was now explaining how the strangers had journeyed all the way from Isarre, or so they said, to seek an alliance with the Azkhantian warriors. Apparently, they had no understanding of the different independent clans and their territories. They'd traveled east from Isarre, across the Sand Lands, and then north toward the steppe, and so had stumbled upon the Golden Eagle lands.

The crowd buzzed with astonishment. Everyone knew of Isarre, a nation of seafarers and stone-dwellers. For all practical purposes, they were indistinguishable from their Gelonian enemies. They were not Azkhantian, and they had nothing of value to the steppe dwellers and so were of little interest. Isarre was too distant to present either a credible threat or an opportunity for raiding. Now these men had come all this distance to bargain for help in defending themselves.

"What kind of moon-blind fools do they think we are?" one of Shannivar's neighbors muttered.

She had no answer. Certainly, the fate of Isarre was of no concern to the Golden Eagle clan. They shared ties of neither blood nor honor. Yet she could not help thinking what a grand adventure it would be, to journey to a country so far and strange. To travel the reaches of sand and ocean, farther than the eye could see or an eagle could fly. Perhaps even to carry war into the heart of Gelon, to see the invaders tremble as their own lands and flocks were trampled beneath the hooves of her horses.

She did not know if these two men were in truth what they claimed. For a moment, she hoped they were, so that she might go with them.

Words were all very fine, but those who dwelled in stone could not be relied upon to tell the truth. Their story must be verified by the blessing of Tabilit, as revealed through the dream visions of the shaman. Esdarash brought the audience to a close so that Bennorakh, the *enaree,* could examine the outlanders.

The crowd began to disperse. Esdarash's wife scolded the younger women for lingering, for the day was still young. "The felt must be properly rolled or it will dry unevenly! You'll never get a good husband if the men see how lazy you are!"

"I'll be along in a moment, auntie," Shannivar murmured. She watched as the *enaree* took the two strangers into his own *jort.* Doubtless, they would remain there for the rest of the day or perhaps longer. The vision could require several days.

Shannivar felt a shiver of pity for the two strangers. She had been examined by the clan shaman only once, before her first foray against the Gelon. The memory was still vivid, the smoky closeness of the *jort,* the strange designs painted on the felt panels, the sonorous chanting. She had been frightened of the *enaree*, this strange, wild-eyed half-man in women's clothing, and fascinated as well.

At the time of Shannivar's initiation, Bennorakh had but lately joined the community, for their old shaman had died of a lung-fever two winters before, leaving no apprentice to take his place. Half-starved and covered with mud and brambles, Bennorakh had stumbled into the winter encampment on the very changing between the Moon of Darkfall and the Moon of Wolves. Unerringly, he had gone to the *enaree*'s *jort* that stood dark and empty, as if waiting for him. No one had questioned his right to be there. Every family had placed offerings of food and other necessities outside the door flap. The hunting had been good all that season, and the grass especially plentiful in the Moon of Foals.

When Shannivar had presented herself for his blessing, he had drawn the point of his sickle knife between her breasts and said that her heart would never rest in Azkhantia. When she heard this, she knew that Tabilit had not destined her for a peaceful life.

As the sun crested the eastern hills the following morning, Shannivar set out on Radu, accompanied by Mirrimal as her closest woman friend and Kendira as her cousin's wife. The felt had been properly rolled, smooth and straight, then set out to dry. Now was the proper time to assemble the framework for Shannivar's *jort*.

The women traveled slowly, laughing and singing. This was partly for Kendira's comfort and partly for the simple pleasure of the day. Mirrimal rode her rangy gray, leading an old she-camel that carried supplies and would carry the completed lattice back. Shannivar set aside her own gloomy thoughts, pleased to see her friend bright and happy once more.

They came across a stand of willow, unloaded the camel, hobbled the horses to graze, and set about cutting and shaping the long, flexible strips for the lattice. As they worked, Mirrimal told a hilarious story about her younger brother at the last *khural*, how he had won honor in wrestling on horseback, but fallen off while attempting to pick up a dropped kerchief at full gallop.

"And so," she concluded, "the girls told him that the Gelon had nothing to fear, if only they would go to war in their skirts!"

"Perhaps we should teach the Isarrans the hat-stealing game!" Kendira said, holding her sides. Shannivar had never seen her so relaxed.

"I don't know that game," Mirrimal said. "Is it one your people play?"

Kendira looked down, her cheeks coloring faintly. "Among the Black Marmot clan, it is a bridal game. When a young woman is ready to be married, she wears a special hat—this tall and shaped so," she gestured with her hands and set the other two giggling, "and *red*!"

The giggles erupted into outright laughter. Kendira's eyes crinkled merrily. "She rides her horse along a flat field, toward a pole set at the very end."

"We know what the pole symbolizes," Shannivar said.

"Any man who wants her follows," Kendira went on, grinning. "Of course, she has a whip to fend them off. So only the one *she* wants will catch her. That man must steal her hat and place it on the pole."

"Ooohh," Shannivar groaned appreciatively.

"What if—what if she wants none of them?" Mirrimal asked.

Kendira shrugged. "Then I suppose she must reach the pole first and place the hat there herself."

In the awkward silence that followed, Shannivar said, "I cannot believe a man so foolish as to live within a stone dwelling would be able to catch *any* Azkhantian woman."

The three friends laughed heartily at the follies of the stone-dwellers. How strange it must be, Shannivar thought, to live in only one place, a place she had not made with her own hands. The love of her friends, her kin, indeed, her whole clan would be woven into the lattice of her *jort* and the layers of felt. Wherever she went, their memories would sustain her.

Watching Mirrimal and Kendira bind the flexible laths, lulled by the music of their voices, she felt something pull at her heart, an unexpected heaviness like the first intimation of farewell.

Chapter 6

SHANNIVAR and her friends returned to the *dharlak* three days later with the completed lattice tied to the camel's back. The she-camel, true to the capricious nature of her kind, turned surly the last few miles. The beast spat at the horses and tried to kick Kendira.

Shannivar, who had been riding ahead, halted Radu and twisted in the saddle to watch. The camel lifted nose to the sky, baring long, orange-streaked teeth.

"Wretched beast!" Kendira snapped. The last few miles, she had been massaging her low back and leaning heavily on the saddle pommel.

"Gray-ears is usually sweet-tempered. For a camel, that is. Something troubles her." Instead of beating the camel with a stick, as any man would do, Mirrimal slipped from the saddle. Rumbling noises came from the camel's throat, though she made no attempt to either spit or bite as Mirrimal drew closer. Crooning, Mirrimal stroked the camel along its narrow, bony chest. The rumbling softened into a sigh.

Shannivar watched in admiration. "I don't know how you do that."

"It's not all that different from your way with horses."

"Better horses than camels!"

"On the other hand, *I* prefer camels to babies." Mirrimal cast a sidelong glance at Kendira.

Sniffing, Kendira tucked a stray tendril of hair back under her head scarf and pretended not to notice.

Mirrimal gave the camel a last pat and returned to her horse. Clucking encouragement, she shortened the camel's lead line. For a moment, it looked as if the camel might resist, but the beast, although reluctant, was resigned and took one swaying step after another.

Ahead lay the *dharlak*, peaceful and tidy. Children laughed as they splashed in the lake. Horses and sheep grazed on the slopes, unconcerned by their approach. Curls of smoke, easily recognizable as cookfires, rose here and there. In the direction of the *enaree's jort*, however, Shannivar thought she saw a cloud like greasy smoke that refused to dissipate.

At the edge of the encampment itself, the camel's cooperation came to an end. The beast dug her forefeet into the dirt and whipped her head around in unmistakable threat. Mirrimal would not force the camel to go any further, so the women were obliged to unload the *jort* lattice and baggage, and carry them into the *dharlak*. Kendira protested, but not too much, when Shannivar and Mirrimal lifted the lattice between them.

"You have other duties to attend to," Shannivar insisted, seeing that Kendira was near the end of her strength. "Go now, for if your husband is not sufficiently impatient for your return, then surely your mother-in-law must be! You cannot leave her to do all the work herself."

"Yes, you are quite right," Kendira said, clearly relieved. "A married woman has responsibilities and cannot always please herself."

Mirrimal watched Kendira walk away, rolling with the awkward gait of pregnancy. "Can *never* please herself, more like."

It was Kendira's own affair whether she was happy or not, satisfied with her life as wife and mother or not, whether she longed to return to hunt and battle, whether she missed her own clan and its customs.

Shannivar was not afraid of hard work, but when she thought of spending the rest of her life confined to *jort* and cookpot, weaving, and tending babies, she felt sick at heart, as if she had unwittingly traded Eriu for Gray-ears. There must be more to a woman's life than what Kendira had accepted.

The two women deposited the lattice beside the pile of folded, dried felts outside Grandmother's *jort*. Scarface came out to greet them, making a motion that Grandmother was sleeping. From the pot on the banked cookfire, she dipped out three cups of butter-laced tea. They moved away from Grandmother's *jort* to talk more freely.

"What's the news?" Shannivar asked. "Has Bennorakh released the strangers?"

No, indeed, Scarface told them, in between sips of her own tea. The strangers were still sequestered with the *enaree*. Day by day, smoke rose from the opening in the roof, sometimes white, sometimes black, and once—here Scarface made a grimace of disapproval—it had been *green*. Drumming had filled the air, pierced for an instant by screaming.

Shannivar could well imagine how the smug, slightly malicious speculations about the strangers had died down, to be replaced by with muted awe. Rarely was one of the clan put to such a testing. At least, Scarface qualified with a carefully guarded expression, so Grandmother had said.

Shannivar and Mirrimal exchanged glances. This must be a matter of serious prophetic importance for the *enaree* to examine them with such vigor.

Grandmother emerged from the *jort* at that moment, querulous at being awakened. Mirrimal bowed and took her leave while Scarface asked if there was anything Grandmother needed. Shannivar diverted the old woman's irritation by asking her to inspect the new lattice. Grandmother did so, and although she ran her gnarled fingers over every strip of wood and every joining, she could find no fault. The perfection, Shannivar reflected wryly, was in part due to Kendira's near-obsession with detail. At the time, Shannivar had thought her cousin's wife excessive, as if a woman's value—or her eligibility for marriage—were determined by the evenness of her *jort* lattice. Apparently, Grandmother thought so, too.

A hubbub from the direction of Bennorakh's *jort* brought an end to the examination of the lattice. Shannivar walked at Grandmother's side, Scarface supported her on the other, and together they passed through the gathering crowd.

Esdarash and the other senior men took their places in a semi-circle around the *enaree*'s *jort*. As was proper, Esdarash sat on his stool of stitched, painted camel skin. At Grandmother's approach, he gestured for a second seat to be brought for her.

Grandmother settled herself. Scarface sat at her feet, but Shannivar remained standing. The crowd grew still, as if holding its collective breath.

The door flap lifted and Bennorakh emerged. Even the most excited onlooker drew back respectfully. The shaman looked haggard, as if the hours of smoke and chanting, of visions and fasting, had etched themselves into his features. For a moment, he struggled visibly to focus on the waiting assemblage. He seemed not to know them, or perhaps he had forgotten himself and what he was doing there. Then his gaze fell upon Shannivar, where she stood behind Grandmother. His expression shifted.

Grandmother made a censorious noise in her throat. Shannivar had no doubt it was meant for her. Although she made no response, she could not take her gaze away from the shaman. A fire burned behind his deep-set eyes. What could it mean, that intense look? She wanted to dismiss it as the result of fasting and too much dreamsmoke. Something roused within her, stirring to life.

Shannivar sensed a wordless bond between her-

self and the *enaree*. She did not know whether to be
elated or terrified. A thought gathered in her mind,
like a storm condensing across the winter sky. She
had the distinct impression that Bennorakh had
seen her in his visions, that Tabilit had interwoven
her destiny, and perhaps her death, with that of the
outlanders.

*How could she, Shannivar of the race of Sara-
mark, daughter of the Azkhantian steppe, have anything to do with stone-dwelling outlanders?*

A moment later, the strangers themselves stumbled from the dark interior of the *jort*, red-eyed and
pale. The older one could barely stand. Sweat matted his hair to his skull, giving him a cadaverous
appearance. His jaw muscles stood out in stark relief against the stubble on his cheek. He seemed to
be holding himself erect by willpower alone. The
younger man, the one Shannivar had marked for a
warrior, carried himself better. From the way he
looked around the audience, his gaze flickering
from Esdarash to the other men, he was ready to
respond to any physical threat.

The moment stretched on. The older of the Isarrans wavered on his feet, Esdarash waited in stony
formality, and Bennorakh stared at Shannivar. Then
the *enaree* raised his dream stick. As he shook it,
the bones and shells, the sacred stones and amulets
of carved horn rattled. The brittle sound pierced the
air.

"The strangers have spoken truly!" Bennorakh
proclaimed, his voice hoarse as a raven's.

The older stranger closed his eyes, lips moving

silently. His gods had answered his prayers. Or perhaps, Shannivar thought with another glance at the *enaree*, the Sky People had a use for even moon-mad stone-dwellers.

Esdarash ordered drink and food for the Isarrans. People turned to their neighbors, speculating about what might happen next. Everyone seemed to have a different opinion.

Surprisingly, Grandmother said nothing. Shannivar bent to whisper a question in the old woman's ear. She felt a curious stillness in the aged shoulders. The next moment Grandmother toppled sideways, and Scarface burst out screaming.

Shannivar caught the old woman in her arms. She staggered under the sudden, inert weight. Tiny as she was, Grandmother was surprisingly heavy. Kneeling, Shannivar lowered the old woman to the ground. Someone was shouting—Esdarash, she thought, although she could not make out his words through Scarface's rising shrieks.

"Grandmother!" Shannivar cried. "Grandmother!"

There was no response. The old woman's head lolled to one side. Her eyes were closed so that only a thin line, like the first glimmer of a new moon, shone between her lids. Her lips had gone dark, almost black.

Don't leave us. Don't leave us. We need you.

Shannivar, not knowing what else to do, bent down and placed one ear over her grandmother's chest. She might not have been able to hear even a strong pulse through a traditional quilted vest and woven wool shirt, but Grandmother wore Denari-yan silk.

For a long, terrible moment, Shannivar heard nothing. Then, muffled, as if far away, came a doubled drum-beat. *Ta-thum* . . .

Another.

Against her cheek, Shannivar felt a faint stirring of air from her grandmother's parted lips.

Relief swept through her. The air turned too bright.

She sat back on her heels and entwined her fingers with Grandmother's. The assembled clan crowded around her. Esdarash pushed forward, his face ashen.

Quickly Shannivar said, "She is not dead! She breathes! Her heart beats!"

He stared at her, then at Scarface, who was still wailing as if Grandmother were certainly dead.

Shannivar rounded on Scarface. "Be still! Would you shame us all by your weakness?"

It was exactly what Grandmother would have said, and in the same tone of voice. Scarface scrambled backward, almost falling over her own feet. Her howling died instantly. An intimation of calm settled over the crowd.

"Take her to her *jort*." Shannivar pointed to the nearest men. She had no idea who they were, nor did she care. "Carefully, now."

"Do as she says!" commanded the *enaree*. He shook his dream stick for emphasis. The bones and shells clattered like hooves over barren rock. "Go, *go!*"

The men jumped to obey. Composure recovered,

Scarface went along, instructing them in the properly respectful way of carrying Grandmother. Bennorakh trailed after them. He glanced behind once, to meet Shannivar's astonished gaze. In that moment, she saw flames, red and gold, behind the lightless dark of his eyes.

Esdarash, having recovered from his first moment of shock, began shouting orders. His son, Alsanobal, stood beside his father, glowering at the Isarrans as if they had somehow caused Grandmother's collapse. The two strangers watched the commotion, uncomprehending. Shannivar had no thought to spare for them as she hurried away.

Esdarash's wife, Yvanne daughter of Liritark, had positioned herself outside the door flap of Grandmother's *jort*. She kept the crowd away, achieving a modicum of quiet. Scarface waited nearby. Shannivar drew herself up and marched up to the *jort* as if to battle. For an instant, Yvanne held her ground, but at the last moment, she moved aside to let Shannivar step across the threshold.

The air inside was thick, making it difficult to breathe. The *jort* seemed not to belong to the rest of the encampment, existing partly in another world, a place of spirits and shadows.

Grandmother was already resting in her own bed. Its ancient carved wood looked almost black, charred. Bennorakh crouched beside her. He had set his dream stick aside and was speaking to Grandmother in low, intense tones.

"I'll have none of it!" Grandmother's voice, hoarse and querulous, broke through his murmured words.

"You must listen—" The *enaree* raised his head to stare at Shannivar.

Shannivar strode to the bed. "Grandmother, I see you are awake. Can I bring you anything? Tea? *K'th?*"

Despite her outward calm, Shannivar was thinking, *Would you like me to throw the* enaree *out for distressing you at a time like this?*

Grandmother dismissed Shannivar's offers with a flick of her fingers and kept her attention on the *enaree*. Breath wheezed in her lungs. "Bennu, my friend, we must all bow to Tabilit's will. I have already seen far more winters than have any other of my people. I will not—I do not wish to—see this doom. This doom upon those I love."

Doom? Shannivar's belly went cold.

"It is not certain," Bennorakh's voice was urgent, almost pleading.

"We have seen what we have seen, you and I. Do not cling to foolish hope."

Bright as bits of sun, Grandmother's eyes lit on Shannivar. The old woman beckoned her close. Something in the fervor of her gaze chilled Shannivar even more deeply.

She is like the flare of a torch before it goes out.

Grandmother held out one hand, trembling so badly that Shannivar had to clasp it between both of hers to hold it still. "Go—you must go."

"Go? What are you saying Grandmother? I cannot leave you like this! What if—" *What if you should die, and I am not here? How can I then sing you to the Sky?*

"I should . . . have sent you away . . . before this. But I did not want to part with you . . . my Saramark."

A long, heart-wrenching pause, and then:"Forgive an old woman's selfish love." Another pause, a hush, a falling away of that fevered strength. "Now—it is too late. You cannot escape—what lies ahead."

Grandmother's lids fluttered closed, and her head drifted to one side. For a heartbeat, and another, and third, no breath came from between the withered lips.

Every resentment Shannivar had ever felt against the old woman, every moment of rebellion, vanished.

"Go," Grandmother had commanded. Had begged. Had foreseen. *"Forgive me . . . You must go."*

The hand between Shannivar's own felt as brittle as an old feather.

The door flap jerked aside and Esdarash swept into the *jort*, trailing turbulence like a Darkfall Moon storm. Shannivar hardly recognized him. He was no longer the uncle she had known, stern and just. His face was flushed, his eyes rimmed with white, his mouth distorted. The scent of his fear hung in the air like burned silver. In that moment, Shannivar saw not the aging chieftain nor the warrior, but the son.

Shannivar hauled herself upright, half afraid that if she remained in Grandmother's *jort* for even a single minute longer, she would shatter like ice.

*   *   *

Alsanobal and his brothers waited outside, and behind them, Kendira and a few women cousins. As one, they looked to Shannivar. She did not know what to say. What assurance could she give them? Had Grandmother clung to life only long enough to utter her final command? Where had Bennorakh gone?

As if in answer, the *enaree* emerged from the little crowd. He carried his dream stick, a large leather bag, and a skin like that used for storing *k'th*, only this one was painted with strange symbols. Pointing to Scarface and Kendira, he gestured for them to follow him into Grandmother's *jort*.

"The outlanders have brought this curse upon us!" Alsanobal said, his voice tinny with emotion. "It is all their doing!"

Shannivar restrained herself from challenging him. The Isarran strangers had just been accepted by the *enaree*. He had vouched for them and the sincerity of their mission. What motive could they have for harming the clan matriarch?

Yet, she admitted, it was natural to look for someone to blame. How could anyone rail against Tabilit for the simple passing of years? Grandmother had outlived her brothers, husbands, and some of her sons. Yet even she could not live forever.

"My Saramark . . ."

Alsanobal allowed himself to be led away by Mirrimal's two brothers. They would talk sense into him, or at least keep him from doing any permanent harm.

Shannivar remained behind. A keening rose from her heart.

> *May the strong bones of my body rest in the*
> *   earth.*
> *May the black hair on my head turn to*
> *   meadow-grass.*
> *May my bright eyes become springs that never*
> *   fail . . .*

"Come away, Shannu." Mirrimal appeared beside Shannivar and touched her gently on the arm. "Her spirit is in Tabilit's care. There is nothing more any of us can do."

Chapter 7

SHANNIVAR allowed Mirrimal to lead her away. Her belly had gone stiff and cold, as if she had swallowed too much snow. They left the ring of *jorts* and passed the smith's hut. No sound of tapping filled the air; a silence had fallen here, as well. She wondered about the people who had built the hut, piling stone upon stone, and wondered, too, if one day, her own clan might be nameless, their deeds and dreams forgotten.

What did it matter if she followed custom and accepted a husband or lived as she wished? In the end, the only thing that endured was the steppe, the wind over the grasses, and the arc of the sky. Tabil-it's Bow, as the new moon was called. The stars that were her tears.

They reached the edge of the horse field, although Shannivar had no memory of passing beyond the *dharlak* outskirts. Eriu nickered and ambled toward them, his head low and swinging easily with his stride. His tail swished flies from his glossy back.

As Shannivar approached, his posture shifted subtly, nostrils flaring, both ears coming up. He dipped his nose. She stroked his chest, his shoulder, inhaled his scent. He turned his head sideways, and one dark eye regarded her calmly. She pressed her cheek against the smooth, sun-warmed neck. He stood like a rock, except for his slow, regular breathing.

For a moment, Shannivar thought she might weep, but no tears came. Grandmother had made sure she could not return after the *khural*. Had she known that Shannivar meant to shape her own destiny? Or was that what the old woman had intended all along?

Eriu's breath thrummed through his strong body. Shannivar twined her fingers through his long, coarse mane. This, she thought, *this* is real. *This* she could depend upon.

> *By day, you are my wings,*
> *By night, you never fail me.*

How long she stood there, Shannivar could not tell. At moments, she became aware of Mirrimal moving through the herd, murmuring to other animals.

She came back to herself slowly, as the shadows shifted, as the scents of feathergrass and sage deepened in the twilight. The day no longer seemed too bright. Eriu blew out through his nostrils, then bent his head to snatch a clump of grass. Whatever had held them there, woman and horse in silent communion, drained away into the ordinary demands of the day.

Mirrimal was sitting on a grassy rise. She unfolded her legs and stood up as Shannivar approached. There was no need for speech.

By the time they returned to the circle of *jorts*, the other women were busy with dinner preparations. No one sang as they worked, and even the usual clatter of pans and stirring sticks was hushed.

The *enaree* signaled for the family, including Shannivar and Kendira, to come forward. As they entered Grandmother's *jort*, he prayed aloud, blessing Tabilit for endowing the threshold with protection from evil spirits for those who dwelled within.

Incense swirled in the dim interior. At each corner of the hearth, a small butter lamp burned. The light felt warm and close. It pressed on Shannivar's senses, a weight on her heart. Grandmother's wooden bed had been folded and put away, and her body arranged on the floor, lying on one side, her face covered with a white cloth.

Esdarash and his sons sat at her head, stern and silent, for it was their responsibility to keep watch for evil spirits. Yvanne, Kendira, and Shannivar dismantled the latticed wall section to the right of the threshold. When they were done, the men carried the body through the opening. When Bennorakh was satisfied with the position of the body, Esdarash brought out the drum, and the *enaree* sang.

Let her return to you, O Tabilit,
Let her pure spirit rise up to your Sky Kingdom,
Carried by the wings of the Golden Eagle.
Let her take her place with the chosen ones.
Let her sit at Onjhol's strong right hand.

When the song ended, the ritual was complete, and everyone dispersed, some to rest, some to quiet reflection.

The funeral procession set off the next morning as the last stars were fading from the sky. Bennor-akh tied Grandmother's body to the back of her favorite horse, a gray mare now white with age, and led the mare at the front. Esdarash and his sons followed, then the women of the family, and finally the other mourners.

On the way, the *enaree* sang of a great horse, a chief of horses, who was captured by outlanders and taken far away. After years in exile, the horse longed to breathe the free air of the steppe again. One night, heartsick and weary, he escaped, but the years had exacted their price. With each passing mile, his strength waned. He prayed to Tabilit that he might see his homeland once again. Tabilit, Mother of Horses, answered his prayer. As he galloped across the desert, the wind in his mane carried him home.

Shannivar knew the song by heart. She had sung it at the death of her comrades, slain in battle. Never before had she heard it sung for anyone but a warrior. Never before had she wept at the words. It was not unseemly to shed tears during the last journey of a family member. Esdarash's cheeks shone and from time to time, he uttered a loud, keening wail. The emotion that swelled in Shannivar's heart was different. She did not grieve only for Grandmother, although she would miss the old woman and could not imagine the clan without her guidance. This was something more, like a knife turning in her heart, a shadow across the brightness of the sky. She did not know what it was, only that she ached deeper than words. No one spoke to her or remarked on her emotion, and for that small favor, she was grateful.

Through the morning and into the high sun, the procession wound between the rolling hills. The land grew harder, with stunted weeds clinging to barren soil. Even the wind took on a mournful note. Once or twice, an eagle hovered high overhead.

They came to a flat area, the ground cracked from seasons of heat and cold. Wiregrass poked through the matted, desiccated stems of last spring's wildflowers. Bennorakh signaled a halt. He slipped the bridle from the white mare and slapped her rump. The horse sprang into a trot.

They caught sight of the mare a little while later. She was grazing, moving stiffly. The saddle was empty. Esdarash pointed to where a shapeless bundle lay on the earth only a short distance away. Reverently, they gathered around as Bennorakh straightened the body. He smoothed the white cloth over her face.

"O Tabilit, Giver of Life," he intoned, lifting his arms to the sky. "I speak for our sister, who is about to join you. Among your many blessings, you have given her the bounty of the steppe, animals to eat, to clothe her, to ornament her dwelling. Let her last virtuous act be to return nourishment to those animals. To the vulture, to the snake, to the wild fox. May they live in peace because of her gift. May their lives, and the continuing life of the world, praise your goodness."

Esdarash went to catch the white mare. After wandering a short distance, she had come to a halt. Her head drooped to the level of her knees, and her legs splayed wide. Suddenly the mare's knees folded under her. She fell heavily. Her sides heaved as she struggled to breathe. She rocked from side to side, attempting to bring her legs under her, to rise again. Just as Esdarash, who was in the lead, reached her, she fell back. The others caught up to him a moment later.

A pang ripped through Shannivar, and in that moment, she saw the horse, no longer bleached with age, but gray as a thundercloud, skimming the earth, racing the wind. On her back rode a young woman, guiding her mount without bit or rein. They were one, woman and mare and storm.

Someday it will be my turn. Someday I will lie on the earth and give back a small measure of its bounty. And Eriu as well—

Shannivar's breath caught in her throat. The day went dim. She had never felt so weak, not even during her initiation testing. What was this omen brushing her heart like the shadow of a vulture's wing? Was something going to happen to Eriu?

The mare lifted her head as Esdarash bent down to stroke her. She regarded him calmly as he murmured to her. Her head sagged once more. Then, with a sigh, she lay still.

Esdarash remained as he was, one hand still resting on the mare's shoulder. He looked as if he could not quite believe the stillness beneath his hand.

How much of the spirit of the horse had been in the woman, and of the woman in the horse?

* * *

For the next three days, Bennorakh directed the preparation of special foods, barley porridge with sheep cheese, flat cakes, and lake fish. The women took down Grandmother's *jort*, untying and rolling the felts, carefully severing the bindings that held the laths together, then stacking the age-darkened wood. Esdarash distributed most of the furnishings and bedding, as well as the carpets, chests, and clothing, among the poorer members of the clan. The jewelry went to Kendira, as Alsanobal's wife. Shannivar could have put in a claim to it, but she was too sick in spirit to care. She wept as she accepted one of the chests, decorated with stylized images of horses dancing beneath the moon.

Scarface received a portion of the felts. By the next morning, rumors sped about the camp that she had accepted Timurlenk's marriage offer. She would have to wait to assemble her *jort*, but she would have a place, and she would be a good step-mother to his sons, their wives, and their sisters. Even Yvanne, Esdarash's wife, who had never been particularly kind to Scarface, seemed pleased.

On impulse, Shannivar gave Scarface the washed-out gray mare, one of the two horses she herself had inherited from her own mother. Shannivar was shy about the gift, uncertain how it would be received. The mare was too old to bear another foal, and too weak for hard riding and the long journey to the gathering.

For a moment, Scarface stared, still and mute, at

the aged mare. Slowly she reached out a hand to stroke the thin gray neck, as if the animal were the most precious thing in the world. In that moment, Shannivar saw the mare not as worn out, of value only for having birthed Eriu, her single extraordinary foal, but as a jewel in herself.

The mare blew through her nostrils and nuzzled the scarred woman's shoulder. Tears glimmering in her eyes, Scarface bowed low to Shannivar. Shannivar felt a moment of shame, that she had never seen the other woman's longing. Scarface had never owned a horse nor ever hoped to. Like all Azkhantian folk, however, her heart had yearned for Tabilit's Gift. Now, because Shannivar could not take the old mare with her to the gathering, another woman's dream had been fulfilled.

On the third day, Bennorakh returned to the burial area and ascertained that no spirit lingered over Grandmother's corpse. The lattice was then burned. Watching the fire consume the birch and willow, Shannivar felt as if the last bonds linking her to her past were rising up in the smoke.

Life returned to the business that had been set aside due to Grandmother's funeral. Esdarash called the entire clan together for a speaking circle, for the matter of the outlanders remained to be settled.

Shannivar sat with Mirrimal, across the fire from Alsanobal and the other young men. For the first time since Grandmother had been stricken, she thought of the two Isarrans, what they must be thinking, their fears, their motives. During the mourning period, they had been confined to their trail tent, guarded in turn by the men. Now they watched from the edge of the fire's light. The ruddy glow burnished their features. Timurlenk stood beside them, hand resting on his sword, eyes wary. She could not believe they possessed the power to curse Grandmother or cause her death. But Grandmother might well have taken their coming as a sign that her own time had ended.

Esdarash, as chieftain, spoke first. He lifted the speaking stick, staring at it as if trying to draw answers from wood and beads and eagle's claw by sheer force of will. Then the speaking stick was passed as every adult, women as well as men, contributed their share.

The shaman had confirmed the story given by the strangers, that they were indeed emissaries from Isarre. Listening to what Esdarash said, and in particular what he did not say, she gathered the *enaree* had uttered a great deal more, undoubtedly his usual confusing but portentous prophecies.

There was no question of the importance of the Isarran proposal—and the danger. Even a fool could see that such an alliance could mean either the ruin of Azkhantia or its ultimate freedom from Gelon.

Two things, moreover, seemed clear to everyone. Firstly, the clans of the Golden Eagle could not act alone; they had neither the numbers nor the military strength, and to dispatch all their able warriors would strip their own defenses. Any action must be taken by the assembled tribes acting together, and the final decision should be one of consensus. No clan would be forced into participation.

Secondly, and perhaps more importantly, Esdarash was determined to get these inconvenient strangers out of the encampment. They were therefore to be escorted to the *khural*, leaving as soon as they could load their possessions on their donkey.

In other years, the entire clan might travel to the gathering. Now, with Grandmother dead and newly given back to the steppe, it was unthinkable for everyone to travel so far. Esdarash would not leave the clan-site. Shannivar could see that he had no heart for the journey. Therefore, he determined that a small party of warriors, young and strong, would accompany the strangers. He appointed Alsanobal as their leader.

At this pronouncement, Alsanobal puffed out his chest. He basked in the murmurs of praise from his friends and admiration from the young women. Kendira looked resigned, for it was not likely he would return before their child was born.

Shannivar seemed to be the only one with reservations about giving her cousin so much power. She liked him, but she did not entirely trust him. He had been quick, perhaps too quick, to blame the Isarrans for Grandmother's collapse. He was far too likely to act on impulse, in the heat of emotion and not wisdom. Shannivar decided then that it was up to her to make sure the strangers arrived safely at the *khural*, even if she had to defy Alsanobal's authority.

Chapter 8

WITH Eriu saddled and Radu on a lead line, Shannivar took her place near the head of the caravan. Mirrimal called a greeting as she checked the straps on the camel that would carry their *jorts* and trail tents, the rest of the baggage being distributed among the pack ponies. Shannivar waved back, glad that her friend was included in the party.

Alsanobal rode at their head, followed by Shannivar and Rhuzenjin, then the Isarrans, Mirrimal and her two brothers, the camel, several pack ponies, the Isarran donkey, and the other riders. The party included Jingutzhen, the clan's strongest archer, and his brother, Senuthenkh. Ythrae, one of Shannivar's cousins, was the third woman. She was the youngest, shy and quiet, and Shannivar suspected that Esdarash had included her to give her more confidence.

Bennorakh came with them. This was unusual, but no one questioned his right to come and go as

Tabilit directed him. In many ways, they were more a war party than merrymakers—strong young adults, and all except Ythrae with fighting experience, all able to ride quickly and strike hard. Gelon could be fought with arrow and sword, but it was even better to have an *enaree* at hand, should the strangers prove other than they seemed. They could be madmen or demons.

Shannivar had little to say to the Isarrans as the party left the *dharlak*. She had enough to do, managing her own animals and baggage, plus the awkward bulk of the *jort*, the lattice and felts, the door flap and carpets that had been her mother's. Mirrimal was in a strange mood, half crazy, half bereaved. She roused a little at her brothers' affectionate teasing, then lapsed into silence.

They settled into an easy traveling pace, having no need to hurry. The journey itself was part of the holiday. For Shannivar it was a pleasure to tend her horses, set up her own *jort*, and take her turn at hunting to supplement the usual trail food: parched barley and dried, spiced meat cakes called *bha*. The weather was so mild, she needed only a single layer of felt for the walls. Except for Bennorakh, who as an *enaree* had his own *jort*, the men used lightweight trail tents. Mirrimal and Ythrae shared Shannivar's *jort*; working together, they quickly set up and took down the structure, sometimes finishing before the men.

Alsanobal rode up and down the line as they traveled. The red horse pranced and shook his head, and Alsanobal encouraged this useless display.

Shannivar could not decide whether horse or rider were more full of flash and bluster.

Curious to see for herself what manner of men the Isarrans were, she tried to strike up a conversation with the strangers. Leanthos, the elder, would not look directly at her. His companion glared as if she were a snake, readying to strike. At first, Shannivar was incredulous, then angry when she saw them speaking freely with the men of the party.

When Shannivar complained, Mirrimal said, "What did you expect? These outlanders keep their women penned within their walls like sheep. They forbid them to ride or shoot or wield a sword, even to defend their own lands, or so I have heard."

"Surely, no people could be so foolish as to cut off their right arm when the enemy approaches."

"You know little of the foolishness of men," Mirrimal said.

Shannivar refused to be drawn in. The Isarrans talked readily enough with Alsanobal and with Senuthenkh, ever inquisitive and not a little inflated by the attention. Mirrimal's brothers were too shy to venture a conversation, and as for Jingutzhen, he rarely spoke two words together, even to his own kin. Rhuzenjin, too, seemed to be keeping his distance.

"Perhaps," Shannivar said thoughtfully to her friend, "they are not accustomed to forthright women." She watched how awkwardly the older Isarran rode. He was a poor horseman, and from the way he straddled his rough-gaited mount, his bare lower legs must surely be rubbed raw.

That night, after the women erected the *jort*, Shannivar strolled over to the tent used by the Isarrans. She brought a leather bottle of camel's-fat liniment. Grandmother had taught her how to prepare herbs to soothe sore muscles and abraded skin, or strengthen sinew and muscle. Shannivar had learned which ones eased women's pain or prevented pregnancy, remedies every woman warrior needed. Sometimes the contraceptive herbs failed, and the woman either married or lived with her women kin, who helped to raise the child.

The younger Isarran, Phannus, met Shannivar outside the tent, barring the way. There was no sign of Leanthos, so she supposed he must be within. Phannus regarded her with suspicion, eyes slightly narrowed, weight balanced on the balls of his feet. "Good evening," he said.

She could not get used to the odd greetings of the outlanders. Azkhantians traditionally welcomed one another with a wish for good luck. "Yes, it is a good evening. May your days be lucky and your arrows always find their mark. I have come to visit your uncle." She used the term for any older male relative.

Something like surprise flickered across the Isarran's features, or so Shannivar interpreted the twitching of the corners of his mouth. "He is resting and cannot be disturbed."

Shannivar reminded herself that these outlanders had no sense of politeness, no understanding of the Azkhantian way to behave. He ought to have invited her into the tent, or at very least, apologized while the older man prepared to receive her. It was an unthinkable breach of hospitality for her to be kept waiting, or worse yet, to refuse her request. Patiently, she replied, "He will rest all the better for the gift I bring."

"*K'th.*" Phannus pronounced the word as if he were spitting.

"No." Shannivar suppressed a smile. "Although he might prefer it."

From within the tent came a querulous voice, speaking Isarran rather than trade-dialect. Phannus answered in the same language. A moment later, Leanthos emerged. He moved as if his joints hurt him.

"Isarran man, may your dreams this night be glorious." Shannivar made a fist with her free hand and tapped her chest over her heart.

After a moment's hesitation, he repeated the gesture. "You are the chief's niece. How may I serve you, lady?"

"I have brought a gift. Come, let us sit together."

Shannivar lowered herself into an easy cross-legged position, and the two men followed her example. She offered the leather bottle, explaining its purpose. Phannus reached out before Leanthos could take it. His nose wrinkled as he sniffed the contents. He spoke to the older man in rapid, angry-sounding Isarran.

Shannivar scowled at this rudeness. Phannus acted as if the liniment were poisoned. She pushed back one sleeve and rubbed a little of the pungent-smelling liquid into her forearm. "This is how it is applied. Work it deep into the skin." She sat back, feeling the familiar pleasurable healing warmth.

Leanthos exchanged a dubious glance with his companion, then nodded acceptance. From the way Phannus took the bottle from him, Shannivar suspected he would be the first to try it, just in case. She allowed herself a moment of amusement at such foolishness. Perhaps living in stone houses had deprived these people of all land-sense; certainly, Tabilit could not speak to them through wind or cloud or dreams under the full moon.

"Thank you for your gift," Leanthos said in heavily accented trade-dialect. "May I ask a question? Why do the women sleep in a—a portable house? Why do your men except for your priest use tents instead?"

"You are truly strangers to our ways. A man lives in his mother's *jort* until he moves to his wife's. If Kendira had come with us, Alsanobal would have slept in her *jort.*"

Leanthos was silent for a moment. "It is different in Isarre. We build our dwellings to last for generations, stone and hard wood that endures." Shannivar could not think of a suitable reply so she got to her feet and said, "May your journey be lucky." Tapping her hand over her heart, she turned and strode back to her own place.

The Moon of Golden Grass grew thin as a drawn bow, promising the coming Moon of Gathering, also called the Moon of Stallions. They followed the river valley, their horses fresh and eager. Around the nightly fire, the *enaree* chanted tales from long ago, when Tabilit walked the land and conversed freely with men, when the stars had voices and the land answered them. The Isarrans listened, politely participating with a chant in their own language. Even without understanding the words, Shannivar heard the sweet-sad longing behind the lyrics as one voice held a note and the other rose and fell, perhaps like the waves of the ocean.

Shannivar tried to imagine so much water, endless as the rolling steppe. Lakes she knew, and rivers, and torrential downpours. Such were fleeting ripples upon the land, the deep eternal land. She tried to picture the ebb and flow of tides, walls of water surging in storm or quiet as glass. Something roused in her, a mirror to the Isarrans' song, and she understood the call of that unknown sea.

As they struck out across open territory, the late summer days turned the grasses golden and then gray-brown in the heat. Feathergrass and ripening second-crop barley filled the air with musky sweetness. Insects whirred, and skylarks dove and swooped as they feasted on them. From time to time, Shannivar spotted an eagle soaring against the sky. Her heart rose at this omen of good fortune, that their party should be under the watchful protection of their totem animal.

Sometimes she glimpsed Leanthos making marks in a little sheaf of papers that he carried close to his person. She wondered if they were counter-spells, but Bennorakh, who had clearly noticed this strange behavior as well, did not seem alarmed, so she let it pass.

Days melted into days, and the Moon of Stallions

swelled in the night sky. The land rose, and rose again. The ground here was drier, the soil scoured by the wind. Rocks jutted skyward like the bones of the earth.

Shannivar and Mirrimal rode side by side, a little ahead of the others. This day, Shannivar was riding Eriu to give Radu a rest. Rhuzenjin passed by at a brisk trot without speaking to either of them. Shannivar thought he was showing off, or else too shy, after what had passed between them, to converse with her in the easy way of trail companions. Ythrae often followed him with her eyes, but he seemed unaware of her attention.

As Shannivar and Mirrimal neared the top of a ridge, a brisk wind blew from the west. Eriu lifted his head and nickered.

"He's ready for the Long Ride," Mirrimal said, reining in her own horse, a tough gray with a long, narrow head.

Shannivar settled the black with a touch. Eriu was bored with the pace set by the camel and the Isarrans' donkeys. A horse like him would never be content to walk everywhere. He wanted to run.

As if sensing her thought, Eriu broke into a jig-trot, coming even with Rhuzenjin's horse. As Shannivar drew near, she saw the tension in Rhuzenjin's body, his attention focused on a distant point. Before them stretched another valley, as green and golden as their own. A westerly tributary cut across its bed and flowed into the main river.

"Shannivar, look there!" he said, pointing. "Do you see it?"

Shannivar followed his gaze, angling obliquely away from their path. She inhaled sharply.

Smoke. And not far away, although the source was hidden behind the jagged horizon.

Her first thought was of fire, ever a danger on the steppe. In the dry season, wildfire could devour the sun-parched grasses faster than a horse could run. All the rich bounty of the steppe, creatures as well as vegetation, could be destroyed in a single day.

Shannivar assessed the terrain, noting that the ridge with its sparse vegetation and rocky outcropping would act as a natural fire break. Her brows drew together as she studied the pattern of the smoke. It issued from a single point and was not spreading. Ordinary grass fires did not behave in such a controlled fashion.

Alsanobal brought his red stallion to a halt beside them, the horse snorting and blowing. Eriu laid his ears back and snaked his head out, warning the bigger horse to come no closer. The red swerved, neatly avoiding Eriu's teeth.

Shannivar said, "I think we have trouble."

"I agree," Alsanobal said. "This does not look like a normal fire. It is most likely outlanders—more of these stupid Isarrans."

"Or Gelon," she said grimly.

A feral grin spread across Alsanobal's broad features. He reined the red to face the rest of their party, who were climbing the ridge more slowly, encumbered by pack animals. "You, Isarrans! Remain here, where you are safe."

"Safe? What? Is there is danger ahead?" Leanthos turned to his companion and gabbled in their own tongue, but neither of them came any closer. Shannivar wondered what they would do in the face of true danger—stand and fight, or run like rabbits for the sake of their mission?

"Ythrae, stay with the outlanders!" At her startled protest, Alsanobal explained, "Keep them out of trouble! Everyone else, with me!" He kicked the red into a ground-eating lope, heading toward the fire. The other Azkhantians needed no further urging. Whooping, they urged their mounts after him.

Shannivar shifted her weight and touched Eriu with her heels. The black leaped forward, his ears pricked in excitement. His powerful haunches drove him on, and his back flexed and extended with each stride.

As she rode, Shannivar used her teeth to pull the laces of the wrist guard tight, and reached for her bow in its case beside her left knee. The smooth, curved wood remembered her touch. Without causing Eriu to miss a step, she strung her bow. Beside her, her clan mates did the same. Shannivar glanced back to see Jingutzhen, his face alight with ferocity, bow ready, body moving with the reaching strides of his sturdy bay.

They followed the ridge for a time, eating up the distance, and then dipped into the long slope to the river tributary. Tabilit favored them, for the ground was relatively smooth. Here and there, a boulder punched through the grassy cover or a deer trail wound along the slope.

The source of the smoke came into view. Shannivar drew in her breath. It was as she'd thought, not a natural fire, nor any started by those wise in the ways of the steppe.

An encampment had been erected along the smaller river. She noted the felled trees and the partially constructed outpost. The invaders had thrown up a crude palisade, a row of saplings, sharpened and lashed together. Beyond the wall lay a perimeter of earthworks, and the stone foundations of a bridge had been erected.

They must be Gelon. Who else would be so insolent?

A thin stream of smoke arose from a hut in the center of the fort. It was most likely a cookfire set by Gelon ignorant enough to burn unseasoned smokebush.

Alsanobal cursed aloud. They were all thinking the same thing: What was a Gelonian garrison doing here in nomad territory? How dare they plant such an obscenity on free Azkhantian soil? Stonedwellers were as crafty as they were rapacious. Once they had fully fortified this place, they would control the river crossing. Entrenched, they might withstand even a determined assault. More than that, they could use this stronghold to push even deeper into Azkhantia.

Alsanobal bent over his horse's neck. Anger flushed his features, and his eyes glowed like firelit obsidian. He barked out the order to split into two wings, encircling the site. If there were a weakness anywhere in the palisade, they would discover it.

The riders parted smoothly, picking up speed as

they reached the bottom of the hill. Alsanobal headed to the right, closely followed by Mirrimal, her two brothers, and Jingutzhen.

Shannivar shifted her weight to turn Eriu to the left, away from Alsanobal's riders. The strength of the Azkhantian warriors lay in the speed and maneuverability of their horses. Not Gelonian onagers and chariots, nor men on foot, could stand against the lightning strikes of the clan riders. Like their totem, the Golden Eagle clan had always swooped in, rained down their arrows upon the enemy, and raced away, or taunted the Gelon deeper into their territory and then encircled them, slashing at their flanks.

What will we do if the Gelon hide behind their walls, like rabbits in their burrows? Shannivar thought. *We are eagles, not ferrets to dig them out.*

It was too late for questions now. Whooping, the riders rushed forward. Eriu flew across the grass-tufted ground, easily pulling ahead of the others. Senuthenkh and Rhuzenjin pounded at her heels. Alsanobal's red cleared the nearest mound before disappearing on the other side of the palisade. Mirrimal's brothers followed, and then Jingutzhen and Mirrimal herself, a length behind. Her gray scrambled over the earthworks and sprinted to keep the pace set by the big red horse.

As Shannivar approached, the weakness in the Gelonian defenses became clear. Behind the torn-up earth, she made out gaps in the palisade where the poles had been propped together instead of being properly bound and reinforced. She felt a surge of elation. The fort was vulnerable, then.

The next moment, a path opened before her, a ribbon of smooth, packed earth between the outlying mounds. The nimble Azkhantian horses negotiated the route without reducing their speed.

The piles of dirt and rock reminded Shannivar of marmot burrows. Her moment of elation faded. Gelonian soldiers could hide themselves there, not cowering rabbits but jackals with teeth, ready to jump up once the enemy had gone by, ready to attack from the rear.

Alert for any sign of a Gelonian counter-assault, Shannivar continued her circuit around the fort. Here and there, she spied other places where the palisade might be forced.

A short time later, Shannivar and her companions reached the riverbank. Here the normal profusion of lush, low-growing browse had been torn up, obliterated. Ruts and hoofprints had gouged deep into the soft earth, and silt clouded the river's edge.

The mud slowed the horses, so that even swift Eriu struggled to keep his pace, fighting the soft footing. His hooves sank into the moist, sticky soil, but with each powerful stride, he pulled himself free. Once he slipped and almost stumbled, but found his balance and surged on. With relief, they reached drier ground.

War cries sounded from the other side of the encampment. Alsanobal's wing had encountered the enemy. He must have chosen one of the unfinished portions of the palisade as a point of attack.

Shannivar shifted her weight, and Eriu answered with a renewed burst of speed. Like one of her own arrows, he flew down the alley of smooth packed dirt.

She breathed deeply, gathering herself, praying for the fierce, hot heart-fire to sustain her through the fight, praying for Tabilit's protection. For victory or death. Both lay but a few strides away.

Chapter 9

PICKING up speed, Shannivar and her riders rounded the last section of the Gelonian fort. The ground here was hard, and the footing sound. A section of the palisade was down. Screaming out their battle cries, Alsanobal's riders had already crowded single-file into the gap. The Gelon would be trapped in their fort like badgers in their dens.

Behind Shannivar, Rhuzenjin burst out in a victorious yell, eager to join their comrades. She frowned, her lips tightening, and shouted for him to hold his place. Despite her own surge of triumph, she disliked the prospect of fighting in such close quarters. There was no space for free use of sword or bow, and no way to use their best asset, the speed and agility of their horses. If anything should go wrong, there would be no way to escape to regroup and strike again. Alsanobal, hothead fool that he was, had risked everything on a single easy opening.

Sensing her uneasiness, Eriu slowed, ears cocked back toward her. He arched his neck, gathering his hindquarters beneath him. A touch of her heels, and he would launch himself forward.

"Gelon! Gelon!"

Suddenly, enemy soldiers sprang up from the earthworks. The space outside the fort boiled over with armored men on foot. Even as Shannivar feared, they had hidden themselves between the irregular mounds, waiting to strike.

The Gelon outnumbered the riders by two or three times. Pale-skinned and muscular, they seemed huge compared to the Azkhantian riders. And they were well prepared for the fight. Helmets covered their upper faces and shields protected their bodies. They brandished their spears and the steel points flashed blue-white in the sun.

Tabilit's silver ass! How many are they?.

"Gelon! Gelon! Gelon!" The soldiers fell upon Alsanobal's wing from the rear. The hindmost of the riders was Mirrimal. She twisted in the saddle to fire an arrow over the rump of her horse. A Gelon stumbled, her arrow in his chest, only to be replaced by another. And another and another, their shields raised.

Mirrimal could not bring down the mass of oncoming Gelon by herself. The space was too narrow to maneuver. None of the riders in front of her could get a clear shot.

The gray reared as Mirrimal struggled to turn him. The horse's legs tangled in one of the fallen palisade stakes. With an almost human scream, the gray lost his footing.

Mirrimal managed to keep her seat as her mount

struggled for balance. With incredible skill, she loosed another arrow. Her face was pale and set, determined. Resigned.

There was no way out. The enemy would be upon her in a moment.

The foremost Gelon rushed at Mirrimal. Wielding a spear, he protected his own body behind his raised shield.

Shannivar clapped her heels against Eriu's sides. The black horse shot forward. She nocked an arrow to her bow and let it fly. The shaft struck the Gelon attacking Mirrimal in the side of the neck, slipping just above the top of his shield. He staggered to his knees.

Two more arrows, then three, found their targets. Some bounced off the Gelonian shields, but others pierced flesh.

In a movement of astonishing speed, Mirrimal slipped her bow into its case beside her knee and whipped out her sword. Shannivar thought that her friend caught her own gaze for a moment, that some grim understanding flowed between them.

With trained precision, the Gelon divided into two groups. Some turned to face the hail of arrows from Shannivar's force. The second group continued their assault on Alsanobal's trapped riders. Not a single Gelon faltered.

In an instant, Shannivar understood the Gelonian strategy. This was no desperate, ill-planned defense. The commander must have known that the Azkhantians would discover the fort, sooner or later. The palisade may have been incomplete, still being erected, but this particular gap was the perfect snare, an opening irresistible to the clan riders. The Gelonian commander had dug hiding places outside and placed his men there at the first sign of an attack.

If I were this commander, I would not commit all my men to such a defense. Not when there might be another wave of riders.

He might well have held more men in reserve, still crouched behind the earthworks. If she led her own party after Alsanobal's, they might be caught in the same trap, with enemies before and behind them. Once within the fort and hemmed in by walls, the Gelon would cut them down. She must eliminate that threat before she could help Alsanobal.

How to draw them from their burrows?

Shannivar was close enough now to see the patterned layout of the earthworks.

"Rhuzenjin! Senuthenkh! Follow me!" With a shift of her weight and pressure of one knee, Shannivar swung the black away from the direct approach to the gap and headed along the narrow path beside the earthworks.

She saw no sign of any soldiers in hiding. *Not yet . . .*

Shannivar's gut clenched. Had she made a terrible mistake, drawing away badly needed reinforcements? Abandoning Mirrimal?

Shrieking insults, she loosed an arrow into the ditch.

A howl answered her.

Shannivar turned her head to see a Gelon

emerge from behind a pile of dirt, clutching the arrow that protruded between his breastplate and shoulder guard. *Onjhol's bloody balls!* She could hardly believe the luck of that shot.

"Here they come!" Rhuzenjin shouted.

Gelon burst from their hiding places and rushed toward the riders. But, Shannivar noted with feral glee, they were only a handful. Aiming another arrow over Eriu's tail, she twisted in her saddle as he galloped past the Gelon. Behind her, Rhuzenjin and Senuthenkh drew and shot. Following Shannivar's lead, they wheeled their horses for another pass. Drew and shot again.

Arrows pinged off shields, but others found their marks. Gelon went down and some did not claw their way up from the trampled dirt again. Someone shouted commands in Gelone. The remaining soldiers rushed to join their comrades.

The gap was open now, although littered with broken palisade stakes. Alsanobal and the others had forced their way into the fort itself. Sounds of fighting—war cries, screams, the neighing of horses, and the clash of metal blades—came from within.

It went against Shannivar's instincts to urge her horse through the tangle of splintered wood. The risk of injury to Eriu was terrifying, but do it she must. There was no time to lose. Inside, Mirrimal was fighting for her life, and Alsanobal beyond her, as well as those clansmen who had followed him. Even as her own riders followed where she led.

Eriu slowed, arching his neck. Shannivar slipped her bow back into its case and drew her sword.

"Go now," she whispered to the black horse, "and may Tabilit guide your steps."

Shannivar and her riders reached the shattered palisade. Eriu lifted like an eagle taking flight, and cleared the tangle of fallen stakes. Once past the barrier, they came out into a yard filled with horses, men, and half-finished wooden buildings. It was impossible to make out what was happening in the roiling chaos.

A moment later, the gray stumbled free of the riotous fighting. The horse was riderless and limping badly, eyes wild, ears flattened against the thin neck. Red streaked one shoulder.

The Gelonian soldiers had gathered in the center of the fort. Shannivar and her riders hurtled through their defenses. As she passed, a soldier lunged at her. She slashed down on a diagonal, taking advantage of her greater height. He raised his shield just in time to meet her blade. The force of the block shocked up her arm, but she had the advantage of momentum. Grunting with effort, she threw her weight into the blow. The man staggered. Her blade slipped over the top of his wavering shield, slicing into his neck. His legs gave way beneath him, and he dropped.

The Gelon continued to fight, clinging to their discipline and struggling to maintain their formation. Each one's shield protected the sword arm of his fellow. They moved together, as if each knew the other's next move; they slashed and drew back, again and again.

Two soldiers, separated from the rest by Shannivar's charge, were fighting back to back. Something in their hopeless loyalty touched Shannivar. So would she wish to die, sword in hand, beside her comrades.

A moment opened up in the fighting, a stillness around the embattled Gelon. Only three were left now, the two and a third, striving to rise, helmetless, his face a mask of blood and dust.

Then the riders swept over them, and it was over. Shannivar turned away from the sight. A moment before, men had stood here and fought. Invaders and outlanders, true, but brave men nonetheless. Worthy adversaries. Now she looked upon a heap of broken bodies. For a terrible moment, she saw Grandmother's white mare among the dead.

"Alsanobal! Where is he?" Shannivar cried, shaking off the strange, sad feeling.

A moment later, she found him, lying half under the body of the red horse. The animal had fallen on him, hamstrung and thrashing, until someone slit its throat. Its head rested at an unnatural angle. Its eyes, not yet filmed in death, stared at the sky.

Alsanobal lay in a pool of the horse's blood. He roused as Shannivar bent over him. Pain mingled with despair in his eyes. His mouth twisted as he gathered himself to speak.

"You always said . . . that horse . . . would be the death of me." His voice sounded thin, as if his life were already spent.

"I was wrong," she said, her voice suddenly thick. "You will live."

He shook his head. "My thigh bone is broken. I'll never ride again." He inhaled sharply. "What life is that for a son of the Golden Eagle? I am no Scarface, Shannu. I cannot live as a cripple . . . useless, an object of pity. Far better that my life end here. Promise me . . ."

Alsanobal's breath failed him. He closed his eyes, biting down on his lip as he fought for control. His face had gone Gelon-pale. "Promise me you will tell my father that I died in glorious battle."

Shannivar looked away, refusing to believe what he asked of her. The smells of blood and excrement and death washed over her. She felt sick at the waste of it all.

The Gelon were not demons or cowards. They had fought well, with courage and loyalty. They must have kin as well, wives and families waiting for them. Waiting and hoping, even as Kendira waited and hoped.

What was this weakness in her belly? Why should she care what sorrows the enemy endured? Where was the fierce, wild joy she ought to feel in battle?

Angry, she grabbed her cousin's shoulders. She forced him to meet her gaze. "Don't talk nonsense! Enough have already died on this day. I will send you back to your father, and next year you will ride to the *khural*!" *But I, I will never return to the Golden Eagle, no matter what happens.*

"Shannivar."

She glanced up. Rhuzenjin stood at her shoulder. The brightness of the sky cast his face into shadow.

"My cousin's injuries need tending." Briskly, Shannivar got to her feet. She was unwilling to let Rhuzenjin see her moment of weakness. "Send for the *enaree* and the Isarrans," she said. "Let them earn their keep."

"I will go myself. But—"

What more?

"It's Mirrimal. I know she's your friend."

Shannivar's heart shivered. Mouth dry, she followed Rhuzenjin's gaze to the far end of the gap, where Senuthenkh crouched beside a fallen rider.

She glanced down at Alsanobal. "Cousin—"

"Go to her, while there is still time. I saw her fall. I . . . could do nothing." Alsanobal's breath rasped in his throat, each word an effort. "I will be well enough . . . until Rhuzenjin returns with help." As if to prove his point, he lifted his head, attempting to raise himself on one elbow.

"Lie still!" Shannivar snapped. "Do not do yourself further injury!"

Alsanobal eased back into the mud, teeth gritted hard. "I am not . . . going anywhere."

Shannivar, meeting his pain-darkened eyes, understood him to say that he would do nothing to bring an end to his own life. His moment of temptation had passed. He was too honorable to hold her when she was needed elsewhere.

Freed from her family obligation, Shannivar rushed to the side of her friend. Mirrimal lay where she had fallen, half on her side, her legs a tangled clump. Blood seeped from wounds on her arms and belly, and one bone-deep gash in her thigh. A Gelonian spear had pierced her just below the heart. The point protruded through her back.

Senuthenkh, crouched beside her, had made no attempt to pull it out. As Shannivar knelt by her friend, he bowed his head and left them.

"Alsanobal . . ." Mirrimal's face was pasty white, her lips colorless except for a smear of drying blood. "Is he . . . ?"

"His leg is broken, that is all," Shannivar reassured her. "His wits are as sound as they ever were. That idiot of a red horse fell on him, the last thing the poor beast will ever do. My cousin will recover, although he's none too pleased at having to ride home in a Gelonian cart instead of enjoying the *khural*."

The ghost of a smile spread across Mirrimal's bone-white lips. "You always said that horse would be the death of him."

"I was wrong. I told him so." Shannivar brushed a few limp hairs back from the other woman's temple, surprised to feel how cold the skin was.

"I could not . . . stop them. . ."

"Lie still, Mirru. Rhuzenjin is bringing Bennorakh. He will surely be able to help you." Shannivar forced a smile. "I'm afraid you will miss the *khural*, as well as having to endure Alsanobal's company."

A spasm of pain swept Mirrimal's features. "Do not . . . lie to me, dear friend. And do not waste the time we have left. No magic can heal me. You know this."

Shannivar could not think what to say. They had fought together and seen many battle injuries. They knew what could be survived and what brought a mercifully swift end. Perhaps Tabilit herself might be able to save Mirrimal. Certainly, Bennorakh could not.

Shannivar had expected to bid her friend farewell at the *khural*, but she could not imagine the world without her.

First Grandmother and now Mirrimal. Who next, O Tabilit, must I lose?

"I never told you . . ." Mirrimal's words came haltingly, "what happened . . . that night . . . with Alsanobal."

"You do not need to explain. What do I care that you found joy in his arms?"

With a gasp of effort, Mirrimal lifted one hand and touched a finger to Shannivar's lips. For a long moment, neither woman spoke. Death-pale lips moved. "I could not . . ."

Mirrimal's eyelids fluttered half-closed. The pressure of her finger against Shannivar's mouth fell away. Shannivar grasped her friend's hand, feeling the flesh already growing cold.

"Shannu . . ." A breath, a whisper, drew Shannivar close. Her lips brushed Mirrimal's.

"It was you I thought of, that night." Mirrimal breathed the words into Shannivar's mouth. "You I wanted."

Shannivar sat back, too numb to know what she felt. Her heart ached. Mirrimal's confession hung in the air between them. There was nothing to say, nothing to do, only to hold steadfast and watch the last fading of the light in Mirrimal's eyes.

When the light was gone, Shannivar dared to

breathe again. *So that is your secret, my friend, my dear friend, and now it ends with you.*

What was her own secret? When would she know it, and who would she tell with her own dying breath?

The Isarrans, it turned out, had some skill in medicine. Phannus had clearly seen battle injuries before. They helped the *enaree* straighten Alsanobal's leg and strap it between two lengths of wood from the fort. Bennorakh had dosed Alsanobal with poppy syrup, so for the moment, he was quiet.

If only, Shannivar thought, there were a poppy syrup for the spirit. She would drink a river of it for a night's forgetfulness.

One of Mirrimal's brothers was dead, along with his horse. For all her experience harrying the Gelon and beating back their incursions, Shannivar could not entirely overcome the numbing sense of shock. Shock and anger. And, for the first time, fear.

In her mind, Shannivar went over the battle. In retrospect, she was far more terrified than she had been at the time. It could so easily have ended with all of them dead. The attack on the fort had been badly executed, without cunning or plan. The Gelon had used the terrain, the lure of the gap in the palisade, and their own superior numbers to force the riders into disadvantage.

Alsanobal had paid for his rashness. But Mirrimal, her brother, and two fine horses had paid as well. Surely, Tabilit must weep.

Shannivar told herself that Mirrimal was now beyond pain, beyond fear, beyond disappointment.
She was galloping free and wild over the endless
Pastures of the Sky with Grandmother and Saramark. With Tabilit herself.

Bennorakh seemed to have no such recrimina-
tions, no thoughts about how the riders had died.
After a brief period of solitary meditation, far
shorter than for Grandmother's death, he began
directing the disposal of the bodies. They had not
the time for burials, but it was a common practice
to burn those fallen in battle. Under the *enaree's*
direction, the surviving riders erected a funeral
pyre inside the ruins of the Gelonian fort. The
wooden stakes of the palisade were dry enough to
burn hot and clean.

The afternoon wore on. Shadows stretched like
wavering, elongated ghosts across the battle ground.
Shannivar studied what remained of the palisade,
the huts and half-constructed strong house. She
knew little of building with stone and wood, yet it
seemed to her the Gelon had intended this fort to
stand for many years. This was their way, even as
the way of Azkhantia was to follow the herds, to
wander from one moon to the next, drifting from
summer *dharlak* to the shelter of winter *kishlak*.
Only there and at the ancient gathering place did
they leave any trace of their passing.

The surviving riders laid out the bodies of the
slain enemy, along with their belongings. These
Gelon were soldiers, accustomed to traveling light
and hard. Besides their weapons, they carried mili-

tary necessities, tiny boxes of salt, cakes of dried opium juice, packets of steel needles, bone fishing hooks and silk thread, and small, slender knives. Shannivar also noticed more personal items: a chain bearing a small copper medallion, so worn that its image could not be deciphered; a ring, silver set with a small, poor-quality ruby, too small for a man's finger; a scroll covered with close writing that Leanthos identified as a collection of prayers to the Gelonian god known as The Protector of Soldiers.

As she handled and sorted these possessions, Shannivar felt a kinship that bordered on intimacy with the dead Gelon. What would one of them make of her life from the examination of her own effects? Her bow, her bag of women's contraceptive herbs, the wooden chest from Grandmother, carved with horses dancing beneath the moon? *That I was a warrior, a woman, a rider.* Nothing more.

As he straightened the last Gelonian corpse, Rhuzenjin muttered that the entire fort should be burned to the ground. Mud and ash, he said, would be a fitting memorial for the invaders.

Shannivar considered his words. Certainly, this was as safe a place as any for such a blaze. Between the earthworks and the river bank, there was little chance of the fire spreading.

A idea crept into her thoughts—to give the Gelonian soldiers and these tokens of their lives, as well as her comrades, to the fire. And why not the fort as well, the symbol of Gelonian arrogance? All would be erased in Tabilit's cleansing fire.

Dharvarath, Mirrimal's surviving brother and the most conservative of the party, was horrified when she proposed it. "You cannot mean to accord these—these *dwellers-in-stone* such an honor? To send them in glory to the Kingdom of the Sky? Who knows what they will do there? Pile stones on Tabilit's sacred earth?"

Ythrae, standing nearby, flinched under the strength of his outburst. Shannivar held her ground. "What else are we to do with them?" Shannivar countered. "Throw them into the river and foul the water? They were warriors, not beasts."

"Beasts! Yes, evil beasts! Not to be treated as men!"

Rhuzenjin looked as if he were about to intervene on Shannivar's behalf, to defend her. Impatiently, she gestured for him to stay out of the quarrel. If she allowed a man to rescue her, she would lose all hope of setting her own terms in marriage. She would arrive at the *khural* as just an ordinary woman rider, when she most needed to be a Saramark.

"The Gelon were most certainly wrong. Wrong to desecrate the land with stone and wrong to violate our territory. But they fought bravely and with cunning. No one can deny them that. I will not send them without honor to whatever lies beyond their lives."

"*You* will not? Did the battle so addle your wits that you have forgotten it is Alsanobal son of Esdarash who leads this party?" He narrowed his eyes. "Or do the deaths of Mirrimal and my brother mean nothing to you?"

Heat shot through Shannivar's veins. Even as her hands curled into fists, she held herself firm. More lay at stake here than her own grief. Dharvarath was challenging her, deliberately provoking her to a fight he was sure he would win. When they were children, she could have wrestled him to the ground, but now she could not prevail against his greater height, his weight, his raw muscular power. She must use her own strength to advantage.

Until now, she had not realized that she had indeed stepped into Alsanobal's place. Unless she faced Dharvarath down, she would lose all hope of control. She moved toward him, feeling her pulse speed up and her muscles tense for action.

Levelly, without flinching, she met his eyes. Despite his taunts, Dharvarath took a step back.

"Treating the dead of a noble foe with respect will not bring our friends back to us," she said, her voice low and tight. "It will not restore your kin. But *not* doing so will diminish the meaning of their deaths. Should we do the enemy's work for him and destroy the best of who we are, simply because we are angry and stricken with grief?"

Ythrae gasped and Rhuzenjin murmured something to her. Without waiting for Dharvarath's answer, Shannivar turned and walked away. Dharvarath made no attempt to follow her. He had already lost.

In the few moments it took to locate Bennorakh, Shannivar had time to assume the appearance of being reasonable and calm. She found the *enaree* in conference with the Isarran emissary.

"We must make provision for the bodies of the Gelon, as well as our own," she told him. "They were outlanders, true, and dwellers-in-stone, but they died under Tabilit's Sky, and we—it is our duty—" She drew in a breath, then went on in a rush. "We should make one big funeral pyre and burn them all."

Leanthos turned to her with an astounded look. She could not tell if his reaction were due to a woman speaking so forthrightly or to a difference in funeral customs. Or was he, like Dharvarath, disgusted at according such dignity to an enemy?

Bennorakh considered her gravely. "You speak what is in my own mind, Eagle Daughter."

Silently Shannivar sent up a prayer of thanks.

"In ancient times," the *enaree* went on, shifting into a high-pitched sing-song voice, "enemy captives were slain and burned with a fallen hero, and their horses and weapons as well. The mightier the warrior, the more sacrifices would be sent to the Sky Kingdom as tribute to Onjhol, to stand with the gods against the coming of Olash-giyn-Olash, the Shadow of Shadows."

Shannivar knew the legends. Tabilit and her consort would not reign forever. The time would come when the fate of the worlds, the one above and the one below, would depend upon a mighty battle. Then the people of the steppe would rise up, the dead as well as the living, to fight against the Shadow of Shadows. It was an honorable fate for a vanquished foe, to have the hope of fighting in that final, cataclysmic battle.

"The Gelon fought well," she nodded. "Therefore, they will serve Tabilit well."

They built the funeral pyre inside the ruins of the Gelonian fort. When all the preparations were complete and the fires lit, the Azkhantian warriors withdrew to the heights to watch. The *enaree* burned incense and chanted the ancient invocations. The Isarrans offered prayers according to their own ways.

The pyres burned brightly at first, then fitfully. Shannivar feared the wood was either too wet or there was too little of it to consume so many bodies. Bennorakh took a torch and went down to the fort, his path marked only by that single bobbing light. It winked out, then reappeared as he moved about the burning ground. A wind sprang up, fanning the sputtering flames.

Shannivar caught snatches of chant in the quavering falsetto of the *enarees*, although she could not make out any words. The wind beat about her ears, muffling the ordinary sounds of the hilltop camp. She could not even hear the voices of the other riders, although they were only a short distance away.

The chanting of the *enaree* grew louder and louder. Insistent, demanding. The darkness seemed to pick out the phrases, to lift them to the heights and swirl them around her . . . *through* her.

Shannivar had walked through snowstorms in the long steppe winters. Each mote of sound reminded her of an ice-edged flake. She opened her mouth to cry out, only to inhale an eddy of sound-flakes. She could not breathe, could not move, could not cry out. The whirlwind intensified, flaying skin, shredding flesh from both the outside and inside. Bone lay bare and then blew away into dust.

Tabilit, help me!

Her vision went white in the pummeling storm, or perhaps she no longer had eyes. Yet through that raging vortex, a shape emerged. A woman of snow, of ice, mounted on a mare whose coat shimmered like polished steel. Slowly the woman rode toward Shannivar, sitting as firm and supple as if she and the horse were one being. The mare's head swung from side to side, revealing that she bore no bridle, only ribbons of silver braided into her mane.

Tabilit, Mother of Horses?

Terrified yet ecstatic, Shannivar waited as the rider grew even closer. Then she saw the rider's face. *Grandmother*.

She was no longer the withered crone, the tyrannical matriarch, but a woman young and strong, a warrior such as Shannivar had never seen. A Saramark.

Then the winds howled once more. The voice of the *enaree* returned with renewed strength. The young-old woman who was Grandmother smiled at Shannivar. The shimmering-steel mare turned and disappeared into the storm. A moment later, a heartbeat, an eon, a second figure took shape. Again, it was a woman, a warrior. She sat astride a big horse whose colorless flanks were tinged with red-bronze, laughing as if her heart were the cradle of all joy. *Mirrimal.*

Am I dead, too? Is that why I can see them?

The white-against-white figure of Mirrimal shook her head gently. The red stallion dipped his head. Then they were gone.

Shannivar peered into the fast-flowing currents of white and wind. There was something else, something she could not quite see. Mirrimal's brother and his horse. The Gelon. Shannivar could *feel* them moving with deliberate grace. In the same way, she could *feel* a lineage of women riders, their features engraved upon her own—her own mother, whom she had never known, and Aimellina, and the first Shannivar.

And behind them, infusing them with her courage, Saramark.

Without warning, Shannivar came back to herself. A sound like thunder, only sharper, resounded through her skull. She blinked, and the next moment, the fires in the fort below surged skyward. They erupted into volcanic brightness, spewing forth glowing, garnet-red cinders. The flames burned white over the pyres. Around Shannivar, the others cried out and pointed.

One of the men said, "There will be nothing left but ash by morning."

"Hush," said Ythrae. "Tabilit herself has laid her hand upon them."

*   *   *

They watched long into the night and chanted to
the dead as the fires raged below. Eventually the
songs died into the velvet quiet of the night. The air
turned cool and river-moist. The others retired for
the night, except for Shannivar and Rhuzenjin.
Bennorakh had not yet returned from tending the
fires below.

Shannivar sat staring at the fires. Something
within her coiled upon itself like a tangled knot.
She could not stop thinking of how quickly everything had changed. The red horse had been so
strong, so full of life, as had Mirrimal and her
brother. Men and women fell in battle or under the
weight of years or disease. She had seen it and had
accepted that it would happen to her as well. Over
and over, she told herself that what they did was
right and noble, keeping their land free from the
Ar-King's menace. And yet—

And yet.

The something in her belly would not let go.
Somewhere at the back of her mind, Grandmother's white mare stumbled and fell. The wind howled
across the steppe like a wolf in winter. She shivered
in the warmth of the summer night.

Across the campfire, Rhuzenjin watched her. The
light of the flames filled his eyes. If she spoke the
words, he would come eagerly to her bed. He was
strong and fit, and from the way he looked at her,
passionate. He would cover her in eager kisses; she
imagined the hardness of him inside her, the scent
of his arousal, the power of his body between her

thighs. She could, for the space of a night, escape this strange dark mood. His ardor would sustain them both. But it would be only for a night. The next morning, his eyes would follow her, filled with longing for what she could not give.

Alone, she strode away from the fire to the horse lines. Radu nickered a greeting and Eriu nuzzled her shoulder as she stroked him. The comfort of horses was uncomplicated. They never told each other to set aside running beneath the wild Moon of Birds, nor sought to steal the sky from another herd. When they coupled, it was for an hour's mutual need, nothing more.

A shape flickered in the darkness. She was not alone, but her horses gave no sign of alarm, as they would at the approach of a stranger. She caught a whiff of incense but did not entirely relax. Bennorakh posed no threat, not physically, but he confused her, sometimes frightened her. He was always full of prophecies that no one could understand.

"What do you want?" she demanded.

"What do *you* want?"

Shannivar could not tell if the *enaree* were asking the question or repeating her own words back to her.

What did she want? Once she would have said, *to ride, to fight, to be free.* Now, with the taste of blood and ashes in her mouth, she did not know.

The *enaree* lifted one hand with a soft jangling of the bits of bone and carved antler threaded into his hair. He pointed north, toward the *khural-lak*, the gathering-place. *Go*, he seemed to say. *Go where your spirit leads you.*

For a long moment, she stared into the night. Around her, the land lay quiet, shrouded. The Road of Stars glimmered overhead. When she turned back to the *enaree*, he was gone. She wondered if she had seen him at all.

Chapter 10

THE next morning, Shannivar's throat ached, and her eyes felt as if she had spent the night weeping. Death, by sword or fever or the simple wearing away of years came to everyone. Mirrimal had died in honor, young and strong. No cookpot or infirmity would ever hold her in its grip. For all her grief, Shannivar could not begrudge her friend that measure of peace.

Shaking off her pensive mood, she began setting the camp in order. Mirrimal's personal belongings must be given to Dharvarath to bring back to their father, along with those of her brother. Mirrimal had no sisters to inherit her few bits of finery, and her mother was dead. Perhaps Dharvarath would marry and present them to his wife.

As for Alsanobal's return to the *dharlak* encampment, one of the carts appeared undamaged and sturdy enough to carry him, and the Gelonian onagers were accustomed to drawing it. Convincing her cousin would be another matter.

"A *cart*?" Alsanobal glared at her, brows drawing together. "You expect me to ride in a *cart*?"

Shannivar suppressed a sigh. "Be sensible, cousin. You cannot mount a horse, let alone ride one, with a broken thigh bone."

"It's bad enough to be still alive, to not have perished in glorious battle!" He glowered at her as if his survival were a malicious act on her part. "Have I offended the Sky People so deeply that I must return to my father as a cripple? All this I could bear as the will of Tabilit. But now you tell me I must do so in a *Gelonian cart*, like so much baggage or like a child too young to ride properly? No, it's too humiliating! I would be shamed forever! There must be another way. Or if there is not, I will sit here until I am fit to ride again."

"Who else can I trust to carry the looted treasure back?" Shannivar shifted tactics. "Is this not the matter of songs and legends, to lay before your chieftain the captured weapons of the enemy, their armor and swords of good steel? Is this not the deed of a hero?" Alsanobal's expression softened minutely as he considered this. Shannivar pushed on, knowing she had the better of him now. "Not to mention five sacks of lentils and wheat, the oil to cook it in, and even a good-sized box of salt."

A portion of the food would go with Shannivar to the gathering as gifts to the elders there, to be meted out among those clans who had supplied fresh meat for those who had traveled the farthest. In this traditional manner, the burden of feasting was fairly distributed.

At last, Alsanobal relented. "Very well, since it will bring honor to my father and our clan, I suppose I must do it. But I do not like the thought of dividing our strength. My father charged me with the safe conduct of the Isarran emissaries. The Gelonian outpost may not be the only danger along the way. I dare not deprive you of a single warrior—"

"And I dare not allow *you*, the son of the chieftain of Golden Eagle, to travel alone for exactly the same reason!" Shannivar checked herself, took a breath, and tried to sound reasonable. "Not even a warrior of legendary prowess could defend himself against a serious assault while lying in a cart."

Alsanobal raised one eyebrow as if to say she had proved his own point.

"Sitting in a cart," she amended.

"Driving a cart."

"Driving a cart. Certainly. But can you do this *and* at the same time shoot your bow? Or use your sword?"

Reluctantly he shook his head.

Shannivar's attention was drawn to Jingutzhen as he checked the gear on his saddle, the bow and arrow-case, and the sword in its sheath, all of them properly cared for and ready for travel. Satisfied, Jingutzhen led his horse to them, with one of the pack ponies on a lead line. His impassive face showed no sign of fatigue or the aftermath of the battle and deaths. He nodded to Shannivar, took a stance, and waited.

"I believe," Alsanobal said dryly, "that my escort has been chosen for me."

Shannivar opened her mouth to protest, then thought better of it. Jingutzhen was by far their strongest archer, and the range of his arrows would be the best defense for a slow-moving cart. Alsanobal could, if braced properly, manage the onagers during a fight. If only all her problems could be so easily resolved.

After the cart trundled away in the direction of the *dharlak* with Jingutzhen leading the way, Shannivar took charge of the remaining riders. This time, no one questioned her right to lead.

Compliant but sullen, Dharvarath attempted to load the camel. Perhaps sensing his mood, the animal would not kneel to be loaded. It whipped its head around and sank its teeth into his shoulder. He gave a strangled yelp, for the long jaws exerted tremendous leverage. His legs gave way, and only the camel's grip kept him from crumpling to the ground.

Shannivar started toward them, although she could not reach him in time. One shake of the camel's head, and Dharvarath's shoulder would be mangled, the muscles wrenched and torn, leaving him crippled. Ythrae, who had been standing nearby, tightening a harness strap on one of the pack ponies, dashed to the camel's head.

"Spawn of Shadows! Let him go!" Ythrae struck the beast across the nose with her short whip. "Hideous beast!" She lashed out again. "Behave yourself!"

Tabilit save us, now she's gotten the camel angry!

The camel, however, merely released its grip on Dharvarath. It turned its large, long-lashed eyes toward the furious girl but made no attempt to attack her. Clutching his bleeding shoulder, Dharvarath scrambled out of the camel's reach.

Ythrae, chest heaving, raised the whip again. With a sigh of resignation, the camel folded its knees and lowered itself to the ground. Belching, it flicked its tail, as if nothing untoward had happened.

For a moment, no one moved. Then Ythrae flashed Shannivar a grin. Taking hold of the camel's halter, Ythrae gestured for Senuthenkh to bring up the baggage. After that, there was no question of her stewardship of the camel or of the camel's meek obedience and devotion to her.

Once the party was assembled, Shannivar took the lead. A residue of her strange mood prompted her to ride Eriu again, instead of steady, soft-gaited Radu.

She was not afraid of battle. She accepted the perils of a warrior as natural and necessary. Yet the world had changed and grown dangerous in a way she did not understand. Mirrimal had said she was not afraid of death. At the time, Shannivar had thought of a life as wife and mother as confinement; the crushing sameness of days, the narrow world of *jort* and cookpot, were the things she had feared most. Now she was not sure.

And so, she rode Eriu. Eriu had no doubts, no hesitation, no moments of startling awake, heart yammering, in the darkest hours of the night. He moved forward willingly, as if he had not been ridden in a battle the day before.

As they went along, the others talked about how they would tell the story of the fight at the gathering, the partners they would win with tales of their exploits, the *k'th* they would drink.

Rhuzenjin composed a song-poem about how Shannivar had won the battle and saved them all. She did not want such adulation, but to refuse the honor would shame him, so she made no protest. Ythrae was delighted with the song, clapping her hands as Rhuzenjin chanted the verses and glowing when he added a reference to the camel. Shannivar's cheeks burned and she turned away, uncomfortably aware of his gaze on her.

Several days later, they swung out on one of the few roads through the steppe. In places, the way was broad and smooth, hard-packed soil where little grass grew, and edged with tumbled lines of stones. How old these paths were or who had made them, no one knew. In places, they disappeared, eroded by the endless wind and the cycles of heat and frost.

Traders often used these roads. They came to buy camel-hair cloth and the intricately worked gold ornaments produced by Azkhantian smiths. In exchange, they offered sandalwood and frankincense, rough gemstones and knives of tempered steel. Before long, Shannivar and her party encountered one such caravan, a line of laden donkeys trudging behind a ponderous wooden-wheeled cart. The oxen drawing the cart were black and rough-coated. Bells clanged softly as they swung their heads from side to side.

Shannivar guessed the traders were Denariyan based on their burnt-copper skins and their clothing of brightly-colored silks instead of wool or camel-hair. She nudged Eriu forward. He arched his neck and lifted his feet high, as if challenging the oxen.

"I am Shannivar daughter of Ardellis of the Golden Eagle clan," she cried out in trade-dialect. "By whose leave do you travel the steppe?"

"Traders we, out of Denariya, with permission of the Reindeer Clan," the trader called back in the same language. Despite his heavy accent, he spoke with the ease of long usage.

Shannivar gestured for him to approach. He walked slowly toward her, holding his hands well away from his body. His only visible weapon was a long curved knife in an ornamented leather sheath, tucked under his sash. Shannivar had no doubt that he carried more.

"May your journey be profitable and your enemies foolish." Greeting her, the trader halted a respectful distance away. Solemnly he tapped one fist over his heart. Clearly, he had learned the value of good manners.

At Shannivar's invitation, the Denariyan trader came closer. From the folds of his sash he removed a small leather purse. He drew out an Azkhantian token of gold, fashioned in the shape of a reindeer,

a safe-passage from the clan of that name. Shannivar nodded in approval.

With formal courtesy he then offered her tea, the
universal ritual of friendship. She accepted, gesturing for her party, especially the Isarrans, to remain
at a distance. Undoubtedly the traders were already
aware of that a pair of outlanders traveled with her
and news would spread across the steppe at the
speed of ox-cart, but it was best to avoid direct contact. At least, until the council of elders and chieftains had examined the Isarrans and made their
judgment. For this encounter, she and Rhuzenjin
were sufficient to meet with the Denariyans.

While one of the traders prepared the tea over a
small copper oil-lamp, another unrolled a carpet
beside the road. They took their places on it, sitting
cross-legged. Shannivar admired the intricate designs of indigo and madder red.

The water came to a boil, and the trader added
wedges of dried pressed tea and spices. When the
tea was ready, he poured it out with solemn ceremony. Shannivar cradled the finely glazed cup in
her hands and wondered who had made it, how far
it had traveled, and what strange lands it had
passed through. The tea was strong and sweet, fra-
grant with dried orange peel. Shannivar praised
the tea and the fine carpet, and accepted compli-
ments on her horse, the weather, and the valor of
her people.

When the tea had been drunk and the amenities
completed, the trader politely inquired of news of
the road. He had given no sign of curiosity about

the Isarrans, not even a surreptitious glance a
where they waited with the pack animals.

"Two days ago, we burned a Gelonian outpost,'
she told him. Let the trader carry word of their
defeat.

"None but madmen or Gelon enter these lands
without permission." The trader made a warding
sign against ill fortune. "Very bad for trade."

Before parting, the trader presented Shannivar
and Rhuzenjin with silk scarves. Hers was dyed
bright yellow and embroidered along the edges
with tiny butterflies and bits of mica. Such finery
would look well at a festive dance at the gathering.
She tucked it inside her vest, and they bowed to
one another and then continued on their separate
ways.

The meeting with the Denariyan trader had eaten
up the better part of the morning, but Shannivar
and her party pressed on. Toward the end of the
afternoon, she decided they had gone far enough.
The Isarran horses were flagging, and Leanthos
swayed in the saddle. The camel's temper had wors-
ened with every passing mile, despite Ythrae's at-
tempts to placate it. The Isarran animals needed
water, even if the hardy Azkhantian horses did not.
Ahead, a line of trees with lush foliage suggested a
spring or at the least, grazing. Bidding Rhuzenjin
remain with the outlanders, she rode ahead to make
sure the place was safe.

The trees were tall and slender, like maiden

dancers in a row. A breeze played through the branches. The air carried the smell of moist growing things, grass and pungent herbs. Although Shannivar saw no cause for alarm, Eriu nickered as in greeting another horse. She came alert, trusting his sharper senses. At her touch on his neck, he quieted.

With battle still fresh in her memory, Shannivar set an arrow to her bow. Eriu moved closer, silent now. In the underbrush, she made out the shapes of two horses. Camouflaged by the dappled sun, two men sat over the remains of a meal. What she could see of their clothing was sensible enough, muted, trail-worn garments in shades of brown, neither ragged nor gaudy nor impractical like the short tunics of the Isarrans.

One of the men started to draw a sword, but the other put out a hand in caution, pulling him back with a gesture and a few phrases in Gelone. Shannivar recognized the word, *Azkhantian*.

Shannivar nudged Eriu from the underbrush and, keeping her bow at the ready, addressed the two strangers with the usual challenge, "By whose leave do you travel the steppe?" The man who had restrained his comrade rose fluidly to his feet and stepped forward. As he moved toward her, the slanting afternoon sun illuminated his features. At first glance, Shannivar thought him Denariyan, but his skin was closer to the honey color of her own people. His shoulder-length hair, as dark as her own, was tied back with a strip of leather. He was young, no more than a few years from her own age.

He held his hands open and away from his body, but she did not think he was by any means helpless. Something in the way he moved gave off the perfume of danger.

"We in peace, no harm to man or beast," he spoke trade-dialect with a peculiar lilting accent that was not at all unpleasant, "ask to pass these lands."

"That will be decided once you speak your names and purposes."

The man hesitated, his reaction quickly masked. In the brief pause, no more than two beats of the heart, his companion got to his feet.

Shannivar inhaled sharply. No one could mistake the race of this second man, that milk-fair skin, the red-gold hair, the strong lines of nose and chin.

Once Shannivar would have been astonished to find a lone Gelon so deep in Azkhantian territory. After the battle of the fort, however, there could be only one explanation. She took aim.

The second man blanched but held his ground. He said in halting trade-dialect, "You ask for names? I answer truly. I Danar son of Jaxar, a nobleman of Aidon."

"What purpose has a Gelon here?" Shannivar said. "If you are not a spy, then you must be a soldier, strayed from your company or run away. We want none of your kind here!"

"I swear by what god you choose, I mean your people no harm. We never intend come this way. Bad luck we set foot on your lands."

Eriu shifted uneasily, responding to Shannivar's tension. At this distance, she could kill both of them before they reached her. "Where bound, then? Why?"

The two men carefully avoided glancing at one another, then the Gelon lifted his chin, resolute, and answered, "Isarre."

Shannivar shook her head in disbelief. Was Onjhol's trickster younger brother toying with her, testing her? The coincidence was unbelievable. The outlanders must be mad, or they thought her an ignorant simpleton, to believe such a thing. Isarre was Gelon's sworn enemy, for all that their people looked alike and dwelt alike in their tombs of stone. She might not be able to tell one from the other, although she was certain that they themselves could.

Another thought occurred to her. A Gelonian deserter might seek refuge in Isarre, beyond the Ar-King's reach, but so might a criminal. The Gelon, she had been told, were capable of unspeakable acts, the slaying of kinfolk, building stone walls across rivers, or the laying of salt upon an enemy's fields so that no grass would grow, as they were said to have done in Isarre.

"And your companion?" she snarled, to cover her indecision. "Cannot speak his own name?"

"Called Zev," said the black-haired man.

Called, he'd said, not *named*. A crafty one, that, who would not betray his name. Did he fear that to do so would grant the listener power over his spirit?

"*You* are no Gelon," she pointed out, stating the obvious.

Again came the slightest pause, the flicker of dark-lashed eyes away from hers and then back again. "No," he said quietly. "Born in Meklavar, mountains far south. True name Zevaron. I only living son of Maharrad, last *te-ravot*—last king—of city."

Comprehension swept through Shannivar. Eriu, sensitive as always to her shifts in mood, danced sideways. Most of the time, Azkhantians cared little for the affairs of lesser nations, their wars and follies. At the *khural* four years ago, however, she'd heard rumors of how the Ar-King had conquered yet another smaller land. *Meklavar*, yes, that was it.

The fate of one city mattered little to her. Let the dwellers-in-stone slaughter one another to the last child, and let the grass grow free when their walls had crumbled into dust.

This man standing before her, this exiled prince, had reason to hate the Gelon. Why would he make common purpose with his enemy?

"You also for Isarre?" she asked Zevaron, easing the tension on her bow and lowering it, but only slightly.

"Friend seeks asylum there. Ar-King threaten his life. I swear protect him and see him to sanctuary. I say to you because you are no friend to Cinath. Cinath send soldiers, take your country for his own. You people fight. You people still free. Me, someday I free my city. I make—what is word?—*pact?* with anyone to help my people."

Shannivar thought of the two Isarran emissaries, who also sought an alliance with Azkhantia. It seemed the entire world wanted her people's help. If so, it was better that the clans continue as they were, relying upon none but themselves, defending their own borders, rather than getting drawn into one foreign war after another.

Isarre, the outlanders had said. The easiest route to that land from Gelon lay across the great sea, and the fact they had not taken it confirmed that they traveled in secret. They might be outlaws or spies, or madmen. Who could tell?

Shannivar made her decision. She had no stomach for killing these men as they stood, not before the gathered chieftains had a chance to evaluate their stories. Instead, she would observe the two parties when they met. Their behavior might well reveal the truth of their respective stories.

"I cannot grant you leave to travel free in our lands," she said. "Might involve Azkhantia in Isarran war with Gelon. I do not have authority, nor is it simple decision. Some say we have enough troubles with Gelon and that such a move would be foolhardy."

"What do *you* think?" Zevaron asked. The coiled tension in his body had eased. He was still wary, but curious.

She shied away from his question. She had already stated that she lacked the power to make this decision, but perhaps the outlander knew nothing of the ways of the steppe. "The matter must be laid before the clan chieftains," she explained. "We are on our way now to the yearly gathering. If you surrender to me and swear no harm to man or beast in these lands, then I will take you under my protection for the journey."

Shannivar lifted her bow again. The muscles of her arm and back flexed, readying. If they refused, then she would have to kill them. She dared not allow two uncooperative strangers, whether enemies or spies or hapless exiles, to venture any deeper into Azkhantian territory.

A glance passed between the two men. Danar, the Gelon, said something in his own language. Shannivar knew only a few words of Gelone, enough to gather that he was saying they had no choice.

Moving slowly and carefully, the two men laid their weapons on the ground and backed away. Shannivar dismounted and gathered them up. The Gelon's sword was serviceable and reasonably sharp, although the steel was not as fine as Denariyan fashioning. Its balance was rough, and it had clearly seen rough usage. She suspected that the Gelon had come by it lately, for if it had been forged for him, the smith was utterly incompetent.

The knives the Meklavaran drew from boot, sash, and an inner pocket of his vest were clean-lined, their steel bright. They were of Denariyan make, she would swear, but their beauty lay not in ornamentation but in the perfection of balance and edge.

Shannivar studied the man who carried such blades. His face gave away nothing as he watched a savage—ah, yes, he would think of her as a savage—handling his weapons. She doubted he'd surrendered all of them, but from the way he carried himself, he did not need steel to fight effectively.

Behind those shadowed eyes lay a keen intelligence, a restless spirit. He might be a foe temporarily disarmed or a powerful ally.

"We will camp here," she told them. The clearing, with its shade and water source, was as good a place as they would find to spend the night. "Do you know the law of hospitality?"

Danar looked puzzled, but Zevaron nodded. "No guest may provoke or take advantage of another."

"Or answer a challenge, no matter how valid," she pressed. "Give your word that you will keep this truce."

They considered for an instant. Danar said, "Does this mean you—your party includes someone who might be our enemy?"

"This means there are no enemies in my camp. No blood shed on the trail or at the *khural*. Any guest who tries will find the hand of every rider against him."

"She means it," Zevaron said to his friend. "Cinath himself could ride among us, unmolested, under such a truce."

Satisfied that the two strangers understood and agreed to the conditions, Shannivar signaled for her people to approach. The rest of the Golden Eagle party entered the grove, first the warriors, then the *enaree,* and finally the two Isarrans.

Shannivar readied herself for the moment when each pair of outlanders would recognize the nationality of the other. She would shoot whomever made the first offensive move.

Both looked surprised to see the other. The older

Isarran acted even more frightened than usual, his comrade more suspicious. Perhaps they thought the Gelon and his friend were assassins sent to thwart their mission.

The Meklavaran, Zevaron, maintained his composure. He seemed to be assessing the Isarrans as possible allies, not enemies. Shannivar was willing to wager that he could hold his own against Phannus. But a physical fight? That she would not allow.

Shannivar ordered the camp to be set up with the Isarrans on one side and the strangers on the other. There were not enough riders to watch all four outlanders, and short of tying them up at night, she had to make sure they were convinced of the folly of any rash move.

Before setting up his *jort*, Bennorakh approached Shannivar. "Who are these two strangers? One of them is touched with light and poison. Why have you given him leave to join us?"

"The one named Zevaron says he is from Meklavar. I have never encountered any of his race, so I cannot tell. Certainly, he is no Gelon. The Gelon is Danar, from the city of Eithon, no— Aidon. What strange names the Gelon give their stone dwellings! They have offered us no harm," she added, surprised to find herself defending them when they had done nothing to earn her allegiance. "They asked for safe passage through Azkhantia, in the hope of an alliance with the clans. I have undertaken to bring them to the gathering, where the Council will decide what to do with them."

The *enaree* nodded. The small carved stones in

his hair and beard clanked gently. His focus turned inward. He tilted his head, as if listening to something only he could hear. As he did so, Leanthos drew close. His face, like pale weathered leather, reflected his agitation. His companion hovered, a pace behind, eyes watchful.

"A thousand pardons for my presumption, Reverend Bennorakh, Lady Shannivar," the Isarran emissary said, inclining his head to each. "In these unsettled times, with the fate of so many at stake, we must make certain of our facts before deciding how to proceed. It serves no one to rush into rash decisions. However, I must ask: *Danar* is the name of the Gelon yonder?"

"That is what he told me," Shannivar said carefully. She did not like the fervor behind the Isarran's questions.

"Danar, the son of Jaxar of Aidon?"

Shannivar wondered if Leanthos had some blood-feud with Danar. If so, Danar was very young to have offended an enemy so far away. Or possibly, the quarrel was with his father. Phannus, ever at the side of his master, turned stony, dangerously still.

"I don't care if he's the Ar-King himself, there will be no trouble between you," Shannivar said sternly. "You will stay on opposite sides of the camp and do nothing to violate the hospitality of the camp. You and the Gelon are both under my protection. No one fights without my leave. *No one.* Do you understand?"

"Even if it is a matter of honor?"

Once Shannivar would have cared nothing for

the honor of one who dwelled in stone, but now she was not so sure. She thought Zevaron and his friend were men of integrity, at least enough for her to trust their word. And she had seen for herself how Gelon fought with courage and loyalty.

Shannivar replied, as temperately as she could, "My uncle, Esdarash son of Akhisarak, has given his word that you will be able put your case before the assembled chieftains, and *I* have given *mine* to these strangers that they may also do so. Once the Council has heard your petition, you will no longer be my responsibility. For now, however, I require your promise that you will not provoke a fight while we are on the trail. In fact, if you so much as sneeze in their direction, I will interpret it as an assault, and you will answer to me."

Leanthos exchanged a look with his companion, who nodded with obvious reluctance. "I will do as you say, Lady Shannivar," the older man said, "but if they come at us, if they—then we must and will defend ourselves."

"They will not," she said tightly.

"Then we will not, either. I beg leave to retire as far as possible away from that—from those—as far as possible." With one of his odd, bobbing bows, Leanthos retreated.

At least, Shannivar thought as she settled down for the night, leaving Rhuzenjin on first watch, there did not seem to be any conspiracy between the strangers and the Isarran emissaries. Let them argue their cases before the assembled chiefs, and let the *enarees* read their omens in smoke and dream visions.

Let me go on with my own life.

Still, she felt a measure of hope. Her own journey had turned out to be even more adventurous than she'd expected. She would ride into the gathering with important news and with Rhuzenjin's victory song on the lips of her riders. She would win the Long Ride and then dance through the night, drunk on *k'th* and glory. What man then would dare to forbid her to ride and hunt and shoot as she willed?

PART III:

Shannivar's Race

Chapter 11

THEY rode on, following the pattern of wind and stars. Around them stretched the steppe, a rich velvet mantle draped over the shoulders of the land, rolling hills broken by wooded river valleys beneath the endless dome of the sky. The wind sang in the grasses.

After the first few days, when it was clear the Isarrans would grudgingly observe Shannivar's truce, Zevaron of Meklavar occasionally left Danar's side. He rode apart from the rest of the party, as if scouting the territory. His small brown mare, Shannivar noted, was poorly bred, of indifferent Gelonian stock. She had not fared well on the tough Azkhantian grasses or the lack of water. Eriu or Radu could, in necessity, drink but once a day, but outlander horses were far less hardy.

Zevaron treated his horse kindly, offering her words of encouragement and never pressing her to go beyond her strength. This consideration was so different from everything Shannivar had heard about the barbarity of outlanders that it aroused her interest. Now she slowed to allow Zevaron to ride beside her.

"That is a fine horse." Zevaron still spoke trade-dialect with his curious, distinctive accent although, with continual practice, he sounded less stilted. "I have never seen one with her gait."

"This is Radu," Shannivar said, patting the dun mare's neck.

Radu cocked one ear back, the other softly sideways to express her contentment.

"She is of ancient lineage. *Tabilit's Dancers*, they are called. It is said that a rider can travel the length of the steppe on such a horse without damaging a feather held between his teeth. Of course, her breed is strange to you. We do not sell or trade our horses to outlanders." *Although sometimes*, Shannivar thought, remembering the *enaree*'s song from Grandmother's funeral about a chief of horses who was captured by outlanders, *sometimes they can be stolen. But always, always, their hearts yearn to return to the steppe.*

"They are like your children." When Zevaron smiled, light spread from his eyes across his features. "The true treasure of your people."

Surprised by Zevaron's insight, Shannivar looked more closely at him. He did not carry himself as one who had spent most of his life in the saddle, but neither was he stiff and awkward, like his friend.

"You know something of horses?" she said.

"I was taught to ride as a child, but we had only a few horses, and those mostly of the Sand Lands breed. Do you know them? They are small like yours, but more lightly built, with short backs and dense bone, made for swift flight."

Shannivar nodded. She had heard of Sand Lands horses, although she doubted even the fleetest of them could outrun her Eriu.

"Each people values something different," Zevaron said. "For you, it is your horses and the freedom to ride as you will. For my own people, we value our books and our history."

Books? Shannivar thought this very strange, to reverence something so easily stolen, lost, or corrupted. History was another thing, song-poems and stories, laments and ballads passed from one generation to the next. The legend of Saramark, the tales of the Sky People, the lament of the exiled horse, all these defined her own people.

Now Rhuzenjin's song, about the battle at the Gelonian outpost and the wounding of Alsanobal, would be added to the repertory. She, too, would be remembered, and that was not so bad a fate. Yes, she decided, the stories of one's lineage were indeed a treasure, a way to bind courage and honor across the ages.

"And your friend? What does he cherish?" Shannivar shook her head and spoke again before he could answer. "I have never understood those who dwell in stone. What do the Gelon seek, that they are always trying to take the steppe for their own?"

"I cannot speak for all of them. My mother used to say there are good men in every land. As for Gelon . . . I say it is rotten to the core. The Ar-King and his kind have no care for honor or valor. They crave only power, power over others, power to destroy, to crush, to plunder—as my people have found to their sorrow."

Anger and grief and something darker ran through his words. Shannivar had no illusions about the Gelon. She fought and killed the Ar-King's soldiers, and her own father had died by their swords. The deaths of Mirrimal and her brother weighed heavily upon Shannivar's spirit, yet she had never felt such implacable hatred as she now heard in the voice of this stranger. It was one thing to glory in triumph, to see the invader driven back and to hear his screams of terror, to ride across the wild grass-swept hills and know that her people were free by the strength of her own hand. But this darkness in Zevaron was something different.

She knew very little of Zevaron's people, of his life. Unlike Meklavar, Azkhantia had never fallen to any invader.

She said so aloud. His mouth twisted, a wolf's savage grin, and he said, "Exactly."

Oh.

"You wish to be free, as we are," she said carefully. "Do you then seek an alliance between my people and yours?"

"I will make such a bargain with anyone or any force that can free my city. You, Isarre, the tribes of the Fever Lands, for all I care." He lowered his voice, damping the vehemence, so that she almost missed his next words, "Just so the Ar-King is destroyed and the ashes of Gelon blown to the winds."

"That will be for the chieftains to decide," Shannivar said temperately.

"You are right, it is a shame to spoil a fine day with desperate thoughts. Will you sing me a song of your people, so that I may know them better?"

She considered, watching him from the corner of her eye, and then lifted her voice.

> May the strong bones of my body rest in the
>   earth,
> May the black hair on my head turn to
>   meadow-grass.

As Shannivar sang, Radu bobbed her head in rhythm.

> May the bright eyes of my forehead become
>   springs that never fail.

She finished Saramark's lament, and with each phrase, she felt Zevaron listening more intently. He sat his brown mare with the same almost-grace, but something inside him had fallen still. She thought she saw the glimmer of tears in his eyes, but when she looked again they were dry. A radiance shimmered just beneath his skin, but that could have been a momentary parting of the clouds. She might have imagined that faint glow, like a dusting of tiny golden crystals. Or it might have been only a trick of the light.

Zevaron, perhaps alerted by some interaction between the other riders, turned his horse and kicked her into a trot back to Danar's side. Shannivar

watched the two men, puzzled at their easy manner
with one another. They were friends, that much was
clear, but whether they were master and servant, and
if so, who was which, she could not tell. Loyalty and
care marked Zevaron's behavior toward the Gelon,
utterly at odds with his bitter words. She wondered
how Tabilit, or whatever god they prayed to, had woven their lives together and for what purpose.

The party settled into a routine of daily travel and
nightly chores. The Azkhantians managed their own
affairs, each tending to his or her own mount. Ythrae
continued her attentions to the recalcitrant camel as
well. The men set up their tents and, between them,
Shannivar and Ythrae put up and took down her *jort*.
The nights were so sweet and mild that only a single
thin layer of felt was needed and only for privacy.

Shannivar's primary concern was keeping the
peace between the two pairs of strangers. Fortu-
nately, Danar seemed willing to abide by her rules,
or else Zevaron ensured that he did. Leanthos was
another matter. Shannivar did not think the older
man would do anything overtly hostile, but she was
not so sure about his companion, or that he wouldn't
give Phannus secret orders to provoke a fight.

She went up and down the caravan, as was her
habit, passing Danar and Zevaron at the back of
the party. She rode Eriu this day, and he expressed
his disapproval at there being so many horses in
front of him, but he settled easily enough at the side
of Zevaron's mare.

After some casual trail talk, Shannivar said, "You have heard Saramark's Lament, a great poem of my people. Will you now sing to me of your own land?"

Zevaron did not respond at first, and she wondered if his people did not sing. That would be very strange, but who could tell about outlanders? The Meklavarans built stone houses out of the face of the mountains, or so she had heard. They might be capable of anything.

Then he lifted his face and began in a clear, strong voice, a voice that rang like burnished bronze. The language was strange, yet akin to the ancient words of the *enarees*. As the song went on, she heard phrases in her own tongue. It was as if the source of the song flowed into many streams, or perhaps the bond that had grown between her and the Meklavaran carried its own magic.

"'What seek you, O my sister,'"

Zevaron sang.

"'So far from the mountains of your birth?

'When I left the tent of my fathers, O my
brother,
I yearned for fame and treasure,
But I found only sand and empty skies.'

'Then seek no more, but abide with me,
And I will pour cool water for your thirst,
And fill all heaven with songs of rejoicing.'"

When he finished, Shannivar was unable to speak. The images of sand and cool water, of thirst and loneliness, lingered in her mind.

"I—I seem to have offended you, and truly that was not my intent," Zevaron said, responding to her silence. "The words are from a book called *Shirah Kohav*, the Song of the Stars. It was my—" his voice caught, "—my mother's favorite. There is more, but I do not own a copy, and this is all I can remember, as she sang it to me."

Shannivar looked away, stung by the desolation behind his voice. Never in her life had she heard a man so bereft, so set apart, not even Bennorakh, who would never marry, who had not even taken an apprentice, who for all anyone knew had no living family. In that moment, she felt she could see into Zevaron's spirit, torn and radiant, brimming with anguish and obsession and, somehow, not entirely his own. Her heart ached for this strange, compelling man.

"Your mother sang it to you?" Shannivar was surprised to hear her own voice so gentle. She had no memory of her own mother, although surely Ardellis must have sung to her infant daughter in the way of their people. In Zevaron's few words, Shannivar felt how much he had loved his mother. She must be dead now, for her memory to evoke such deep sorrow. Dead by Gelonian hands? That, more than the fall of his city, would explain his hatred. But then why the friendship with Danar?

Zevaron's shoulders shuddered, as a horse in the winter sheds falling snow. He cleared his throat. "I do not sing well, I am afraid. At least, not such a song. Shall I try something else, a drinking song, perhaps? I learned many such when I was at sea."

He sang a lively Denariyan ditty that he told her was the story of three peddlers, a donkey, and a weaver-woman. She laughed heartily at hearing the antics of the donkey in the leaps and bounds of the melody. He smiled, looking more at ease than she had yet seen him.

"You sing very well indeed," she said, "especially for an outlander. But I think your people must be a gloomy sort, that you must borrow merriment from others."

"It is true the Denariyans love a jovial tune and a hearty drink." He faltered, his gaze shifting inward. "There is as much joy in Meklavar as anywhere. Or rather, there was. The only songs sung there now are dirges. It has been so long . . . but I would not spoil your day with my own sorrows. What shall I sing next? A ballad of the sea?"

"That is enough singing for now." Shannivar touched Eriu with her heels, and the black surged forward, skimming the tufted earth. She was on her way to the gathering, to the Long Ride and her future. What right had this outlander to move her so deeply?

Yet she could not shed that vision, half-glimpsed, of brilliance shimmering beneath smooth golden skin.

Chapter 12

THE place of gathering, the *khural-lak*, was one of the few fixed points in Azkhantia. At its heart lay an oasis that never ran dry, not even in years of drought. Here the ground was flat and easy, smoothed by generations of use. A rocky prominence rose above the fields, as if some giant beneath the earth had stretched up in greeting to the sky. A single narrow trail, a zigzag of switchbacks, led to the top of the prominence, where a ring of ancient stone structures formed a crown. The heights were sacred to the *enarees*, for here they met in their own private council and performed their secret rites.

Shannivar and her party arrived in late afternoon, before twilight muted the sky. *Jorts* and summer tents, many of them bright with clan emblems, dotted the central encampment. Here and there, a standard on a long pole towered above the tents. Reed screens had been erected to provide shelter from sun and wind while sipping tea and exchanging gossip. Horse pickets and groups of resting camels occupied the surrounding fields. Spaces had been cleared for dancing and contests of strength and skill, and a long flat field for races and mounted games.

Other septs of the Golden Eagle had already established their camps in the area traditionally reserved for their extended clan. Shannivar and her party set about doing the same, according to the routine they had used on the trail: the *enaree* in his own *jort*, Ythrae in Shannivar's, and separate trail tents for the men. As before, the two Isarrans kept to themselves, as did Danar and Zevaron.

One of the young men from a neighboring site strode into their camp just after the *jorts* were assembled. He was young and handsome, his hair oiled and tied back with thongs wrapped in colored wool, his boots and belt clearly new and of the finest leather. Shannivar did not know him, but she recognized the stylized ptarmigan on his jacket.

Shannivar set down the armload of blankets she had just unloaded from the camel and went to greet him, although it was rude for him to present himself before the new arrivals had sufficient time to settle in. Shannivar hoped he did not expect the customary hospitality, since the means of preparing tea had not been made ready. Senuthenkh, who had taken this responsibility for their party, was still unloading and sorting the chests containing the necessary supplies.

"May your day be lucky." The visitor greeted Shannivar politely, tapping one fist over his heart, yet without staring directly at her. "I am Kharemikhar son of Pazarekh of the Ptarmigan Clan. Where is Alsanobal son of Esdarash? I desire to speak with him."

"May your arrows fly true, Kharemikhar son of Pazarekh. Bitterness sits upon my tongue," Shannivar replied formally, "for my cousin Alsanobal was wounded in battle with the Gelon as we traveled here. I am Shannivar daughter of Ardellis, leader-by-acclaim of this party."

Kharemikhar blinked, quickly masking his surprise, though whether at news of the battle or at her leadership, she could not tell.

"Sorrow enters my ears to hear of it. Yet this is lessened by the greater sorrow of the women of Gelon, whose husbands will never return to them." He glanced at the horse lines Rhuzenjin had set up.

"If you are looking for that crazy red horse of his," Shannivar continued, dropping the ritual phrases for everyday speech, "save your sight for better things. He grazes now in the Pastures of the Sky, and there may he serve his master better than he did my cousin."

Seeing Kharemikhar's reaction, she smiled, although it was not respectful. "I hope he had not challenged you to a horse race?"

The Ptarmigan youth nodded. "I was looking forward to besting him in the Long Ride this year." He preened a little. "Now there is no one left to match me."

"No one? Surely you and my cousin were not the only contestants?"

"Alsanobal was my only serious rival. I shall win without him, but the victory will not be as sweet."

"If you hope to win the Long Ride, you must first beat *me*," she answered with a touch of heat.

A flicker of disdain crossed Kharemikhar's handsome features. Shannivar thought that it would make her own victory all the more glorious to see his face when she took the prize. At that moment, however, Danar and Zevaron came into view, their arms laden with rolled carpets for Bennorakh's *jort*. As they had on the trail, they worked together, doing their share. They had earned a measure of respect for their willingness to do even the most arduous and menial tasks without complaint.

Kharemikhar had been about to reply to Shannivar when he saw the two outlanders. "Who is that? A Gelon?" He glared at Shannivar. "What is he doing here? We do not take prisoners, as even the smallest child among us knows."

"He is not a prisoner."

Kharemikhar grasped the hilt of the short, curved sword at his belt. "No enemy may set foot in the *khural-lak*! It is the law. If that man is a Gelon, then his life is forfeit."

"And what of the law of hospitality? Would you shed the blood of a guest?" Shannivar moved quickly to block his path. "The Gelon and his comrade are under my protection."

"Your—?" By his expression, Kharemikhar clearly thought she had gone mad. "For what purpose would you bring such men among us?"

Trying to sound reasonable, Shannivar replied, "They have business before the chiefs."

"What business?"

Now it was Shannivar's turn to get angry. "It is no concern of yours. I have judged it important enough to bring them here, and that should be enough. If I am in error, the Council will tell me so. Either way, you have no cause to concern yourself."

With a dip of his head, Kharemikhar refrained from challenging her outright, but his gaze flickered again to the two strangers. "I leave them to the wisdom of the chieftains, then. For the time being. But if these outlanders should break even the smallest custom of the gathering, that mistake will be their last."

Shannivar watched him stride away. This, at least, was one husband she would not be seeking.

Having deposited his burden beside the threshold of the *enaree*'s *jort*, Zevaron came to stand beside her. His expression was intent and vigilant, his eyes steady on Kharemikhar's retreating back. "That man searches for trouble."

"What has he to do with you, or you with him?" Shannivar replied, still angry. "Your business is with the Council."

"I've seen his like before," Zevaron said evenly. "He's out for blood. Neutrality is all very well, but some matters must be settled before half the young hotheads in the camp join in."

Danar, who had followed a pace behind, said, "Zev, don't do anything stupid. Promise me."

"I gave your father my word I would protect

you." Heat edged Zevaron's words. "That doesn't include taking your orders against my better judgment."

"But it includes taking *mine*," Shannivar interrupted. "If either of you draws blade or bow against any man or woman here — including that ptarmigan-brained hothead — I will withdraw my protection and have you thrown out of the *khural*."

Zevaron struggled visibly to refrain from answering her. Danar, his expression earnest, stepped between the two.

"I know our position here is difficult," Danar said to her, "and I am grateful for all you have done on our behalf."

Zevaron was right, however. The *khural* encampment was full of young warriors who would like nothing better than to kill another Gelon, and in a manner devised to attract the greatest public attention. Zevaron, as Danar's protector, would suffice in his stead, for one stone-dweller was very much like another. Kharemikhar would carry word to his friends, and together they would find some excuse to instigate a fight.

Shannivar could see only one way to resolve the problem, and that was to get the business of the Isarrans and of Zevaron and Danar finished as soon as possible. According to gathering custom, the chieftains heard cases from dawn until dusk. There was still time to get the business settled on this very day.

"I will go now to the Council," Shannivar said to Danar and Zevaron, "and ask them to hear your case without delay. Until I return, you must remain here. Even better, keep within your own tent."

"Out of sight and out of trouble?" Zevaron shook his head, clearly skeptical that would stop someone like Kharemikhar.

"The Isarran mission, at least, could be settled," Danar said thoughtfully. "They would soon be on their way, eliminating one source of trouble." He paused, rubbing his chin. "Even if our own petition is delayed, the simple fact that we *intend* to present one grants legitimacy to our presence. Besides, curiosity is a powerful motivation. We pose no present threat, but we do present a tantalizing mystery. Who would kill us before learning what brought us here?"

"You mean," Zevaron replied dryly, "they'll wait to kill us *afterward*?"

"They'll wait to see how good a story we tell," Danar replied, unperturbed.

Shannivar nodded, impressed by the young Gelon's acumen. He refused to be irritated by his friend, which showed he had good self-control. She agreed with his reasoning. More likely than not, once word spread through the *khural* that these outlanders had traveled through many dangers in order to address the chieftains, their status would be secure. At least, it would be until they had laid their case before the Council. She wondered if Rhuzenjin might agree to compose a song about them to enhance the mystery of their mission. After the dark looks Rhuzenjin had given Zevaron, however, she did not think asking him would be a good idea.

She found Phannus standing guard outside the trail tent with such an expression of protective vigilance that she thought he would challenge anyone who even suggested that his master break his rest. She inquired politely and waited while the Isarran demurred. Hearing her voice, Leanthos emerged, moving as if his knees pained him from so many hours in the saddle. He had been resting, perhaps asleep, and looked disheveled. The journey had been hard on him. He had aged visibly on the trail.

"So soon?" Leanthos sputtered, when Shannivar told him to prepare himself in case the Council would hear his case today.

"Why wait any longer? Are you not anxious for your words to be heard?" Shannivar demanded. "For your case to be settled?"

"I beg your indulgence, Lady Shannivar. I expected my reception to be a bit more . . . formal. Such is my error. But if it is your command and the way of your people that we proceed at once," Leanthos visibly braced himself, "then I am grateful for even a little time in which to prepare."

"Make yourself ready, then. If they agree, I will send for you."

With a repeated admonition to Zevaron, Shannivar prepared to present herself to the Council. She paused only long enough to gather up the small portion of loot from the Gelonian fort: a wooden box of salt, a dagger of Denariyan steel in an ornate sheath, and a jar of oil.

She had not gone far when she was greeted by a handful of younger people. They had noticed her arrival and waited for an appropriate moment to approach her, as full of gossip as of curiosity. She recognized two or three of them from previous gatherings—Antelope, Falcon, Black Marmot, even one older woman of the Skylark clan.

"Heyo, Golden Eagle daughter! Your cousins have been waiting for you."

"You're here at last!"

"We thought you might not come. Took your time, did you?"

"Heyo! It's good to see you, too," Shannivar replied with a grin. "May your tongues be nimble and your horses fleet."

Laughter answered her, along with more questions.

"Shannivar daughter of Ardellis, is it? Who could forget the black horse with the dancing feet?"

"Are you racing this year?"

"Where is Esdarash son of Akhisarak? Does he not sit on the Council this year?"

"Yes, I'm Shannivar, and Esdarash was brother to my father, and yes, the Long Ride. As to why we are late, it's a long story."

"Stories we have time for, with plenty of *k'th*."

"And dancing!"

Shannivar sobered. "The greater part of my clan, including my uncle, could not leave the *dharlak* so soon after the death of my grandmother—that is, Jannover daughter of Koranit."

"Jannover daughter of Koranit!" Awed whispers echoed through the others.

"I didn't know she was still alive."

"She must have been as old as winter itself!"

"Ai, sorrow sits upon my heart! Her death marks the passing of an age," the Skylark woman lamented. "We shall not see another like her, not in all our years."

"Do we see outlanders among you? Who are they? Why have they come?"

"What's the news here?" Shannivar asked, to divert attention. "Why so many empty spaces?"

"Snow Bear has not yet arrived, nor Raven. No one's heard from them all year."

"Yes, but they may still come, Snow Bear that is. It's a far journey from the north."

"Is Mirrimal daughter of Sayyiqan here? Last gathering, she said she would come again."

Shannivar forced words through a throat suddenly tight. "Bitterness sits upon my tongue this day. Mirrimal daughter of Sayyiqan now dwells in the Sky Kingdom, along with her brother, Tamoferath son of Taraghay. They perished in battle against the Gelon."

"Ai, sorrow! Jannover daughter of Koranit, and now Mirrimal! So many brave women lost to us! How did this come to pass?"

"There will be time enough for the tale," Shannivar promised, unexpectedly moved by the expressions of sympathy. "You will hear the whole story at the proper time. Rhuzenjin son of Semador has composed a song-poem about the battle."

The younger women expressed their eagerness to hear the song-poem, for Rhuzenjin was known for his musical compositions from past gatherings.

"Now you must be patient," Shannivar said, "for I must speak to the Council."

Bidding her friends a bright day, Shannivar passed one area after another. The Golden Eagle people were not the only ones to send a diminished party to this year's gathering. The space reserved for the Snow Bear from the far north was indeed empty. The chief of the Ghost Wolf clan, who was still ailing from last winter's lung fever, had sent his son in his place. Alsanobal would have represented their sept of Golden Eagle, but Shannivar would not be permitted to sit with the Council. Grandmother had done so for many years, and she'd rendered judgments that were still respected, but Shannivar was no Jannover. A Saramark, perhaps. Someday. If Tabilit willed it.

Meanwhile, there would be games and races, singing and dancing, courtship and gossip. Nothing had changed, not the duty she was about to discharge nor her own plans.

At the base of the rocky promontory, a pavilion had been prepared for the Council. A small audience had gathered, so a hearing was most likely still in session. Shannivar slowed her pace respectfully as she approached. A few spectators, recognizing her from past gatherings or else in simple courtesy, moved aside for her.

The Council members normally sat in a half-circle on their stools of camel-skin stretched over light wicker frames and painted in designs representing Tabilit's gifts, the many animals that enriched the clans and the fire that warmed their nights. To Shannivar's disappointment, all but two of the stools were empty. She waited until the current case drew to a close. It involved failure to pay the agreed-upon price for a she-camel after the animal was found to be barren. The two elders conferred briefly with one another and rendered their judgment. The parties withdrew, apparently satisfied. Shannivar stepped forward, presented herself, and offered the gifts.

One of the elders recognized her. Ardellis, her mother, had been born to his clan, Silver Fox. He was very old now, his skin pleated with the passage of seasons. The wispy hairs of his moustache were white. His voice quavered, but pleasure suffused his features as he greeted her. He addressed her affectionately as "niece," and she called him, "Uncle Sagdovan," which seemed to delight him even further.

After the proper courtesies, Shannivar presented her request. Both Sagdovan and the other man, a chieftain of the Antelope people, looked grave as she explained that she had escorted not one but two parties of outlanders, each with their own petition for the Council. She did not need to explain the urgency of the matter.

"Esdarash son of Akhisarak of the Golden Eagle clan is wise indeed, to place such questions before the Council," said Sagdovan. "But we two alone cannot determine such a weighty matter. It requires the combined wisdom of our chieftains and elders, and we must consult the *enarees* as well. You say that your *enaree* has already examined these strangers through his dream visions?"

"Yes, but only the Isarrans," Shannivar reminded them.

"We must consider the possibility that Tabilit has brought these two groups of outlanders together for her own purposes," the Antelope chieftain said.

"Who can tell the intentions of the Sky People, until their results are revealed?" Sagdovan shook his head. "I say again, we must consider this matter carefully."

Chapter 13

THE next morning, Shannivar and her warriors led a procession through the *khural-lak* to where the Council met. Only Dharvarath stayed behind, saying he had seen enough madness brought about by dwellers-in-stone. The pairs of supplicants, the Isarrans and Danar and Zevaron, followed solemnly. As the party passed through the encampment, they caused ripples of excitement. Overnight, word of their mission had swept through the gathering. As Danar had predicted, everyone from the youngest child to the oldest grandmother now clamored for a glimpse of these outlanders.

This time, every stool in the pavilion was occupied. As was customary, leadership of the Council rotated annually among the various chieftains. This year, Tenoshinakh son of Bashkiri, a chieftain of the Falcon clan, held that office. Not yet in his middle age, he was strong and clear of sight, respected for his prudence as well as his daring in battle. He was a large man, almost as tall as a Gelon, with a forbidding aspect. Most of the other Council members, chieftains and elders, had seen far more winters, with the notable exception of the son of the Ghost Wolf chieftain, who watched the proceedings with the proper degree of respectful silence.

Three *enarees* stood in a cluster to one side, Bennorakh among them. His eyes were reddened from lack of sleep or perhaps from the ceremonial smoke. Shortly after their arrival, he had withdrawn to the top of the promontory with the other *enarees*. Because they followed the customs of neither men nor women, the shamans were said to dwell between worlds. What they did when they came together in such a time and place was not for ordinary people to know.

Shannivar's kinsman Sagdovan nodded to her as she approached. After the ritual that opened that day's business, and after beseeching the favor and wisdom of Tabilit, Tenoshinakh invited Shannivar to begin.

"May Tabilit grace your words with wisdom and your *jorts* with laughter." Shannivar tapped one fist over her heart and inclined her head. "I bring you greetings from my uncle, Esdarash son of Akhisarak, leader of the Golden Eagle clan."

"Esdarash son of Akhisarak is honored throughout all Azkhantia," Tenoshinakh replied gravely. "Sorrow enters my heart that I do not see him here."

"And mine as well, that I must stand in his place," she answered. Several of the elders nodded in approval of her modesty.

Another chieftain asked, "What has befallen the clan of the Golden Eagle, that Esdarash sits not among us?"

Although the Council would have been aware of the rumors flying through the gathering, courtesy demanded a formal question and answer. This way, there could be no misunderstanding based on gossip.

"He is well, my fathers." Shannivar explained that the death of Grandmother had caused Esdarash to remain behind. Exclamations rippled through the audience. Shannivar was again moved by the many expressions of grief.

"If Jannover daughter of Koranit now sits at Tabilit's right hand, the Sky Kingdom shines all the brighter," Tenoshinakh said after a moment. Then his gaze shifted again to Shannivar. He nodded, encouraging her to continue.

"My uncle appointed his oldest son, Alsanobal, to sit among you as his representative," she said. "On our way here, we came upon a Gelonian fortification. Alsanobal fought bravely and defeated the invaders, but was too badly wounded to continue the journey."

Shannivar hesitated for an instant. She had already boasted to Kharemikhar about being leader-by-acclaim of her party. She had earned the honor, as much as any man, but it might not be wise to bring it up now, before the assembled Council. Her present responsibility was to carry through her uncle's charge, as well as to see the Gelon and his friend safely to this place. Later, when her own fu-

ture was at stake, she could bolster her position
with the honors she had earned.

With an effort, she set aside her own pride. "In
the name of Esdarash son of Akhisarak, I present
Leanthos of Isarre and his assistant, Phannus, who
have traveled through many dangers to speak with
our people. It is by my uncle's command that they
now submit their case before you. He felt the matter could not wait, nor should it be decided by him
alone, for it concerns all Azkhantia."

Several of the chieftains stared at the strangers,
their weathered faces betraying no hint of friendli-
ness. Shannivar's kinsman bent to whisper to
Tenoshinakh. For a few moments, the chieftains de-
liberated, their words too hushed to be overheard.

Tenoshinakh said, "We will hear them."

Shannivar asked the Council to consider whether
the mission of the second pair of outlanders, a
Gelon and his companion, might relate to the first,
if not in their own intentions, then in the importance of their presence to Azkhantia. Her kinsman
had apparently informed the other elders of their
conversation the afternoon before, for they speed-
ily confirmed their decision to hear both parties of
strangers without delay. She requested and was
granted permission to translate the proceedings
into trade-dialect for the benefit of the outlanders.
No one wanted any unfortunate consequences to
arise from a faulty comprehension of language.

Leanthos began by presenting formal greetings
on behalf of his King. He spoke smoothly, advancing a well-reasoned argument for an alliance be-

tween his nation and the Azkhantian clans. The
long journey and brief rest had impaired neither his
tongue nor his determination to gain the advantage
for Isarre.

With a glare at Danar, Leanthos emphasized the
growing threat of Gelon. The Ar-King must be
stopped, he said, before the world fell beneath his
armies, field and city alike burning in Cinath's wars.
For too long, Isarre had stood alone against Gelonian aggression, but now her own borders were vulnerable. Her ships had been captured on the open
seas, and the port city of Gatacinne now lay in Gelonian hands.

Zevaron's face tightened, and the faint movement drew Shannivar's notice. Something in the
Isarran emissary's argument had caught him by surprise, had perhaps raked an old, festering wound.

Gatacinne, port city of Isarre. What could such a
place matter to a man from land-locked Meklavar?
Yet it did, she would have sworn it. She had not
imagined the tightly masked emotion on his face.

Returning her attention to the argument, she
heard rumbles of suspicion in the Council. Fine
speeches were all very well, but not worth the price
of their own blood. Why should they bind themselves to a weakened nation?

Leanthos had evidently considered that point.
Perhaps he felt, with some justification, that if he
described Isarre as too mighty, the Azkhantians
might well decide their help was not needed. If too
weak, they might think they would do all the fighting for an ally who could not materially contribute

to its own defense. He modulated his tone, pausing at the end of each of his points to make sure the audience had time to fully take it in. "If Isarre falls, there will be none to stand against Ar-Cinath-Gelon." Leanthos pitched his voice so that the exclamations from the audience fell away into silence. "He will direct the fullness of his wrath to Azkhantia. You know he will."

He turned, making eye contact with first one and then another of the Council. "This time, however, he will have more than the resources of Gelon to draw upon. He will have the wealth of his many conquests as well. Gelon will be more powerful than ever, and *you* will have to face them alone."

"What is this to us?" said one of the chieftains, a man of the Snake clan. A long-healed scar from a Gelonian spear marked one side of his face from temple to cheek and narrowly missed his eye. "We will throw him back as we have always done."

Shannivar translated, although Leanthos, and Danar as well, clearly understood the Snake chieftain's meaning.

"No one doubts your skill at arms, your love of your country, or your determination," Leanthos said. "You alone, of all the peoples of the world, have held fast against the Gelonian horde. But . . ." he let the syllable trail off for dramatic effect, "but you have done so because Gelon was limited in the number of men and swords it could send against you." He paused once more, letting the words sink in. Even the Snake clan chieftain listened intently, brow furrowed in concentration. Leanthos had made them think, and not only that, in the direction he wished.

"What if Cinath sends ten times that number?" Leanthos continued. "Twenty times? They will sweep across your plains like locusts, consuming everything in their path. The steppe will run red with the blood of your warriors. If you retreat to your far places, thinking to weather this storm, you will find yourselves encircled and penned there. Starved like animals until you are too weak to fight."

Now the listeners raised their voices, laden with scorn and yet with fear as well. Every person there had lost a father, a brother, a sister, or a friend. The Azkhantian tribes had never been numerous, so each loss struck at their strength.

Leanthos, perhaps sensing the quicksilver temper of the crowd, rushed on before the mood could shift to outright defiance, before they could turn on him as the source and cause of such a dire prediction. "I tell you, your only hope is to join us now and defeat Gelon before it grows too strong."

"What would your King have us do?" Shannivar's kinsman asked, and then paused for her to translate. "Fight his war for him, while he sits on his stones and grows fat?"

Nervous laughter burst out here and there in the crowd.

"If we are far from Gelon," Sagdovan continued calmly, "we are even farther from Isarre. Perhaps Cinath will be so occupied with conquering you that he will forget about us."

"What should you do?" Leanthos faced Sagdovan, once the titters had died down. "Act not in defense of Isarre but of Azkhantia! Come down from your high plains. Strike at Gelon and carry the war to their own territory!"

The muttering shifted tone, becoming less disapproving. This sounded more like the stuff of glory, the way of war in the steppe. Here and there, even under the Council pavilion, heads nodded. Only Tenoshinakh and Sagdovan looked unmoved. As for the *enarees*, they gave no sign of any reaction. Their expressions looked so blank and their gazes so inward, that Shannivar wondered if they were listening to the Isarran's speech or to the whisperings of the goddess.

What would Tabilit have us do? What would she say if we were to leave the steppe, the land she created us for, and carry war to the Land of Stones?

"Meanwhile," Leanthos went on, "we of Isarre will not be idle. While you draw away the Gelonian armies, we will attack from the sea. Cinath will be forced to divide his forces. Each victory will weaken him further. We will catch him in our pincers like a crab crushing its prey."

This did not seem a powerful image, for even a child could snap the claws of a river crab. Shannivar glanced at Danar, curious to see how a Gelon received such a speech. Although Danar held himself with dignity, listening politely, he looked troubled. She could not blame him. He might be an exile, but he loved his country. Why should ordinary people, even Gelon—the good men Zevaron had spoken of—suffer for the greed of one tyrant? And why should she consider the enemy as anything but power mad city-dwellers, to be slain whenever possible?

Zevaron, however, listened with an expression of dark intensity, almost rapture. His wordless fervor—so different from the moment of quickly masked pain at the mention of Gatacinne—stung her.

Leanthos ended his speech. There was a short pause, and then Tenoshinakh straightened on his stool. The audience listened even more intently. "We have heard your words, man of Isarre," the chieftain leader said, using the time honored expression to mean that he recognized the legitimacy of the speaker, "and we will deliver our decision in the fullness of time."

Heads bobbed in agreement and, for some, not a little relief. Still the shamans gave no sign of either approval or censure. Bennorakh kept his place among them, his eyes unfocused. He might have been a carven image.

"Now," Tenoshinakh continued, "let us hear this other petition. Perhaps, as is often the way of things, one question may cast light upon the other."

Leanthos bowed to the chieftains in the Isarran manner and stepped back. If he were displeased by this response, he gave no outward sign.

Danar moved forward to make his own case. In comparison to the rehearsed, polished phrases of Leanthos, he offered no flowery speeches, no impassioned call to battle. Instead, he spoke of his family, of his father's studies and love of learning, and how the greater part of the Gelonian people wished only to live in peace with their neighbors.

As Danar went on, Shannivar saw that his arguments were personal, flowing from his heart. Her people had a long tradition of such discourse. Passionate and quick-tempered, they recognized that men often acted from emotion instead of reason. It was said that Tabilit often guided men through their hearts without them knowing it. The chieftains listened patiently, yet Shannivar sensed they, too, were listening to something deeper and more resonant in Danar's words.

Leanthos, on the other hand, appeared to have no patience for listening. Although he was too experienced a diplomat to let his agitation show, his mouth tightened into a thin line. His brows drew together. He stood very still, and his gaze on the Gelonian youth was unwavering and merciless.

As Danar described how the Ar-King had launched into a campaign of aggression far beyond the territorial aspirations of his fathers, Leanthos could no longer contain himself. He strode forward, placing himself squarely in front of Danar.

"Enough excuses! Enough fabrications and justifications!" he exclaimed. "Esteemed and worthy judges, I cannot permit this charade—this *travesty*—to continue. In another moment, this scoundrel—" fixing Danar with a venomous glare, "will have you believe he is only an innocent victim of the Ar-King's tyranny. Nothing could be farther from the truth!"

Shannivar drew in her breath at this, as did every

clansman there. Danar trembled visibly at the affront and the blood drained from his face, but he held himself with exquisite dignity.

"Tell them who you are, Danar son of Jaxar!" Leanthos demanded. "Admit that you are the *nephew* of Cinath, Ar-King of Gelon, their mortal enemy!"

Exclamations of disbelief and revulsion rippled through the audience. "What!"

"What did he say?"

"The Ar-King's own kin?"

"You cannot conceal your place in the line of succession!" Leanthos gathered momentum from the crowd's response. His voice soared above their exclamations. "*Tell them the truth!* With the death of Thessar-Ar-Gelon, only Cinath's younger son and your father—an invalid!—stand between you and the Golden Throne!"

While Leanthos spoke, Phannus glided into position at his shoulder. Shannivar saw the assistant's fingers encircle the hilt of his sword, ready to draw it forth. He was no mere servant but, as she had suspected from the first, a skilled bodyguard. An assassin.

"*Tell them!*" Leanthos repeated, then went on, his voice now calmer but resonant with fervor. "Tell them the real reason you have come here—to convince the clans to support your bid for power. To enlist them as your army so that you can take the throne of Gelon for yourself. The rivers of Aidon will run with Azkhantian blood, but what do you care, so long as it is not *yours*, so long as you take the prize in the end?"

Throughout the onlooking crowd, people shifted, hands going to weapons, faces darkening in anger. Shannivar had only the knife tucked into her boot, and she could not match these men in strength or reach. Zevaron, she noted, had moved closer to his friend, balanced with one foot slightly in front of the other, eyes reflecting steady alertness. Although his hands were empty, he looked confident.

Tenoshinakh surged to his feet, shouting, "Enough!"

The onlookers hesitated. In that fractional pause, a sound ripped the air. A high-pitched wail accompanied the ghostly clatter of bone and shell, of antler and stone.

Shannivar stiffened, as if an icy hand had clamped down on the base of her skull. Her breath froze in her throat, and she realized that everyone else in the audience suffered a similar paralysis. The chief of the *enarees* shook his dream stick once more. Red light glinted from his eyes. Then he lowered the ornamented staff, and Shannivar found she could move again. In the audience, men exchanged dubious glances. Some hung their heads, while others shuffled back to their places.

"Enough, I say!" Tenoshinakh repeated. "Such charges are easily made, but blood once spilled cannot be recalled. We will take no action until we have considered all sides of this quarrel." After a moment of stunned silence, he gestured to Danar that he might answer the Isarran's accusation.

Danar's fair skin had turned even paler, but he held himself proudly as he faced the pavilion. "What the Isarran emissary says is indeed true but only in part. The line of succession to the Golden Throne passes by law and custom from Cinath to his younger son, then to my father as his only brother. And then," with a flicker of those peculiar sky-green eyes, "to me. Beyond those facts, which anyone can learn, the rest is lies."

He paused, letting his words sink in. "Do not let your fears deceive you into believing that *all* Gelon are mad for power," he went on. "That *all* Gelon thirst for blood. That *all* Gelon have no care for justice or honor. My father does not want the throne, and because of his condition, he himself could not rule, as has been the case from his birth. This too is the law."

"All the more reason for you to secure the throne for yourself!" Leanthos sneered. "Do you expect us to believe you would refuse it out of some lofty nobility of spirit?"

Danar frowned, a faint crease between his brows. "Until now, I would have said, *Yes, I refuse it. I am not fit to rule.*"

This statement provoked another expression of incredulity from the Isarran emissary, who now made no effort to disguise his contempt. In Shannivar's eyes, Leanthos appeared so blinded by hatred of his country's enemy that he could perceive nothing else.

Danar lifted his head, and something in his earnestness, the simplicity and directness of the movement, touched Shannivar. "At first, I sought only sanctuary," he said quietly. "I fled my own country on my father's command when Cinath plotted my death. But after what I have seen . . . I would *not* refuse the throne. In fact, I now believe that I *must* become Ar-King."

A rush of emotion, shock and disbelief, passed over the chieftains and the assembled clansmen. Even Zevaron looked startled. Two of the *enarees* huddled together, whispering.

"There!" Leanthos cried, pointing at the Gelonian youth. "You have it from his own mouth, from the monster who means to drive his soldiers into your lands, even as his fathers have done!"

"That is *not* why—" Danar stepped toward Leanthos, onc hand outstretched.

"No more lies! No more Gelonian deceit!" Leanthos cut him off with a sharp gesture of negation. "I challenge you, Danar son of Jaxar, heir to the Golden Throne of Gelon, by honor and by blood, by tide and by moon, until last breath!"

Shannivar's first reaction was to intervene as she would have during the journey. The responsibility for maintaining peace had become habit. Now she forced herself to step back. It was no longer any concern of hers how these stone-dwellers behaved toward one another. She had done what her uncle asked. She had fulfilled the requirements of honor.

"What are you saying?" Danar recoiled, clearly appalled by the Isarran's challenge. "I cannot—no, you are no swordsman—and we must not become personal enemies!"

"I make the challenge for my country, not myself," Leanthos responded, "and my champion stands ready to fight in my stead. As for *becoming enemies*, that relationship began generations ago and was sealed in blood by the vicious aggression of your own kinsman. You cannot undo what has been done or bring all the fallen Isarrans back to life. Or change who and what you are. I will listen to no more of your lies! Do you expect me to believe that *you*—of Cinath's own blood—would swear neutrality—or friendship—with Isarre?"

Before Danar could utter another word, Phannus stepped between his master and Danar. Assuming a fighting stance, he drew his sword. His features were composed, his expression intent, and only the momentary glitter of anticipation in his eyes betrayed any emotion.

The onlookers moved back to give them more room. A duel, yes, that was the proper way to settle such matters. Curiosity lit their faces, for none had seen a match between city dwellers. They were eager to see how the outlanders would conduct themselves.

The fight would be brief and final, Shannivar thought. Danar was young and reasonably fit, but he lacked the cold, deadly focus of the Isarran bodyguard.

"I say again, no!" Danar backed up, hands raised well away from his sword. "I will not fight you! You must listen—"

"What is wrong with him?" someone in the crowd demanded. "Is the Gelon a coward?"

"All Gelon are cowards! Everyone knows that!"

"What is the stone-dweller saying? He will not defend the honor of his clan?"

"Quiet, hear how he answers!"

"Chief Tenoshinakh," Danar cried, "I appeal to you! How can the death or maiming of one of us resolve our differences? Stop this madness!"

"We will not interfere." Tenoshinakh's brows drew together, and his voice took on a harsh tone. "This quarrel is an outland matter. Now is your chance to prove your case. Show us what is behind your fine words. If you refuse to fight, we will know them for a coward's lies."

Danar flushed, two spots of heat spreading across his cheeks. His gaze, which had been fixed on Tenoshinakh, wavered. He gulped and reached for his sword.

The instant Danar moved, Phannus closed with him, blade slicing through the air.

The Isarran's steel never reached its target.

For all the speed Phannus had displayed, Zevaron moved even faster. He was not only fast, but lithe and balanced. One foot swept out in a lightning arc, his movement a blur. His boot struck the Isarran bodyguard's wrist with a slap of leather against flesh.

Phannus grunted in pain. His sword went spinning through the air. It landed point down in the earth. The blade vibrated with the force of the impact.

Propelled by the force of the blow, Phannus spun away. He stumbled but quickly regained his balance. His face darkened to an ugly red, but his expression remained unperturbed, his concentration as keen as ever. With a flip of the wrist, a knife slid from a sheath hidden inside his sleeve and into his uninjured hand. He leapt forward, closing quickly. Zevaron held his ground until the very last instant. Then, just as the tip of the Isarran's knife was about to pierce him, he dropped to the ground. He crouched beneath the oncoming blow and turned sideways, bracing himself on both hands. Before Phannus could react and redirect the blow downward, Zevaron's foot swept out, low to the ground. Phannus had just shifted his weight to put power into his attack. Zevaron's swift, circular motion hooked the ankle of Phannus's leading foot and jerked it out from under him, and he fell heavily. The impact sent up a billow of dust. Onlookers murmured appreciatively.

Zevaron straightened up, again moving with preternatural feline grace, and nodded to Danar.

Tenoshinakh threw back his head and laughed from deep in his belly. "Let the one who calls the challenge do the fighting! Is that what you mean, friend of Gelon? That's the Azkhantian way as well!"

So there could be no misunderstanding, Shannivar translated into trade-dialect.

As the meaning of Tenoshinakh's words sank in, Leanthos looked terrified. In issuing his challenge, the Isarran had never intended to place his own life at risk. He did not even carry a sword. He had been counting on his bodyguard's skill. Shannivar did not envy his position. Danar could take him down in an instant.

"There has been enough blood shed between

Gelon and Isarre." Danar's voice rang out, resonant with conviction. "It comes to an end now. I say there will be no fight."

"You must!" One of the chieftains exclaimed. "He has insulted your honor before this Council. And you, Leanthos, you must back up your accusation with action or else withdraw it."

"That will not be necessary," Danar said before the Isarran could respond. "There can be no insult given if none is taken."

The crowd grew very still, heads angled to listen to Danar's astonishing words. This was a moment they would relish telling their grandchildren, the day a Gelonian prince shrugged off an insult from his traditional enemy.

"Leanthos, much of what you said is true," Danar said, "and the rest reflects only your admirable loyalty to Isarre. Yes, I am the son of Jaxar, nephew and heir to Ar-Cinath-Gelon, standing in the line of succession only after his own son. But it is also true—and I will swear by any god you name—that Cinath has betrayed the allegiance I once owed him. Loyalty must be earned as well as rendered. My uncle has sought my death, and for all I know, my father's. It is by his malice that I am outlawed, sent into exile. I have no love for him.

"But," Danar went on after a pause, "I love everything that is true and good in Gelon. By the breath of my soul, I pledge myself to restore Gelon to what it should be, a nation of justice, of learning and prosperity, a nation worthy of the blessings of its gods. A nation," his voice fell, and in the hushed silence, every syllable rang clear, "at peace with its neighbors." He slipped his sword free and offered it, hilt first, to Leanthos. "I swear to you that the second thing I will do when I take back the Golden Throne is to end this war with Isarre."

Heads nodded, everyone recognizing that in order to take the throne, Danar would first execute Cinath and put an end to his ambitions. And therefore, his threat to Azkhantia.

"In return," Danar said, still speaking to Leanthos, "I ask for safe conduct to your King, that I may say the same thing directly to him."

Leanthos did not take the proffered sword, but simply placed his hand over Danar's on the hilt. "I do not know whether such a thing is possible, but it is not my mission to judge. I am charged with bringing what aid I can to Isarre. The friendship of a Prince of Gelon—even one who is moon-mad—" Leanthos paused as Danar laughed aloud, "—must be deemed an advantage. I will do as you ask, and will speak for you in Isarre."

Withdrawing his hand, Leanthos turned his attention back to Tenoshinakh. "You have seen how enemies can become allies, and thus Isarre is strengthened. Will you not join us as well? Our unity in common cause will ensure our triumph."

After a brief conference with the other chieftains, Tenoshinakh said, "We of Azkhantia have never concerned ourselves with outland matters and see no reason to do so now. We have no fear of Gelon, but neither will we provoke further aggression in a fruitless cause. If you dwellers-in-stone have made an alliance between yourselves, so much the better for you. But it has nothing to do with us."

The chief raised his voice. "Leanthos of Isarre, you and your clansman are free to remain, but when you return to your cities, you may not take a single Azkhantian with you, not one horse or one arrow. As for you, Danar son of Jaxar, you may remain with us for the length of the gathering. If you are the salvation Leanthos seeks, may it be so, but do not trouble us further with your concerns."

Tenoshinakh glanced to the chief of the *enarees*. After a moment, the shaman nodded gravely. He lifted his staff and shook it. The sound of the bones and shells rattling against one another signaled the end to the hearing.

Neither the Isarrans nor Danar seemed unhappy with the decision. Only Zevaron looked pensive as he withdrew with his friend.

Chapter 14

DESPITE the excitement of "Shannivar's strangers," the usual festivities of the gathering continued. Young people engaged in contests of strength and skill throughout the day, while their elders traded livestock and gossip. Through the lingering dusk, everyone enjoyed feasting and music, ballads sung to reed flutes, drums, and two-stringed bowed *khurs*. There was *k'th* and dancing for everyone young enough to care about such things. Older folk discussed marriages and planned grandchildren while debating the finer points of hospitality and embroidery. Herb-sellers did a brisk business in the rarer plants but also in those used to prevent pregnancy. The chieftains, once freed from their daily Council duties, gathered to swap tales of great horses, heroic deeds, and fabled winners of past games.

When the sounds of drums and flutes signaled the night's dancing, Shannivar went with Ythrae to join in. Shannivar felt as if a weight had been lifted;

the relief of no longer being responsible for not one but two sets of unpredictable, troublesome strangers, men who knew nothing of the customs of the steppe, whose honor was unknown and unknowable. That was over now, and their fate was their own. Soon they would be on their way to make whatever alliances they could. They would ride over strange lands or perhaps take ship across the wide seas, never to trouble her again. She was free of them, and they of her.

The dance circle was small at first, but it grew rapidly. A handful of musicians spun out a merry tune, drummers, flute-players, and one old man squeezing music from a goatskin bagpipe.

Rhuzenjin was already there, dancing with a dozen other young men from different clans. Ythrae went to join the women's line. Shannivar paused, watching, and the old bagpiper, his eyes crinkling in his weathered face, glanced in her direction. Gnarled fingers danced over the holes on the pipe and seamed cheeks puffed out, sustaining the long, wailing notes. The music wound through her blood. It made her want to dance, to weep, to run.

She remembered the morning the strangers had arrived at the *dharlak*, the sound of Grandmother's breathing, the creaking leather straps of the old woman's bed, and the sight of the muted outlines of pillow, of caskets and chests containing the treasures of her family. She remembered wondering what it would be like to live in a place where nothing smelled of memories, of family, of home. A shadow fell across her heart.

Zevaron would not, could not, return to his city. She wondered if the home in his heart was his hatred for Gelon. The thought filled her with sadness, as if it were she herself who had no hope of anything better.

She tried to dispel the moment, unable to understand what troubled her. What had the fate of one city-dwelling outlander to do with her? She was among her own people at the gathering. She had discharged her obligations with honor and was now free to seek out her own future. Grandmother would have been pleased. Tonight she would dance and flirt and perhaps choose one of those fine young dancers for her bed. Tomorrow she would take part in contests of agility and horsemanship, or archery, and she would gossip and laugh. But she would never return to the home of the Golden Eagle.

Was exile what Mirrimal had feared most? Had exile sharpened Kendira's tongue and cast such shivering darkness across Zevaron's heart? Would the same thing happen to her?

Shannivar reminded herself that the steppe was her home. No one part of it might claim her any more than another. Like the Golden Eagle that was her totem, she would go where she willed, where the winds took her. Her home was in her wings, the fleetness of her horses, and Tabilit's endless sky.

The dance had come to an end. The bagpipe wheezed to a halt, releasing her. The lines broke apart. Ythrae lingered for a moment, watching Rhuzenjin with hopeful eyes. As usual, he seemed utterly unaware of her attention. The youth who had led the men's line, the son of the Ghost Wolf clan chieftain, approached Ythrae. Shannivar could not hear what he said, but she caught the blush and quick smile on the younger woman's face.

Looking up at the Ghost Wolf youth, Ythrae tilted her head and laughed at something he said. Watching them, Shannivar felt glad and unexpectedly wistful. Ythrae was, after all, as deserving of happiness as anyone. Shannivar could not wish her young cousin anything less.

The music started up again, the opening strains of a courting dance. Out of the corner of her vision, Shannivar saw Rhuzenjin glance in her direction. The next moment, he would approach her. She was certain of it, and she could not refuse him outright without insult.

Just then, Danar and Zevaron stepped into the firelit circle. The orange light warmed the Gelon's features pleasantly, but the effect on Zevaron's honey-gold skin took Shannivar's breath away. He had paused at the edge of the beaten dirt, his head turned toward the musicians. Gold touched the lines of his cheek and nose, the strong neck, the lean curves of shoulders and chest. His hands hung at his sides, momentarily at rest yet eloquent with power and the promise of gentleness.

Before Shannivar could form a conscious intention, she was moving toward him, a moth to his flame. Flame, yes, as if a fire burned just below the surface of him. A fire that, as his gaze shifted and his eyes met hers, ignited them both.

In that moment, Shannivar could not breathe. It was if the two of them had become trapped in amber, their hearts frozen in flame between one pulse and the next. An image rose up to blind her sight: Tabilit bending low from the Road of Stars to breathe upon the two of them.

Then Shannivar found herself at Zevaron's side, one hand reaching for his. The music dimmed, distant. She inhaled the scent of far-off mountains, of sea and storm and foreign winds. Something tugged at her, evoking an answering surge of longing. His fingers closed around hers.

Shannivar blinked, and the stars were now only stars, the fire only fire, the music sprightly but the instruments slightly out of rhythm with one another.

"Will you teach me this dance?" he asked.

Wordless, she took his other hand, lifting both to shoulder level, straightening and turning so that their right shoulders faced, their joined hands in front of her heart and his. His gaze remained on hers. He moved with her, one deep gliding step, rise and pause, then another. They revolved around the center point like creatures of legend, slow and elegant, deliberate in their movements, and unwavering in their gaze.

As they circled, Zevaron's gaze never faltered, not even when he missed a step and recovered. Shannivar saw in his eyes an expression of wonder, as the other dancers faded like mist. Only the two of them remained, flowing with the music, treading the sacred land. They became every man and every woman who had ever come together in this dance. They were Tabilit and Onjhol, Saramark and her noble husband.

At last, the music dimmed and then fragmented as one instrument after another fell silent. Tabilit had withdrawn; magic no longer seeped from the earth, from the sky. Dancers stepped apart, laughing or murmuring to one another. Shannivar still gazed at Zevaron, not knowing what to say.

Rhuzenjin appeared, moving from night into the circle of light. He scowled, his lips twisting. His brows drew together, tight and hard, as he tried to disguise his displeasure. "Shannivar, you bring no credit to your clan by behaving in this way."

For a moment, she thought he might strike her, or at the least grab her arm to draw her away. His glare shifted to Zevaron, who calmly returned it.

"I will dance with whomever I please!" she retorted.

"It looks like that means *everyone*," Rhuzenjin said, pointing rudely at Zevaron.

"I do not understand what is going on," Zevaron said to Rhuzenjin in trade-dialect. "If I have given *offense*—" He used the word that meant a rude, vulgar act, rather than a violation of honor, but his intention was clear.

"Stay out of it, outlander!" Rhuzenjin snarled, still in Azkhantian. "Shannivar, what are you doing, to openly favor a stone-dweller! Think of how it must look! Consider your uncle's honor—"

"My uncle has nothing to do with this!" Shannivar's temper flared. "You mean I have no right to choose my own partner, that now I must dance with *you*! If you want to dance with a woman, there are many who would be glad of it. Ask Ythrae and bring her joy. Or the camel, for all I care! I will not dance with any man who speaks to me in such a manner."

"Has there been some misunderstanding?" Zevaron said.

"None at all," Shannivar returned, switching back to trade-dialect. She kept her gaze steadily on Rhuzenjin. "We understand one another perfectly well. We just don't agree."

"Shannivar, I'm thinking only of your happiness," Rhuzenjin insisted, still in Azkhantian. "Why turn away from a man of your own people—one who can give you a secure place, honor, respect—for an outlander? All he can offer is misery and exile. Consider what you are doing."

"Since when does one dance mean a commitment to marriage? Or anything else?" Shannivar demanded. "Or is it your own pride that speaks—?"

"Not just any dance." Rhuzenjin paused, breathing hard. His pupils dilated in the failing light. His face tightened with emotion. Then he repeated, low and intense, "Not *any* dance."

So he had felt it too, the breath of Tabilit. The Blessing of the Sky.

It had been a moment's grace, nothing more. Whatever her feelings for Zevaron or his for her, that moment had ended. He would go to Isarre with Danar, and she would follow wherever Tabilit beckoned her, here on the steppe. The world was too vast and too unpredictable to offer even the smallest hope that they would see each other again after this gathering.

"If I have given offense or caused difficulty, the fault is mine," Zevaron said. "Please do not quarrel with your kinsman on my account." He spoke calmly, but with quiet confidence. Something in his bearing reminded Shannivar of the moments before he had trounced the Isarran bodyguard. "I ask your pardon, Rhuzenjin, since I do not know your customs—"

"May bitterness sit long upon your tongue." Without waiting for a reply, Rhuzenjin stalked away.

Zevaron watched his retreating back. "There goes an unhappy man. If I have made him my enemy, it was not my intention."

"Him?" Shannivar snorted, then felt ashamed. It was improper and disloyal to speak ill of a clansman.

Rhuzenjin had never treated her poorly until now. He was jealous, and there was nothing she could do about it. At least she had never taken him into her bed, or the situation would be even worse. She tossed her head, wishing it were as easy to shed the certainty that she had caused pain to a man who meant her only good.

She turned back to Zevaron. "Forget about him. If you must worry about anyone in this camp seeking to cause trouble for you, it would be Kharemikhar."

"Oh, *him*." Zevaron's lips curled in a wolfish grin. "That matter is already dealt with."

She saw the small bruise darkening one cheek. Before, it had been hidden by shadow, then masked by Tabilit's golden breath. "Kharemikhar—"

Zevaron gave her another grin, a flickering glance of dark-lashed eyes. Shannivar followed his gaze.

Kharemikhar had entered the circle, favoring one leg as he moved through the opening figures of "Onjhol's Dance." He spotted Zevaron and touched one fist to his chest in salute.

"We—ah—settled things," Zevaron said in response to Shannivar's expression of astonishment. "He wanted to learn the foot sweep I used on the Isarran bodyguard. I taught him."

And a few other things as well, she had no doubt.

"He let me know I'm welcome to join the wrestling contest tomorrow." A glint of mischief lit his eyes. "Shall I?"

Shannivar shrugged. "You must decide such matters for yourself. I am no longer responsible for your good behavior. But since you ask my advice, and there are many games to choose, I know you ride as well as a camel drunk on *k'th*."

"Oh, as bad as that?"

"No, but I don't think you should try the handkerchief race or mounted wrestling. Can you shoot?"

"As a boy, I was pretty good with a sling, but the best that can be said about my archery is that I usually don't hit things I'm not aiming at."

From the lightness of his tone, he had no inflated vanity and seemed to find his own lack of skill a source of amusement. And although he had accused himself on the trail of being a poor singer, his voice had been clear and strong.

"Then you had better follow Kharemikhar's advice and try the wrestling on foot," Shannivar said, "since you seem to be good for very little else."

As they talked, they strolled to the edge of the dancing circle. Ythrae had gone off with the Ghost Wolf youth. Danar was talking with two other men, Senuthenkh one of them. The Gelon nodded, looking serious but not uneasy. Zevaron joined the conversation, but Shannivar declined.

She sat down with the unmarried women and took a sip from the skin of *k'th* they were passing around while calling out encouragement or ridicule at the men who were dancing for their benefit.

The men moved in a circle, improvising steps to display their athletic prowess. One after another, they stepped low and wide, kicked their legs, leapt high in the air and landed crouching like cloud leopards on the hunt. Kharemikhar had taken the lead position, still limping but performing the most strenuous steps anyway. Shannivar smiled, thinking how much he was like Alsanobal: prideful, stubborn, with more courage than sense. Still, what did it matter if he injured himself even worse by showing off, so long as the young women smiled at him?

The dance ended and another began, this one a women's courting dance. Shannivar set aside the *k'th* skin and stood up with the others. She felt Zevaron's attention turn to the dance as she extended her hands to the women on either side, elbows bent, fingers clasped loosely. Ythrae, flushed and excited, took a place beside her. Several unfamiliar women joined the circle, colorful in their holiday finery. Their dresses and jackets were embroidered in clan emblems and edged in ribbons of bright Denariyan silk. Shannivar was one of the few who had not set aside her loose riding trousers.

"You'll never catch a husband looking like that!" The girl beside Shannivar wore a flowing skirt and tight-fitting vest that showed the shape of her breasts and hips, and the narrow waist between them.

Shannivar shook her head, stepping to the beat of the drums. Smoke from the fire and *k'th* whirled through her veins. The men fell silent, their focus on the dancers. One of the girls broke free to dance alone inside the circle, spinning so that her skirts and the long braids of her hair flew outward. Laughing, she returned to her place.

The music carried Shannivar forward. Stomping her feet, she felt the earth beneath her as a living carpet. The sky seemed to be singing with the music, the stars dancing with her. She hurled herself high into the air, her arms extended in imitation of her clan totem. Her blood sang in her ears. The audience whooped in admiration. Shannivar heard Rhuzenjin's voice, and then Zevaron's. She whirled and leapt again, as the music shifted, deep and throbbing.

When the dance ended, Ythrae slipped her hand around Shannivar's elbow and drew her aside. Shannivar glanced quickly at the knot of onlookers but could not find Zevaron. She turned her attention to her young cousin, whose eyes glittered as if she had drunk too much *k'th*. She blushed as she stammered out the news that the young man she had been dancing with, the son of the Ghost Wolf chieftain, wished to marry her. He had been watching her since they arrived, and only this night approached her. He was—and here Ythrae's babble failed her— "everything wonderful in a man." Only the absence of both their families prevented an immediate agreement. That would have to be negotiated over the winter and culminated at next year's *khural*.

For a moment, Shannivar wondered why the younger woman confided in her. She was, she then realized, Ythrae's only kinswoman at the gathering, as well as the leader-by-acclaim of their party.

Shannivar felt a twinge of envy at Ythrae's exhilaration. How simple it was: you saw a person who attracted you, you danced, you married. Rhuzenjin had not wanted Ythrae, so she had found a man who did.

She took Ythrae into her arms, kissing her forehead in blessing. Yes, she agreed, it was all very wonderful, and the anticipation of waiting would make it even more so. He was a very fine young man, and there was no reason they would not be as happy as any other couple. At least, she thought wryly, their camels would be content under Ythrae's skillful handling.

Beaming, Ythrae skipped back to the circle. Another dance had begun, men and women in two lines, facing one another. Shannivar took her place in the women's line.

"*Wey, wey, wey*," sang the men, clapping in rhythm, "*Where is your bridegroom?*"

"*Wey, wey, wey*," the women answered. "*He remained behind in the mountains.*"

"*Wey, wey, wey! Let him stay there, stay there*," the men responded.

"*Wey, wey, wey*," they sang together. "*His horse grows old while being tethered.*"

Shannivar finished the dance, hurrying away before any of the young men could ask her for the next couples dance. The last song had wound itself through her skin. The strange mood of earlier had returned, stronger than before. She felt wild and sad all at once and had no words to explain why. She wanted to run barefoot beneath the moon, to dance across the silvered grasses, to swim to the bottom of the deepest lake. She did not know what she wanted.

Voices, low and urgent, reached her as she passed one of the reed mat shelters. The words were neither Azkhantian nor trade-dialect, but Gelone, of which she knew a little. She paused, straining to hear them above the sound of her heart. In the pale brilliance of the moon, she discerned two shapes, hunkered down together.

Danar said in a low voice, "I don't understand." Shannivar could not make out his next few words, then: "You won't come."

"I promised to get you to safety," Zevaron said. "You have safe passage to Isarre."

"Yes, and I expected you to seek—" *safety? sanctuary?* "there . . . your mother's kin." Danar went on, but Shannivar's understanding of Gelone was not good enough to follow him.

A pause. Then Zevaron said, "From here your way is clear. Mine is not."

"What, then?" Danar's voice rose in pitch. "Where else would you go—not Meklavar—" more phrases, too heated and swift for Shannivar to catch. ". . . throw your life away in a useless rebellion? Think, man! Think of Tsorreh! Do you want her death to mean nothing?"

"How dare you bring Tsorreh into this?" Zevaron flamed.

Tsorreh? Someone important to Zevaron . . . now dead. Shannivar held her breath, waiting for more.

"Keep your grief, then. But do not let it make you stupid. Wait until the time is right," Danar urged. "Gather your allies. You know I will stand at your side—"

"I *said* I will decide! Now leave me alone. I will hear no more of this!"

With a rustle of cloth, Zevaron got to his feet and strode away. Shannivar thought that if she stayed still, Danar would also leave, with no knowledge they had been overheard.

Danar stood looking in the direction Zevaron had gone. "You fool," he said to himself. "The *first* thing I would do is free Meklavar."

Chapter 15

EARLY the next morning, Shannivar went down to the horse lines to check on Eriu and Radu. She missed the simplicity and familiarity of their company. So many things in her life were changing, uncertain. And though horses changed, it was according to the pattern Tabilit had set for them. They grew from capricious foals to steady adults and then declined, but they remained forever themselves: Radu with her calm regard, the slightly cocky tilt of one ear, as if to say, *Silly two-legs, where have you been?* Eriu with his inwardly-curved ears up and alert, eager for the next adventure. Particularly one that involved flying over the land.

Soon, she promised both him and herself.

To her surprise, Zevaron was there before her, tending to the brown mare. He had lifted one hind hoof to examine it but, not knowing the ways of horses, had placed himself almost directly under her hip, so that the horse leaned heavily on him. Zevaron's body folded over into a painful looking crouch.

"Heyo, Zevaron!" Shannivar called.

He looked up, face dusky with exertion. Sweat beaded his forehead. She tried not to laugh.

"I'll show you an easier way." When Zevaron let go, the mare dropped her foot with a thump. Shannivar took his place at the animal's side. She bent down to run her fingers along the tendon in the lower leg. The mare responded to the pressure and allowed Shannivar to lift the hoof. Before the mare could settle her weight, Shannivar pulled the leg back and to the side. The mare gave an aggrieved sigh and balanced her weight on three legs.

"You see?" Shannivar said.

"I suppose horses are like people. Some will take advantage of any opportunity."

Shannivar set down the hoof, but not before noticing it was narrow and weak-walled, badly suited to rough terrain. She rubbed the patches of white over the mare's withers, scars from old saddle sores.

"Is there anything I can do for her so she doesn't break down on the road?" Zevaron asked. "I didn't have much choice in a mount, so I must make the best of her."

Shannivar considered. "About her feet, not much, except to not give her too heavy a burden or push her too hard over rocky ground. She needs better food and a thick blanket so the saddle does not rub. And a breast strap and crupper for hills, because her chest is so narrow."

"I am sadly ignorant of how to care for animals and their equipment, how to hunt or find edible plants, how to travel long distances overland and in all sorts of weather. I learned a little about riding horses as a boy, but others did this sort of work. Now I must learn everything." He sighed. "If this were open sea instead of land, I would know what to do."

"You are a sea man, then? A . . . sailor?"

The hint of a grin quirked one corner of his mouth. "*Was.* In all likelihood, never will be again. But yes, I did travel the waves. For four years I served on a Denariyan ship, the *Wave Dancer.* Her captain, Chalil, was like a father to me. He taught me shipcraft, hand-to-hand fighting, and a little piracy."

Shannivar lifted one eyebrow.

Zevaron's grin broadened. "Well, more than a little. That's what the Gelon called us, certainly. We thought of ourselves as free men, seekers of fortune. That is one thing about life onboard. There are no walls, no boundaries. You go where you will or where the ocean wills. Storm and tide and other things, these are powers no mortal man can resist. But everything else . . ." He spread his hands wide, "everything else is there for the taking."

"I do not wonder that the Gelon called you *pirates,*" she said. "They want the whole world for their own, and then they would cover it with stone fences."

He looked intently at her, his smile fading, then nodded. "That they would."

Again she heard in his voice the resonance of something so deep and hard, she could not call it hatred. Puzzled, she wrinkled her brow. "Then how did you come to travel with one of them? To be his friend and protector? For that matter, how did a man of a far mountain city find his way to the sea?"

"It is a long story."

"I have time. And we Azkhantians love stories."

"Well, then. You have convinced me. Before I met Danar, I was at sea, and before that, I was at Gatacinne."

"Gatacinne? In Isarre?"

His gaze slipped past her, past the horse lines and the *jorts* of the *khural-lak*. Past, she suspected, the wide reaches of the steppe. To Isarre? To the mountains of his home? To the sea?

"Gatacinne, in Isarre," he repeated in a hollow voice. "When Gelon conquered the city."

That was four or five years ago, Shannivar thought. He must have been just barely a man. She felt as if she were standing on the brink of a cliff. She had seen cascades tumble through deep-cut ravines, had seen them swollen in flood. She did not fear such rivers, but she respected them. No one could fight against their power or command them, perhaps not even Tabilit herself.

"The story begins a long time ago," he repeated, "when Meklavar fell. That is how we came to Gatacinne, my mother and I. She had kin in Isarre, and we hoped—it does not matter what we hoped. We thought we were safe at Gatacinne. And so we were, until the Gelon came."

Shannivar peered curiously at him.

"Danar and I are indeed peculiar companions," he said. "It was, after all, on the orders of his own

King and uncle that my city was attacked and its gates burned, that my mother and I fled into exile."

In the way he spoke of her, Shannivar heard great love and even greater grief. "Your mother . . . Tsorreh?"

He looked startled. "You know her name?"

"I overheard Danar mention it, yes."

"He would," Zevaron said in a thick voice. "He has no difficulty speaking of those he loves."

Yes, that was right. For all his strangeness, Danar was clearly a man who loved deeply, without reservation. Shannivar could not imagine how the nephew of the Ar-King could have met the exiled Queen of Meklavar and known her well enough to love her. But with dwellers-in-stone, who could say? Patiently, she waited for the rest of the story.

"Tsorreh—my mother—and I, we made it across the Sand Lands to Gatacinne." Whatever had stopped him before now gave way. His words spilled out like a river too long dammed. "We thought the worst was past. Then the Gelon attacked at night, from the sea. We got separated in the fighting. The city was burning, and there was carnage everywhere. She—" He paused, looked away. "She was taken to Gelon as a hostage. I tried to find her, to rescue her before her ship set sail, but the Gelon were everywhere. They were too many, too strong. I nearly—I ended up—"

Zevaron skittered to a halt, chest heaving, face touched with the hint of flush. Shannivar could well imagine his rage.

"In the end, Chalil took me onboard the *Wave*

Dancer. I was more than half-crazy, I think. All I wanted was to kill as many Gelon as I could lay my hands on, and there was nothing I could do. Nothing except get myself killed, that is. He talked some sense into me, taught me, and gave me hard work to occupy my mind. Gradually I made a life for myself. Sailing. Trading." He paused, the hint of a grin tugging at one corner of his mouth. "Pirating."

Nodding encouragement, Shannivar listened.

"Years passed, and I almost gave up hope. But she was still alive, in the custody of Danar's father, Lord Jaxar. By chance, or perhaps not chance at all, I found her . . . for a time."

"Were you forced to leave her there? In Gelon?" Shannivar asked in sympathy. What a terrible fate, to languish in the hands of such an enemy. Shannivar could not decide if it would be worse for the woman herself, or for the son who had no choice but to abandon her.

"In a way. She died there." A pause, a breath like the steam of a heated sword plunged into ice. "On Cinath's orders."

Shannivar was not sure if his next words were spoken aloud, or if the two of them were joined in such sympathy that she heard them in her own heart.

Cinath will pay for her death, for the enslavement of my people. All Gelon will pay.

"I promised her I would take care of Danar, and I have. He will go to Isarre and make an alliance there."

"And you? You will not join them? Is that not

the way of stone-dwellers, to band together against a common enemy?"

He shook his head. "Isarre cannot conquer Gelon. I saw that at Gatacinne. They have neither the strength nor the determination to put a final end to their enemy. They will settle for keeping their own borders secure. But that is not enough for me."

With that strange harmony of feeling, Shannivar felt his passion for revenge as if it were her own. Perhaps the bond Tabilit had woven between them during the dance endured, giving Shannivar the ability to sense the images behind his words. Or perhaps the intensity of his feelings—and that glimmer of gold beneath his skin—was a kind of magic in itself. He wanted nothing more than to tear apart the glimmering palaces of Aidon, capital city of Gelon. Stone by bloody stone. In her mind, as in his, fire raged across the seven hills, as hot as the pulse pounding through his temples, and the ashes of the conquerors blew away in the wind.

The Golden Land crumbled into salt, and no man remembered those who once lived there.

By the Shield of Khored, whispered through her thoughts, *by the memory of my mother, by everything holy and by all that is unholy if need be, I swear that Gelon will pay.*

Chapter 16

ON the morning of the Long Ride, the sun spread across a perfect, cloudless sky. Dew still clung to the grasses, but by the time Shannivar had finished saddling Eriu, the ground was almost dry. It would be a hot day, a final lashing of summer before the seasons turned, and that would make for a grueling race.

Shannivar had risen well before first light and eaten a cold meal of *bha*, spiced meat cakes. It would keep her going for a long time without overly filling her stomach. She carried more of the concentrated food in her saddlebags, as well as skins of water and honey-grain cakes for Eriu. They both would need all their strength for the last distance.

"You will win for me, my Eriu," she murmured, stroking the black's muzzle. He regarded her calmly, his eyes pools of glossy darkness, and swished his tail at the flies. She checked the girth again, took a double handful of mane, and swung herself lightly up on his back.

A good portion of the gathering had come to see them off. Bennorakh was there, along with two other shamans. One held the age-scoured brass gong that would signal the start of the race. Tenoshinakh waved the winner's banner, a length of white silk, and tied it to a pole at the finishing-place.

Everyone from the Golden Eagle contingent stood to the forefront, cheering as Shannivar approached. Ythrae waved to her and even Dharvarath, who had been desolate and sullen since the death of his brother and sister, smiled.

Shannivar could not count the number of riders. There must be more than a hundred, she thought, although only a few were women. Kharemikhar was already there, mounted on a big silver roan. *Not a bad horse*, Shannivar thought. *Well coupled with good bone below the knee.*

Kharemikhar wheeled the horse as he boasted to the other riders. A cluster of young women watched him with admiration. Shannivar thought that if Kharemikhar were looking for a wife, he would have no trouble winning one.

Rhuzenjin nudged his horse into place beside her. "A fair morning to you, Shannivar daughter of Ardellis. May your day be lucky."

Politely, Shannivar returned his greeting. "Let the promise of the dawn be fulfilled in the glory of the evening." Rhuzenjin had said nothing of his intention to enter the Long Ride, but if he was willing to behave properly, she would do her best to treat him as a clansman.

A stir in the crowd caught her eye. Zevaron and

Danar had joined the onlookers. They looked relaxed and at ease with one another, with no trace of lingering tension from the conversation she had overheard.

Kharemikhar, following the custom of taunting the other riders, swerved his silver roan closer to Eriu. Like many of the others, he brandished a short whip of braided camel leather. He snapped it in the air.

"So Golden Eagle clan is to have a champion today, after all," he cried. "Two of you, in place of Alsanobal! Pah! I had hoped for a real race!"

"Look to your own dust," Shannivar replied in a loud voice. "I will win this day! Eriu is the fastest horse of all the Golden Eagle clan, and I am the best rider!"

The riders brought their horses to face east, for the Long Ride customarily began facing the dawn and ended facing the sunset. Eriu arched his neck. Through pad and saddle, Shannivar felt the long, powerful muscles of his back flex, the rise of his ribcage.

They will see how well I ride, as they try to catch me!

The gong sounded, and the horses leaped forward. Riders whooped and flailed at their mounts with whips and sticks. They broke into a trot for a few steps and then a full-out gallop.

Hooves churned the ground and threw up clods of hard-packed dirt. The galloping sounds filled the air like thunder. Black and bay, sorrel and dun and gray, the bodies of the horses rippled like a multi-hued river.

Kharemikhar passed Shannivar, shouting insults and slashing the silver roan with his whip. Something in his expression, that arrogant, triumphant gloat, stung Shannivar. She had never used a whip on Eriu, had never needed one.

"Go! Go! *Go!*" Yelling, she dug her heels into Eriu's sides.

The black sprang forward like an arrow. He was smaller than many of the other horses, but within a few moments, he had passed them.

Suddenly a horse diagonally in front of Shannivar went down. She could not see what happened, if it had stepped into a marmot burrow, been knocked off balance by another horse, or maybe broken a leg. Clinging to Eriu's mane, she twisted around for a better view, but the poor horse was already lost to view.

The horses rushed forward, jostling each other, their riders struggling to maneuver them into the best position.

Another horse fell, and two more dropped aside.

Shannivar kept her eyes ahead and her hands quiet on the reins. The slightest lapse might throw Eriu off his stride. He drew even with the pair of horses just in front. Lather had already broken out on their necks. She could hear the hoarse sound of their breathing, could almost touch their straining bodies. Kharemikhar's silver roan was still ahead, but now not so far.

Eriu raced on, fighting to pass the leaders. Streaks of sweat appeared on his shoulders. Shannivar knew his temper. He would not give up until he was ahead, even if it meant bursting his heart. Only last night, one of the chieftains had chanted a song-poem about how such a horse had run unto death to save its rider.

The thought shocked Shannivar out of the madness of the race. No horse alive, not even Eriu, could maintain such a breakneck pace. What had she been thinking, to risk him in this way? Was winning worth the cost of his life?

The Long Ride was a race like none other, a test not only of speed but of endurance, of patience, of steadfastness. Of cunning.

Shannivar hauled on the reins, guiding Eriu to the edge of the mass of horses. He fought her, but not as much as if she had tried to stop him outright. He still wanted to run.

Once free from the main body of the race, Shannivar was able to slow Eriu from a gallop to a trot. He danced sideways, wringing his tail in frustration and tugging at the bit.

Shannivar stroked his hot, wet neck as she forced him to a walk. "Save yourself, my beauty, my Eriu. The time will come. We will fly, you and I together. Soon, soon. You will need all your strength for later."

She was not the only one to let the headlong rush pass by. A handful of riders, Rhuzenjin among them, had held their horses back. One of the few women, a stocky, cheerful girl from Badger clan, circled her restive horse at a walk. She waved at Shannivar, in no apparent hurry to get on with the race. Rhuzenjin seemed far more interested in staying close to Shannivar than in keeping up with the others.

When the dust had settled, and Shannivar judged the mass of riders to be sufficiently far off, she loosened the reins and gave Eriu the signal to go forward. After a few minutes of shaking his head and jittering, he settled into an easy trot, the gait used in long journeys. After a short time, she felt him relax.

The ground swept by, shifting from beaten earth to tufted grasses. The sun rose higher, heating Shannivar's shoulders. She drew Eriu to a walk and let him recover his breath and drink from the water skins. She hoped she had not sapped too much of his strength by letting him gallop so hard.

After a time, a couple of other horses caught up with them, ridden by older, experienced men who had known better than to get caught up in the frenzy of the beginning of the race. One such rider walked beside her for a time. The faded embroidery on his vest depicted a stylized Skylark. He rode a mottled sorrel, thin and gangly in the manner of young horses, yet moving with a long rein and an easy stride.

The rider gestured a greeting and wished Shannivar a lucky race.

"You were wiser than I, to stay behind while the others galloped their horses," Shannivar said ruefully.

"My grandfather taught me, as his father taught him, the best way to train horses for the Long Ride."

Shannivar saw now that the man was older than

she had first thought. His face was weathered like dark leather, crinkled around the eyes, and he spoke slowly, as if there were no cause for hurry under Tabilit's wide sky.

"That is a fine, spirited horse you have. Do not force him to walk too early," he advised her. "He will build up too much rancor. When I am training a young horse like this one, I allow him to trot for the distance that is safe for his strength. Only then do I ask him to walk. If I cannot achieve this, if there is still too much fire in his blood, then I dismount, and we walk together. All my horses are taught in this manner."

"Do you mean to win the race on that horse?" Shannivar asked. The sorrel had the makings of a good horse, but she thought it would be some years yet before the animal came into his full strength and balance. Some horses were slower to mature than others, and could be ruined by asking too much of them too soon.

The old man grinned and bent to stroke the sorrel neck. The young horse cocked one ear back, listening to his voice. "I have already won."

Shannivar thanked him, feeling more hopeful about the outcome of the race. Once Eriu recovered his breathing, she allowed him to trot again. He kept his head low, his stride easy.

After a time, they began to pass other horses that were trailing the main group. She continued to alternate walking and trotting, just as the old man had suggested. Eriu settled into the rhythm, no longer pulling on the bit.

By the time the sun was directly overhead, Shannivar judged that she had passed over half the main pack. Eriu did not seem overly tired yet, although Rhuzenjin's mare was flagging. They stopped to give the horses water and honey-grain cakes. Rhuzenjin's horse would not eat, but stood with her head lowered, her eyes dull.

"You must not go on, for the sake of your horse." To her surprise, Shannivar felt a little regretful. Rhuzenjin had said very little so far, even when they walked their horses. Clearly, he had no aspirations toward winning the race, but had come only to be near her. For a moment, she wished she could return his devotion.

The half-way point of the Long Ride was a spring at the base of a huge rock. The rock was shaped like a camel, making it easy to spot from a distance. A grove of trees cast a welcoming shade. Eriu, scenting the moister air, nickcred.

A representative of the Council met Shannivar at the edge of the oasis. He handed her a strip of blue-dyed cloth to prove that she had completed the outward journey. She tied it around her upper arm and dismounted. Eriu was warm, but not too hot, and he was breathing easily. She checked his feet and legs, then led him to drink. He thrust his muzzle into the water and gulped noisily, but did not stomp about in the mud or sully the water.

Beside the spring, Kharemikhar and some of his friends took their ease, sprawled against the trunks of the largest trees. Their horses, coats still dark with sweat, tore at the few remaining clumps of grass.

"So you've caught up with me at last." Kharemikhar did not rise from where he sat, his back against the largest tree. He seemed so confident of his lead that he could afford to rest in this pleasant place. "Where's your shadow gone?"

Shannivar refused to be taunted. "His horse was not strong enough, so he returned to the *khural-lak*. When you have finished with your nap, I will see you there." Seeing that Eriu had drunk his fill, she swung up on his back.

Behind, she heard Kharemikhar's bitten-off curse and then the commotion as he and his friends scrambled to tighten their girths and jump into their saddles. Clearly, they had expected her to need time to recover, just as they had. They'd been counting on bursts of speed to put them far ahead of the rest. Now they whipped their horses into a gallop and quickly passed Shannivar. Smiling to herself, she made no attempt to match their pace. Eriu shook his head, jingling the bridle rings, and kept on at his even, ground-covering pace. His willingness to let them pass was a measure of his trust in her.

The day lengthened. Shannivar passed more riders, but not Kharemikhar. He remained in the forefront. She grew anxious, wondering if there were enough time to catch him, if Eriu's stamina would hold for a final sprint. Somehow, she must remain steady to the end. No matter what happened at the finish, she had made a good race, and she had not crippled her horse. But it was not the same as winning, and she knew it.

The rocky prominence above the *khural-lak* rose stark and shadowed, the setting sun behind it bright on the horizon. Crimson smeared the sky.

Shannivar nudged Eriu with her heels, and he lengthened his stride. They passed a handful of contestants; one led his badly limping mount. Only a few riders remained ahead. Squinting against the sunset glare, Shannivar recognized Kharemikhar and the Badger clan woman. She could not tell at this distance how much strength remained to the silver roan. She knew only that if she did not make her move, she would not have enough time to overtake them.

She bent over the black's neck, feeling him respond to the shift in her weight, and whispered into his ear, "Now, Eriu!"

Gathering himself, Eriu shifted into a lope and then a gallop. Wind sang against Shannivar's face. She clung to his mane. Her knees gripped the saddle pad. Eriu ran freely, reaching for the ground, but there was no joy left in him, only weariness and determination.

The other horses were running now, too, making their final sprint to the finish. Drained, they could not hold the pace for long. Kharemikhar and the Badger clan woman were still ahead, urging their horses on.

Shannivar passed the Badger clan woman. The finishing-place lay before them. The crowd cheered as they approached.

Eriu's body heaved with each panting breath, but he did not falter.

Now only the silver roan was ahead. The light burnished his hide, red in the setting sun. The muscles of his hindquarters flexed and stretched. His hooves kicked up puffs of dust.

Gallantly Eriu kept on, but his strides were shorter now and rough. Shannivar felt the jarring of each footfall in her teeth.

Kharemikhar drove his horse hard, switching the whip from one hand to the other, slashing again and again. Shannivar felt a spasm of pity for the poor beast. She had never struck Eriu or any of her horses; they served her from love, and because it was their nature. *In daylight,* went the Song of the Horse, *you are my wings.*

Be my wings, Eriu!

Eriu dipped his head. He seemed to draw renewed strength from the land. As if the air itself lifted him, his stride turned silken. Like an eagle, like the Golden Eagle, he skimmed the ground.

The silver roan was failing. Yellow lather covered his neck. Foam dripped from his jaws. Blood oozed from the reddened stripes over his sides where the whip had cut him. Shannivar drew even with Kharemikhar. Exultation surged through her. In just a few more lengths, they would reach the end.

The silver roan no longer responded to the whip. His eyes had gone dull, as if blind. His gait was broken and ragged. He had nothing left to give. Kharemikhar's face flushed a dusky red. He shifted his whip to the side nearest Shannivar, a motion so quick, a flicker only, that she had no time to react.

Thwack!

With a sound that cut the air like a lightning crack, Kharemikhar brought the whip down. The braided camel-leather tails slashed Eriu across the head.

The black staggered under the blow, missing his stride and almost going down to his knees. Shannivar caught herself, her hands braced on his withers. Her muscles responded instinctively, knees gripping hard against the saddle roll. Luck was with her. She managed not to tumble over his head.

The silver roan rushed past them.

Shannivar regained her balance as the black lurched to his feet. She bent low over his neck. "Go!"

Eriu scrambled into a gallop, but it was too late. In those few precious moments, Kharemikhar had seized the winner's banner. The white silk rippled as he waved it above his head. The gong sounded wildly. The onlookers shouted their approval. Some threw their hats into the air.

The first of the other riders arrived a few moments later. They circled the finishing-place, laughing and talking. The air filled with dust, the mingled reek of horse sweat and adrenaline.

Shannivar slowed Eriu to a walk. He fought her, tossing his head. Around her, people were cheering. Several came over to praise her. Their words passed through her like ghosts.

Eriu came to a halt. His nostrils flared, gulping air. Sweat drenched his hide, and his sides heaved like bellows. Shannivar kicked her feet free and jumped to the ground. Her legs almost gave way beneath her. Trembling, she took hold of the bridle and brought Eriu's head around to examine him. The whip had caught him diagonally across his forehead, narrowly missing one eye. Drops of blood oozed from the welt.

Throughout the steppe, it was considered shameful to strike a horse—any horse—in front of the girth. But there were no rules in the Long Ride.

Shannivar was too furious to speak. A vision rose up behind her eyes; she saw herself rushing up to Kharemikhar, naming him *coward* and *dishonored* before the assembled gathering. She could almost feel the sword in her hand, the weight and swing and bite of the blade as she cut him down.

She looked for the silver roan, but horse and rider had disappeared in the milling throng. The Badger clan woman rode past, and as her gaze lit upon Eriu, her face turned hard. She had seen what Kharemikhar had done. Everyone at the finishing-place had seen.

In that moment, Shannivar knew they would do nothing. A heat and a stillness fell around her. She was no stranger to bloodshed, but neither was Kharemikhar a stone-dwelling Gelon. He was born of the steppe, brave and arrogant and deceitful, no better and no worse. Azkhantians did not fight one another.

They had all seen. Tabilit had seen. What Shannivar did now was as much a measure of her character as it was Kharemikhar's.

Eriu rubbed the uninjured side of his head, itchy with sweat, against Shannivar's shoulder. Her anger receded. Whatever Kharemikhar had done, she would not let Eriu suffer. What happened was not the horse's fault. He had run honestly, with great heart. They should have won, and perhaps, in Tabil-it's eyes, they had.

He needed to be walked so that his tendons would not become brittle as he cooled down. Only when he was no longer sweating could he be safely watered and then fed. *And then* . . . Shannivar could not think what came next.

Shannivar led Eriu to the horse lines. As she went through the motions of caring for her mount, she became aware that others were watching her. The old rider looked up from massaging clove-pungent paste into the lower legs of the young sorrel. His eyes flickered to the swelling welt on Eriu's face. He said nothing, but Shannivar remembered his words, *"I have already won."*

Zevaron stood at the edge of the horse area, silent. He saw that she noticed him, and he came nearer. Gravely, he studied the black's wound. Eriu tolerated the attention, although even a gentle touch on the welt must have caused him pain.

"This needs a poultice of comfrey and firebane. Do you know these herbs?"

Comfrey she knew, but not the other. He described it, and she nodded. "*Pemmeche*, we call it."

"Yes. It will draw out the pain and keep the skin supple. I have a small supply in my pack."

She straightened up from picking out Eriu's

hooves. Zevaron might claim to know little of horses, but he did not hesitate to offer his knowledge freely. He was no *enaree*, to hoard his secrets. She thought of how he had handled himself against Phannus, ending the confrontation without serious injury. He must have had many such fights in his years at sea. At Gatacinne. She wished he had broken Kharemikhar's neck in wrestling when he'd had the chance.

"When men are willing to use any means to get what they want," he said, "it is the innocent who suffer."

She had no idea what to say to that. He meant far more than one individual horse.

Zevaron went to his tent to make the poultice and returned quickly. She was grateful for his speed.

At the first touch of the mashed herbs Eriu flinched, but Shannivar murmured to him, stroking his neck, and he quieted. Watching the gentle way Zevaron applied the poultice, she felt a growing respect for, and also an odd kinship with the outlander. They were both on their own. If the chieftains of the gathering would not act regarding the race, neither would they ever risk a single rider to help Zevaron free his city.

Eriu would heal, and most likely bear an honorable scar. She need never speak to Kharemikhar again. But Zevaron would not be so easily turned away from his goal. A fire burned in him, the shift of golden light just beneath the skin. She had no words for that fire.

* * *

With Eriu settled and resting, Shannivar went to wash herself with the cedar-infused water that had been prepared for the contestants. Her arms and legs felt leaden. She could remember few times when she had felt so drained in body and spirit. Reluctantly, because to refuse would have appeared spiteful, she joined the celebration around a bonfire. Kharemikhar was already drunk, cavorting through a men's dance to the adulation of several young, unmarried women.

Rhuzenjin pressed a skin of *k'th* into her hands and urged her to join in the next dance. "You rode magnificently! Saramark herself could not have equaled you. I will compose another song-poem to sing to our clan!"

How could she explain her disappointment? She had been a fool to think that winning the Long Ride, or any other achievement, could buy her the life she wanted. And what did she truly want? A marriage to someone like Kharemikhar? Not even when drunk could she endure such a fate.

"Everyone saw what happened," Rhuzenjin went on earnestly. "How shameful were Kharemikhar's deeds this day! But take heart. Everyone knows what he is. No one regards you any the less because of *his* foolishness."

Shannivar was annoyed at his solicitude, but said nothing. Rhuzenjin was her friend, even if he clearly wanted to be more. Except for that moment of ill temper at the dance, he had always treated her with respect. She saw that he still had hope, that he had not accepted that she would never return to the clan of the Golden Eagle and marry him. Bear his children.

In her mind, she saw Grandmother as a young woman, full of the same fire that burned in her own breast. And then she saw the old woman again. *Someday, that will be my face. Someday, I will ride Eriu beside Grandmother and Saramark through the Pastures of the Sky.*

She did not fear old age. She feared only arriving at the end of her life without having lived it.

The celebration following the Long Ride went on most of the night. As the young men got drunker, the dancing got wilder. The musicians played in a frenzy. Skin after skin of *k'th* flowed down the throats of the revelers. Eventually the old people retired, but the festivities continued. Couples went off together. Rhuzenjin glanced hopefully at Shannivar, but she gave him no sign of invitation. She danced a few times, but only with other women.

At last, one of the Antelope clan men stumbled into a fire, scattering burning sticks and embers everywhere. Everyone scrambled to help him. Shannivar slipped away, not to her *jort* in the Golden Eagle camp, but to the horse lines.

As she drew near, the familiar, comforting smells of the horses swept through her. She remembered how Mirrimal had brought her to this refuge on the day Grandmother died. Grief rose up in her like thunder and then subsided. Mirrimal would have understood without words.

Eriu was lying down, resting deeply. Radu stood only a short distance away, alert, keeping guard over her companion. She nickered in the manner of a mare greeting a trusted friend. Eriu lifted his head as Shannivar approached, but did not rise. His nostrils flared to catch her scent. She spoke his name, and he sighed.

Curled against the solid warmth of his body, she slept.

Chapter 17

SHANNIVAR rose at dawn, fed and watered Eriu and Radu, returned to her *jort*, and lay down again. The interior of the *jort*, with its familiar objects, the smell of the old carpet, the small carved chest from Grandmother, soothed her jangled nerves. As she drifted in and out of sleep, the ordinary sounds of the camp lulled her further. She heard familiar voices and the clink of cooking implements. Inhaling the aroma of buttered tea, she imagined herself at home again, in a place where she belonged, a place where no one would dare to strike her horse. Someone lifted the door flap and left a plate of sheep's milk cheese and boiled barley with wild onions, along with a cup of tea, just inside the threshold. It must have been Ythrae, Shannivar thought, and sank again into half-formed dreams. She did not want the next day to come, for then she must face Kharemikhar. And Rhuzenjin. And Zevaron.

She woke again, this time to the sounds of excited cries. Still groggy, she could not make out what was going on. She stepped from the *jort*, rubbing sleep from her eyes as she sought the source of the disturbance.

A girl of ten or so, mounted on a spotted pony, rode into the clan area in a cloud of dust. Feathers fluttered from her single long braid, and her face glowed with excitement. Shannivar recognized her as belonging to another sept of Golden Eagle, although she could not recall her name. The entire party, including the Isarrans and Danar and Zevaron, gathered around the girl. Even Dharvarath, who in his mourning had kept apart from the others, peered at her curiously.

"Come, everyone!" the girl called, wheeling her pony. "Come and see!"

The last dregs of sleep dropped from Shannivar's senses. "What is it? What has happened?"

"The Snow Bear party has just arrived and brought with them a thing of wonder! You must all come at once!" Without a backward glance, she kicked her pony into a canter toward the *jorts* of her own family.

Shannivar and the others glanced at each other with expressions of puzzlement and delight. Ythrae clapped her hands and exclaimed, "What a mystery!"

"Is it permitted that we view this wonder?" Danar asked, clearly as interested as any of them.

"Oh, yes," Shannivar said. "You are free to participate in any of the gathering events. Did Tenoshinakh not declare so?"

"I know that he did, but I am so much a stranger here, I was not certain—"

"Shannivar! Rhuzenjin! What are you waiting for?" Ythrae called over her shoulder. She trotted away in the direction the young girl had indicated, and everyone rushed to follow, skirting the tents and cook fires. Danar and Zevaron came with them, as did the two Isarrans.

The caravan of the Snow Bear people had just arrived at the northern side of the *khural-lak*. To everyone's surprise, there were no women among them. Their horses were light gray with heavily-feathered lower legs and dorsal striping, sturdy and thick-boned. The newcomers brought no camels, only a string of laden reindeer. The beasts' hooves made odd clicking sounds on the dirt. The two largest had been harnessed together to draw a sledge, to which was lashed a large irregular shape, wrapped in tattered blankets. Under its weight, the wooden runners had carved deep gouges into the earth.

Tenoshinakh and several of the *enarees* stood talking with the Snow Bear party. As the crowd gathered, the oldest of the Snow Bear clan turned to survey the newly assembled audience. He assumed a formal stance, legs braced wide and chest thrust out.

"I am Chinjizhin son of Khinukoth, chief of the Snow Bear people!" he proclaimed in a voice roughened by the passage of many harsh seasons. He introduced his son, Chinzhukog, and the other Snow Bear kinsmen. The northern people called themselves 'tribes' rather than 'clans,' and made no distinction between one sept or family group and another, considering all fellow tribesmen as brothers. Everyone could see that Chinjizhin came from a distant land. His vest was strangely cut and a fur-lined hood instead of the usual felt cap lay folded back across his shoulders. His skin, although weathered into creases, was unusually pale, his skull oddly shaped. The hair that was drawn back into a complicated single braid was almost as colorless as his skin.

"On behalf of all the northern tribes, I bring you greetings, news of dire portents, and also a thing of wonder," he announced.

"Dire portents?" someone cried, and another, "What has happened?"

"We have had no bad news from the north."

One older man said to his neighbor, "Some say all manner of ill fortune began last year when the white star fell from the sky."

"So it was," the Snow Bear chief said, "for the night sky turned bright as day, and the ground trembled."

"What is he saying?" Zevaron bent toward Shannivar. By now, he knew a little Azkhantian, but the Snow Bear man's accent was too difficult for him to follow.

Shannivar translated the Snow Bear man's words into trade-dialect. Behind them, Senuthenkh did the same for Leanthos and his bodyguard.

"Smoke rose up to cover the Road of Stars," Chinjizhin said, accompanying his story with dramatic gestures, "but our *enaree* prayed to Tabilit and it blew away."

Shannivar nodded, remembering. At that time, Bennorakh had spent many days in prayer, fasting and chanting and inhaling dreamsmoke. If Tabilit had granted him any visions, he would not speak of them. Nothing dire had happened afterward, so everyone believed his magic had prevailed. The white star's passage had faded into just another story.

But perhaps it had, indeed, been a portent. Perhaps Grandmother had known. What had she said? *"I do not wish to see this doom upon those I love."*

"It is not certain," Bennorakh had answered.

And Grandmother had responded, *"We have seen what we have seen. Do not cling to foolish hope."*

"We thought all was well," Chinjizhin went on. "Some of our young men rode off to find the fallen star and returned saying the mountains themselves had been broken."

Zevaron's head shot up. Shannivar felt the leap in his attention as if she herself had been stung. Until that moment, he had been curious in an ordinary way. Now he radiated preternatural alertness.

"How can that be?" someone asked, astonishment overtaking courtesy. "The land endures forever, for so Tabilit has promised. Mountains do not just fall down. Anyone who says so must have drunk rotten *k'th*!"

A few of the onlookers laughed, but others looked grave. Tenoshinakh and Shannivar's kinsman, Sagdovan, scowled. The mockers quieted. It was one thing to deride outlanders with their strange notions and uncivilized manners, but an

outright breach of courtesy to treat another Azkhantian in this way.

"I myself saw this thing," the Snow Bear man insisted, pounding his chest with one fist. "Where
once the mountains stood as Tabilit had shaped
them at the beginning of time, a wall reaching to
the sky, there I found only shattered stones."

Murmurs swept the audience. No one would
dare to question the word of a chieftain, especially
one who had witnessed the sight himself.

"Then in the winter, in the night," Chinjizhin's
voice dropped into the cadence of a storyteller,
"even stranger things were seen."

The crowd hushed and drew closer, even those
who only a few moments ago had been loud in their
skepticism. Shannivar continued to translate for the
outlanders, in a voice barely above a whisper.

"The Veil of the North was torn asunder. Wolves
came howling into our *kishlak*, our wintering-place,
although there was still ample game for them to
hunt. They threw themselves on the fires, as if they
had gone mad."

The tale sent a shiver through Shannivar, as if
her bones had been brushed by shadows. Not natural shadows, but Olash-giyn-Olash, the Shadow of
all Shadows. Certain things—unlucky men, dis-
eased animals, ill-fated actions, cursed objects—
were said to have fallen under that malevolent
influence.

Shannivar had never seen anything to make her
believe in curses, not when fortune, illness, or sim-
mering blood vengeance could so easily explain the

stupidity of men. Like all Azkhantians, she regarded predators such as wolves and cloud leopards with respect, as one warrior race to another. Usually, there was little reason to fear them, unless hunger drove them to stalk the herds. Everyone knew that an old or injured predator could be dangerous. But the madness of animals, and totem animals at that, defied ordinary explanations.

The Snow Bear chief spoke of how his people had fortified their wintering-places and of the rites and sacrifices they had performed according to the received visions of their *enarees*. For a time, their lives had continued as before. The Snow Bear tribe believed that all ill had passed.

But it had not, his voice and manner clearly indicated. That spring, more than a few babies were born dead. Other infants bore strange growths upon their bodies, toes and fingers stuck together like hardened daggers. One of the women in the audience cried out and cradled her pregnant belly. Her friends made signs to ward off evil as they hurried her away.

The Snow Bear chief told how, when the men gathered in their reindeer herds, they found carcasses with throats torn out but not by any wolf. The flesh had been mangled, chunks of meat ripped from splintered ribs. The livers and hearts had been left intact, something no natural predator would do. The men had followed the trail of blood to find a huge bull reindeer, the leader of the herd, standing in a circle of bodies. Antlers and jaws dripped with hot blood. Several of the fallen reindeer still lived, but barely. Strips of hide had been slashed from the bull's sides, and many of the others were injured in like manner, as if the ordinarily placid beasts had turned cannibal on one another.

The voice of Chinjizhin shook as he told this part of the tale. His eyes gleamed, glassy and half-blind, as if he had looked upon far more terrible sights. He reminded Shannivar of an aged cloud leopard she had once come upon at the very end of its last hunt. Encircled by jackals, it had been too exhausted to run and too feeble to fight. As it gathered itself for a final charge, she had seen in its eyes that same expression of desolation.

The Snow Bear chief explained they would have arrived sooner, except that a party of their young men had gone exploring in the mountains and brought back a thing of surpassing strangeness. An omen, some had said, but there was no agreement of whether it boded ill fortune or good. Their *enaree* had inspected the find and then entered a dreamsmoke trance, only to emerge no wiser. In the end, the *enaree* had determined the object must be brought to the gathering.

At a gesture from Tenoshinakh, the Ghost Wolf chieftain's son went to summon the *enarees* of the *khural*. The men around Shannivar muttered and drew back from the sledge. None would dare to come any closer until the shamans had declared it safe.

While they waited, Shannivar inched her way to where she could see more clearly. Zevaron followed, as if he were personally drawn to the object.

Shannivar had never seen reindeer closely before, although the smiths of the northern tribes often depicted them in ornaments. Their backs were smooth, their coats gray and soft brown. Tufts of pale undercoat dangled from their bellies in tangled clumps. The two drawing the sledge were males. By their hoarse breathing, the crusted foam on their nostrils, and the way their heads drooped, they were near the end of their strength.

As for the sledge, it seemed an awkward affair, clearly not designed to travel across the tough steppe grasses. A camel would have been far more efficient in carrying even a larger load. The bundle of tattered blankets masked the shape of its contents.

After a time, the *enarees* proceeded at a stately, measured pace into the cleared space. None gave any sign of haste. All was in order, their motley garments and magical implements, even their dignified expressions. Gravely they examined the bundle. One by one they peered at it and passed their hands over it, carefully avoiding direct contact. From time to time, one would straighten up, close his eyes, and mumble a chant; another would shake strings of bells and pause, listening to the jangling echoes. When each had performed some test, according to their own enigmatic protocols, they withdrew a short distance to confer. The onlookers, who had watched in awed silence, now whispered among themselves.

At last, the chief of the *enarees*, from the Rabbit clan, announced that the omens were conflicting, that the object seemed to present no threat, and yet it did. No proper determination could be made without viewing it. Such a move might carry grave risk. At the same time, everyone understood that the greater the danger, the greater the honor. Several young men, Rhuzenjin among them, rushed forward to remove the wrappings.

While this was going on, Zevaron stood transfixed. He seemed to be barely breathing. His brows drew together, and his jaw was set, giving him an expression of barely contained ferocity.

By this time, the audience had grown even larger than before. Nearly everyone in the encampment was present, except for the pregnant women. Newcomers strained for a view of the mysterious object. Someone jostled Shannivar from behind. She held her ground.

"Out of the way!" Kharemikhar elbowed his way to the front. He glowered at the youths who were wrestling with the knotted cords, although he made no move to help them.

"Oof!" cried the man he had pushed aside.

Someone else said, "Can you see it?"

The wrappings fell away, and the onlookers surged forward. Shannivar glimpsed a human-sized piece of stone, elongated and twisted, mottled gray and brown in color.

At that moment, the reindeer threw back their heads, eyes rolling. The larger gave a cry like a strangled grunt and reared up on his hind legs. Two of the Snow Bear men, the chief's son one of them, seized their halters, or they would have bolted.

Shannivar heard Zevaron's quick inhale, the breath hissing between his clenched teeth. He muttered words beneath his breath, but whether they were curses or prayers, she could not tell.

The object resembled an oversized lizard, lying partly on its side. Despite the contorted posture, there was no question that the creature was deformed. The hind legs were too long and too heavily muscled for an ordinary reptile, yet the hips were placed as if the thing walked upright like a man. It might be a natural rock formation that happened to resemble a lizard-man. Or it might have been formed into this shape by human hands. Shannivar frowned. She had never seen a carving this perfect, the proportion of snout and limbs so realistic.

Murmurs of astonishment rippled through the onlookers. Many drew back, their eyes wide. Some made ritual gestures to ward off bad luck. A swathe of empty space quickly cleared around the sledge, except for the two Snow Bear men, who were still struggling to hold the reindeer. One of the younger *enarees* began chanting in the eerie, high-pitched voice used for invocations of protection.

The man in front of Shannivar exclaimed, "What is that thing?"

"Aii! It is a devil!"

"A devil come to eat us up!"

"What, have we all become cowards now, to fear a thing of stone?"

"Onjhol defend us!"

"Cursed!" someone else exclaimed. "We are all cursed to have laid eyes upon this thing!"

During the ruckus, Danar slipped quietly through the crowd and knelt beside the sledge with its mysterious, repellent burden. Several onlookers cried out in warning, but Danar paid them no heed. He bent this way and that, inspecting the lizard-shape from every angle with frank curiosity. Although Shannivar heard rumbles that the Gelon must surely be demented, she did not think so. His expression showed no trace of madness, only curiosity. He made no move to touch the object, but that seemed more out of carefulness than fear.

"Extraordinary!" Danar glanced up, grinning broadly. "It's perfectly marvelous! Such a magnificent specimen! I had never hoped to actually see one."

"You *know* what this is?" Tenoshinakh asked, astonished.

"Unless I'm very much mistaken, it is a stone-drake. I've read about them in my father's books." Eyes alight with enthusiasm, Danar rushed on, interspersing phrases in Gelone with trade-dialect. "The scholars of Borrenth Springs say they result when lightning strikes a gigantic salamander resting on volcanic rock. They like to bask in the heat, you see. Because the rock was once molten, the lightning causes a merging of the elements of stone, fire, and light. The result is an artificial semblance of life, a—a counterfeit of a natural creature."

Danar paused, perhaps noticing for the first time the expressions of incomprehension in his audience, but only for a moment. "The stone-drakes are said to be invulnerable to fire and steel, impossible to kill—"

Kharemikhar gave a derisive snort.

Danar's smile faded. "Well, perhaps that's just another of those old stories, things men of times long ago invented to explain the mysteries of the world. But if I may—" Rising, Danar bowed to Tenoshinakh and to the head *enaree*. "With your permission, I would very much like to examine this specimen. Perhaps I can correct the errors of past scholarship, or at any rate learn something new about these marvelous creatures."

For a long moment, no one said anything.

Tenoshinakh looked to the Rabbit clan *enaree*. "Is this lizard-man a thing of spirit or of ordinary matter? A sculpture created by human hands, like the idols worshiped by the Gelon? Or a once-living creature, magically turned to stone?"

"Turned into stone!" someone echoed.

"Or a man, slain by some terrible curse?" one of the other chieftains muttered.

Around Shannivar, people nodded sagely. Legends told of foolish or greedy men corrupted by Olash-giyn-Olash, the Shadow of Shadows. Shannivar had been deliciously terrified as a child, listening to these tales around a winter fire. Now, seeing this thing, she wondered if it had been wise to take such stories lightly.

"Why has it come to us?" Tenoshinakh asked the chief shaman. "What do the gods require of us?"

Eyes closed, half-crouched but swaying now, the head *enaree* passed his stick over the stone figure and began to chant. Shannivar could not understand his words. Perhaps no one could, for the *ena-rees* were said to be gifted with divine speech.

Around her, the audience murmured in consternation and awe, but Zevaron nodded, as if he could follow what was said, in sense if not in specifics. That was impossible, wasn't it? Then she remembered that the song he'd sung on the road had been in a language that sounded like that of the *enarees*. She still did not understand how she had been able to sense the meaning of his song, but Tabilit must surely have brought them together and given them this harmony of mind. There was no other explanation.

The *enaree* fell silent at last. He remained still for a long moment, his eyes open but blank. Then he shook himself and began to speak.

"I cannot see clearly. The spirits remain silent. This object, this drake of stone, must be studied further before the uninitiated," he glared pointedly at Danar, "may be permitted to examine it. The council of *enarees* will search the dream world for answers."

The *enaree* pointed to the rock promontory, indicating that the stone-drake should be brought there. "Meanwhile, until Tabilit has made her will known, the object shall be deemed taboo, tainted by evil. We must safeguard it from idle eyes and even more idle hands. No man may touch it, lest a curse fall upon him, his clan, and all the people of the *khural*. Every person who has had contact with it must be purified."

Rhuzenjin, who had helped others to strip away

the coverings, blanched, but quickly assumed a determined countenance, so that he would not be thought lacking in courage. Danar, unfamiliar with the steppe beliefs regarding curses and ritual cleansing, looked confused.

A curse was bad enough, Shannivar thought, but one that affected an entire clan, perhaps the assembled *khural* itself, would be terrible indeed.

"Cover it up!" Tenoshinakh ordered. "Hurry now! Get that thing out of camp! And bring wood to build the dream fires!"

The young men who had so eagerly unwrapped the strange object hung back. What at first had seemed an exciting novelty and an opportunity to show off, took on a more sinister aspect. Even the bravest warrior might be slain, maimed, or left witless by a sufficiently powerful evil spell. Horsemanship and courage would avail little against an enemy that had no physical body.

Impatiently, Shannivar pushed forward. Let the others cower behind their mothers' skirts! *She* was not afraid.

She grabbed the edge of the nearest blanket and pulled it across the stone legs. This close, she could discern the contours and texture. No crudely hacked rock sculpture or clay-daubing this, but one of exquisitely precise detail. The toes of the lizard-shape were long and clawed, as were those of the forelimbs. Its eyes were closed, or else crusted over with a rocky membrane. The neck was flexed forward and tilted, so that the creature seemed to be twisting to look up at her.

Shannivar shivered. At any moment, the stone-drake might sense her nearness, open its eyes, and reach out with those clawed hands. As she jerked the braided leather cords tight, Rhuzenjin moved to help her. Perhaps he was embarrassed by his former hesitation. "I do not need your help," she snarled. "Stay back. Do not expose yourself to whatever curse this thing carries."

"Shannivar, be reasonable. If there is a curse, I am *already* subject to it."

"You must be, to insist in this manner."

"It is you who should have kept away. Or do you mean to carry the entire burden of glory yourself, in this as in everything else?" Rhuzenjin did not wait for her reply. He grabbed another corner of the blanket. On the other side, Zevaron also bent to the task.

Fool! Shannivar fumed. Zevaron clearly did not understand the risk. Or perhaps he, like Danar, had some knowledge of the stone lizard, some reason to investigate it further. She remembered his reaction to the tale of the Snow Bear chieftain, especially the mention of *broken mountains.*

At last, the bundle once more tied securely to the sledge, they started off, Shannivar and Rhuzenjin on one side of the sledge, the reindeer driver and Zevaron on the other. The *enaree* leader strode ahead, leading the way, and the rest of the shamans followed behind.

The sledge moved without too much difficulty over the relatively flat, beaten ground, until they came to the base of the promontory. The runners had been constructed for snow and then adapted for grass. They caught on the irregular stony path, often bringing the sledge to a jerking halt. The reindeer lunged forward, half-staggering under their burden. Shannivar, lifting and shoving the sledge over yet another rock, felt pity for the poor animals.

They halted in the little clearing between the stone mounds. The *enarees* clustered around it, talking animatedly. After a short discussion, they erected a tent around the sledge. The tent would allow them to perform their magical investigations with additional secrecy, and the symbols painted on the fabric would prevent all but the most potent supernatural powers from escaping.

The Snow Bear man unhitched his reindeer and led them back down the trail to the camp. The poor beasts trudged after him, released from the terror that had driven them.

"Come, we must return for the purification rite." Rhuzenjin touched Shannivar's arm, clearly anxious not to linger. So far, no curse had manifested, but no one could tell how long their luck would hold.

"Zevaron?" Shannivar turned to their companion. "We should let the *enarees* be about their work."

Zevaron showed no sign of being in a hurry to leave. He lingered, staring at the wrapped stonedrake. A strange light glimmered beneath his skin, as if a cloud had parted and a beam of sunlight touched only him. He pressed one hand over the center of his chest as if to ease a pain there. When

Shannivar spoke to him, however, awareness returned to his eyes.

At the edge of the *khural-lak*, well away from the sleeping and cooking areas, a tent had already been prepared for the purification. It was large enough for the Snow Bear party as well as all those who had handled the sledge or the bundle. Pungent smoke curled skyward from the central opening. When Zevaron hung back, one of the older clansmen, who wore the stylized emblem of a Ghost Wolf, noted his hesitation.

"Outland man, you are a good fighter, but you do not know our ways." The Ghost Wolf man's face was stern, and his tone gruff but not unkind. "You may pray to different gods, but you are now in our lands and subject to Tabilit's laws. For the safety of us all, you must go with the others and spend the night in purification and fasting."

Shannivar translated for Zevaron. "The smoke tent is not a punishment," she explained, "but an honor on behalf of the entire clan. It is not pleasant, but it is necessary. We willingly take the spiritual danger upon ourselves and thus protect our people, even as we might ride into battle in their defense. Do you not do the same in your own country?"

"No, not in that fashion." Zevaron shook his head. Shannivar caught the faint movement of his eyes toward the promontory. "How long must we remain within?"

"Until dawn. We take no food or water during that time. In the morning, however, we will feast." Seeing his continued hesitation, she urged him, "Do not delay further. Come inside the tent. You will insult the *enarees* if you are seen to refuse their command."

Two old women stood outside the door flap, arranging a pile of wood chips soaked with dream resin. Shannivar bent low to follow Rhuzenjin into the tent. The air was hot and close. A firepit had been dug in the center of the dirt floor and lined with blue stones. It put forth resin-laden smoke.

Danar was already inside, along with the Snow Bear men and the others. By custom, those undergoing the purification were almost naked, so that the medicinal smoke would penetrate more deeply. Shannivar glanced at Danar, not wanting to be rude but curious about what manner of man this stone-dweller might be. She was a little disappointed. He was nearly as pale as snow beneath the reddish fuzz that covered his chest and legs, but otherwise quite ordinary.

"Heyo, Shannivar," one of the young men said, "can't find a husband any other way?" He threw back his shoulders and flexed his muscles.

"As if any of you would be worthy of her!" Rhuzenjin shot back.

She laughed. "Take no heed of such babble. The smoke has already stolen his wits!"

Shannivar stripped off her own clothing until she, like they, wore only a brief loincloth. One of the old women took her clothes and boots away. In the morning, they would be waiting outside, neatly folded and sweetened with dried spring flowers, the sign of Tabilit's pleasure.

Settling between Danar and one of the Snow Bear men, Shannivar crossed her legs comfortably. The drug-laden smoke wafted over her. Within moments, she was glad not to be wearing her padded vest and woolen trousers. Her skin turned sticky and then slick. She forced herself to breathe slowly and evenly. Dizziness hovered at the edge of her vision. It was going to be a long night.

While she undressed, Rhuzenjin had also taken off and handed out his clothing. Zevaron followed their example, but more slowly. He kept his gaze carefully away from Shannivar. She found his shyness endearing but a little puzzling. Surely he had seen a woman's breasts before. How could a man travel to distant lands and across oceans, and remain ignorant of the most basic things? Perhaps he did not care for women in that way—no, she was certain that he did. He looked away because of how much he wanted to see.

The conversation continued in a desultory manner, the men no longer teasing Shannivar but boasting of the tales they would tell at home, the women they would impress, and the *k'th* they would drink the next night. The pauses between each comment grew longer.

Shannivar glanced at Zevaron from beneath her half-lowered lids. The skin of his body glowed like honey in the light from the coals. Softly curling hair marked his chest and formed a dark line down his belly. It fascinated her, for Azkhantian men had scant body hair.

When Zevaron had turned to hand his clothing

outside, Shannivar saw the reddened slash of a recently healed wound on his side, and older scars, pale knotted stripes across his back. No battle wounds these, criss-crossing the otherwise smooth skin. She had heard that the Gelon whipped their slaves, sometimes unto death. Had Zevaron, with his fighting skill and his pride, been a Gelonian *slave*? But that was impossible.

She looked away, heat from more than the fire rising to her cheeks. She wanted to ask, yet she could not bear to know. She felt his presence through her skin, a spreading fire along the curve of neck and shoulder to her breasts, to the hollow below her ribs and along her thighs. And Zevaron kept his gaze lowered, as if he could not bring himself to look at her. As if he knew what she had seen and surmised. Did no one else notice the ruddy flush rising to his face and throat, the way he held his hands so still? What was wrong with him? What was wrong with *her*? This was not her first time in a smoke tent, undergoing the ritual along with the men. She had never felt so conscious of her body—or of a man's—before.

Rhuzenjin was laughing now, telling the others of the song he was composing about the day's events and the parts they had all played. Danar smiled, as if he understood. Certainly, Rhuzenjin's determined cheerfulness needed no translation.

"Ah, but the tale is not yet done," said the youth who had teased Shannivar about finding a husband. "We still do not know what the *enarees* will decide."

"Perhaps they will send the stone lizard off to

Isarre, for it's no good to anyone here," one of his fellows suggested.

"Yes, they can use it to frighten away the Gelonian gods, it is so ugly," another suggested to a round of laughter.

"Unless they mistake it for your mother-in-law."

"Aiee! You insult the lizard!"

Unable to summon enthusiasm for idle talk, Shannivar let their words roll over her. Ever since she had looked upon the stone-drake, a part of its eerie nature had remained with her. She did not know what it was, except that it was not a thing to be taken lightly.

Perhaps, she thought as she folded her arms around her knees and laid her forehead against them, the best thing would be to send it to Isarre with Danar, who was clearly enraptured with it. At least, that would get it out of Azkhantia.

She was still drained from yesterday's race, and the heat made her dizzy. Her thoughts drifted on the billows of smoke. *What if there were more stone lizards? What if they crawled—or walked—or ran over the land? What if they were, even now, making their way from the frozen north across the steppe?*

In a dreamy vision, Shannivar saw herself mounted on Eriu, bow in hand, galloping across a plain. The ground underfoot glimmered, as if encased in frost. Eriu's hooves churned beneath him and she swayed with the rocking of his gait, yet they hardly moved. The air itself held them prisoner. Ahead, mists boiled out of the ground, thick and gray. A shape moved within the mists, looming closer. With every passing moment, it gained in size and substance.

Shannivar opened her mouth to call out a warning, but no sound came forth. The mist had stolen her voice. In dismay, she glanced to one side and then the other. No comrades rode beside her. She and Eriu were alone in this strange world.

The black horse was laboring now, struggling. His ribs heaved, as they had at the end of the Long Ride. Flecks of lather blew back to encrust her chest and arms. Stop, they must stop, or even his brave heart would fail him. Try as she might, she could not move her hands on the reins, nor could she signal Eriu with her weight. Her body was frozen in the saddle.

All the while, the thing within the mists grew larger, already many times the size of the stonedrake. Lightning flashed above, and storm clouds piled high and higher. Any moment now, the mist thing would burst free.

Cry out! she begged herself. If only she could make a sound, the dreadful spell might be broken. *Cry out!*

Suddenly, Shannivar came back to herself, sitting bolt upright within the smoke tent. Her lungs burned as she drew in the thick, acrid air. Within her chest, her heart galloped as fast as Eriu's frantic hooves. Around her, the tent lay dark and silent. She heard the muted sounds of the encampment at night and the distant whinny of a horse. Some time must have passed while she dreamed, for the fire had died down, and someone had put new chips upon it. The smell of the dream resin was stronger than before. She raked back damp hair, trying to clear her thoughts.

The shadow thing, what was it? Why did it terrify her? Was it a sacred vision, sent by Tabilit? A nightmare born of an exhausting race the day before and the sight of the hideous stone-drake? A dream from the resinous smoke?

A dream . . .

The others might well be dreaming, too. Danar lay back, one hand twitching. Rhuzenjin seemed to be lost in his own visions, too, and Zevaron . . . Zevaron was gone.

Chapter 18

CURSING, Shannivar scrambled for the door flap of the tent. Behind her, one of the men stirred and mumbled something about a goat. As she crawled outside, she heard another comment, this time about the feebleness of women who could not endure the smoke.

The night air shocked her senses after the heat of the tent. She drew it into her lungs to clear her head. Overhead, the moon shone just past full in a cloudless sky, bright enough to cast faint shadows. The encampment lay still, quiet except for a few scattered voices and the last of the evening's singing.

Shannivar could think of only one place Zevaron might have gone, the worst destination possible. Surely he did not believe he could sneak up there without the *enarees* learning of it.

Pausing only long enough to pull on her trousers, vest, and boots, she dashed back toward the circle of *jorts*. As she passed the banked remains of one of the wood fires, she yanked a half-burned stick free. The wind of her passage fanned the embers into flame.

Breaking into a run, she sprinted toward the promontory that rose up before her, its bulk blotting out the stars. Halfway up its side, a barely visible figure moved slowly upward.

Muscles burning, heart pounding against her ribs, she climbed the narrow, twisting trail, pushing herself to go quickly. Hours of sweating had left her light-headed, and she wished she had taken the time to grab a water skin. There was no help for it now. Zevaron could not be far ahead. He was just as weak, and he would have to feel his way along the difficult trail by moonlight. She at least had a torch.

When she reached the top, she found no sign of him. She hurried to the tent the *enarees* had put up around the sledge. The door flap was askew, as if it had been jerked aside in haste. Shannivar lifted it and plunged inside.

The air inside the tent reeked of adrenaline-laced sweat. The sledge and its contents occupied the center. Zevaron knelt beside it, back hunched, hands tearing at the cords that bound the wrappings.

Fool! Onager-brained outlander fool! He had not only trespassed on the sacrosanct territory of the *enarees*, he was violating their specific taboo!

"Tabilit's silver ass!" she cried. "What do you think you're doing?"

Zevaron made no response, only continued his

efforts. His breath came quick and hoarse. He might have been deaf. Deaf, or under an evil spell.

Shannivar plunged the unlit end of the torch into the ground, taking care to keep it away from the side of the tent. Curling her fingers in his shirt, she grabbed Zevaron by both shoulders.

"Stop! Think what you're doing!"

Trying to turn him around was like trying to move the promontory itself. She jerked and tugged, but he continued to work at the cords with such determination that several of the knots came loose. She set her stance and shifted her grip, slipping one forearm around his neck. With a sharp exhale, she threw her own weight backward. This time, she was able to break his balance. Panting with effort, she dragged him away from the bundle.

Snarling, Zevaron pivoted to face her. He rose from his knees into a fighting crouch. The speed and power of his movement broke her hold, and for a terrifying instant, Shannivar feared he might strike her. She recalled how easily he had taken down Phannus, a trained fighter. But Zevaron simply stared at her, reflections of firelight in his eyes. He looked drunk, ensorcelled. Obsessed.

She could not give up now. When he turned back to the bundle, she grabbed him again.

He moved more quickly than her mind could follow. His shoulders shifted, and he reached for her opposite hand. His fingers encircled her wrist. One thumb pressed into the back of her hand. In a small, subtle movement, he bent and twisted the joint. Pain lanced up Shannivar's arm, almost sending her to her knees. The torch-lit interior of the tent wavered in her vision. Other than a single sharp gasp, she could not speak or cry out. Her free arm flailed about but could not reach him.

Maintaining his grip upon her wrist with one hand, Zevaron bent sideways, grasped one edge of the blanket, and pulled it away.

Through blurring vision, Shannivar glimpsed the stone-drake's snout and opaque eyes. The creature seemed even more eerie in the flickering light of the torch than it had by day, and at that moment, it looked like the mummified corpse of a living creature and not stone at all.

Zevaron began murmuring in his own language, too muffled for Shannivar to hear the words clearly. Whether he was praying to his own gods, invoking some protective magic, or simply talking to himself, she could not tell. She had not thought him a man to waste his breath on chatter. He was *afraid*. She could smell it, feel it through the unrelenting leverage on her wrist, see it in the taut lines of his muscles and the set of his jaw. But he was no coward.

Zevaron bent over the stone form and peered into its unseeing eyes. Again, Shannivar caught that flash of muted sunlight just below the surface of his skin. For an instant, the air shimmered with it. He raised his hand and reached for the stone-drake—

"No!" The word burst from her throat. *"Don't—"*

Zevaron hesitated, then visibly gathered himself. With a cry that seemed to come from the depths of his being, he slammed his palm flat against the stone creature.

For a long moment, the space of a half-dozen heartbeats, nothing happened. Then Shannivar realized that Zevaron had frozen in place. He might have turned to stone, like the lizard thing. She could not make out any movement of his chest. His grip on her wrist loosened minutely. She managed to twist free. His hand fell to his side, limp. The light beneath his skin flared and died.

Just then, the improvised torch guttered out, plunging the tent into near darkness. The only illumination came from the opening at the top, where the faintest glimmering of the moon sifted in.

"Zevaron—Zevaron, please."

Shannivar closed her fingers around his shoulder. Beneath the thin, summer-weight shirt, she touched muscle, smooth and hard. Too hard, more like polished stone than flesh.

With only a little effort, she was able to pull him free. This time, he did not resist her. He seemed to weigh no more than if he were made of bird bones. As soon as she broke his contact with the twisted stone figure, heat flared beneath her fingers.

"Ah!" Zevaron exhaled like a swimmer rising from the depths of a lake. Locked muscles gave way. He sagged against Shannivar's braced legs. Shudders rippled through his body.

"Up! Get up!" she snarled, but he did not respond. She did not know how she was going to get him out of the tent if he could not walk on his own.

The door flap opened suddenly. Torchlight flooded in. Squinting against the sudden brightness, Shannivar made out several *enarees* as they peered inside.

"Out!" one of them shouted. "Get out!"

Zevaron offered no resistance as Shannivar hauled him to his feet and shoved him through the opening. She scrambled after him, into the chill night outside. Her vision went gray, but she managed to remain steady on her feet.

The *enarees*, some holding torches, formed a circle around the two of them. Their expressions ranged from incredulity to outrage.

"Daughter of the Golden Eagle," Bennorakh growled, "you have brought great shame upon your clan this night!"

Shannivar stifled a protest that she had only followed Zevaron, who knew no better. He was an outlander, a dweller-in-stone, ignorant of spirit matters and proper behavior. But she could offer no excuse for her own actions. More than that, she was certain that Zevaron had not acted lightly. He was neither witless nor irresponsible. Something great and terrible had compelled him to transgress as he had. Something, she realized, that had roused from the very moment he heard Chinjizhin's story.

"Shannivar." Zevaron moved closer to her, his voice low and urgent. "Help me."

"Help you?" *After what you've done? Are you mad?*

She wondered if Zevaron realized what he was asking. Surely it was a point of honor in his people as well as hers to accept the full consequences of one's actions. In this case, the offense was grave. The enarees might exile them, curse their arrows, or sever their spirits from their bodies.

"I have done wrong in your eyes," he said to her. Some harmonic in his voice, dignity mixed with sorrow, reached into her heart. "I deeply regret the trouble I have brought to you. You, who have shown me nothing but kindness. For myself, I saw no other choice."

Shannivar stared at him. She had not been kind. She had threatened him, lectured him, taken him under her protection—how was that *kind*?

Then she thought of the moments of quiet conversation, of how they'd shared songs and stories to better understand one another. Of the loneliness she sensed in him. How her heart had ached for him because his closest friend was the blood kin of his most bitter enemy.

"I don't understand," she said, shoving aside the uncomfortable feelings. "How can you not have had a choice? Who held a knife to your throat and forced you to do this?"

He shook his head, as if the answer were utterly beyond words.

"Why did you defy the taboo?" she pressed on. "Do you not understand that the *enarees* speak for Tabilit herself in these matters? Yet you set yourself against the Mother of Horses and the laws she established."

"No—no, I meant none of these things! It was never my intention act disrespectfully or to violate the shamans' commands. I do not know how to explain myself to these holy men, and I do not wish to offend them any further. Shannivar, please. Help me to explain."

She turned to look him full in the face. Torchlight burnished his skin to molten bronze. His eyes were dark and pleading.

"I will accept whatever punishment they see fit to impose," he said. "Will you tell them for me?"

"I will try."

By this time, the Rabbit clan *enaree* had arrived. The others drew back to let him through. Shannivar bowed, one fist over her heart. He looked at her as if he had never truly seen her before.

Praying that Tabilit might look into her soul and guide her words, Shannivar began to explain. She did not know the correct shamanic words to describe the situation. She tried to convey that the stranger meant no lack of respect. According to the customs of his own people, he had important spirit business with the stone-drake. He did not understand the importance of the taboo, and he begged to be allowed to make amends for his offense.

The *enaree* nodded from time to time, closed his eyes, and swayed back and forth. He might be listening to her or communing with the spirits, or about to break into a dance. When she finished, her words spent, he peered at Zevaron for a long moment.

"Ha-ya-heh! Eez-ma-cha-kovh'ar!" The shaman raised his staff and shook it vigorously.

At the outburst, Shannivar flinched, but Zevaron stood firm.

"Don't ask me what that means," Shannivar whispered. "It is a mystical language that only the *enarees* know."

"I can understand it," Zevaron said. "At least, in a general sense. It is very like the ancient holy tongue of my people, but how your wise men came to speak it, I cannot tell."

"What did he say, then?" Shannivar demanded.

One corner of Zevaron's mouth tightened. "*Fool of an unbeliever*, or something to that effect, only less generous."

The *enaree*, who clearly understood their exchange, responded by tilting his head back and laughing uproariously. Several of the others followed. Bennorakh scowled and crossed his arms over his chest.

"We will hear this story," the *enaree* chief said, "and then you will be purified again. Properly, this time."

The Rabbit clan *enaree* directed that a fire be built up a short distance from the tent. The lesser shamans and the apprentices hastened to obey. They unrolled reed mats, some to sit upon and others, hung from wicker frames, to keep off the worst of the wind that blew around the promontory. One of the apprentices produced cups of buttered tea. Shannivar sipped hers, welcoming the savory warmth.

"The sacred writings of my people tell of many things," Zevaron began, his command of trade-dialect much more fluent than when Shannivar had first met him. "Some are like this stone-drake, neither alive nor dead, but a combination of fire and ice, utterly inimical to all that lives. Until recently, I had thought them to be mere legends, like the fables Danar spoke of, entertainments for the simple-minded."

Several of the *enarees* seemed to look upon him with increased respect, or at any rate, diminished hostility.

"Do your people have legends of the beginning of all things?" Zevaron went on. "Ours tell of the making of the world, and also of the great enemy. Fire and Ice, it is called in the common tongue."

"Olash-giyn-Olash," the Rabbit clan *enaree* said, nodding in agreement. "The Shadow of Shadows."

Shannivar said to Zevaron, "I do not know if it is the same as your Fire and Ice or only an invention to frighten disobedient children."

"Once I would have said so. I was taught, as is every Meklavaran child, how Fire and Ice tried to reshape Creation to its own will. How it almost succeeded, except for a great king, Khored of Blessed Memory, and his six warrior brothers. As it is told in our sacred text, the *te-Ketav*, so hear it now."

Zevaron lifted his head and began to recite. Shannivar recognized the language as a very old form of Meklavaran, yet it also sounded a little like the holy tongue of the *enarees*. From the first syllable he uttered, they looked startled. They stared at him, mouths open and eyes wide. He paused at the end of each section to translate into trade-dialect, sometimes pausing to search for the right phrase.

"At the beginning of time, the world was formed in Fire and Ice, in darkness and light. The Holy One caused the elements to become separate, and thus did

earth and heaven come into being. But as the sun set on the first day, twilight opened the gates to evil. Fire once more embraced Ice, and that which had been made separate now joined in unholy union. Defying the Holy One, it gave itself a secret name . . ."

His words flowed in a rhythm that was strange and yet compelling. Hearing the original language, even though she could not understand it, sent ghostly lightning through her. The clear meaning in trade-dialect heightened the uncomfortable sensation of hearing a dreadful and wonderful tale.

"In the hidden places of the world, the union of Fire and Ice conceived a terrible hatred for all who dwelt beneath the sun. Slowly, it gathered an army unto itself, dragons of frost and flame, ice trolls, and, most dreadful of all, the invisible shadows that cast themselves upon the souls of men.

"And as the minions of Fire and Ice swept across the land, men fought against their domination . . ."

In her mind, Shannivar glimpsed the creatures of Fire and Ice marching across the living land, stone-drakes creeping inexorably onward, monstrous giants crushing the earth itself. She heard trumpets calling, the neighing of horses, and the ringing sound of drawn swords. And over it, through it, a force luminous with magic, with pure radiant light.

"From them emerged a te-ravot *both powerful and wise, Khored of Blessed Memory, and his six warrior brothers. Khored forged a magical Shield: six perfect* alvara *crystals like the petals of a flower, surrounding a single luminous center. Each* alvar *was a gem of utmost clarity, a vessel of light, but*

none was more pure or more powerful that Khored's own gem, the te-alvar, *the soul of the Shield.*

"With the power of the Shield, Khored learned the secret name of the incarnation of Fire and Ice. He conjured forth the ancient enemy and bade it submit to judgment."

The rhythm of Zevaron's chant, the very sound of his words shifted. She sensed the clash of battle: rivers boiling, mountains crumbling into sand and then melting into glass, green fields charring into ash. Then came bitter rains, flooding the battlefield. And silence. And mourning. And remembering.

"But Khored in his wisdom knew the enemy was vanquished but not destroyed. Long he pondered, thinking of the ages to come, when the will of men might weaken and evil arise once more."

It no longer mattered to Shannivar that she could not understand the original language or that the translation into trade-dialect was occasionally halting and stiff. The repetition created a resonance in her mind that built with each phrase, words and something numinous and terrible sounding through them.

"And Khored took the Seven-Petaled Shield, and gave each brother one of the alvara *crystals, reserving the* te-alvar, *the heart of the Shield, for his own. With all his arts, he worked upon the stones, so that each* alvar *might be placed in the heart of a living man, hidden from profane sight. Each brother undertook the stewardship, and they swore eternal fidelity to one another.*

"And ages passed, and descendants of Khored

and his brothers kept faith with the pledge their fathers had made. The seven petals and their guardians are the hope and refuge of the living world, for as long as the Shield of Khored endures, the ancient enemy remains imprisoned and righteousness reigns.

"May it be forever so."

The last phrases in Zevaron's clear, strong voice echoed softly against the rock of the promontory. One by one, the *enarees* reverently touched fist to breast, but not to honor Zevaron the man. They offered their respect to the power that flowed through his words, to the merit of those who had first spoken them, and through them, to the valor of those who had performed these deeds.

While he related the tale, an animation, a glamour almost, had suffused Zevaron's features. Now he seemed to diminish, once again an ordinary man.

"This is what I have been taught. How much is true, I cannot tell," he said as the shamans once again seated themselves. "The *te-Ketav* tells us that Khored exiled the forces of Fire and Ice far away. Two things kept them imprisoned. The—" he broke off, massaging his breastbone, took a deep breath, went on, "the magic of Khored, and the wall of mountains in the distant north."

Shannivar's breath caught in her throat. Something swept through her, a soundless whispering, as if some unimaginably immense being bent low and whispered inside her mind.

The mountains, she thought, *that were broken when the white star fell.*

"The might of men has waned with the scattering

of Khored's Shield," Zevaron went on, "as I have reason to know only too well. Now your own people from the north bring this thing—this stone beast, unlike anything known to you. Yet when I touched it—" He held out his hand, fingers spread wide, and for a moment, his expression shifted to one of amazement. "When I touched it, I felt—I *knew*—it was a thing of Fire and Ice. Here, in the lands of men. If the warnings of the *te-Ketav* have come to pass, if the ancient enemy has breached the walls of its mountain prison, if the magic of my ancestors no longer holds it at bay . . ."

"This is a noble tale, strong in spirit. But what does it have to do with you, outlander?" one of the *enarees* asked in a polite tone.

"My people—my own forefather, Khored of Blessed Memory—once stood against this thing. If it has arisen once more, how can it *not* concern me?"

"Ah. It is a matter of family honor." Heads nodded all around. "This we understand."

"There is much I do not yet know," Zevaron said, lifting his head. "I beg your leave to travel to the north, to the country of the Snow Bear people, so that I may see with my own eyes."

"Man of Meklavar," intoned the Rabbit clan *enaree*, "you take on a great deal, to involve not only yourself but all the clans of the steppe in these spirit matters. Azkhantia may fall under a curse because of the rash actions of a man who is not one of us, who has no regard for our own traditions. Do you understand the consequences of what you propose, outlander? No matter how honorable and praiseworthy were the deeds of your fathers, you are not among your own people now. If such evil as you have described may fall upon us, then we claim the right to say what may or may not be done. Why should we trust your judgment in matters that concern us, when you have failed to observe the proper rituals of purification?"

Zevaron rose and bowed deeply, after the manner of his own people. "The fault is mine, and I will undertake whatever penalty you set. Only allow me to follow this trail to its end."

"For that, you need permission from the Council of chieftains, as well as the Snow Bear tribe," Shannivar told him.

"If the *enarees* agree, will the chieftains forbid it?" he countered.

Perhaps in his own country, holy men made the laws, but it was not so on the steppe. The *enarees* read the omens; they might attempt to persuade or intimidate, but they did not command, lest their powers be set against the authority of the chieftains and thereby lead the people into disorder.

"You have courage, man of Meklavar, but we do not yet know the truth of the matter." The Rabbit clan *enaree* raised his dream stick and shook it gently. "You both will return to the purification tent and remain there until summoned. We will eat the smoke of dreams once more. We will dance through its magic and pray for guidance. If it is will of Tabilit, a prophecy will be revealed to us. Then you may come before the Council and make your petition."

Without further deliberation, Shannivar and Zevaron were ushered back down the trail to the main encampment.

Rhuzenjin and the others were still inside the purification tent, completing their own, lesser ordeal. One of the *enarees*, Shannivar couldn't see which one, flipped the door flap closed with a decisive snap. One glance told her that the flap was tied down, weighted with warning bells and stones. The *enarees* were taking no chances this time.

The fire had died to a mound of embers and ash, yet dreamsmoke still drenched the air. The others looked very much as she had last seen them, eyes half-closed, some rocking gently, caught in their own visions.

Rhuzenjin roused as Shannivar sat down beside him. In the dim red light, he looked worried. "What happened?" he whispered. "Where did you go? What trouble has the outlander dragged you into?"

The dreamsmoke stung Shannivar's eyes and throat. She swallowed a cough. "It is a spirit matter. The *enarees* will make a prophecy about it."

"What did he do?" Rhuzenjin persisted.

"Tell him," Zevaron said grimly. He had evidently learned enough Azkhantian to follow the conversation.

"He touched the stone-drake," Shannivar said to Rhuzenjin.

"He *touched* a thing pronounced taboo?" Rhuzenjin clenched his hands into fists, shoulders tensing.

Zevaron's eyes glinted in the uncertain light.

"Leave him alone, Rhuzenjin. He did not do it merely to annoy you. His reasons have to do with the honor of his people. As it is, he has troubles enough, between this new evil arising in the north and the wrath of the *enarees*."

"Why are you are defending him?" Rhuzenjin shot back. "He has put you under an evil spell, forcing you to take his side!"

Refusing to argue, Shannivar turned her back on Rhuzenjin and settled herself beside the door flap. Zevaron hunkered down beside her, close but not touching. She felt him shivering and wondered if the stone-drake had set a fever on him. To give him courage, and because it was going to be a long, uncomfortable night, she touched his hand. His skin was smooth and surprisingly warm.

Shannivar had more questions, a dozen, a hundred, but something in Zevaron's manner, the undeniable effect the stone-drake had upon him, and the earnestness of his confusion stilled her tongue. She had not the heart to press him.

The brief refreshment of the tea drunk on the promontory faded. The dreamsmoke worked on her, loosening her thoughts and her muscles. She had no strength or will to resist. She drifted on its currents.

Some time later, Shannivar jerked awake. Someone had pulled aside the door flap. Morning light streamed in, along with a gust of chill air. Rhuzenjin and the others were pulling on their clothes.

"Come, come!" One of the *enarees* stood outside.

Your time is up. Do not linger!" Shannivar did not now him, but she thought he was of the Falcon lan. He was very young, too young to have completed his apprenticeship.

As Rhuzenjin left, he scowled at Zevaron, sitting unched beside the opening. The apprentice *enaree* anded in more wood and resin, gesturing for Shannivar to build up the fire again. Slowly, with hands nade clumsy by dreamsmoke and thirst, she complied. Within a short time, billows filled the tent. Her eyes stung.

Zevaron shook his head, as if to clear his vision. The movement set off a spasm of coughing.

"It may be many hours before the *enarees* summon us," Shannivar said. "Try not to fight the dreamsmoke. The visions are part of the purification. Perhaps you will learn something of value."

"I dare not sleep again." He rubbed reddened eyes. "My dreams have been uneasy enough of late."

"Evil dreams can sometimes work upon a man and steal his courage, or lead him into foolish hopes," Shannivar said, nodding agreement. "In such cases, it is better to stay awake."

She paused, considering. "Once you asked me for a song of my people, that you might better understand them. It would be disrespectful to sing at such a time as this, but will you not tell me of your home, some story of your people?"

For a long moment, he was so still, she was not sure he had understood her. Perhaps the dreamsmoke had taken him suddenly, as it sometimes did. Then he lifted his head. His eyes reflected the glow of the fire.

He began to speak, not in an ordinary voice but i a rhythmic chant, as if he were reciting one of th great story-poems, translated into trade-dialec Shannivar felt herself carried along by the words, a she had when he recited the great story of his peopl to the *enarees*. Vivid images formed behind her eye:

She looked upon a land of mountains, a city o towers and market places, and a room filled witl rainbow-hued light. Dancers lifted their hands to the sound of drums and cymbals and singing. A line of men and horses, many thousands of them, rode across a plain. Wind sent ripples through the sun burnished grass. The men raised their swords Brightness flashed from a thousand blades.

Her vision paled. The plain fell away, and she stood in a place lapped by mist. A figure moved toward her, a woman. She could not make out the woman's features, only her eyes. They glowed like bits of the sun. The woman folded her hands across her breasts. Cupping something between them, she stretched her hands out, but not to Shannivar. Rather, she reached *through* Shannivar to someone standing behind her. Shannivar's body had become as insubstantial as the curling mists.

Shannivar spun around to see the woman holding a golden sphere, then saw Zevaron reach out to take it. It seemed a perfectly innocent action, and yet, somewhere in the pit of Shannivar's belly, she knew that to touch the sphere would change Zevaron for-ever. It would consume him, as surely as fire or death.

Zevaron turned to her, and she saw with horror that his eyes now burned with the same fire as the woman's. He tilted his head, his blind gaze searching for her. Then he opened his mouth, and she saw that his teeth had turned to jagged shards of ice. In an instant, frost coated his skin. Breath roared out of him, bitter as a winter storm.

She whirled and sprinted away. The mists closed around her. With each step she took, the world around her grew brighter and colder, a chill that seared down to her bones. Everywhere she ran, that same ice-white figure appeared. She could not escape.

He was everywhere and nowhere, this man who was Zevaron and not Zevaron, human and something infinitely more terrifying.

Do not run.

Shannivar stumbled, caught between surprise and disbelief. The voice—the words ringing so clearly in her mind—

Do not run away.

"Grandmother?" It sounded like the old woman, and yet with no hint of the quavery uncertainty of age. The voice was strong, strong as Saramark.

Shannivar came to a halt. Frost coated her skin and yet, with the sound of that voice, familiar and not familiar, she no longer felt the cold.

Do not run away. He is in terrible danger. He must not face it alone.

With a gasp, Shannivar came back to herself. Her heart pounded in her ears. She shivered. The tent was dark except for the fading light of a few ash-coated embers. Zevaron lay on the other side of the banked fire, curled in on himself.

Outside lay the sleeping camp, the dense stillness

of earth and night sky. From the promontory came the faint chants of the *enarees* as they danced and sang, petitioning Tabilit and Onjhol for the true sight. The residue of dreamsmoke hung in the air, stinging her lungs. The taste of ashes filled her mouth, and her belly cramped with hunger. As she tried to settle herself, she heard Zevaron cry out.

She wanted to go to him, to wrap him in her arms and feel the warmth of his skin, not the ice of her vision. She knew she should be ashamed to even imagine such a thing during a purification ritual. If she could not control her thoughts, at least she could behave properly. She turned her back on him and closed her eyes.

After a time, she felt herself wandering through half-remembered territory, vast sweeps of plain and rising hills. She came upon a forest-lined river, an oasis of the steppe. Herds of horses, goats, and camels browsed along banks lush with new grass. None bore any halter or harness, and they gave no sign they were aware of her.

Always before, her heart had risen in joy at the sight of the animals feeding so peacefully. Now, a wordless dread crept over her. Was this her fate, her personal prophecy, to sacrifice herself for the land and its creatures?

Why were there no people at the oasis, no trace of riders or kinsmen?

Chapter 19

"WAKE up! Wake up!"

Shannivar blinked awake at the voice. For a moment, she was not sure she had heard the summons or if it were the effects of the dreamsmoke. Gummy residue blurred her vision. Her stomach growled, leaden. When she tried to swallow, her mouth felt as if it were lined with felt. Moldy felt, at that. Muscles trembling, she crawled from the tent into the overcast dawn. Zevaron followed, looking as drained as she felt. The camp was peaceful. Smoke curled skyward from scattered dung-fires.

Morning. Gathering. Enarees. *Purification. Breakfast?*

Tabilit's golden knees! The stone-drake! And the vision . . .

"Come! Come!" A woman who looked older than Grandmother stood outside the tent. She pointed to Shannivar. One of the Antelope men was already leading Zevaron away.

Trying her best not to show weakness, Shannivar

followed the old woman to a *jort* on the periphery of the camp. A few children stared as they passed, then went back to their games.

The painted symbols that surrounded the door were familiar—Ghost Wolf, Shannivar thought, and wondered how Ythrae and her suitor fared. Inside, she inhaled the familiar smells of incense and cedar chips. Platters of food, water skins, and implements for bathing had been laid out.

"Drink, drink," the old woman said, filling a horn cup and handing it to Shannivar. Her accent was so thick and her words so garbled by missing teeth that she was barely intelligible. "Get strength back. Big council today, chieftains, *enarees*. Everyone."

Shannivar wished her head was not buzzing with a thousand insects. Was she to sleep here? As a guest or a prisoner? She sank to her knees. Her tongue felt thick and stupid. "Have the *enarees* received their prophecy, then?"

The woman cackled. "*Enarees*, witch-men, all yesterday chanting, chanting, chanting, smoke-dancing. Prophecy, yes. *Important* prophecy, yes, yes. You look proper, do respect to gods. Drink now. Eat. No more questions."

Shannivar accepted the cup gratefully. The herb-laced water was cool and refreshing. She finished it all, then a second cup, more slowly. After disrobing as instructed, she knelt down. The old woman smeared her bare torso with a paste of cedar and frankincense, and massaged it in vigorously. Tension drained from Shannivar's taut muscles. The mixture was warm, the old woman's hands strong.

The paste dried quickly, and the old woman scraped it off, leaving Shannivar's skin soft and sweetly scented.

Her clothes had been brushed clean and neatly folded. After she dressed, the old woman combed out her hair and rebraided it, then presented her with a bowl of barley boiled to a mush and laced with dried fruit and bits of smoked rabbit. The old woman nodded approvingly as Shannivar devoured the food, thinking she had never tasted anything so delicious in her life. Her head cleared as she regained her strength, and the last effects of the dreamsmoke faded.

Outside, the campsite hummed with activity. A few clans, having no further business, were breaking down their tents for the journeys back to their own territories. Once the chieftains had met for their final session, the *khural* would end.

Shannivar had run out of time and not yet found a husband.

That was never your fate, my child, a voice whispered, but whether it came from Tabilit or Grandmother or some other power, she could not tell.

At the Council pavilion, the chieftains and elders had already assembled, seated on their camel-skin stools. The Rabbit clan *enaree* stood behind Tenoshinakh, but the other shamans had not yet arrived. Although the audience was smaller than before, everyone from the Golden Eagle contingent was present, including Danar and the Isarrans. The Snow

Bear tribesmen stood apart from the others. Their worn, trail-stained garments and haggard expressions contrasted with the general mood of festivity that usually accompanied the close of the *khural*.

Zevaron waited among those to be judged. Like Shannivar, he wore the shirt of one who has emerged from a purification tent, and his hair had been oiled and braided in Azkhantian fashion. He looked strikingly handsome, but smudges of exhaustion ringed his eyes. Catching her glance, he gave a quick nod. Darkness hung about him, a barely perceptible shadow, or perhaps that was only a blurring of her own eyesight.

The session opened with the usual ceremony. The Rabbit clan *enaree* offered invocations and prayers to Tabilit for wisdom. Then, before the assembled dignitaries, Ythrae and the Ghost Wolf son, whose name was Tarabey, married one another in the style of warriors in the field, called an "arrow-wedding." A generation ago, before Ar-Cinath-Gelon's ambitions spurred wave after wave of Gelonian invasions, arrow-weddings had been rare. Most nuptial ceremonies had been formal affairs, "fire-weddings" arranged by both families. A couple such as Ythrae and Tarabey would have returned to their respective homes, and their parents would engage in protracted negotiations that, if all went well, culminated in three days of feasting and ritual. Constant raiding created uncertain futures, so the old battlefield tradition—binding together an arrow from each one's quiver, then shooting the arrow into a fire—had become more common.

After the arrows were tied together, Ythrae handed them to Tarabey, in token that she would now lay down her own bow, becoming wife rather than warrior. He shot the arrows cleanly into the fire, and everyone shouted out their approval.

Shannivar cheered with the others, offering wishes of luck, fertility, and long life to the new bride, but her heart was not in it. To make matters worse, Rhuzenjin was watching her with an intensity that made her uncomfortable.

The Council listened to a few late complaints, an accusation of a curse laid upon a camel, a quarrel arising from insults hurled after drinking too much *k'th*, and a disputed price of a saddle. Since these matters had arisen during the gathering, here they must be resolved or else wait until next year. The claimants accepted the verdicts quietly, without discussion, as if they cared more to have the matter done with than to prevail.

Speaking on behalf of the Snow Bear tribesmen, Chinjizhin son of Khinukoth asked for whatever help might be supplied to his party. They had traveled long and far with an onerous burden. Freely the Council offered food for their return journey, as well as fodder for their beasts and a few small luxuries for the clan—bone hair combs, crystallized honey, and tea.

Shannivar contemplated requesting to join another clan, Ghost Wolf perhaps or Badger, as an unmarried warrior. It was an unusual move but not without precedent. The songs mentioned several such examples. She was still undecided when

Tenoshinakh motioned her forward. She bowed respectfully, tapping her right fist over her heart, and wished the Council a lucky day.

"Shannivar daughter of Ardellis of the Golden Eagle clan," Tenoshinakh addressed her, "have you undergone the rite of purification, according to the traditions of our people and the command of the *enarees*?"

"I have done so," Shannivar replied formally.

"Then you may return to your place free from any obligation, your honor clear."

"I wish to remain with the outlander, Zevaron of Meklavar, until his own case is decided. It was by my decision as party-leader that he stands here among us."

"He is a grown man, even though he is not one of us," said Uncle Sagdovan. "By law and custom, he is responsible for his own actions." The other members nodded their agreement.

Shannivar bowed again to the Council. With those words, they had already accorded Zevaron a certain degree of respect. A true outlander—one who had no honor—would have been dismissed outright.

Tenoshinakh spoke again, asking Zevaron the same question he had asked Shannivar. Zevaron replied that he had completed the purification rite. He spoke halting Azkhantian, stumbling from time to time over an unfamiliar word. Shannivar wondered how long it had taken him to rehearse the speech. After a hesitation, he asked permission to address the Council.

A few members of the audience, Rhuzenjin

among them, muttered their disapproval. This ignorant outlander had broken the taboo, thereby proving that he had no sense of proper behavior. Shannivar glared at them.

"We will hear what the outlander has to say," Tenoshinakh said, putting an end to the discussion. "Then we will judge the worth of his words."

Zevaron came to stand directly in front of the Council. He bowed, first in the manner of his own people, then with one fist over his heart. The stern expressions of several Council members, notably Sagdovan, gave way to guarded approval. "I had long heard of the courage and ferocity of the Azkhantian clans," Zevaron began, speaking trade-dialect. "Now that I have seen with my own eyes, I know the stories to be true."

This seemed to please the chieftains. During the *khural*, Zevaron had comported himself honorably, with a craftiness that had earned him the approval of some.

"Perhaps someday," Zevaron said, "Azkhantia and Meklavar will unite in common cause. Until that time, I ask you to consider me a friend to Azkhantia." He was not repeating the mistake of the Isarrans in trying to cozen them into an alliance with all the benefit on one side and all the risk on the other. "A matter has arisen that concerns both our peoples. I speak of the stone-drake brought here by the Snow Bear clan. You have seen it for yourselves. You know this is no an ordinary, harmless thing, but an object tainted by malignant supernatural influences."

Tenoshinakh's quick glance questioned the Rabbit clan *enaree*, who had thus far listened immobile and stony-faced. "Nothing the outlander says is untrue," the shaman admitted. "The stone lizard is but the forerunner of a greater evil to come. All the omens are sinister." He paused. "We suspect it is a creature of Olash-giyn-Olash, the Shadow of Shadows."

Hearing these words, it seemed to Shannivar that a shadow passed over the assembly, bearing a chill of the spirit. Familiar faces turned strange, for a moment both desolate and terrible. Whispers rustled through the crowd like the first intimations of a winter blizzard.

The Shadow of Shadows.

"My own people have knowledge of such things." Zevaron spoke out of turn, but in a manner so calm and respectful that no one objected. "That is why I have begged leave of your wise men to travel to the north to discover what more may be learned. I ask now for your permission as well."

Before any response could be made, Bennorakh and the remaining *enarees* marched single-file into the hearing-place. Shannivar could read little in their stern visages. The audience grew very still. The usual comments and scuffling, each person elbowing his neighbor aside for a better place, died down. No one wanted to miss what came next.

Tenoshinakh asked, "What prophecy have you received regarding the stone-drake?"

The head shaman turned to face the Council. He rattled his dream stick so fiercely that the assembled men and women drew back. Glaring first at Zevaron, then Shannivar, he lifted his arms and began to speak. Phrase after phrase rumbled like summer thunder from his mouth. Shannivar did her best to translate for Zevaron:

> *"When the city lies in shadow*
> *A fire burns in the snow.*
> *Blood flows across the steppe.*
> *The horse gallops on the edge of a knife.*
>
> *When the heir to gold is drowned,*
> *He returns with treasure.*
>
> *When the heir to light goes to the mountain,*
> *He does not return.*
>
> *When the woman finds what is lost,*
> *She gives it to the stranger.*
> *Thus the gods have spoken to us."*

When the *enaree* came to a halt, Zevaron whispered, "Ask him if this means I have their permission to investigate."

"Investigate? Investigate what?" she hissed.

"The stone-drake, of course," he shot back. "Where it came from, the broken mountains where the white star fell—*everything*!"

When Shannivar translated the question, the head *enaree* answered, "If the outlander goes to the north, he will fail. His gods are not our gods. Tabilit does not spread her blessings over him, nor does

Onjhol lend his strong right arm except to our own kind."

"What did he say?" Zevaron asked in trade-dialect.

"You will not find what you seek, says the prophecy." Shannivar turned back to the *enaree*. "What have you seen? What will happen to my friend?"

"If he goes to the north," the *enaree* repeated, "a terrible fate will befall us all."

"He sees disaster for more than you yourself," Shannivar said to Zevaron.

"Does he forbid me to go? Will he stand in my way?"

He reminded her of a great hunting cat, not a lion but something sleeker, swifter. Deadlier. She remembered how he had dealt with the Isarran bodyguard and his light, inexorable touch on her wrist. He would find a way to the north, with or without permission. Something in his bleak determination, his *aloneness*, struck a resonant chord in Shannivar. If he had no clan to ride at his back, neither did she.

When Shannivar conveyed Zevaron's question, the *enaree* shook his head. "This is a matter for gods, not men. We do not command. We speak only of the visions they have sent us."

"What fate did you see?" she persisted. "If there is an enemy in the north, should we not ride out to meet it?" *The horse gallops on the edge of a knife . . .*

The Rabbit clan *enaree* made a warding sign and struck the ground with his dream stick. The rabbit bones clashed together with a hollow sound.

"Are there not many meanings in even the simplest prophecy?" Bennorakh turned to his senior *enaree*. "Could it be possible that this outlander has come to fulfill it, to draw out its poison as from a festering wound?"

"The stone lizard and the power it embodies bode ill for Azkhantia." Tenoshinakh's gaze flickered to Zevaron and then to the Rabbit clan shaman. "Might we avert the curse by sending it beyond our borders?"

The corners of the Rabbit clan *enaree's* mouth drew down. Clearly, he wished the stone-drake to remain where it was, guarded by shamanic magic.

As she translated, Shannivar appreciated Zevaron's timing. Now it seemed as if he were offering his service to the clans instead of begging their favor.

Tenoshinakh went apart with the other chieftains for a brief conference. The audience turned to one another, discussing the situation in hushed, expectant voices.

"What is going on?" Zevaron asked Shannivar.

"Tenoshinakh is looking for a way to divert the curse from the clans," she explained. "He thinks that if you go to the north, you will take it with you. The only problem is the prophecy."

"That I am doomed to failure, and that some catastrophe will befall me?" His eyes, as he met her gaze, were full of darkness, but she could not make out any fear. "I am certain of one thing. If I do not go, something terrible will indeed come to pass. Perhaps it will, whether I go or not. But I have no choice. I am summoned. I cannot turn away from this destiny, regardless of the outcome."

She stared at him, stung by his sense of dreadful purpose. What did he see with those haunted eyes? An army of stone-drakes, an upsetting of all natural order? Surely he could not think a mortal could defeat such a force. Arrows could not bring down monsters of rock and fire, and a sword could not prevail against the Shadow of Shadows. He bowed his head, and Shannivar could almost hear his thought, *The curse has already fallen upon me.*

"From here, your way is clear," Zevaron had said to Danar, that night in the darkness. *"Mine is not."*

Now it was.

Something stirred within Shannivar, admiration for this man of Meklavar and a feeling she could not name.

Zevaron once more faced the Council. His gaze encompassed not only the chieftains and elders, but the *enarees* as well.

"If you go to the north, the curse might well fall upon you," Tenoshinakh said. "Are you prepared to take that risk?

"I must go, regardless of the cost." Zevaron's voice was so resonant with unspoken passion that no one could mistake his meaning, even without Shannivar's translation. "I prefer to do so with your blessing."

"You have our leave to travel as you wish throughout the steppe," Tenoshinakh announced, "so long as you do no harm to man or beast."

"I promise," Zevaron said. He went to the Snow

Bear men and saluted them. "Will you take me to your country and show me where you found this thing?"

"We will undertake to guide the outlander, if it is the will of the Council," their chief answered.

Tenoshinakh grunted. "Now, who goes with him, for he is a stranger among us and does not know the ways of the steppe?"

The audience shuffled back a few steps. "The outlander claims this spirit matter belongs to his own people," someone said. "What has it to do with us?"

"It is not proper to interfere."

"Why should we share the curse? He is not our kin."

"The stone-dweller has taken this burden upon himself. It is the will of Tabilit."

"It is his own rashness, his own thirst for glory speaking. Then let him suffer the consequences."

They were justifying themselves, Shannivar knew. *Cowards. They would send one man—a stranger and outlander—where they themselves fear to go.* Why did Tenoshinakh not chastise the men for their timidity? Did he intend Zevaron to perish alone?

Perhaps that was exactly what the chieftain planned. Zevaron would carry away the curse with him when he died. The prophecy would be satisfied, for he certainly would not return, and no clansman would suffer.

Shannivar was so furious, so embarrassed at the cowardice of her own people, that for a long moment she could not speak, for fear she might burst out in a tirade against the Council, the *enarees*, and anyone else who was too spineless to seize this chance for a glorious adventure. Then she came to her senses, realizing that they were only doing what they had always done—acting prudently for the good of their people. It had never been their way to involve themselves with outlanders, and they saw no reason to do so now.

It seemed to Shannivar that all her life, she had longed to prove her valor, to accomplish feats worthy of Saramark herself, and now Tabilit had chosen her for this task. Once again, she heard the voice of her dreamsmoke vision: *Do not run away. He is in terrible danger. He must not face it alone.*

She came to stand beside Zevaron and raised her voice so that everyone could hear. "I, Shannivar daughter of Ardellis, will go with the outlander!"

Chapter 20

EXPRESSIONS of surprise greeted Shannivar's announcement. Rhuzenjin cried out, "No, not you!"

"I am a warrior of the steppe," Shannivar went on, her voice soaring above his protest. "My horses are swift and my arrows fly true. I am not afraid. I will do this thing, and I will return covered in glory!"

Zevaron, at her side, said, "Shannivar, you do not have to—"

She cut him off with a gesture. This was not the time for private conversation, for explanations and misgivings and negotiation.

A hush settled over both the onlookers and the Council. Even Rhuzenjin fell silent. The *enarees* stood as witnesses, neither giving nor withholding their blessing. Zevaron's quest had already passed from their hands.

Tenoshinakh nodded gravely. "Then the matter is concluded in honor. May Tabilit guide your steps and may Onjhol of the Silver Bow grant you his strength."

With these words, he rose to signal that the session was over. People turned to their neighbors, chattering away about this latest news. Shannivar had no doubt that by the time each clan returned to their own territory, the story of the stone-drake and the outlander would have grown. As for the stone-drake itself, the *enarees* would decide how best to safeguard it.

With the end of the formal hearing, the assembly began to disperse. Uncle Sagdovan approached Shannivar with words of encouragement, as did several others, so that within a few moments, she found herself surrounded by well-wishers and those curious about her. No one attempted to dissuade her, for to do so would be to go against the will of the Council. At another time, Shannivar would have felt uncomfortable being the center of so much attention. She was an arrow in Tabilit's bow, and her dreams of glory arose from the goddess, not her own limited self. The crowd was useful in keeping Rhuzenjin calm. He would not embarrass himself by airing his personal feelings in so public a setting.

Shannivar answered questions and accepted wishes for luck until her audience drifted away. Rhuzenjin watched her pass as she strode off.

She would not look at him. Zevaron and Danar were deep in conversation. Danar, clearly unhappy, gesticulated emphatically, and Zevaron shook his head. Shannivar recognized that stubborn expression. She did not think there was anything Danar could say, or any persuasion or threat he could bring to bear, that would change Zevaron's mind, especially now that she had committed herself to go with him.

Although the Council had concluded its affairs, the day was yet young. Those clans that had come the greatest distances began preparations for departure on the following day. Old men sat in the shelter of the reed mats, drinking tea. Billows of dust and distant whoops from the playing fields indicated the final games.

In the horse field, a few men were inspecting one animal or another, clearly engaged in some friendly trading. Shannivar recognized the old man from the Long Ride. He held the lead line of the young sorrel he had ridden. With a grin, he swung himself on to the horse's bare back and, using weight and a nudge of his knees, set the sorrel trotting in a circle. She remembered his words, *"I have already won,"* and realized the same held true for herself. Tabilit had not sent her to the *khural* simply to win a horse race or to choose a husband.

At Shannivar's approach, Eriu nickered, clearly hopeful of another adventure. His summer coat was smooth and glossy. The weal left by Kharemikhar's whip was healing fast. She pressed her cheek against his neck and inhaled deeply, as if she could draw his solid animal strength into her lungs.

Radu ambled over, sedate as always, and lipped a stray strand of Shannivar's hair as if to say, *Silly two-legs, aren't we going riding?*

"Not today," Shannivar murmured, stroking the sleek dun shoulder. "Enjoy your rest."

She saddled and bridled the black, then rode him at a walk to the playing field. He moved a little stiffly, but the gentle exercise would be good for limbering up any strained muscles. She promised herself not to demand too much from him.

She found a good spot from which to watch, not too near the other mounted viewers. Ythrae gestured a greeting while keeping her attention on the game. By now, the playing fields had been trampled so many times, the earth was packed hard. Scattered cheering came from the onlookers, most of them mounted. In the middle of the field, surrounded by a cloud of dust, a knot of riders scrimmaged over possession of a pole. A dusty, tattered felt hat had been tied to one end. Clearly, it had been dropped and ridden over a number of times, and from the enthusiastic cheers of the contestants, the game was a heated one. Contests on horseback had few if any formal rules, so anyone on the sidelines might spontaneously join in. In the heat of the competition, the players often changed sides.

One of the onlookers circled his restive horse, then galloped onto the field. His friends cried out in encouragement. Almost immediately, Eriu was infected with the excitement of the game. He pawed the dry dirt. Shannivar patted his neck sympathetically. If he had not run the Long Ride just a few days before, she might have taken part in the hat game. It was unusual but not unheard-of for women to compete with men in this particular event, where strength and size counted less than riding skill.

The current possessor of the hat was Tarabey, Ythrae's new husband. He rode a spotted horse, bright sorrel and creamy white, and was grinning broadly. He broke free of the others and wheeled his horse toward the goal, two standards set at the end of the field. But he was too slow, too full of himself and the exhilaration of having seized the prize. Another rider was after him in an instant, the Badger clan woman who had done so well in the Long Ride. This time, she rode a different horse, a tall, leggy bay. She looked like a child, clinging to its back.

Zevaron joined the onlookers. He met her gaze and walked over to her, moving slowly like a man approaching a skittish horse. "I appreciate the gesture of support," he said, a little diffidently, "but I would not have you—you are under no obligation to me."

"We are not all cowards!" Shannivar said, surprised at the heat in her own voice.

"I never said that you were."

"Listen to me, Zevaron Outlander. I believe that this thing, this stone-drake, concerns us as much as it does you. Even if it did not, you have been a guest among us. You have acted with honor and have made amends for your mistakes. It shames me that my own people are so lacking in courage they let an outlander venture, alone and friendless, where they dare not go. I would not have it said of us that we are too timid to search out an enemy in our own lands."

"Even so, it was not necessary for *you* to volunteer."

"You cannot travel to the north alone," she pointed out. "It is too dangerous for anyone not wise in the ways of the steppe."

His face closed. "I will find a way." Again, he rubbed his chest, as if to ease some deep, abiding pain.

"You misunderstand me," she said, gentling her tone. "I meant only that you need someone who knows how to live on the steppe. How to hunt, where to find water and shelter, when to rest, how to read the skies for direction, how to tell which plants can be eaten and which are poison."

He stood very still, his gaze straight ahead, fixed on the game.

"I chose this quest freely," she repeated. "It is as much mine as it is yours." She smiled. "They will sing songs about our valor for generations to come."

"I do not do this for fame," he answered, and Shannivar thought he also meant, *I did not choose it, either*. To that, she had no answer.

They watched as the game proceeded to a round of cheering. Tarabey had seen his danger and was making a run for it. He pummeled the sides of his horse with his heels. The horse surged forward, spotted hide gleaming over bunching muscles. An instant later, the long-legged bay had caught up with him.

"I'm a little surprised to see the festivities continue," Zevaron remarked.

"The *khural* won't officially end until the *enarees* give the blessing of leave-taking," Shannivar explained, grateful to have an uncontroversial topic. "That's tomorrow. For today, we have the last of the games, as you see, and everyone runs around, saying farewells."

The Badger clan woman leaned over, her movements neat and deft, and snatched the pole with the hat. The bay whirled with amazing speed for such a large horse and sprinted for the other goal. The onlookers hooted in approval.

Tarabey started after her. The other riders followed in a bunch. A moment later, the Badger woman galloped between the standards.

Flushed with excitement, Tarabey trotted his horse to where Ythrae waited. He didn't seem upset by the loss. On the contrary, his good nature and the distraction of the game had erased his former shyness.

Ythrae glowed with happiness as he flirted with her. She looked on her new husband with the same pride as if he had won a hundred games. There would, Shannivar reflected, be the usual difficulties of an arrow-wedding—the frictions of joining a new family, of pleasing a new and unknown mother-in-law. But the couple seemed well-matched, and there was no reason why they should not be happy.

Watching them, Shannivar felt even more isolated than before. She had seen enough loveless marriages to know how rare this mutual delight was. She had also seen the longing in the eyes of the widowed in unguarded moments. Was it worse to

be alone than to share one's *jort*, bear children, and
grow old in an uneasy, loveless marriage? Mirrimal
had said no, but Mirrimal was dead. She would
never face the long years of solitude.

Eriu pulled at the bit, frustrated at standing still
when the other horses were having so much fun.
Shannivar dismounted, took firm hold of his reins,
and led him back in the direction of the horse fields.
Zevaron followed.

"I saw you at the horse fields earlier," he said. "It
looked like there was some horse dealing going on.
Would you help me acquire a pack animal? I have
a little money. It's from Gelon, but the gold is
good."

Shannivar agreed to help him, although she refrained from saying that the only use anyone of the
steppe had for Gelonian gold was to melt it down
into something else, not to mention that Azkhantians did not sell their horses to foreigners.

Together they walked back to the encampment,
discussing what they must prepare, what to take
and what to send either with Danar or with the returning Golden Eagle party. Shannivar had her
own *jort*, her horses, her bow, and her knowledge of
how to live off the land. She could legitimately take
the camel as her share of the clan's herds, or two of
the pack ponies. On the other hand, Ythrae was
also entitled to a share and had far greater skill in
managing the camel. Shannivar smiled to herself.
Given a choice, she would far rather deal with ponies.

Shannivar and Zevaron arrived back at the clan

encampment. In Shannivar's absence, the others had prepared for departure. All that remained now was to fold the tents, take down the *jorts*, and load the pack animals. The Isarran party was almost ready to leave. Leanthos was clearly anxious to return to his homeland. Danar waited with them. When he saw Zevaron's expression, his own reflected his disappointment.

Zevaron said something in Gelone, at which Danar shook his head and replied kindly. Shannivar recognized the word for *friend*. Ashamed at overhearing yet another private conversation, she turned away. The two men must exchange their farewells in privacy.

"Shannivar daughter of Ardellis, I would speak with you!" Rhuzenjin had been attending to his tent. He waited until she left Zevaron to his friend before approaching her. Her heart sank when she saw his expression. Her mind was clear that she had not deliberately given him false hope, but now she wished she had done more to discourage his attention.

"May your day be lucky," she replied.

"Have you gone mad?" Rhuzenjin blurted, without further preamble. "Or has the outlander cast an evil spell on you, to cause you to abandon your own people?"

Shannivar made an impatient gesture at his rudeness. Clearly, he wasn't going to part ways in a dignified manner. "Keep your voice down, Rhuzenjin son of Semador! Do you seriously think a stone-dweller who rides like a sack of rotten *k'th* and barely knows how to string a bow could induce me to do *anything* I did not want to do? I'm going as his guide, of my own free will."

"He has seduced you, bound you to him with forbidden sorcery—*forced* you! That's it, isn't it?"

Shannivar's temper flared. "Tabilit's silver ass! There is far more at stake here than your broken heart! You saw the stone-drake, you heard the story told by Chinjizhin son of Khinukoth. You witnessed the prophecy of the *enarees*."

She lowered her voice and fixed him with a direct gaze. "Something evil stirs in the mountains to the north. Is it Olash-giyn-Olash, the Shadow of Shadows? I don't know, and neither do you. The outlander says he is spirit-called by this thing. I believe him. I saw him when he touched it. I felt its power. Should he go alone to defend all of us? Should we cower in our *jorts* like frightened rabbits? Or should one of us ride out to meet this evil with him, whatever it might be?"

"But you, Shannivar, you must not risk yourself!"

"Risk? I am a warrior of the steppe, a daughter of the Golden Eagle. No man has the right to tell me what I must or must not risk. I have stood against the Gelon. I will face this enemy as well."

"You must return home," Rhuzenjin went on, his eyes dark with pleading, "with me."

What could she say? She did not want to be cruel. "I will never return to the clan of the Golden Eagle," she said, as kindly as she could manage. "If I have seemed to encourage you, it was without my conscious intent, and I am sorry."

Over Rhuzenjin's protests, she said, "We will speak no more of the matter. Nothing you say will dissuade me, and I cannot promise anything that will put your mind at rest. Life is as Tabilit wills it."

"Life is as we make it."

He was right, but Shannivar refused to be drawn in. "I must confer with Chinjizhin son of Khinukoth regarding travel conditions, so that I can better divide the gear and pack animals. While I am gone, will you help Zevaron and make sure he has suitable travel gear for the north?"

She was offering Rhuzenjin the chance to show himself magnanimous, to act as a friend and kinsman. He shook his head, his lips white and tense.

"I will not aid you in this folly."

He strode away, and Shannivar watched him go. She had not meant to injure him, and saw now that his hurt was deep. There seemed no remedy she could offer. To say she wished their friendship to continue would only make things worse. Time and the blessing of Tabilit must ease his pain.

Danar and Leanthos each thanked Shannivar for her efforts on their behalf. As a token of their friendship, and because she genuinely wished the young Gelon well, she presented him with the yellow silk scarf that had been the gift from the Denariyan trader. His eyes lit up when he saw it, for he clearly recognized what it was. He touched it to his lips and then hung it around his neck. Shannivar smothered a giggle, for it looked almost comical, so bright and cheerful against the drabness of his clothing. It was as good a farewell as any.

Then Danar and the Isarrans turned the noses of their mounts to the south. They left a pile of supplies, everything they could spare, for Zevaron.

Shannivar showed Zevaron how to sort and pack the goods they would take, blankets and jackets, wool hats, gear for hunting and then cooking what they had caught, a small axe, a jar of oil, skins of water and *k'th*, packets of herbs, dried meat and *bha*, and supplies for mending the harness. Zevaron also carried a small kit with soap, cloths, and a razor for shaving, which Shannivar thought a bizarre and unnecessary custom.

The night being warm, she curled up in her blanket under the sky, apart from the remaining attendees. Someone had left one of the reed screens up, but the wind had died down. A fragrance rose from the earth, the musty sweetness of late summer. Around her, she heard sounds of people settling down to sleep, soft talking, a woman's laughter. Already, she seemed to belong to them no longer.

She would have had to leave Golden Eagle clan in one way or another. All things changed in their season. Girls became women and then wives and then grandmothers, and in the end, they lived on only in the memories of those who came after them. She sang to herself of Saramark, who had lived so long ago, and wondered who would sing of her.

The familiar sounds of a camp readying for sleep, and the deeper silence of the earth, had no answer for her.

"Shannivar?" Zevaron pitched his voice low, to avoid disturbing the other sleepers. He made her name sound like something beautiful.

"I am still awake." She sat up. The blanket fell from her shoulders. Although she still wore her shirt and trousers, as was the custom on the trail and in *khural*, she felt naked.

The darkness revealed more than it hid. On all their nights on the trail, they had never been this close. Zevaron moved like a liquid shadow to kneel before her. She had no fear of him, only a sense of anticipation.

"I thank you for all you have done, everything you—" His words caught in his throat. She felt his breath, quick and hot.

Before she could react, he took both her hands, turned them over, and kissed each palm.

Shannivar pulled away, startled. She had never felt anything so soft, so stirring, as the touch of his lips on her skin. Heat flooded her blood.

In the dark, she felt the shadow fall across his eyes once more. She thought she would drown in those secret depths, that her heart would break utterly open.

In an instant, he was gone. It was a long time before she could sleep.

Shannivar woke to a milky gray morning, well before the sun had cleared the horizon. Tatters of her dreams clung to her like wisps of fog. She took down the *jort* and finished packing away its contents. Rhuzenjin evidently had second thoughts and relented enough to help load the gear on the ponies. He said very little and would not look her in the face. She decided to treat his helpfulness as an apology.

She frowned as he added an additional pack to one of the beasts. "That is not ours," she said, bracing herself to refuse his parting gift.

"It is mine," came Bennorakh's voice, behind her. He held the reins of his own horse. His dream stick was tied to the saddle.

"I don't understand," she said.

"Do you think you can go off on a spirit journey, tracking down something as dangerous as that stone-drake, by yourself? Not even you, Shannivar daughter of Ardellis, can face such a trial unprotected."

PART IV:

Shannivar's Hunt

Chapter 21

AS Shannivar, Zevaron, and Bennorakh journeyed northeast with the Snow Bear men, the rising sun slanted across their eyes. Overhead arched the endless sky, clear as far as the eye could follow. Beyond the trampled earth of the gathering place, the late summer grasses rose lush and tall. Feathergrass, sage, and wild barley covered the gently rising hills. Here and there, strawflowers dusted the horizon with yellow or purple. A scent rose up from the earth, musty and sweet. The horses bent their heads to snatch stalks heavy with grain.

The days had already begun to grow shorter, for midsummer was past, but there was yet light enough to travel many hours each day. The nights were mild as the land slowly released its heat.

They traveled slowly, for the reindeer had not yet recovered from their arduous trek, and the Snow Bear men on their shaggy little tundra horses were in hardly better condition. Shannivar did not attempt to draw them into conversation beyond the ordinary exchanges of finding water, setting up camp, caring for the animals, and sharing their evening meal. They seemed weary in spirit, worn down by worry. Shannivar noted the glassy look in their eyes as they gazed north, and the slight hesitation of their hands on reins or harness.

Zevaron had made no attempt to repeat the kiss. The memory faded until she wondered if she had imagined the warmth of his lips on her palms. Perhaps she had taken his thanks and exaggerated it into something more.

She did not want Zevaron for a husband. She did not want any man to be the purpose of her life. Tabilit had opened her eyes to this warrior's quest, and it was to Tabilit alone that Shannivar owed her devotion. If it were the will of the goddess to weave Shannivar's life journey with Zevaron's for a time, she would comply with pleasure, but if their ways parted . . . She hoped for the singleness of spirit to hear only the commands of the Mother of Horses. And the strength to obey.

Let me go where you send me, with a warrior's honor, she prayed. *Let me never look back.*

The Snow Bear chieftain, Chinjizhin, and his men treated Zevaron with courtesy. In his faltering Azkhantian, Zevaron offered thanks for being allowed to travel with them. They glanced away, uncomprehending and a little embarrassed. Even Chinzhukog son of Chinjizhin, who was more open in his manner than the others, looked uncomfortable. Surely, Shannivar thought, Zevaron must realize that the Snow Bear chieftain acted not out of his own choice, but in the service of the Council, the *enarees*, and Tabilit herself. To thank him made as much sense as praising an arrow or a saddle. She let the matter rest; she was Zevaron's guide, not the guardian of his manners.

One afternoon, Zevaron reined his mare beside Chinzhukog's sturdy tundra horse and opened a conversation about the merits and ancestry of the breed. Shannivar, riding Radu a little distance behind, did not intend to overhear the exchange, although there was no presumption of privacy under the open sky. Radu's walking pace, although slower than her silken gait, outstripped the shorter strides of the tundra horses. Within a short time, Shannivar had drawn near to Zevaron and Chinzhukog, and they were no longer discussing horse breeding.

". . . the stone-drake," Zevaron's words came clearly to her. "Where exactly was it seen? How far from the village? You are certain it came from the mountains where the comet—the *white star*—fell?"

Shannivar could not make out Chinzhukog's answer, only the reluctance of his lowered eyes.

Zevaron did not seem to notice. "Did any person, a child perhaps, see it fall?" He pressed on, stumbling on unfamiliar Azkhantian words as he asked about the deformed babies and mutilated reindeer, and whether any in the village had strange dreams or visions.

Why could Zevaron not see the anguish his questions caused? Shannivar fumed inwardly. This was too much! Was it possible he did not know that a curse, spoken aloud, gained in potency? The stone-dwellers could not be so different in their nature as to be ignorant of all decency. The Snow Bear chieftain had already told their story for the entire gathering to hear. Why force his son to recite the agonizing details once more?

Despite her disapproval, Shannivar recognized the relentless hunger behind Zevaron's questions. She had seen his face in the tent on top of the *enarees'* promontory just before he slammed his hand down on the stone-drake. She had seen the shifting play of darkness and light behind his eyes. She had heard the determination in his voice, the unspoken vows he would keep at the cost of his own life. Something more than human ambition drove him.

It reminded her of the way Tabilit's will had taken hold in her own spirit. Understanding that, she could not condemn Zevaron for faithfulness to his own gods.

All the same, Shannivar took Zevaron aside when they had stopped for the night and the western sky glowed like embers. One of the Snow Bear men had found a fine campsite with a grove of willow surrounding a natural spring that kept the grasses lush. The horses and pack ponies had been watered and hobbled to graze. The reindeer lay close together, eyes half-closed, legs tucked under their bodies, as they chewed their cud. As Shannivar and Zevaron walked past, Eriu lifted his head, ears pricked, a stalk of feathergrass hanging from his jaws.

Shannivar laid her hand on Zevaron's arm. He turned toward her, and she felt his response as if through her own body. They were alone, with the horses between them and the rest of the camp. "Zevaron," she said, speaking softly yet firmly, "you must not ask the Snow Bear men to speak of the stone-drake and other such things."

"Why not? Everyone at the gathering knew about them. I am not asking anyone to reveal a secret."

"You speak of secrets? You, who tell your own story only in mysterious hints?"

"My history is not the issue here. The situation in the north is another matter. Do you suggest I go blind into enemy territory? Or is it forbidden to ask questions?"

"It is *cruel*, surely you must see that!" she said hotly, then reined her temper under control, lest their voices be overheard. She did not want the discussion to turn into a public argument. "These men have suffered greatly and now you remind them of what they must return to. At least, let them have a little peace on this journey. It will end all too soon."

Dusky red flushed Zevaron's face, expressing shame rather than anger. "You are right. I have thought only of my own need for information and not of the effect of my words. But—surely you must agree—it is better to learn as much as possible of what I may face." He shook his head. "Preparation is half the battle, or is that not true on the steppe?"

"In a physical fight, certainly. But in the realm of magic, a man's own mind can be turned against him."

"I am not unprotected."

"So you think."

"So I know."

Shannivar stared at Zevaron. How could any man except an *enaree* safeguard himself from supernatural malevolence? Understanding seeped into her thoughts. Each people had its own defenses against evil. His must be powerful indeed. "If you would learn more," she suggested, "you would do better to take your questions to Bennorakh."

"Bennorakh? Why, what could he tell me?" Zevaron sounded snappish. "He has never been in the north."

"You once spoke of ancient legends," Shannivar pointed out, "of Fire and Ice, of the sorcery of Khored the King. Your Khored had just such protection as you speak of, did he not? Just as every land has its own gods and its own customs, so it has its own demons. If we go now to a land beset by that ancient evil, would it not be better to seek advice from one who is learned in such matters?"

For a long moment, Zevaron gazed at her. In his expression, she read astonishment, although quickly masked. "I thought," he said slowly, "from the way you look at your shaman, that you did not like him."

Shannivar wanted to laugh. One did not like or dislike an *enaree*. His kind were set apart from other people, neither men nor women, living half in the ordinary world and half in one she could only imagine. They were to be pitied as much as feared, but always respected. "Bennorakh has lived among the Golden Eagle people since I was a child. I do not always understand what the gods tell him, but he has always been their faithful messenger. He has come with us for their reasons and not his own."

"And you?" He turned to her, and the air between them shimmered as if a wave of heat had suddenly arisen from the earth. "Do you come for the reasons of your gods, too?"

"I am called, even as you are."

"No, not as I," he answered in a tone that was terrible in its desolation. "By the Most Holy, I hope not as I."

One day melted into another, and only the slow waning of the moon and the shortening of the days hinted of the season's passage. The party settled into a comfortable routine of travel and rest, of silence and song, the relentless rhythms of waking, tending to the animals, riding, hunting, and settling for the night in a place very much like the last. After his initial missteps, Zevaron made friends among the Snow Bear men, in particular Chinzhukog, the chieftain's son. The difficulties of language quickly gave way to Zevaron's willingness to learn and his good humor when he made mistakes. The Snow Bear men sat with him, chanting the legends and lineages of their tribe. In turn, they pressed Zevaron for knowledge of his own people and his travels. Like Shannivar, they were particularly fascinated by his tales of life at sea. None of them had seen any body of water larger than a lake, and the notion of endless gray-green waves struck them as exotic, yet almost laughable.

They passed through the territory of one clan and then another, sometimes stopping for a night of hospitality and the telling of tales. Those who had not attended the *khural* this year were eager for news. They peered at Zevaron with shy curiosity, and now and again a boy of two or three would dart out, touch Zevaron's hand, and race away, giggling. Zevaron, far from being affronted, would throw back his head and laugh. From his saddlebags, he would produce a packet of sticky Denariyan sweets, which he presented to the child's mother, to smiles all around.

At one such stop, the chieftain made such a serious effort to buy Eriu to improve his breeding stock that Shannivar urged a timely departure before the man decided to honor the old tradition of horse-stealing.

Riding side by side, Shannivar and Zevaron passed the time by telling one another stories, legends and holy tales, as well as incidents from their own lives. Shannivar sang the ballad of Aimellina daughter of Oomara, who died at the hands of the Gelonian invaders.

Zevaron related how he, a man of Meklavar, came to a friendship with a Gelonian noble. Briefly, as if he feared sounding boastful, he told of saving Danar from the Ar-King's assassins without any idea that Danar's royal father had been given custody of Tsorreh. "Danar and I—I guarded him, for her sake, because she had come to love him like a second son. She found goodness even in Gelon. I wish she had been right! The last time I saw her alive, she gave me—gave me—" He broke off suddenly. His voice trembled, not with emotion but with physical effort. His face flushed. Gasping, he forced out the words, "—gave me a treasure of our people."

For a time, he said no more. His breathing softened, and his color returned to normal. Whatever his difficulty in speaking of this treasure, the parting gift of a mother he so clearly loved, Shannivar understood the sharpness of his grief. She did not press him further. From her own experience, she knew that the pain of loss would subside in time. She thought of his mother, dying in a hostile land so far from her people.

"She must have had a great heart."

"She is here when I speak of her to you," Zevaron said. "I have not been able to say her name aloud since—but you, you understand. Have you also lost family?"

Shannivar could not remember her own mother, who had died giving birth to her, and she had already passed her womanhood ritual when her father was killed in a Gelonian raid. Grandmother had been parent and matriarch to her, and now Shannivar would never see her again. *Nor Mirrimal . . .* Grief rose in Shannivar's breast, but whether her own grief or Zevaron's, she could not tell. He gazed at her with a mixture of curiosity and suspicion. He must be thinking how easy it was to accuse him of keeping secrets while guarding her own.

"You are right," she said. "We have both lost kin and heart-kin. And homes."

"Will they not miss you?" Zevaron asked. "Your clan? Your family?"

"I would not have returned to the Golden Eagle anyway."

"Why did you come with me? I cannot believe it was only out of duty. Is there something in the north that draws you, too? Something you have kept secret?"

Does he think the stone-drake spoke to me as well?

"When, as a child, I learned the ballads of Saramark, I prayed that I, too, might be chosen for such a destiny," she said. "Tabilit has woven together the threads of our lives for a time. We are comrades on the road. I do not know what my part will be, or if we seek the same goal. I know only that something I have longed for all my life waits for me."

After a long pause, Zevaron said, so quietly she could not be sure she heard rightly, "It is not good to be alone."

As they traveled on, Shannivar finished the last of her stores of bittergrass and star-eye, herbs used by fighting women to prevent pregnancy. She gathered more, although the plants she found differed in subtle ways from the ones she knew. She continued to brew them out of long custom.

The Moon of Stallions passed, and the Moon of Fire Leaves as well. Soon a new crescent of light would herald the Moon of Frost and the turning of the season to winter. The land grew more rugged, with broken hills and steep-walled canyons formed by swift-flowing streams. The bones of the hills jutted out from the thinning grasses. Antelope were fewer, but there were plenty of rabbits and marmots to hunt.

On the day the Snow Bear men announced they had passed into their own territory, they set up camp early. The horses grazed contentedly a little distance from Shannivar's *jort,* where she and Zevaron sat beneath the rolled-up door flap. Dinner, a small antelope Shannivar had brought down with a single arrow, roasted over the cookfire.

"I am curious," Zevaron said. "How do the Snow Bear men know the boundaries of their territory? I see no difference."

"Do you not know your own land?" She made a fist and tapped him gently on the arm.

He shook his head. "Perhaps you nomads have such a sense, but I must rely on outer signs—a river, a mountain, a city—to know where I am. At sea, we used the coastline and sometimes the stars. Someday, I would like to take you to Meklavar and show you its treasures. Not gold and precious stones such as the Gelon prize, but the library, the castle with its great window of colored glass that shines like molten jewels, the ancient temple set high within the mountain."

"My people do not care for cities of stone," she said, "but I would willingly visit yours."

"I hope," he said. "I hope it will be possible. Someday."

"There is the small matter of the Gelon."

"The Gelon, yes." His brows drew together. For a long moment, he fell silent.

"Shall we fight them together, do you think?" she said, trying to lighten the moment. What she meant was that if he returned from the north a great hero, covered in glory and celebrated in song, the Council at the next *khural* would surely give greater weight to his proposed coalition with Azkhantia.

"If the chieftains would not ally with Isarre, I cannot hope for their help, not even if you plead my case. But Azkhantia may not be the only force capable of defeating the Ar-King. Somewhere, there must be . . ." His gaze flickered to the north, his face tightening. She could not tell what he was thinking, but when she spoke to him again, he smiled.

After climbing steadily all day, the party came out onto a high rocky plain. The night air was very clear, and the stars burned bright in the moonless sky. A cold wind swept down from the north. When it was time to set up camp, they found neither tree nor rock for shelter. The horses stood together, tails clamped against their rumps, facing away from the wind according to the wisdom of their kind.

Shannivar unrolled the extra layers of felt around her *jort*. The felt was thick, springy beneath her fingers. She remembered sitting with Mirrimal and Kendira, beating the fibers and singing. How long ago that seemed, how far away.

Somehow, young Chinzhukog found enough

dried reindeer dung from a previous caravan to make a small fire. The flames fluttered in the shifting gusts and lasted just long enough to prepare tea before guttering out. They ate their communal meal cold — a mixture of cheese, *bha*, and parched grain moistened with a little *k'th* — and then prepared for sleep. Bennorakh disappeared into his *jort,* and the Snow Bear men, even more taciturn than usual, retreated to their own shelters.

Shannivar finished the last of the tea, savoring the richness of the butter on her tongue. While the nights had been warm, Zevaron slept outside or in his flimsy trail tent. It would have been mildly scandalous for him to share Shannivar's *jort* while the weather was fine. They were not kin, nor were they betrothed, but the steppe had one unforgiving rule in the bitter cold: live together or die.

Why then did she feel shy about speaking? It was not as if she proposed to take him into her bed as well as the warmth of her *jort*. Who cared what the Snow Bear men thought, when they had not invited the outlander to share their own shelter? As for Bennorakh, the *enarees* had their own ways of judging men and women.

Zevaron looked both startled and relieved when she suggested he pass the night in the *jort*. He had been having a difficult time getting his tent set up in the wind. The last of the cookfire embers had gone out, leaving the camp in near darkness.

"What about the horses?" he asked. "Will they be all right?"

"Oh, for them this is a brisk autumn breeze,

nothing more. In bad weather, when we are in *kish-lak*, the wintering-place, they have shelter against the worst storms."

"I do not think my poor horse would survive such a winter."

"Most beasts do. It is only men who do not have the sense to come in out of the wind. Do you mean to stand there all night?"

Shannivar secured the door flap behind Zevaron. Politely, he avoided stepping directly on the threshold, which would have broken its protection against evil spirits. He had learned some manners, then.

The familiar smells of wool and cedar and trail dust filled the *jort*. By comparison to Grandmother's *jort*, the space seemed sparsely furnished. If this were a family dwelling, the areas for men and women would be divided by the central hearth.

Shannivar touched Zevaron's arm. "Here is a carpet to keep out the earth's chill, and there are extra blankets if you need them."

She prepared her own bed and slid out of her outer clothing, her eyes averted. With her skin as well as her ears, she sensed the rustle of Zevaron's movements, the faint sigh of his breathing, and the sounds as he settled his body on the carpets. The air was warmer because there was another person to share it.

Chapter 22

THE land rose, each range of hills higher than the one before. From time to time, Shannivar glimpsed distant gray-purple mountains. They set up their camp in the failing twilight beside an old well, its stones so eroded and crumbled as to be barely recognizable. This place was well known to the Snow Bear people as a reliable water source.

Shannivar and Zevaron worked together, putting up the *jort* and tending to the horses. Bennorakh retreated into his own *jort*, going about his own mysterious business, while the Snow Bear men prepared the evening meal.

As the last light seeped away from the western sky, Zevaron wandered to the northeastern edge of the camp. His back to the cooking fire, he peered into the featureless dark. Shannivar felt drawn to him, he looked so proud and lonely at the very edge of the light.

He pointed to the sky. "Look! Look there!"

Above the northern rim of the world, Shannivar

made out a faint glow. It grew stronger moment by moment, flickering like distant flames of green and red. The flames merged, spreading across the sky. The light shaped itself into an arch as additional ribbons of color appeared, slowly brightening. Then they folded back on themselves. As she watched, transfixed, they merged into a radiant curtain.

"What—what is it?" she asked, her voice half-choked with awe. Surely this rapture unfolding above her must be the door flap to Tabilit's own country.

"I do not know."

"It is the Light of the North." Chinjizhin came to stand beside them. "We call it Tabilit's Veil. It is said that births and weddings under such a sky are greatly blessed."

For long moments, they watched the curtain wave and swirl overhead. The lower edges seemed to catch fire, flaring red and orange. Blues and purples appeared as points of brilliance. The diaphanous display rippled faster, as if caught in a celestial storm. The sky ignited with swirling color.

A hush fell over the watchers. Shannivar's heart ached. In her mind, she saw the draperies part to reveal a far country, like the one she sometimes glimpsed when the rising sun pierced mountains of cloud. She had yearned then to spread wings like her totem, the Golden Eagle, to rise above the earth and sail through those canyons of light to the lands beyond.

"How could I have doubted the words of the *te-Ketav*?" Zevaron murmured, his words for himself alone. "How else could there be such glory in the world?"

Shannivar and Zevaron had drawn together as they watched the shimmering display. She felt his warmth on her face. Almost, she could hear the beating of his heart. No, it was not his heart, but her own, and for a moment there was no difference.

In wonderment, she turned to him, and they gazed at one another in the multi-hued light. His breath was on her skin. His heart beat within her body.

Truly, she had been guided to this moment by the spirit of Saramark, by Tabilit herself, by the thousand tiny decisions that might have turned her path in another direction. She might have let two strangers go on their way, or she might have returned to Golden Eagle clan with Rhuzenjin, or she might have joined some other clan as an unattached warrior . . . She might have died at the Gelonian fort or in any of a dozen raids. Might have let Zevaron go up to the *enarees'* promontory on his own.

There was but one small step yet to take, one veil to sweep aside. She reached out her hand and his fingers curled around hers. An absurd joy bubbled up in her like a never-failing spring. She wanted to laugh aloud.

Together they moved toward the *jort*. Behind them, the Snow Bear men began chanting in praise of Tabilit's gifts, petitioning the goddess for protection.

Inside the enclosed darkness of the *jort*, diffuse light sifted through the smoke hole. Zevaron put his hands on her shoulders, and she moved into his embrace. Her skin tingled with the pressure of his arms tightening around her, the muscled length of his body pressed against hers.

His mouth was surprisingly soft and warm. She had been kissed by men before, and lain with them, but never with such delirious care, such delicately paced arousal. Here she felt no frantic haste, but a deep awareness of each moment. Each movement of his lips on hers, each touch of his hands, each curve of his body carved itself into her memory.

They piled the carpets into a single luxurious layer, then slipped out of their clothing and beneath a shared blanket. She was as eager to explore his body as he was hers. In the purification tent, they had stolen glimpses of one another, but now she could touch and taste him as well.

She rolled him on his back and stretched out on top of him. He put his hands on her buttocks, pulling her closer. Between her parted thighs, she could feel the hardness of his erection. Her own body was ready, moist and swollen, but she wanted to draw out the moment, to savor every part of him. To remember this night forever.

The skin of his torso was warm and smooth, except for the surprisingly soft hair along the center of his chest and downward. Burying her face in the angle between his neck and shoulder, she inhaled his masculine scent. He smelled of the trail and like other men, yet unlike. Cushioning her teeth with her lips, she took a mouthful of his skin and bit down. He gasped, shuddering. From his reaction, this was not a common form of love-play among his people, but from his breathing, she could tell he enjoyed it.

She planted little kisses, sometimes with her lips alone, sometimes with tongue and gentle teeth, in a line down the center of his body. Like most young women who had fought against the Gelon, she'd had her share of celebration afterward, usually after too much *k'th*, but she had never got so drunk that she could not remember the lovemaking she particularly enjoyed. One lover had delighted her with running his hair and lips up and down her body. By his soft moans, Zevaron found the experience as pleasurable.

After a time, he hooked one leg around her back and rolled both of them over. He laced his hands in her hair, tipping her head back to cover her throat in unbelievably soft kisses. Each touch of his lips spread ripples of sensation over her skin. He went farther down, between her breasts, pausing at each nipple. Her breath caught in her throat. She wanted him to stop, to slide into her now, *now*, and yet she also wanted each moment to last.

The farther down on her body he went, the slower and more sensual his kisses became. He breathed across her skin and her entire body quivered.

Yearning built up deep within her, spreading out from the sweet aching between her thighs. In an instant, he lifted himself, and then he entered her, not all in one stroke, but with a rhythmic, rocking motion, easing in and then out. Each thrust was deeper, and there seemed to be no end to them.

She dug her fingers into his buttocks, pulling him deeper inside her body. His muscles flexed and hardened as he pressed against places she had not known existed inside her.

Oh, now!

She was on fire, in an agony of impatience. Any moment, the building storm would break, flooding all through her, and yet each heartbeat, each racing pulse, carried her further.

Just at the moment when she thought she could bear it no longer, a storm of pleasure ignited where their bodies joined. It surged and pulsed all through her. She felt herself as a stream of melting intensity, as if she had been seized and swept into an endless sky of light.

Zevaron shuddered, and Shannivar felt his breath as if it were her own, his wordless cry issuing from her own throat.

The crest of ecstasy peaked and began to fall away, but only for an instant, a heartbeat, a single exhale of amazement before it flared up, as powerful as before. She gave herself over to it, and this time, she sensed, it was her orgasm that transported them both. Zevaron was in her body, in the soaring currents in her mind, in her heart. Her vision went white, then filled with colors that paled the lights of the north.

My blessing upon you, my children. Words formed in her mind, dissolving as she came back to her senses. Laughter spilled from her. He was laughing inside her, outside her, along with her. He said something in his own language, and she did not care what it was.

Spent, he rolled off her and onto his side, one arm still holding her. A slight shift, and he rested his head on her shoulder. Her arms went around him.

She felt utterly content. She trailed her fingertips over the smooth skin of his shoulder. She felt the firm, elastic texture of his muscles, a softening of the indefinable tension that never seemed to leave him. He murmured in pleasure. Smiling, she continued stroking him, over the flatness of his shoulder blade and the bony tips of his spine, like a chain of nubbly pearls.

When her fingers slid over a ridge of harder tissue, she paused. She had seen those criss-crossed scars during the purification ritual. From her own experience with battle wounds, she knew what kind of injury would cause them, how deep the slashes must have been. How deliberate. The scars were white and some years healed, but they were not the work of a blade, not the way they followed the contours of his back.

Not a knife. A whip. A whip laid on again and again, slicing skin and muscle, laying bare the bone underneath.

"Don't stop," he whispered.

She had not realized that her hand was now still, resting on the hieroglyphics of pain etched in his flesh. She wanted to ask and yet did not know how. Would the telling open old wounds, not of the body but of the spirit?

Gelon whipped their slaves, beat them mercilessly and sometimes unto death, or so it was said. Had Zevaron been a Gelonian slave?

He shifted, raising himself on one elbow. She felt his gaze on her. Questioning, testing, demanding. Demanding what? That she not shrink from what must be asked? She lifted her chin. "I want to know about your scars, how you got them. Will you tell me?"

His breath left his body in a rush. In the near dark, she felt him nod. He lowered himself to lie once more on his back, no longer touching her.

So alone, she thought.

"You have heard how my mother and I escaped the fall of Meklavar and made our way to Gatacinne, in Isarre. How the city came under Gelonian assault. She was taken prisoner and then sent by ship to Gelon. To Aidon, where I found her four years later. What I did not tell you is that I tried to find her before she left Gatacinne. The city was in turmoil— Gelonian soldiers and Isarrans fighting in the streets, the port on fire, buildings burning everywhere."

He paused. She felt how the memories crowded around him, enshrouded him. His voice turned hoarse, as if with remembered smoke. "Before the attack began, we had been housed separately. She was in the Governor's mansion, and I was in a barracks with the young men. I didn't like us being apart, but we were dependent on the hospitality of her kinsmen and in no position to demand anything. It turned out I was right. When the fighting began, the Gelon targeted the mansion. It was one of the first places they captured. I couldn't get to her in time. I couldn't—"

Meklavar had come under Gelonian rule four years ago, or was it five? Shannivar tried to imagine Zevaron then, barely grown to manhood, alone in a strange city, cut off from the one person he knew, fighting against men older and more experienced. He was lucky to have survived.

"I heard that a foreign lady fitting her description was on a ship setting out for Verenzza. That's a Gelonian port. I had no money for passage to follow her. I went down to the wharves, and—what happened next doesn't matter. It was a stupid, impossible scheme. I was caught up in a Gelonian raid and became fodder for their oar-ships."

"Taken prisoner?"

"Taken slave. And the first law of the slave—" Zevaron drew a breath, and in that silence, Shannivar heard the echoes of the lash.

"—is that the masters will do whatever they wish, whenever they wish—"

In Shannivar's mind, parallel lines of fire seared his skin. The pain took his breath away. He hunched over and tried to cover his head. Back-handed, the lash struck again, knotted strips of leather biting deep. They landed on Zevaron's back, too fast and heavy to count. He tried to twist away, but his tormentor kicked his legs out from under him. Within a few minutes, his back and shoulders had turned into a mass of cuts, some of them clear down to the bone.

"—simply because they can," he finished.

She breathed in his pain, his bitterness. In her heart, she understood the Zevaron he had been, the boy struggling for the breath to scream, but all that came were sheets of agony, cold and burning at the same time. The hiss of the lash filled his ears. Tears spilled down his cheeks, and he felt the sticky warmth of blood as each new blow landed. *Sweet Mother, he was being flayed alive.*

She reached out and rested one hand on his

cheek. A shudder passed through him. With a sound that might have been a sob, he curled on his side, facing away from her. She moved closer, fitting her body to the curve of his back. Her breasts pressed against those terrible scars. She thought how her breasts might someday nourish a child and provide the sustenance of life. If only, in some illogical way, her woman's body might somehow lift his pain, draw it out as she might draw out venom from a wound, and then change it into a blessing.

His back was adamant, unyielding. On impulse, she shifted her position. Gently, with her heart in every movement, she pressed her mouth against first one line of scars and then the next. Her lips followed the gnarled and corded ridges. She tried to put into each kiss all the tenderness she could express. Over and over, she traced the pattern of his suffering, his humiliation, and his despair. As she worked her way along the lines of indurated tissue, she left a trail of tears as well as kisses.

Finally she came to the end. Of scars, of kisses, of tears, she could not tell. In the pit of her stomach, she felt a silence. There was nothing more she could do, except to hold him.

She had slipped her top arm around Zevaron's waist as she pulled herself to him. Now she felt his hand tighten around her arm. Against her belly, the hardness of his spine and muscle softened. They moved as one with his breathing.

Gradually the movement faded, until he lay almost inhumanly still. As still as a stalking predator, as still as its prey. He gripped her hand, her arm folded under his. They lay in this position for what seemed like half the night, with only the pressure of his fingers betraying that he did not sleep.

The stillness broke when he took a shuddering breath. "That . . ." he began, "that was not the worst of it." He paused, his back still curved into a protective shell.

He could not bear to say what came next, not face to face, Shannivar thought. Only in the dark, only when turned away from her.

"The whip was nothing. Skin and muscles heal. But the Gelonian demon who did it, he flaunted the token my mother wore braided into her hair. He told me he took it from her dead body."

Pause.

"He laughed when he said it."

Another pause.

"Chalil—the Denariyan captain who rescued me—he said it was the nature of such a man to be cruel, even when there was no profit in it for him. The Gelon, seeing that I recognized the token, had aimed his words like a spear at my spirit. To torment me in any way he could. Or so Chalil said."

Shannivar could not tell if the shuddering ran only through his body or through them both. "But she wasn't dead, was she? She was alive. You found her in Danar's stone-dwelling."

Zevaron bent his head, but Shannivar could not tell if the gesture meant agreement or simple endurance. "Losing her the second time . . . I saw her body with my own eyes."

Each phrase, half-whisper, resonated like a bone-deep drum. Slow, irrevocable. Inevitable. "And there was nothing left for me except . . ."

Except to bring down those who took her from you, not once but twice, Shannivar thought. Tsorreh's had not been a natural death either time; not the end of a life lived well and long, not the sweet-sad farewell, the sure belief that the loved one was now gathered into Tabilit's embrace. Not the mist-white image of Grandmother and Mirrimal, riding their fine horses to the Pastures of the Sky. Mirrimal had died in battle, of her own choice, and no one had used her death to inflict pain on another. Shannivar did not know what to say, how to breathe.

Finally he said, "I've never told anyone. Not the whole story. Not until now. Danar knows a part of it, as did Chalil. You . . ."

Gently, he rolled over, carrying her with him. He kissed her brow, her lips, her breasts, her belly. Although his lips were as soft and mobile as before, there was nothing sexual about the contact. Instead, she felt each kiss as an offering of his deepest self.

"You," he murmured as he rested his cheek against her breast, "now you have all of it. All of me. As much as I can tell. As much as I can give."

It was not me, she started to say, *it was Tabilit's grace upon us both.* But she had not the energy to form the words. The goddess, she felt sure, would understand.

Chapter 23

THE next day dawned clear and mild. The Snow
Bear men were cheered, having interpreted the
Light of the North as a favorable omen. Even Ben-
norakh seemed encouraged. Shannivar, riding at
Zevaron's side, could imagine no greater joy.

Every night brought a new display of lights, each
more glorious than the one before, or perhaps that
was because Shannivar saw them through new eyes.
Soon they would reach the *dharlak*, the northerly
summering-place, of the Snow Bear people, where
they would find the rest of the clan. Zevaron would
continue his search for the stone-drake. She would
go with him.

During that night's routine camp chores, when
the glowing colors rippled across the sky, Shannivar
emerged from her *jort* to sit and watch the display.
She wondered if she would ever tire of the sight. As
before, the curtain grew brighter and folded back
upon itself. Motes of brightness dotted the fabric of
light.

Where the spots of light clustered the thickest, a blemish appeared. At first, Shannivar could not be sure she saw anything amiss. As she watched, however, the shadow deepened. Soon it resembled a jagged tear, as if a knife had slashed through Tabilit's Veil.

Shannivar scrambled to her feet. She could not take her eyes from the widening darkness.

Zevaron rushed to her side. "What is it?"

By this time, the Snow Bear men had noticed. They cried out and pointed aloft. Clearly, they had never seen anything like this before. One of them fell to the ground, cowering, barely able to contain his moans of terror.

"Bennorakh!" Shannivar shook herself free from her own trance. "He will know what to do!"

The *enaree* had anticipated her. He strode to the center of the camp, carrying his dream stick and a handful of something she could not make out. He threw it into the fire, which burst into blue-green flames and gave off clouds of eye-searing smoke.

"Stand back!" he cried, but Shannivar had already inhaled a lungful of the stinging fumes. She broke into a fit of coughing.

Zevaron put his arm around her. "Look!"

She lifted her head. Tears blurred her vision, but she made out a tower of smoke shooting upward from the fire and then spreading. Bennorakh chanted under his breath, his words too hushed for her to make out.

Leaning on Zevaron, she straightened up and rubbed her eyes. Seen through the smoke, the rent in the sky shifted its appearance. A shadow blotted out the stars, a vast, dense coldness. Something moved within that utter absence of light. She could not have told how she knew, only that she felt it the same way she felt its chill.

"Olash-giyn-Olash," she whispered. *The Shadow of Shadows.*

Zevaron stepped away from her, peering through the haze of the smoke. Lifting one hand to his chest, he moved toward the smoke. Just as he reached it, Shannivar shouted in warning. The next instant, the smoke fell away like dust, leaving only a heap of embers. One of the Snow Bear men rushed to build the fire up again.

In the sky, the shadow had grown until it now eclipsed the glowing curtain. No stars shone in its depths. As Shannivar watched, the last remaining sliver of brightness flared and went out. For an instant, the entire northern sky turned dark. A Snow Bear man prayed loudly for Tabilit's protection, and another made a sign to ward off evil.

Shannivar searched the sky for any hint of light. What madness had caused Zevaron to disrupt the magical smoke? And what now might be the consequences of that rash act?

Then, slowly, the stars began to come out. The Snow Bear men greeted with sight with expressions of relief, but it seemed to Shannivar that the heavens' brightness was diminished, as if they had been wounded.

"Outlander! Infidel! Heretic! Fool!" Bennorakh seized Zevaron by the shoulders. Shannivar had never seen him or any other *enaree* threaten physical violence to man or beast. Rarely did they touch another person. Bennorakh's features twisted as he peered into Zevaron's face.

Zevaron did not resist. He seemed bewildered. Something had happened to him in those few brief moments. "What—?" he stammered. "What was that thing?"

"Do you not know?" There was no hostility now in the *enaree's* voice. He released Zevaron. "Do you truly not know? Then may Tabilit and Onjhol and all the gods of your own country spread their mercy upon you." With these words, Bennorakh disappeared into his *jort*.

Shannivar rounded on Zevaron. "What did you think you were doing, interfering with Bennorakh's spell? Are you mad or has the stone-drake's curse stolen your wits?"

"I'm sorry, I didn't mean—

"You could have gotten us all killed! Or opened the way for the Shadow to cast itself over all the sky and land!" When she saw Zevaron's expression, still dazed, and the way he recoiled from her words, Shannivar's anger softened. He was an outlander, after all, not born to the ways of the steppe. Then she remembered the relentless way he had been drawn to the stone-drake, in defiance of the taboo. Then, as now, he acted from ignorance, not malice. If he were to succeed in his own quest, he must be brought to understand the dangers. Darkness was not a good time to discuss such matters.

When Zevaron started to speak again, she laid

her hand upon his arm. "It is late and the night will be cold. Come to bed, beloved. We will speak further about these matters in the daylight."

Shannivar woke suddenly, in darkness. She shivered as she sat bolt upright, her blankets in disarray around her. She had no idea how long she had slept, and was not sure if she was truly conscious or dreaming. At her side, Zevaron murmured in his sleep, broken phrases in Meklavaran.

Moving with a warrior's silent caution, she reached for the case with her bow and arrows, and found it, as always, beside her. Noiselessly, she slipped on her trousers and jacket, shoved her bare feet into her boots, and strung her bow. A quick jerk on the cord loosened the door flap.

The wind had died down, and the stars cast a weak light across the camp. Everything looked as it should: Bennorakh's *jort* standing like a solitary sentinel among the tents of Snow Bear men, the dimly glowing embers of the cookfire, and beyond it, the forms of the horses and reindeer. The Snow Bear man on watch nodded to her and went back to surveying the camp from one side to the other, his posture one of heightened vigilance

Although she could not see the horses clearly, Shannivar sensed them moving about. Her ears caught their breathing, faster and deeper than normal. A hoof stamped, muffled. In her mind, she saw Eriu's head come up, ears forward, the flare of his nostrils, tasting the air.

By day, you are my wings,
By night, you never fail me.

Skirting the fire, Shannivar made her way toward the horses. Something moved at the corner of her vision, black against black. She whirled, arrow nocked, but saw nothing. Her heart pounded. Her nerves sharpened, as if on the brink of a battle. The man on watch came to his feet, his own bow ready. For a long moment, nothing more happened, beyond the restless movement of the animals.

Eriu nickered, low and throaty, at Shannivar's approach. He danced a step sideways, as far as the hobbles would allow. Radu, always the quieter of the two, crowded up against Shannivar. The mare was sweating, trembling. The other animals were jittery, too, even the normally placid reindeer. She remembered how the reindeer had reacted to the stone-drake, the wildness in their eyes.

Moments passed without any sign of present threat. Yet something had made the horses nervous, perhaps some taint of the Shadow. The danger was close, but not immediate. The horses could see and hear and smell danger long before she could. She trusted their senses even more than her own.

One by one, she unhobbled the horses and led them into the center of the camp. After a brief discussion, the Snow Bear guard agreed with the prudence of safeguarding their animals and took charge of the tundra horses.

Zevaron's brown mare dipped her head to lip some bits of dry grass, trampled during the set-up

of the camp. Eriu relaxed a little, although his head
stayed up, ears and eyes alert. Shannivar put the
hobbles back on Zevaron's and Bennorakh's horses,
but not her own two, and went back for the reindeer and ponies.

Two of the ponies were missing.

This puzzled her, for usually the equines stayed
close together, preferring the company of their own
kind. Ponies were usually imperturbable, more so
than horses. Perhaps something had startled them.
Why would only two of the ponies have wandered
off? They could not have gone far, hobbled. Shannivar cursed softly as she peered into the dark expanse. The wind tore at the flickering torch.

She returned to camp with the remaining pones,
to find that the other animals had quieted. Whatever had disturbed them was gone now. She could
tell that much from Eriu's posture.

She told the Snow Bear man about the missing
ponies, and they discussed what to do. No natural
predator could have spirited them away, the Snow
Bear man said. He was frightened; she heard it in
the careful way he avoided any mention of Olash-
giyn-Olash, and the way he said it would be foolhardy to pursue the ponies before daybreak. In this,
she did not argue with him. Even with a torch, it
would be impossible to track the ponies, and a few
hours would in all likelihood make no difference.
Either they had broken their hobbles and bolted, or
they were already dead. She returned to her *jort* for
whatever sleep was left to her.

As usual, and even with the disturbed night, she

was the first to rise. The sky was a sullen, slate gray, as if the sun had lost its potency. She built up the fire for a morning meal and heated water for tea.

In the strengthening light, Shannivar went alone to search for the missing ponies. She bridled Radu, pulled herself on the mare's bare back without taking the time to saddle her, and continued her search.

Of one pony, she found no sign, not even broken hobbles. She spotted the other some distance to the north of the camp. Its body lay in a tangled heap, so that she did not recognize it until she was almost upon it. Radu, normally easy-tempered, snorted and arched her back, clearly unhappy about approaching the distorted carcass.

Shannivar slid to the ground and went up to the body. The pony lay with its stiffened forelegs extended in one direction and hind legs in another, as if its spine had been completely dislocated. Its hide was mottled with irregular black patches that appeared to be charred, yet rimed with frost. It smelled of burned hair and more, something dank and sodden.

She did not want to touch it or force Radu to drag it back to camp, for fear of exposing the mare to whatever had killed the pony—some evil spell or disease. It looked as if a terrible convulsion had broken the pony's back. And those strange sores . . . She had handled livestock all her life and had never seen their like. What could have caused the pony's skin to be both burned and frozen?

The answer whispered through Shannivar's mind: *A stone-drake, a creature of Fire and Ice?*

*   *   *

Shannivar watched Zevaron's face as he bent over
the dead pony, and she knew he thought the same
thing. He rubbed his chest in that gesture she was
coming to recognize. It had something to do with
his awareness of uncanny, magical things.

The rest of the Snow Bear men mumbled among
themselves, shaking their heads. To them, this was
only one more unnatural occurrence. If what Chinjizhin said was true, they had seen far worse in the
bodies of their own dead children.

Bennorakh spent a long time crouched beside
the carcass. On his orders, the others cleared the
ground of grass for many paces around and kept
their distance. Chanting, he covered the body with
chips of resin and colored powders. Chinjizhin
handed the *enaree* a stick lit from the morning fire.
Bennorakh touched it to the twisted spine. For a
moment, Shannivar thought the carcass would not
burn. The flame at the tip of the stick fluttered,
shifting from yellow to the dull red of an ember.
The next moment, the carcass ignited. Perhaps the
incantations fueled the resin chips.

Flames, white and blue, shot skyward. Billows of
steam, glowing like clouds before a summer sun,
filled the air. Shannivar recoiled as the sudden blast
of heat stung her face. The Snow Bear men retreated to a safe distance. Only Zevaron lingered,
his eyes gleaming in the brightness. Bennorakh
raised his arms and shouted. Shannivar did not rec-

ognize the words, only the gesture, half summoning, half supplication.

The carcass was quickly reduced to bits of bone and ash, and the tang of the resin lingered in the air to counteract any residual evil. Although she was not cold, Shannivar shivered, remembering how close she had came to the mutilated body.

They broke camp after redistributing the disassembled *jorts* between their remaining pack animals. The reindeer were much more even tempered than a camel. The ample forage and easy pace of the journey thus far had done much to restore their strength.

Shannivar kept waiting for the sky to lighten, but it never did. Through the morning and well into mid-day, it seemed no brighter than in the hours before dawn. The watery light cast blurred shadows. Only the passing of the terrain and her growing hunger marked the shift to afternoon.

Dusk came swiftly, as if on the wings of an enormous vulture. They had barely enough time to choose a site and put up their shelters before darkness swallowed them up. The western horizon flashed red, and Shannivar's spirits lightened in anticipation. If the luminous curtains returned, Bennorakh's magic had prevailed. But the colors died away, stillborn. There were no more patterns of light across the night sky, no trace of Tabilit's Veil. The shadow had eaten them up, leaving the sky as dark as if they had never existed.

A wind quickened as the temperature fell. The cookfire sputtered out as snow drifted down. Huge wet flakes swirled more thickly with each passing moment. Everyone scrambled to make the camp secure. In the center of the camp, the animals huddled together, horses and ponies and reindeer, their tails turned against the burgeoning storm.

"This is no natural snow!" Zevaron said as Shannivar handed him an armful of rolled carpets.

One of the Snow Bear men darted past the hissing coals. His wail pierced the sound of the wind. Shannivar could not at first make out who it was. She watched, horrified, as he toppled to the earth. *Mother of Horses!* It was Chinjizhin.

As Shannivar reached the Snow Bear chieftain, his arms and legs flailed wildly, scattering snow. Instinctively, she flinched away. His head was thrown back, and even in the heavy snowfall, she could see gleaming crescents of white, all that was visible of his eyes. His skin turned blue-black as one paroxysm followed another. For a long moment, she did not think he was breathing.

Zevaron pushed past her and threw himself to his knees beside the convulsing man. He had snatched up a blanket, which he now placed under the chieftain's head.

"Stay away!" one of the Snow Bear men shouted.

"What are you doing, fool of an outlander? He is demon-touched!"

"Get back, or the demon will seize you, too!"

Clearly terrified, the other Snow Bear men backed away. Some made warding signs against evil. Only Chinzhukog remained beside his father, his face a mask of alarm.

Zevaron showed no sign of fear. Calmly he removed his sash, folded it, and slipped it between the man's teeth.

"Zevaron, please! The risk!" Shannivar pleaded. "Remember the purification ritual! Do not make things worse for yourself. You cannot help him with foolhardy heroism. Come away—"

"There is no need for alarm," Bennorakh said, coming near. "Tabilit smiles upon the man of compassion, even an outlander."

Gathering her courage, Shannivar took a step closer. Zevaron seemed to be well enough as he continued tending to the stricken older man. Surely, if a demon meant to seize him, it would have manifested by now. Her curiosity roused. "What are you doing?"

"Making sure he will not harm himself," Zevaron answered. "The fit will pass and then he will sleep. As soon as we can, we must get him inside and keep him warm."

"How do you know this?"

"I have learned many things in my travels," Zevaron said, gently straightening the chieftain's limbs. The chieftain's thrashing was growing weaker, and his eyes were now completely closed. "The Denariyans say this condition sometimes begins with an injury to the head. It is an illness, not a demonic influence. There is no danger to others, only to the victim himself."

"This did not begin with an injury."

"None that we know of," Zevaron pointed out. "Perhaps he took the hurt some time ago."

"Then he might be demon-touched, after all."

Bennorakh gestured to Chinzhukog and the other Snow Bear men. "Come, take your chief out of the storm, even as the outlander says."

They hurried to comply, perhaps more fearful of the *enaree* than of the man now lying as if deeply asleep.

"Bring him into my *jort*. He will be warmer there than in his tent," Shannivar said, despite her lingering suspicion that this was no natural ailment, any more than the death of the pony had been.

Quickly, Shannivar divided her meager furnishings into the traditional arrangement, a women's side for herself and a men's for the Snow Bear chieftain. When Chinjizhin had been wrapped in blankets, the others retreated to their own tents. Only his son, Chinzhukog, remained.

"I will keep watch over my father. Shannivar daughter of Ardellis, surely Tabilit smiled on the moment we met. May your horses ever be sure and fleet of foot. I thank you for your generosity. And you, too, Zevaron Outlander, for your quick thinking."

Bennorakh had watched the proceedings with a grave expression. After the others retreated to their various shelters, he gestured for Zevaron and Shannivar to approach him.

"You have done well, Zevaron of the ancient race of Meklavar. You once asked my counsel, but the signs were not yet clear. Truly, you face a perilous journey. When the time is right, I will do what I can for you."

"I thank you for your help," Zevaron said.

"Help? I have none to offer. All help comes from Tabilit, Sky-Mother, Horse-Giver. Even an outlander must recognize that no merely human strength can match that which awaits you in the north."

Zevaron bowed his head.

"I will not leave him," Shannivar said, moving closer to his side.

In the dim light, she caught a twinkle in the shaman's eye. "Some things, even the gods cannot stand against."

All night, snow-laced wind battered the sides of the *jort*. The thick felt walls kept out the worst gusts, but tendrils of shiveringly cold damp air managed to seep in through the seams and around the door flap. Shannivar slept alone that night, coiled in layers of blanket. Zevaron kept to the men's side, along with the Snow Bear chieftain and his son. Before going to sleep, they had built up a small fire in the central hearth and banked the embers well, so the *jort* retained a measure of warmth.

The next morning, Shannivar awoke stiff and cold. The lattice still quivered under the force of the gale. She sat up, shivering, and pulled on her jacket and boots. The embers had burned down to a drift of frozen ash. Zevaron was gone, but Chinzhukog sat at his father's side. The older man did not rouse, although he snored gently.

She stumbled outside to relieve herself, check on the horses, and exchange a few words with the others. Despite having passed the night in a trail tent, they looked well enough but grave. They gave her a pot of hot buttered tea and a few live coals to start her fire again.

Zevaron came back just as Shannivar finished reviving the hearth fire. He carried an armful of deadwood, although some of it was damp. With the drier wood, the fire soon warmed the interior of the *jort*. Shannivar passed cups of tea to Zevaron and Chinzhukog, set another pot of snow to melt, then added a double handful of parched barley and slivers of *bha*.

"Your father does not wake?" she asked Chinzhukog. It was more a polite statement than a question.

"Not this whole night," the young man said.

Throughout the day, the snow came down and the wind had an edge like a knife. It seemed as if the Moons had been flung out of order, catapulting from Frost directly to Icefall.

In time, Chinjizhin roused. He tried to speak, but his words were garbled, and he clearly lacked the strength to rise. Under Bennorakh's direction, Shannivar, Zevaron, and Chinzhukog took turns spoon feeding Chinjizhin a thin gruel of *bha* simmered into a pulp in melted snow, then seasoned with butter.

They remained in camp for some days. Each morning, one or another of them went out to hunt for fresh meat — all except for Zevaron, who had no skill. He took on the extra duties of seeing to the reindeer and checking their hooves and antlers. The males had already shed theirs.

Chinjizhin improved slowly. Whether from the ministrations of the *enaree*, the rest in relative warmth, or the simple passage of time, he regained his speech. He was able to sit up and to handle bowl and knife. His wits returned, although without any memory of that terrible night. Once or twice he awoke from dreams and sat, shivering and rigid, until dawn.

Eventually, the worst of the blizzard passed. The sun, breaking through the tattered clouds, shone weakly at first. The horses pawed through the snow for what grass there was, and the reindeer nipped the stubble.

Shannivar stroked and soothed first one horse and then another. Each had reacted to the eerie storm according to its temperament. Eriu was vigilant, flaring his nostrils in the manner of a stallion guarding his herd. Zevaron's little mare looked miserable, with her head down and eyes listless. Shannivar did not think the poor beast would survive the winter.

Before returning to the *jort*, Shannivar paused and tested the air. This snow would not hold, she thought, but more would come, perhaps not immediately, but surely. It would be a long, harsh winter, even in *kishlak*.

Chinzhukog and Bennorakh waited for her inside the *jort*. "My father cannot travel far or fast," the young man said with unusual firmness. "But it would be worse to remain here. I do not even know if he can survive the journey to our summering-place. It is too far north."

From the way the Snow Bear chieftain nodded, he and his son had already discussed the situation and come to an accord. They both glanced at the *enaree* for his reaction. Bennorakh sat still, eyes not quite focused, as if attending to some inner voice.

Before the *enaree* could respond, the door flap lifted and Zevaron entered. A gust of air, not as cold as it had been but still chill enough, swirled in his wake. His gaze took in the taut faces of the other men, their expectant expressions. He bowed politely before asking, "What's going on?"

"A change of plans." Shannivar explained that to reach the *kishlak* of the Snow Bear tribe was beyond the strength of their chieftain.

Chinjizhin added, speaking slowly and heavily, "We must make for our wintering-place, which lies to the east. We run the risk that the rest of the clan will still be at the summering-place, but I do not think so. These storms had their birth in the north, so our people will most likely not have lingered there. With such an early winter, they will already have departed."

Zevaron drew in his breath. Shannivar felt the sudden leap of tension in his body, the flare of disappointment. For a moment, she feared he might rage off into the north by himself. Bennorakh watched him with a cool, assessing gaze.

After only the briefest pause, Zevaron regained his poise. "I would not wish my own business to place the health of such a worthy man at risk. Indeed, if I had my wish, no one but myself would suffer from my own choices." He bowed again in the Azkhantian fashion to Chinjizhin. "I am at your service."

"If it is the will of Tabilit, you will find what you seek at the proper time," Chinjizhin replied gravely. "Until then, the hospitality of the Snow Bear is yours."

Zevaron might not understand the terms of hospitality, and he might wrestle with his own frustrated desires, but Chinjizhin offered them as safe and comfortable a winter as possible. Regardless of his previous status as outlander, Zevaron would now be accepted as one of them. He would lack for nothing when it was time to leave next spring. The Snow Bear people would supply him with suitable clothing and weapons, everything necessary to survive the brutal winter; they would ply him with songs, include him in the men's gossip, and teach him whatever skills he wished to learn. No one would turn away his questions, for he now had as much right to hear the entire history as any tribal member. It was a gracious and generous gift, even if Zevaron did not yet know it.

Chapter 24

CHINJIZHIN'S stamina was unreliable at first. Each time he seemed to grow stronger, he faltered. Bennorakh tended him assiduously, but Shannivar thought the *enaree* looked worried. They traveled slowly, often resting at midday.

The wintering-place of the Snow Bear tribe lay near the extreme south of their territory, at the end of a long U-shaped valley. A chain of shallow lakes stretched along the wide valley floor, and the rocky sides rose gently at first and then steeply. Stones, some larger than a camel, dotted the slopes. Stands of coniferous trees alternated with fields where herds of reindeer and white-coated tundra horses grazed. The air tasted different here, as if snow were never far away.

A dozen or more aggregates of extended families had already settled into the encampment. The area looked as if it had been in use for a long time, although Shannivar saw nothing like the ancient stone walls of the Golden Eagle *kishlak*. These walls were low and crumbling, fit only for livestock pens.

As they approached the *kishlak*, a handful of young men galloped out to meet them. Their sturdy tundra horses, shaggy with their winter coats, scrambled over the rocky terrain as nimbly as goats.

"Hi-yeh! Hi-yeh! May this day be lucky!" they cried. "May your horses never stumble!"

"May you father many sons!" The ailing chieftain sat taller in the saddle as they drew near.

Shouting out more greetings, the young riders circled Chinjizhin and his party. Eriu lifted his head, prancing until Shannivar calmed him. Zevaron held himself like a man expecting trouble.

"These are hunters, not warriors," Shannivar said in trade-dialect. Zevaron looked at her, a question behind his eyes. "This far from the borderlands, there are no Gelon to fight."

"Your tribes do not make war on one another?"

Shannivar shrugged. "They raid for livestock, nothing more. With the land here so harsh, who can afford to create enemies out of cousins and allies?"

As Zevaron turned his gaze back to the riders, she realized she had answered the wrong question. He had not been concerned about an imminent attack, he had been asking whether these men might be a fighting force to enlist in his own cause. Quickly she turned her thoughts away. He was a fool to hope that any temptation of glory might lure these men away from their already struggling clan. More than that, she did not like to imagine him the sort who looked upon others only in terms of the uses he might have for them, without any regard for honor or tradition. No, Zevaron was not like that. The weariness of the journey, the anxieties of Chinjizhin's illness and the rending of Tabilit's Veil, the strange and ominous things they had seen and sensed, all these had unsettled her mind. Such thoughts had no power except what she herself granted them.

The enthusiasm of the young Snow Bear men tempered into diffidence at the sight of three strangers. They greeted Shannivar with courtesy, Zevaron with reserve, and Bennorakh with an eagerness that bordered on reverence.

"Honorable Father," one of the youths addressed Chinjizhin with a gesture of sorrow, "bitterness sits upon my tongue. Our own *enaree* no longer walks among us. Three nights after you departed for the *khural*, he entered a smoke dream—"

"To see into the broken mountains—" another interrupted, subsiding at a glare from the first, "or so it was said."

"—and when he did not emerge, I myself went to see how he fared. I found him as stiff and cold as if the winds of the Moon of Darkfall had swept through his *jort*. And yet," he dropped his voice, "the embers in his hearth were still warm."

Chinzhukog uttered a keening wail, as did another of the men, but his father sat still and silent, grim-eyed.

Zevaron turned to the chieftain's son. "I am sorry for your loss. Your people have already suffered greatly."

"We bring good news as well," another of the youths said. "An *ildu'amar* has been seen in the uplands. We shall have fine hunting and meat to smoke for the winter."

"*Ildu'amar*?" Zevaron repeated. "I do not know that word."

"It means 'sword-nose,'" Shannivar replied, "but I myself have never seen one. They are creatures of the north."

Chinzhukog explained that the appearance of such prey was an exceptional stroke of luck, for these creatures rarely ventured from their territory in the ever-frozen tundra.

The young riders devoted themselves to making their leader's homecoming as comfortable as possible. Plainly, they were relieved to have Chinjizhin and the others back again.

At the encampment of Chinjizhin's extended family, Shannivar and her party were welcomed by everyone. The Snow Bear clan's *jorts* were of a different style and shape, and the roofs were more sharply peaked than those Shannivar knew. The colors, muted gray and brown, gave the aspect of giant, misshapen, antler-less reindeer. Instead of the felt caps of the south, the women of the Snow Bear wore elaborately folded head scarves that covered not only their hair but most of their faces. Otherwise, their clothing in no way differed from the men's. They all seemed to be married, bound to cookpot and *jort*. Several of them were visibly pregnant, although there were no young children to be seen, only a few shy, half-grown girls.

Chinjizhin's wife was named Ahnzel, a stout, broad-faced woman. She wore white ptarmigan feathers and lapis beads stitched into strips of reindeer hide that hung, like the strings of Bennorakh's amulets, from the neckline of her knee-length jacket. She bowed respectfully to her husband and then bustled him into his *jort*, leaving no doubt in Shannivar's mind who was the real chieftain in that family.

Shannivar and Bennorakh set about erecting their *jorts* where they were bid. Every man in that area, and a few from the others, came over to inspect Eriu and Radu. There ensued a lively discussion of horse breeding, with many pointed glances at the black and hints about the value of an infusion of new bloodlines.

As Chinzhukog had anticipated, storms had swept down on the summering-place. The tribe had waited, hoping the unseasonable cold would pass, debating the wisdom of staying or going to the more sheltered *kishlak*. Their greatest fear had been that Chinjizhin would arrive at the more northerly site and, finding them gone, face another difficult journey with fewer resources. In the end, Chinjizhin's second son had convinced them to trust his father's good sense. Although the son did not say so aloud, none had wanted to remain near the broken mountains.

With great excitement, a hunting party was organized under the leadership of Chinzhukog. The Snow Bear hunters, mostly men but a few women, prepared themselves with spears, arrows, and knives. Shannivar was curious to see what manner of beast the *ildu'amar* might be, for at home, she had hunted nothing larger than antelope. She bound her breasts with special care, for of late they had been tender and fuller than usual. Zevaron came with the party, his skill at archery having improved markedly with regular practice. He rode steady Radu, for his own horse was not fit for a hunt, and the Snow Bear hunters rode their hardy little tundra horses, not fast but immensely strong. Shannivar had to hold Eriu back or he would quickly have outstripped the others.

They rode north, alternating between an easy trot and a walk. The excitement of the hunt infected everyone. Eriu danced with eagerness. Chinzhukog joked with Zevaron, the two men laughing aloud.

At last, they entered the forest. The air, which had been cold and almost tasteless, now filled with pungent scents: the zest of fir and pine, the moistness of the earth, the tang of melted snow flowing over rock, the barely perceptible undertones of animal spoor. Snow draped the piles of leaf debris to muffle the footfalls of the horses. Their snorts and the clinking of bits and harness rings were the loudest sounds. Shannivar studied the tracks made by small hoofed animals, antelope or deer, and also one set she did not recognize: widely-spaced prints of three massive, splayed toes around a central pad.

They heard the "sword-nose" before they saw it, during one of the passages through denser thicket. Something massive was crashing about, snapping dead branches, snorting and grunting. A flutter of breeze carried an unpleasant musky odor. Motioning for silence, Chinzhukog led the hunting party in a circular path, keeping carefully downwind of their prey.

The *ildu'amar* came into view, its massive head raised from where it had been browsing on the trampled branches. Its shoulder was easily as high as a man's head, its four legs thick as trunks, and its short neck joined its body in a hump. The feet were oddly shaped, almost dainty for the size of the creature. Shaggy gray-brown hair covered the thick body. Two tapered horns jutted from the midline of the tapering skull. The larger of the two horns, easily as long as Shannivar's bow, appeared to grow directly out of the creature's nose. Bits of moss hung from the sharp tip.

For a long moment, no one moved, neither human nor beast. The forest seemed so still, Shannivar could hear the wind in the topmost branches. Cautiously, she slipped an arrow into her bow.

The *ildu'amar* rumbled and lowered its head. Its eyes shone like marbles set in deep sockets. Nostrils flared wide in the square muzzle, slitted shut, and flared again. It pawed the ground, throwing up chunks of ice, soil, and decaying leaves.

Shannivar's vision sharpened, turning every detail crisp. The creature's breaths sounded like distant thunder. The next moment, the *ildu'amar* let out a bellow, tipped its head to level the sword horn, and charged directly at her. She had no idea an animal that size could move so fast.

She loosed her arrow. It lodged in the animal's

shoulder, enough to madden it further but not slow it down. Someone yelled a warning, but she was already wheeling Eriu out of the path of the rampaging prey.

The other hunters shouted above the whinnying of their horses. Leaning over the black's neck, Shannivar searched desperately for a way through the nearest trees.

They plunged into the dense, ice-edged shade. The undergrowth here was thin and choked. Patches of bare rock, fractured and eroded by the harsh seasons, dotted the forest floor. The sky flickered above her in flashes of blue. Behind her, the sword-nose bellowed and kept coming.

Close. Much too close.

She swerved the black and pushed him for more speed. Trees stretched into the misty distance, close and dark in every direction except one. Light glimmered through the trunks, suggesting another clearing.

The next moment, horse and rider burst into the open. The earth dropped away down a treeless slope. Eriu somehow managed to keep his balance, although loose stones slipped out from beneath his feet. Shannivar clung to his back, not daring to glance over her shoulder.

Within a few paces, the slope became steeper and rougher, marked by outcroppings of rock and glacier-smoothed boulders. The wind tore the breath from Shannivar's lungs. She could hear nothing above the clatter of the stones.

Eriu, be my wings!

Suddenly, as if her prayer had indeed given him

wings, the black tucked his forefeet and jumped. His body stretched out, perfectly balanced. He soared through space. Shannivar glimpsed an eroded ravine below, like a fissure carved into the living hide of the earth. The angle of the boulder-pocked terrain had hidden it from her sight until that moment. It did not look deep, but the drop would break a horse's legs.

Eriu landed on the far edge. The impact almost unseated Shannivar. She caught herself on his arched neck. By some miracle, her weight stayed centered. Her stomach muscles tightened, her knees dug into the padded saddle flaps, and the next instant she was once more secure.

The *ildu'amar* came pelting down the hillside after them. It did not so much run as it catapulted. Its stubby legs churned, barely keeping it upright as momentum carried it on. With each step, an avalanche of small rocks broke free beneath it. The stones tumbled into the fissure.

Shannivar watched, half in horror, half in disbelief, as the sword-nose rushed toward the stony cleft. The beast seemed to be blind, or else so maddened that it had lost all sense of danger. Surely, the creature must have seen the crevasse by now, yet it made no attempt to slow its breakneck pace. As it approached the edge, it stiffened its legs. By then, it was too late. Nothing could slow that mad descent. One splay-toed forefoot came down on empty air.

For an instant, Shannivar glimpsed the eyes of the *ildu'amar*, no longer opaque but brown as dead leaves. Crazed, desperate. She had seen that look before, in animals too grievously wounded to live. In Mirrimal's eyes, before she died.

The next instant, the beast plunged into the ravine. The shock of the landing shivered through the rock. The *ildu'amar* collided with the far side of the crevasse. The thick body twisted, legs folding, as the beast fell on one side. A sound issued from its heaving lungs, an inarticulate bellow of pain, but also of confusion and despair.

The other hunters clattered up to the edge of the ravine. Snorting and blowing, their mounts slid to a halt. Chinzhukog shouted for the others to make ready their spears.

Grabbing her bow, Shannivar jumped to the ground. Below her, the great beast thrashed weakly and cried out again. From the painful angle of its motionless hind legs, its spine was broken. Even before it fell, it had already been badly injured. Oozing sores marked its exposed side and belly. They looked like unhealed burns, and yet the skin around them was laced with frost.

Shannivar set an arrow and drew her bow. For an instant, she imagined the creature met her gaze. It lay still, and the crazed light in its eyes grew clear. She could almost believe that it understood her intention and gave its consent.

She took careful aim and loosed the arrow. It buried itself deep in the nearer eye socket. A spasm rippled through the body of the great beast. Then, with a barely audible sigh, it lay still.

"A mighty shot!" Chinzhukog cried. The other hunters shouted in praise.

Ignoring the cheers, Zevaron jumped to the ground and crouched at the edge of the ravine, peering down at the fallen *ildu'amar*. His face had fallen into shadow. One of the hunters made a crude comment that the outlander must never have seen a dead animal of that size before, that he must surely be filled with terror. Ignoring the heckler, Zevaron strode along the rocky margin.

A moment later, he found a ramp of eroded rock and fallen debris. Before Shannivar could stop him, he plunged down the slope. Only a madman would have attempted it, for the angle was impossibly steep. The footing, unsure, collapsed beneath him in a rush of stones and dust. He landed neatly on his feet at the bottom.

"Zevaron!" Shannivar called. "What are you doing?"

He gave no sign he had heard her, any more than he had noticed the hunter who'd taunted him. Instead, he hurried to the side of the motionless giant. An arm's length away, his steps slowed, as if some invisible force held him at bay. Eyes narrowing, he bent closer to the great beast, peering at each of the glistening wounds. As he circled around and returned again, she imagined him caught in a spiral current that carried him ever closer to the carcass. One of the hunters made a half-hearted joke that there was nothing more to be done, for the beast was already dead, but no one laughed. Only the restless movements of the horses and the scuffle of Zevaron's boots on the tumbled stone broke the silence.

Eriu stood like a statue, unmoving except for an occasional tremor through his muscles. Shannivar watched Zevaron even more closely, saw the spot to which he returned again and again, and focused her attention there. Something in his posture, the way he seemed *drawn* to the unmoving sword-nose, sent an alarm through her. She had seen him like this before, intent as a stalking cloud leopard, as he had approached the stone-drake. That had been a thing of cursed magic, but this poor dead animal, on the other hand, with its strange injuries . . .

Those frost-rimmed burns.

The sword-nose been mutilated by the same unnatural forces that created the stone-drake and left the pony a twisted carcass. "Zevaron, no! Wait!" she cried out, even as his hand reached out toward the mangled hide.

For a fraction of a second, Zevaron froze, palm flat against the side of the *ildu'amar*. Then golden light flashed beneath his skin. She caught only a glimpse of that subtle radiance—his bared hand and forearm, and the side of one cheek, yet she felt the power as if in her own body. Power and recognition.

He stood up, slow and silent, and turned toward her. The air around him shimmered, gold shading into silver.

A mist billowed up behind her eyes, muting everything she saw—the ravine, the riders on the far side, forest and sky and broken rock, her own arrow still protruding from the eye-socket of the *ildu'amar*, Zevaron himself.

Something condensed in the swirling brightness.

Shannivar's breath stuttered as she caught the shape of a magnificent horse, silver-white on white. Its mane flowed like a river of milk, and its eyes gleamed like slivers of sun. On its back sat a woman, a tantalizingly familiar woman, who lifted one arm in warning. But whether she was Grandmother or Mirrimal or Tabilit herself, Shannivar could not make out.

The next instant, the vision had vanished, as had the golden light beneath Zevaron's skin. A stench rose up from the ravine, of flesh long rotted, and beneath it the reek of something even more foul. Eriu threw up his head, snorting in outrage. One of the hunters cursed loudly.

Zevaron, his mouth twisting in an expression of nausea, retraced his steps to the steep trail. Sliding and scrambling, he climbed out of the ravine.

"We'll get no meat from that *unholy-dead-thing*," Chinzhukog said, using the term that referred to the most serious taboo, a death that poisoned anyone who came into contact with it.

"Should we bring branches, so that the sight of it will not offend the Sky People?" one of the hunters asked, although by his inflection, he was deeply reluctant to come any closer.

After a quick conference, it was decided to leave the beast where it had fallen and to depart as quickly as possible while they still could.

"Shannivar, will your horse jump across to us?" Chinzhukog called.

Shannivar was unwilling to ask Eriu for another such leap, even if it were not over the body of the *ildu'amar*. "I will find an easier crossing."

She rode a short distance north and found a place where the ravine narrowed. Eriu jumped it without problem, and they rejoined the others.

For a time, the party rode on in silence. The day was rapidly drawing to a close. They were tired and far from home, their horses snorting at shadows. They had taken no prey, and Chinzhukog did not want to return without meat, as much for the morale of the hunters as for the needs of the *kishlak*.

They camped northern style, in a single shelter for hunters and horses alike, assembled from downed branches. Simple trail food, *bha* and parched grain boiled in melted snow, furnished their evening meal. The horses were allowed to browse, pawing through the drifted snow and leaves, and then were led into the shelter. The tundra horses had been trained to lie down in a circle, warming the air and keeping off the worst of the wind from the sleepers. Radu refused to enter the shelter, and Shannivar doubted the mare would have lain down willingly. As for Eriu, he paced in the manner of a stallion who scents a cloud leopard, and she judged it best to let him stand guard, unhobbled.

Shannivar lingered in the last glimmering light outside the shelter. She felt more weary than usual, even after a hard ride. Her breasts ached. Above, clouds muffled the stars. The snow glowed faintly, like blue glass from Denariya.

Zevaron came to stand beside her. Something in the fallen sword-nose had troubled him, and something inside him, that fleeting golden glisten, had *answered*.

"I cannot wait for spring," he said after a long moment of silence. "I must go north without delay."

She heard the truth in his words, felt it shiver through all the world around. This she had already known.

An unspoken question hung in the air between them. A hunger, far deeper than the passion of their bodies.

She answered it, "Then I will go with you."

Chapter 25

THE hunting party returned to the wintering-place late the next day, their horses laden with the carcasses of two wild goats. The women took away the meat to prepare it, while the men lingered, bristling with curiosity. Shannivar and Zevaron followed Chinzhukog into his father's *jort*, so that he might have the honor of being the first to hear their story. They found him with Bennorakh.

Chinzhukog related the hunt and its conclusion in the finest dramatic style—the charge of the *ildu'amar*, Shannivar's leap, the strange injuries of the beast, even Zevaron's inspection of it. Shannivar watched Bennorakh's face but could read nothing in his expression. The chieftain looked grave. Clearly, the appearance of a creature tainted by the menace of the north, wandering so close to the *kishlak*, disturbed him. From time to time, his gaze shifted to Zevaron, as if weighing whether the presence of this outlander, with his uncanny bond to such a creature, was a blessing or a curse.

When Zevaron stated his intention to leave for the north as soon as possible, Chinjizhin's uneasiness lightened. He did not seem at all unhappy about the outlander's departure. When Chinzhukog requested the honor of acting as Zevaron's guide, his father protested.

"I cannot allow it! We have too few able young people. This winter will be full of dangers. I would not deprive the clan of even a single one."

He did not add, but everyone understood, *If anything should happen to me, who else will lead our people?*

"It would be shameful to let a stranger venture where we dare not, especially in our own territory," Chinzhukog insisted.

"The outlander will not be alone." The chieftain nodded to Shannivar; Zevaron might be a stonedweller without skill or sense, but *she* was Azkhantian.

"We must use every means to see what lies ahead," Bennorakh said. "Whatever lies in the north now spreads across the land. For reasons of its own, it calls to the outlander. It summons him." He looked at Zevaron. "You know this, or you would not have come so far."

Zevaron raised one hand toward his chest, then lowered it. "It is true. I am bound to the power in the north. Whether it is what my people call Fire and Ice, or yours call the Shadow of Shadows, or else some offspring of that ancient evil, I do not yet know. Perhaps, as I have been told, they are the same. The farther I go, the more strongly I sense it.

Reverend *enaree*, I am in your hands. Show me what I am to do, read me as a book. Give me your guidance and, if you will, the blessing of your gods."

Bennorakh said, with no trace of disapproval, "You would not have come this far except by the will of Tabilit. You, Shannivar daughter of Ardellis, you also have a part in this quest." Shannivar bent her head in acknowledgment.

"If it is the will of Tabilit that my son depart," Chinjizhin said heavily, "then so must it be."

"The way will be revealed," Bennorakh said, speaking to Shannivar and Zevaron. "Therefore, eat and drink nothing this night," for the aroma of roasting meat now wafted into the *jort*. "There is much to be done—and seen."

After the others had eaten, Shannivar and Zevaron made their way to Bennorakh's *jort*. Draperies of snow already covered the ground, and the wind blew heavily through the encampment.

Shannivar ducked beneath the door flap, Zevaron at her heels. Although she had known the *enaree* most of her life, she had not entered his *jort* more than a handful of times. It was very much like any other with its rounded sides and felt-covered walls. A single layer of carpet, so worn the designs were no longer distinguishable, covered the floor, and his small brazier radiated a gentle, smokeless warmth. His dream stick lay across a travel chest, along with several bronze utensils, a bowl, an incense burner, and other things she could not identify in the dim light. A bitter smell tinged the air.

At Bennorakh's direction, Shannivar and Zevaron seated themselves near the brazier. The *enaree* brought out a leather skin, like the ones used for *k'th*. He explained that the potion was akin to dreamsmoke, only much stronger. Offering the skin to Zevaron, the shaman motioned him to drink. Zevaron tilted his head back and placed the tip in his mouth. He took a gulp and sputtered.

"Again," the *enaree* said.

Still choking, Zevaron obeyed.

Then it was Shannivar's turn to drink. The liquid had no detectable smell, not like *k'th* or one of the herbal infusions. She took a gulp as quickly as she could. A puckering sensation spread through her mouth and throat. Her gorge rose at the prospect of taking more. However, determined not to show weakness, she swallowed again. She hoped it would be sufficient. She did not think she could force down a third mouthful. As it was, her eyes watered and her belly shuddered.

They rested in silence. Nausea hovered at the edge of Shannivar's senses. The crawling sensation in her throat faded, replaced by a creeping chill, a chill that defied the pervasive warmth from the brazier. This chill, she suspected, was not of the body but of the spirit.

Moments passed. The interior of the *jort* blurred and filled with light. She shook her head, struggling to focus her watering eyes.

"Do not fight the visions." Was it Bennorakh's voice echoing so strangely, or a memory of herself speaking those words? Was she back at the gathering, or somewhere else?

"Let the potion do its work . . ."

In the far distance, someone was chanting in a language she did not understand and yet somehow recognized in the very marrow of her bones. The rhythm, rising and falling in syncopation, brought forth resonances in her heartbeat, her blood, her womb. What did it mean? What did any of it mean? She throbbed with almost-understanding.

Phrases spiraled into a pattern, reached out and then returned. Cadences swept her up and dissolved her into motes of sound and light. She had no will to resist.

In the pauses between one breath and another, her consciousness stretched to a veil rising in a golden misty distance, then melted like sunlight pouring over the endless steppe. The images overlapped and bled through one another. She seemed to be looking with more than one pair of eyes, or else the walls between the worlds of gods and men had grown unimaginably thin.

The earth fell away beneath her. For a sickening moment, she plummeted into a well of light. She could no longer hear the chanting or feel the bone-deep shivers of her body. Winds bore her up as if she were no more than a downy feather from her clan's totem eagle. She hovered over a high place like a mountain peak, taller than the promontory of the *enarees*. Overhead, storm clouds collided, and in their turbulent depths, colors writhed and coalesced. Shapes moved, no—one single shape, manlike and erect, but distorted. She made out a heavy-jawed skull, arms, and legs that reached down into the very marrow of the land. It blotted out half the sky.

The figure was moving now, emerging from the clouds to stride across a wide green field. A corona of fire surrounded it. Whatever it touched burst into flames and left cinders of frost. Its shadow spawned smaller creatures—stone-drakes, winged snakes, things that might have been wolves except for their many-forked tails and firelit eyes, and many others too dim and misshapen to recognize.

The mountains glowed, belching molten rock and ash. Shannivar became aware that she was not alone. Rising up behind her, as if she had floated on a banner in their forefront, stood a company of men. One man in particular stood out. Although she could not see his face, and his armor and weapons were foreign to her, she knew him; she knew his hidden face's strong cheekbones, wide mouth, and clean jaw line. He was Zevaron and yet not Zevaron, bathed in an aura of the same gold she had seen glittering beneath Zevaron's skin. The soldiers chanted in unison, but she paid them no heed. Her attention was drawn to the object the man now raised overhead, a rainbow of colored crystals, shimmering with power. At their heart lay a clear faceted gem, forged for a single purpose—to focus that power. Golden light streamed through it and suffused the face of the man. It glimmered under his skin.

"Khored! Khored!" the men shouted. Their voices filled the wind and rose up to the heavens.

The man turned toward her, eyes glowing with the multi-prismed radiance of the crystals. As they met hers, she saw they were Zevaron's eyes. *Khored. Zevaron's ancestor, whose power Zevaron now bore. The golden light beneath his skin . . .*

A wave of frozen fire, sudden and immense, engulfed her. The great king and all his army disappeared. Then she was falling again, twisting in an unseen storm.

With a shock, Shannivar found herself back in Bennorakh's *jort.* She lay on her side, her hands twisted together. Her fingers throbbed, as if she had been clenching them with all her might. She struggled to sit up. Her spine popped, and her muscles felt as stiff as if she had just fought an entire Gelonian army by herself. A faint light filtered through the opening at the top of the *jort.* It was not dawn, but close. She and Zevaron were alone.

He sat, knees drawn up, eyes wide open, staring into an unimaginable distance. He seemed to be caught in a trance, akin to those the *enarees* entered to receive their prophecies.

"Zevaron?" She reached out to touch him. For an instant, he gave no response. Then his eyes rolled up in their sockets. His spine arched, throwing his head back. His body slammed against the ground, so rigid that his skull and hips struck first. He shuddered with the impact. Arms and legs straightened, as if shoving away unseen enemies. His face turned dusky.

No, not like Chinjizhin!

She must find help! Where was Bennorakh? There was no time to search for him—what had Zevaron done for Chinjizhin? Placed blankets beneath him. Yes, that was already done. Shoved something soft in his mouth so that he would not bite his tongue. Shannivar looked around for something she could use, but Zevaron's frenzy already appeared to be subsiding. Perhaps the fit would resolve on its own. It might be only a temporary effect of the potion.

The stiffness was rapidly draining from his limbs. His head lolled to one side, facing her, his features slack. She bent over him and grasped his shoulders. He was not breathing.

O Tabilit, Blessed Mother! He cannot die, not now!

She scrambled for the door flap and jerked it open. "Bennorakh!" she screamed.

Outside, the encampment lay still. No fire was lit, nor was there any sign anyone was awake. The snow had stopped falling during the night. It muffled all sound, as if the earth itself were holding its breath. She could not hear even the normal noises of the horses and reindeer in their stone-walled pens.

"Bennorakh!"

"I am here." The *enaree's* voice came from behind her, from inside the *jort*. Crystals of melting snow dotted his bare head and shoulders. How could she not have seen him before? He knelt at Zevaron's side and placed one hand on the outlander's chest. After a moment, he drew back, rubbing his fingers.

"What is it?" Shannivar cried, her own sense of desperation rising.

"His heart has stopped. He is in the hands of the Sky People now."

"Your potion did this! Surely there must be an antidote, a spell, something you can do!"

"This calamity arises not from the dream potion, but from the foreseeing itself. He has gone—he will go—where no living man dare follow. He has—he will—seek his own doom. I am sorry, Shannivar daughter of Ardellis. There is nothing I can do." The *enaree* did not meet her eyes as he retreated from the *jort*.

Shannivar gathered Zevaron's body into her arms. He had gone as limp as a dead man. Perhaps he was already gone—no, it could not be! There must yet be time!

"Zev!" She pressed him against her heart, calling his name over and over again. "Zevaron . . . Zevaron . . ."

If you were at the gates of death itself, she whispered to him in her mind, *I would follow you there, and if I could not bring you back, I would go with you so that we would be together!*

Shannivar had no magic to summon him back from that far land, nor any idea where it might lie. Nor was she prepared to slit her own belly, as heroes

of old were said to do. Not while there was still hope.
Zevaron had spoken of a treasure of his people, one
given to him by his mother. More than that, he could
not say, but Shannivar believed it was the thing that
bound him to whatever danger lurked in the north,
to Fire and Ice, to Olash-giyn-Olash, the Shadow of
Shadows. In her bones, she was certain that this was
the power that held him now in its grasp.

This must be the purpose of her own vision.

What to do? How to call him back, before it was
too late? She tightened her hold, rocking both of
them. Memory rose up. *Zevaron's eyes focused in-*
ward, the faint scintillation of gold just below his
skin, his hand rubbing the skin over his breastbone,
as if to ease some deep ache . . .

Shannivar loosened her grip, allowing Zevaron
to slide to the floor. His jacket was fastened loosely,
and her fingers slipped beneath the overlapping
folds of his shirt. She placed one hand flat between
the rounded muscles of his chest, where only a thin
layer of skin covered the breastbone. There was no
movement, not even a faint pulse. His flesh was
warm and resilient, and this gave her an unexpected
flare of hope.

O Tabilit, O Giver of Life! O God of Meklavar! I
call on you now. If ever you loved your people, if
ever you showed your favor to Saramark and
Khored the King, to Grandmother and Mirrimal, do
not fail me now. I ask nothing for myself, only for
this man!

She paused. What came to her was that Zevaron,
sent upon a great and dreadful quest, had not

turned back. He had not taken the easy road with his friend to Isarre or stayed in Denariya and become rich. If he were serving the gods, they must in turn protect him. She had no right to conjure them or demand their help. She could only implore their grace. Tabilit must judge what was in her heart, in her soul, even as she judged Zevaron. Bending her head, Shannivar touched her lips to his.

If breath is life, she prayed, *let mine flow into him. Let my life sustain us both.*

Or if need be, she added, trembling, *let my own pass away.*

Beneath her hand, the warmth of Zevaron's body shifted, growing hot and sharp, as if a fire had taken hold of him. A whirlwind of brilliance swept through her own body. She could see nothing except that coruscating gold-white light.

She floated above a misty, radiant sky. Currents swirled around her, not random but in a pattern she could almost but not quite recognize. Colors winked into being, at first blurred and indistinct, then crystalline.

> *Blue, a summer's cloudless sky*
> *Green, as new grass in the Moon of New Foals*
> *Red, as spilled blood, as berries*
> *Gold, pure and new-minted, fresh from the*
>   *smith's shaping*
> *Pink, as a maiden's cheeks, as blood-stained*
>   *water*
> *Purple, deeper and richer than any she had*
>   *ever seen.*

The colors seemed to fade as they came together. The light turned clear, clearer than any spring water, than any polished crystal. It focused all other light into itself. In its depths, she beheld a brilliance beyond description. She had sensed it in the back of her throat in the soaring cadences of song, in the instant before she and Zevaron had first kissed, in the shimmer of moonlight on wind-ruffled grass. Now she felt as if she could spread eagle wings and soar above all ordinary things, that there was no limit to her vision.

To the south, across the sea of bitter waters, a city gleamed like a jewel set in the living rock of the mountains. Ancient patterns glimmered in its walls, in the rhythm of prayer, the holy words echoing through rock and mortar. *Meklavar.*

Never before had Shannivar understood the strength of stone. Fortresses had always seemed as prisons, as obscenities on the earth. Now, through the magic of the gem, she understood this city of walls and mountains. It was not a cage but a garden, a place of nourishment of the spirit. Through its intricate byways, she sensed the resonance of other crystals, like called unto like, and yet incompletely, their harmonies out of tune.

She looked further south, across cerulean waters where huge creatures plunged and swam. Was there a flash of brilliance, as quickly hidden?

The power of her dream vision flung her to the southwest, to Isarre's white cities along the coast, and then north to Gelon. Gelon appeared as a cloud of rust and tarnish, densest over the largest city. Although it shifted like vapor, she could not penetrate it. Instinct urged her to flee, but her warrior's training held firm. The Mother of Horses, to whom she'd prayed, had brought her to this place, as to the others. She must endure the sight of her enemy's stronghold for Zevaron's sake.

Something lurked in Gelon, generating the cloud to hide itself. No human sorcerer could have done this, she knew that much through the magic of the crystals. This was a thing of spirit, preternatural and malevolent. She knew instinctively that this miasma had the power to taint any good purpose, to twist hope and hunger, pride and loyalty, all to its own purposes.

The vision dimmed. Shannivar began to make out the interior of the *jort*, to feel the weight and warmth of Zevaron's body, to see the light sifting through the ceiling opening. She refused to believe that Tabilit had brought her this far, only to fail. Perhaps in order to save Zevaron, she must follow his own quest.

With an effort, she turned her attention from shrouded Gelon to the northernmost reaches of the steppe. Like an arrow, she sped beyond the country of the Snow Bear, straining to make out the mountains where the stone-drake had been found. Peaks rose before her eyes like the curtains of Tabilit's Veil. Row upon row stretched upward. Never in all her dreams had she imagined anything so massive and so steep. She had once heard them called the Pillars of the World, because they held up the sky.

Shannivar's vision faded. Any moment now, she

would return to the ordinary world. Wordless need drove her on. The mountains turned filmy, and she saw, behind their eternal horizon, a jagged gap, sheets of fractured rock opening up like a wound. Beyond, she sensed something stirring, a beast roused from slumber. No, no beast this. It had never been alive, and yet it was sentient. It moved, it sensed, but it knew neither loyalty nor love nor joy, only a slow, frozen hatred of everything living. It turned sightless eyes toward her, orbs of burning ice, of frost-rimed fire—

Run! Run before it sees you! Every fiber of Shannivar's being recoiled, but she willed herself to hold fast. She was a daughter of the Golden Eagle, heir to Saramark. She would not give up until she had wrested Zevaron from whatever held him in its grasp.

The form was turning away, its edges dissolving like fog torn by wind. The light in those eerie eyes winked out.

Shannivar's awareness fractured into confusion, shards of color and form. Muscles momentarily slack, she toppled backward. All sense of the menace of the north and the guardian gem vanished. She scrambled to Zevaron's side. When she lay her head against his bare chest, she heard a faint, spasmodic pulse. His chest rose and fell in a shuddering breath.

He lives! My beloved lives!

She threw her arms around him, her eyes stinging. She felt his hands on her back, drawing her close against him. His lips moved against her hair, and she thought she heard the whisper of her name.

Once she had thought that Tabilit had surely woven their lives into a single tapestry, a single destiny. They belonged to one another, choosing and chosen. Whatever came next, in the north or beyond, across the wide steppe or even in far Meklavar, they would be together.

Chapter 26

BENNORAKH watched as Shannivar and Zevaron sipped their steaming, buttered tea. Her belly clenched at the smell, but she forced it down. Bennorakh's eyes seemed to see right into her mind, as if he were pacing the boundaries of her vision. Only when she and Zevaron had finished drinking and she felt steadier, less drained by the potion's aftermath, did the *enaree* ask them what had happened.

Zevaron stared into his cup, swirling the dregs. Shannivar wondered what he had seen, if it had been so disturbing he dared not speak of it. He might have wandered the borderlands of the Pastures of the Sky, but surely that was not so terrible a thing. She wanted to ask if he too had seen King Khored, or the misshapen giant of frost and fire, or the multi-hued radiance.

To give Zevaron time to recover himself, Shannivar related her own experience as best she could. The vision was already beginning to fade, its details blurring in her mind. She found she had no words to describe many of the things she had seen, things that had been so vivid only a short time ago. As she spoke, Zevaron roused from his daze. His eyes focused, and he looked less drawn.

Bennorakh listened gravely, without interruptions or questions. He did not prompt Zevaron, although it was clear to Shannivar that Zevaron's experience must also be told. Only then could the shaman interpret their combined vision.

"I saw many things," Zevaron said in a voice that sounded as if he hadn't spoken in days, "many of which I cannot clearly recall. I saw an ocean racked by storm, rising to blot out the sky. The heavens rained white fire on the land. A mountain cracked in two and creatures of molten rock crept forth, freezing everything they touched. A woman garbed in white held a poisoned fruit in her hand. I cannot believe these are omens of good."

"Omens are rarely what they appear," Bennorakh remarked.

Shannivar privately agreed with him. Then, to her surprise, the *enaree* refrained from questioning Zevaron further. She wanted to know what happened when Zevaron had almost died—or had actually died. He was concealing as much as he revealed.

Bennorakh dismissed them, and they returned to Shannivar's *jort* to rest. "In my vision, I saw him," Shannivar said to Zevaron, once they were alone, "your great king, your kinsman, Khored. No—" seeing the flicker of disbelief in his eyes, "—not as I imagined him from the stories you told me, the legends of your people. I *saw* him. It was as if I watched the great battle with the Shadow of Shadows—your Fire and Ice—with my own eyes."

His doubt faded into wonder.

"We were spirit-joined," she said. *Tabilit brought us together for this quest.*

"I too saw Khored of Blessed Memory and the battle that vanquished Fire and Ice," he murmured. "I watched him wield the Seven-Petaled Shield, I—" He broke off, rubbing his chest.

Gently Shannivar covered his hand with her own. "I know you cannot speak of this, that some force keeps you silent. But when you were dead, or I thought you were, I prayed to Tabilit, and I touched . . ." Words vanished from her mouth. She did not feel herself restrained, not in the way it seemed he was. She simply had not the speech to describe the shifting rainbow prism.

"There are some things, yes, I cannot speak of," he admitted. "And others I did not tell the shaman."

Shannivar commented that the *enaree* was accustomed to hearing all manner of bizarre visions. "It is not good to keep visions to yourself, no matter how difficult or confusing they are. We are not on this journey for our own private purposes, but for those of the gods."

He set his jaw and looked away.

"Will you not entrust me with what you saw?" she pleaded. "We need not tell Bennorakh if that is what is stopping you."

After a moment, he nodded assent. Some of the

things he described sounded very much like what
she had seen, or what she still remembered. Others
were strange, including the woman with the poisoned fruit, who had clearly drawn Zevaron into
some sort of spell. From Zevaron's embarrassment,
Shannivar thought perhaps he had wanted to take
the offered fruit. Perhaps she had offered something more. At last, he paused, leaving only one
more thing hanging unsaid in the space between
them, one thing he did not want the *enaree* to know,
one thing he struggled to speak aloud.

He drew himself together and met Shannivar's
gaze. "I saw—over and over again—" Here his
voice changed, and she caught a tone of savage exultation, of desire that went beyond craving. "I saw
Gelon. Gelon burning."

Shannivar packed her personal belongings, checked
her weapons, medicinal supplies, and spare clothing. Her supply of women's herbs was almost gone.
The last she gathered had been during the Moon of
Frost along the trail. It was not unknown for a warrior woman to bear a child, although that meant
laying down her bow for a time. Older married
women sometimes used the herbs solely for reasons of health, since children were considered a
blessing to the entire community. Not knowing
what else to do, she sought out Chinjizhin's wife,
Ahnzel.

In the absence of a tribal *enaree*, Ahnzel had

taken over many of the traditional healing functions. Shannivar had noticed how various members of that extended family, and other families as well, came to her with worried expressions and departed looking relieved. When Bennorakh interacted with Ahnzel, he treated her with almost as much respect as he would have shown a colleague. At first, Shannivar had supposed this to be ordinary politeness to the wife of a chieftain, but she had since come to understand that the *enaree* recognized a spiritual kinship with the old woman. She remembered what Mirrimal had said about the strange half-world of the shamans—that it should not matter whether they began as men or women, as long as they ended up in the same halfway place.

It was midday and the men were busy tending the reindeer herds, when Shannivar and Ahnzel went into Ahnzel's *jort*. Chinjizhin was up and about, so they had the dwelling to themselves. Ahnzel pulled the door flap closed and tied it securely against the gusting ice-edged wind. The living space was divided by a central hearth into men's and women's sides.

Ahnzel ushered Shannivar to the women's side and indicated she should sit on a cushion with worn designs of snow hares in flight. The older woman brought out a tea set, a pot and cups of beautiful but chipped blue ceramic. Shannivar waited in polite silence while Ahnzel brewed the tea and offered her a cup. The tea was strong, bitter, and lightly salted.

"Now, woman of the Golden Eagle," Ahnzel

asked, sitting back on her own cushion, "what do you seek from me?"

Shannivar explained what she wanted, bitter-grass or star-eye, whatever grew in this climate.

Ahnzel looked astonished. "You cannot—" She broke off, lowering her voice as if she feared being overheard.

"Why, do the women here not know how to pre-vent pregnancy? Or—" Shannivar faltered, "is such a thing forbidden?"

"Not at all. What do you think we are, animals that drop their young at any season? The life of the Snow Bear is not for the weak of body or spirit, and food must go to those who can best make use of it. Far better to bear fewer children who can be prop-erly cared for than to have many and see them starve. But such things must not be used to uproot a pregnancy."

"No, I mean their use in prevention." Shannivar's throat tightened. She gazed, wide-eyed with aston-ishment, at the old woman.

Ahnzel's dark eyes glinted in the diffuse light fil-tering through the roof opening. Slowly she nodded.

How can it be possible? Had she been mistaken in the herbs she had gathered along the trail? That was more than a moon ago. What if they only re-sembled effective remedies, but lacked true phar-maceutical qualities? She stared at the empty cup in her hands and struggled to gather her thoughts.

"My dear," Ahnzel said, using a strange but un-derstandable term of endearment from older to younger kinswoman. Something in Ahnzel's voice hinted at the question no one ever dared ask, *Do you want this child?* "Did you not know?"

"How could I? I haven't—haven't missed—"

"But you have a lover, and from all appearances he is an ardent one."

Ardent. Oh, yes. Then: *How can she tell if I am pregnant when I myself had no reason to suspect?*

The answer leapt to Shannivar's mind. Ahnzel was gifted with an inner sight akin to that of the *enarees.* The signs had been there all along—the unusual fatigue, the tenderness in her breasts, the queasiness at the smell of morning tea. *A baby. A child? Zevaron's child?* She bent over, arms protective around her belly. *Oh, Sweet Mother Tabilit! I took the dream potion—such strong magic—has it harmed my baby?*

"My daughter, are you well?"

"I am well. And will be well. But—since by your arts you knew of my pregnancy before I myself did—can you tell me, please, is my babe well? Did the potion—" She could not go on.

Ahnzel placed one hand, feather-light, on Shannivar's abdomen. For a long moment, neither woman took a breath. Ahnzel straightened, her spine creaking. Her expression was thoughtful, but a smile hovered at the wrinkled corners of her eyes.

"I can sense nothing amiss at this time. However, it is in my mind that only the strongest babe could have made his presence known this early. I think you have nothing to fear on that account."

Ahnzel patted Shannivar's arm. "Go safely under Tabilit's wide sky until we meet again."

*　　*　　*

Shannivar told Zevaron about her pregnancy that
night as they lay with their arms around one another after lovemaking. His muscles tensed and his
breath hissed in a sharp inhale. She pulled away
and propped herself up on one elbow. She could
not read his expression in the dim light filtering
through the central opening of her *jort*, and did not
know what to expect. Any man of the clans would
have been overjoyed. Rhuzenjin would also have
tried to use the pregnancy to pressure her into marriage. Better to face a problem squarely. "What's
the matter?"

"Matter?" his voice sounded thick with emotion.
"Nothing! It's just . . . I didn't expect—"

"What?" she countered, forcing a laugh. "Do
your people not know where babies come from?"

"Of course we do. I thought—I'd heard talk at
the *khural*—that women of the steppe have ways of
preventing pregnancy. Oh, Shannivar, I would never
have exposed you to the risk had I realized!"

Shannivar frowned. At every turn, it seemed,
some man was lecturing her on *risk*. She set aside
the thought as unworthy. Surely a daughter or son
was a blessing to clan and family, even if she would
not be able to fight for a time. She wondered what
Saramark had done when her children were infants, if she strapped them to her back or carried
them in front of her on her saddle while she went
about her heroic deeds. Or did she stay in camp

until they were old enough to be left with their aunties?

"The chance of pregnancy was small," she said, "and it was mine to take. The herbs sometimes fail, and there are differences from one variety to another. But when you say *risk*, do you mean this news is displeasing to you?"

"No!" The eagerness of his denial surprised her, as did the unrestrained delight with which he embraced her. "That is, if it does not displease you."

This time, she did not have to force a laugh. "A babe is a treasure of the clan."

"I thought you would not wish to set aside your present life—riding to battle, hunting—and this journey. My only sadness is of being parted from you."

"Who said anything about *being parted*? Do you think that the moment a woman becomes pregnant she is helpless? That her skill with a bow, her knowledge, her courage, all fly out of her like a flock of startled ptarmigans?"

She went on in this fashion for a time, growing more vehement, until she realized that Zevaron had made an honest mistake in assuming she would now abandon the quest. He was not blind; he was ignorant of what a woman on a horse, pregnant or not, could accomplish. He had lived in stone houses, and then at sea, among men. She told him how Kendira had ridden out to make the *jort* lattices, how her kinswomen often did the work of managing the encampment, putting up and taking down *jorts*, cooking and weaving, beating felts, and harvesting wild barley, until the very day the babe was delivered. While a mother nursed her own infants, the raising of the children was shared by the women and men of the clan. If a woman died in labor, her sisters and cousins, aunts and grandmothers, took over. "We women are constrained from hunting or going into battle not by childbearing itself but by the customs of marriage," she explained. *Although we should not be.* "It does not often happen that unmarried women bear children and continue with their lives as warriors and hunters. Most women marry first, and then they set aside their bows."

"And you do not wish to marry?"

"I am determined to live my life as I choose," she replied with heat, and then realized he might have been asking if she wished to marry *him*. She touched his face in the near dark. "And I choose to defend my people, to take the man I love into my *jort*, to follow where Tabilit has called me. She brought us together, surely you realize that, and she has blessed us with this child. But she has also put a fire in my heart. She has set me on this path, and I do not—I *cannot*—believe she intends me to give up now."

He was silent for a moment, and she added, "Would *you* turn back, so close to the northern mountains?"

"The danger is for myself alone. You are carrying a child, and therefore placing two lives at risk. How can I allow that, especially when it is mine?"

"The venture is not yours to allow or forbid. And if you think you can go on without me, you are an even greater fool, Zevaron Outlander."

He sighed and turned on his back. "I am a fool, this is true. A fool for thinking I could argue with a woman of the Azkhantian steppe."

"Oh yes," she said, snuggling against his shoulder, "a very great fool. But so have we all been, from time to time."

"Seriously, Shannivar, we may be going into dangers neither of us have faced before—"

She lifted her head. "You're not going to start again, are you? I thought we'd settled that argument."

"—and face enemies that are not mortal flesh and bone."

"Of course. If you tell me you are more prepared and better defended than I am, I will not believe such nonsense. You, who defied the taboo, placed your hand on the stone-drake, and had to undergo purification not once but twice!"

He rolled on to his side, facing her. "You, who followed me!"

"Just so. Anywhere you go, I will go, too. Someone has to rescue you!"

For a moment, he did not answer. She hoped he had the sense to realize when he was defeated. With another sigh, he lay back. She did not press herself against him, although the air between them was rapidly cooling.

"A child, my child . . ." he said. The words came as a whisper, as a prayer. "I wish my mother had lived to hear of it."

*   *   *

For days, they rode north, a caravan of riders and laden reindeer. Chinzhukog and his cousin acted as guides, pack animal handlers, and quartermasters. They knew the way from wintering-place to summering-place, felt it in their blood as inexorably as the turn of the seasons, even when there was no more than a thread of trail across the rock. As they rode, the two northern men chanted stories of great deeds, of kinship with the animals they hunted, of the brief joys of springtime and the enduring struggle of winter. Shannivar sang ballads of her own people, Saramark's Lament and songs in praise of horses.

They made their way over stark, weather-gnawed hills. Winds swept the sky clear, revealing a blue so deep, it was almost black. Despite the brightness of the sun, Shannivar could not see this as a good omen.

At last, they arrived at the *dharlak*. It was far more of a permanent place than that of Shannivar's clan. The summering-place of the Golden Eagle was no more than a lake, good pastures, and a few crumbling stone structures. This encampment had been set up in the lee of a fractured cliff. Flat stones had been stacked and mortared to form livestock pens, the walls high enough to keep out the worst of the wind. Beside them, round-sided buildings held fodder for beasts as well as human necessities — blankets, dried fruit and *bha* wrapped in oiled leather packets, and bows and axes similarly preserved. The well itself was weathered, as if it had grown out of the bedrock itself, but it yielded plenty of water.

Shannivar set up her *jort* in the most sheltered of the spaces, as the men turned the horses and reindeer into the pens. The day had been milder than many on the trail, and Shannivar saw how pleasant this place might be in summer, sheltered by the mountain from the heat. Now it was deserted and bleak.

They slept badly that night, between the eerie lamentation of the wind and a faint but growing feeling of dread that hovered at the edges of Shannivar's dreams. The Snow Bear men went about their chores, preparing the morning meal and tending to the animals.

The next day, they continued on. Wind scoured the barren rock and tore at the manes of the horses. It burned exposed cheeks and penetrated layers of felt and wool. Shannivar pulled her peaked cap low over her forehead and wrapped the collar of her jacket around her neck. She showed Zevaron how to do the same. The tundra horses seemed unaffected by the cold, but Eriu and Radu plodded on with lowered heads.

The further north they went, the more withdrawn Zevaron became. He went about the daily tasks of setting up camp as if in a trance. As if, Shannivar thought, his thoughts and heart were speeding ahead, leaving his body to go about its routine work. When she spoke to him, he answered her, and from time to time, the light in his eyes would return, and she would know he truly saw her. When they lay together, he would touch her belly and enlarged breasts with tenderness. With each passing day, however, those times became fewer and briefer. She tried to hold at bay the fear that she was losing him to his heritage, to the thing beyond the shattered mountains, the rubble of the white star.

A range of tall peaks came into view. At times, the route was no more than a whisper of a trail; at others, it widened into a gap between sheer-sided hills.

Shannivar had been riding with her head down, more concerned with the terrain before her than the larger landscape. When she lifted her eyes to the pass, she saw a line of dusty purple mountains beyond it. Across their lower slopes, the darker hues of green delineated the tree line. The mountain tops shimmered white and gray before disappearing into the low clouds.

"Look there! To the east!" Zevaron shifted forward in his saddle.

At first, Shannivar could see nothing beyond the desolate grandeur of the heights. She nudged Eriu forward, craning for a better line of sight through the gap.

Extending eastward, the immense rocky peaks fell away into a tumble of jagged shards. Her first thought was that some god, perhaps Onjhol himself, had shattered the bones of the earth and strewn them every which way. Here and there, slivers remained, upright spears of stone. Dense mists pooled in the gaps, mists that curled upward, but not like steam from sulfuric vents.

She came even with Zevaron and halted Eriu with a shift in her weight. The black pricked his ears, head up, muscles tense. His breath quivered through his body. He, too, felt something. Not awe at the magnitude of the destruction, for animals could not appreciate such a thing. No, there was something more.

Suddenly the air grew very still and quiet. Radu had also halted. Zevaron sat on her back as a man transfixed. The whiteness of the sky seemed to have infected his eyes, and his features were set, intent. For a terrible moment, she knew that if she spoke to him, he would not hear her, and if she touched him, he would be as ice.

In the space between one heartbeat and the next, the world shifted. Winds brushed Shannivar's cheeks. Eriu pawed the snow-crusted dirt. In the distance, a hawk sounded the *skree!* of its hunting cry.

Chinzhukog, pale and grim, adjusted his position in his saddle. His little tundra horse hung its head, feet braced, back hunched, and tail clamped to its rump. At the rear of their little party, his cousin wrestled to keep the snorting, wild-eyed reindeer from bolting.

Shannivar studied the swirling mists. "What lies beyond that?"

"This is as far as any of my people have come," Chinzhukog replied. "I think the place where the white star fell is close."

She reflected for a moment. "It would be wise to set up camp here. The reindeer cannot go much farther. If you and your cousin will tend to them and the *jorts*, Zevaron and I will explore while the light is still good."

"There was a place a little way back. We will do as you ask. Do not go too far."

She nodded gravely. "Zevaron, let's go."

Zevaron tapped his heels against Radu's sides, but the usually obedient mare threw up her head. She took one tentative step forward, then settled on her hindquarters. Her muscles stood out through her newly shaggy coat. She snorted white vapor from her flaring nostrils.

Zevaron kicked her again, hard enough that she flinched. She lifted one forefoot, then the other, but her hind hooves remained rooted to the ground. Her ears flattened against her neck. He cursed in Denariyan. "What's wrong with her?"

Shannivar reined in closer. The dun mare was trembling visibly. "She's too frightened to move."

"I thought Azkhantian horses were fearless," Zevaron said, but he ceased battering the mare's sides.

"There, Radu, sweet girl." Shannivar reached out to stroke the mare's neck.

At first; Radu did not respond. Fear hardened her body. Shannivar continued her soothing words and gentle, rhythmic touch. The expression of terror faded slowly from the mare's eyes.

"Let me go first," Shannivar said. "Eriu will not fail me, and Radu will follow wherever he leads."

Be my wings . . .

Eriu moved forward, one careful step at a time, proud and wary in the manner of a stallion when a

wolf approaches. He arched his neck and lifted
each foot high; she could feel the coiled strength in
his back. One ear remained cocked back toward
her in trust. Radu followed, as Shannivar had predicted.

They entered the region of shattered rock. The
mist closed in behind them, shutting out the pass. It
crept along the ground, flowed sluggishly along fis-
sures, and gathered around the bases of the upward-
jutting splinters. Some of these fractured strata
were slender, chipped into irregular shapes that
surely could not withstand the erosive powers of
wind and temperature. A few looked ready to shatter at the slightest touch. Others were as massive as
the promontory of the *enarees*. Their heights disappeared into the hovering mist, and over them hung
a stillness, a slow, inexorable waiting.

Step by step, Shannivar and Zevaron made their
way through the forest of shards. The ground was
occasionally covered in snow, and there were no
traces of animal life. The horses remained tense.
Their hoofbeats echoed strangely. Shannivar would
not have believed that such a place existed, not even
in the legends chanted by *enarees*. The contours of
the stones suggested the bent spines or folded limbs
of misshapen creatures. When she peered at them,
the semblance vanished, as if it had been no more
than a trick of light and perspective.

How long they travelled on in this careful, halting manner, she could not tell. The haze across the
sky diffused light so thoroughly that it might have
been any hour of the day. The air grew warmer, or

perhaps that was an illusion created by the mis
The eerie, unnatural quiet swallowed up thei
words.

Shannivar dared not look over her shoulder, fo
fear of seeing the same impossible maze of spire
and pinnacles, the same unsettling shapes, the same
broken ground underfoot, the same mist, as in fron
of her. As long as they kept going, she could pre
tend they were not lost. Would Eriu's animal sense:
be keen enough to guide them back? Or woulc
they be forced to wait here until the mist cleared, in
it ever did?

Eriu tossed his head, flicking out a spray of con-
densation from his mane. When Shannivar stroked
his neck, he halted, as if her touch were a command
His head shot up, and his sides heaved as he sucked
in air. In front of her, the mist thinned.

A gigantic wall of white on white emerged. She
squinted, trying to gauge its size and distance. It
shimmered and crackled like a colorless Veil or
sun-touched clouds before a storm. Its base could
have encompassed a dozen *jorts*, and its smooth,
tapering sides disappeared overhead. Shannivar
couldn't decide whether it was rooted in the stony
rubble or was a mighty spear thrust down from the
shrouded sky. The back of her neck prickled.

Zevaron, silent since they came down over the
pass, muttered something in his own language.

"What—?" her voice came in a whisper, as if the
coruscating brightness had stolen her breath. "What
is it?"

"I do not know," he replied in the same hushed tones, "but I believe this is all that remains of the white star."

She saw then that the wall was not solid. From one moment to the next, eddies of light on its surface turned transparent enough to reveal an interior. Shadows like flickering visual echoes moved and disappeared in an instant. They captured her attention, holding her like a marmot in a snare. Her eyes refused to move, even to blink. Then, as if with a careless disdain, the flickers stopped and she was released. Her muscles felt like paste. She clenched her jaw to keep a rush of nausea at bay. Tabilit had entrusted her with this quest. She would not be sick. She would not be weak.

"What do we do now? What does your . . ." Shannivar searched for a word for the ancient magical device he carried within his breast, "your *guide* tell you?" At least her voice did not tremble.

The horses had halted. Eriu stood firm, but Radu was clearly near the end of her courage. Zevaron slipped from her back, landing lightly on his feet. He gathered the reins and handed them to Shannivar. Without a word of explanation, he started toward the wall.

Onjhol's bloody balls! The next moment, she jumped to the ground beside him, grabbed his arm, and wrestled him back. "What do you think you're doing?"

He stilled her protest by taking both her hands in his. "Shannivar, I want you to stay here, to give me something to come back to. My anchor, my life-line." Seeing she did not understand, he added, "My safe harbor."

None of these references made sense to her, although she understood perfectly well that he meant to leave her behind. "I need no man's protection!" she retorted, both frightened at the fatalistic tone of his voice and angry that the argument had been brought up again. "Whatever danger lies ahead, I will face it with you! I am a warrior of the steppe, a daughter of the Golden Eagle. In my veins flows the blood of Saramark! Do you think I am *afraid*?"

The light in his eyes shifted, fierce and abyssal. "You do not understand. I do not doubt your courage or your prowess, beloved. Or your determination to see this hunt through to the end." He shook his head. "What I mean is that all my life, everything I am and everything I have was given over to someone else. When I was a small boy, my duty was to be a strong right arm to my brother, he who was to be *te-ravot* after our father. But he died, the Gelon slaughtered them both, and then all I had—the only purpose of my life—was keeping my mother safe."

"And the Gelon took her, too."

"I had given up hope, or almost, and then lost it again. Why was my own life preserved, if not to save hers?"

Zevaron hated Gelon more than anyone she'd ever met, but what had his mother's death to do with the uncanny happenings here in the north of the steppe or wanting Shannivar to stay behind?

I saw Gelon burning, he'd said.

"Do you mean to avenge her?" she asked, for it seemed that he must choose between his desire to strike back and the spirit quest that had led him here. By the leap of tension around his eyes, she saw that he had not—perhaps *could not*—give that up.

"Gelon will pay for her pain and her death," he said in a voice that rang quietly like a sword slipping from its sheath. His shoulders lifted and fell. "Gelon and the evil that now rules there. I used to think the enemy was human, with human ambition. Cinath is a man like any other, after all."

"A man who commands many warriors," she added.

One corner of his mouth twitched upward. "Warriors your own people have held at bay. But what if you were to face not mortal troops, men of flesh, men who bleed and die, but an army of stone-drakes?"

Shannivar's belly clenched at the thought of such a force sweeping over the steppe.

"I saw—my mother herself suspected—there's more at stake here, and a far greater enemy to face. I now know what lies beneath all the death and outrage, the ruin of Meklavar." He tilted his head toward the wall.

"The white star?" she said.

"Rather, what pulled the white star from the heavens."

In the midst of the streaming brightness, Zevaron stood like an upraised blade of Denariyan steel. Images rushed to her mind: the sudden, immense power of an avalanche, a wall of fire such as sometimes swept the steppe, lightning-born, consuming everything in its path. She had not come all this way merely to be dismissed when her services were no longer required. She hungered to be the Saramark of her time. To stand between that fire and her people.

Not all warriors had the same strengths, she knew. Some were better riders, some stronger wrestlers, others more accurate with bow and arrow. *Enarees* ventured into realms of the spirit where not even the bravest fighter dared go. She remembered the living gold beneath Zevaron's skin, the shared dream memories of the magic of his people, magic that had once defeated the embodiment of chaos. Magic that was now his to wield. That magic had led him to this place, and so he must go on.

She wanted to follow him and protect him, but perhaps that choice was not hers to make. Tabilit had entrusted her with keeping her people safe. Shannivar had no idea what dangers lay beyond the wall or what were the chances of victory. If the uncanny power that had smashed the mountain were greater than Zevaron's magic, he might fail. *"My safe harbor,"* he'd said.

Her free hand went unthinking to her belly, where their child grew. She thought of the Gelonian soldiers, fighting back to back, each defending the other. Someone would have to remain free, to rescue him if the need arose.

A voice whispered to her: *"When the heir to light goes to the mountain / He will not return."*

So said the prophecy. But prophecies did not always turn out to be what they seemed. She could not—*would not*—believe this one.

"All this time, I have been alone," he said, his voice low not with the strangeness of the place, but with the tenderness she knew so well. "I have never had anything, any one, just for myself. I was always the second son, the last son of Meklavar, the Heir of Khored. But you have never seen me as anyone but myself. A man like any other."

Shannivar looked into his eyes. In that moment, when he opened himself to her, she found the courage to release him.

Tabilit, strengthen his arm! Bring him back to me!

"You are not a man like any other," she said, repeating his own words. "You are a hero, as great as any of my own people. If you are to venture in there—" with a quick glance toward the wall, "and contend with whatever lies within, then you will need a hero's mount." Shannivar handed Eriu's reins to Zevaron. His eyes widened in surprise.

"Eriu—I cannot take him from you."

She set her chin. "Eriu is the finest horse I have ever known. A horse to carry you through frost and fire. A horse to bring you back from the very gates of death."

A horse to bring you back to me.

She held him with her gaze, as if she could force him to understand. He was not steppe-born, so he had not learned to ride before he could walk. He did not see the world from a horse's back. He had traveled over vast waters on wooden ships, and had lived in stone dwellings. But this frozen, shattered land was part of Azkhantia, and no Azkhantian was complete without his horse.

Eriu seemed to understand what Shannivar wanted of him. He stood firm as Zevaron swung up on his back, sheathed sword in hand, and did not hesitate at the touch of his rider's heels but stepped out briskly toward the wall of shifting light.

PART V:

Zevaron's Conquest

Chapter 27

THE fog swirled wildly, as if it were sentient and aware of Zevaron's approach. He dared not look back, for fear his resolve would vanish, dissipating into phantasmal wisps and merging into the mists.

He raised one hand to his chest, although he could not feel his skin beneath the layers of wool and camel's hair. The gesture had become reflexive, a habit, a way of focusing on the *te-alvar*. The further north he had journeyed, the brighter it had shone in his thoughts, and yet it had also grown heavier. Sometimes it felt like an open wound, each throbbing pulse more torment than reassurance. At other times, it filled his mind with golden light. He was never sure what it was trying to communicate, only that something waited for him beyond these broken mountains. That much, he already knew.

Visions stirred at the back of his mind. He had only to close his eyes and the images, as sharp as any real memory, would take him. As if he had been there, he stood on that hilltop.

Looking down on the massed armies, their blades like silvered grass, horses neighing, voices calling out, "Khored! Khored!" Wind whipping his cheeks, edged with ashes and ice . . .

The *te-alvar* was now so hot and bright, burning with memory and urgency, that he feared his whole body would go up in flames. It must sense the power of this place, of these mists and the forms within the luminescent cone. Surely it had led him here. Surely he now did its will.

The mists reached out, as if eager to embrace him. His stomach felt like curdled lead. He wanted nothing more than to turn the black horse around and gallop back the way he had come. He closed his eyes, clenched his hands on the reins, and thought of his mother, lying waxen and motionless in the Justice Hall back in Aidon. He remembered his brother's blood and his father's, and the malicious glee that glowed in Lycian, Jaxar's vain, beautiful wife. Rotten, all of them!

No matter what it takes, he promised himself, *Gelon will pay.*

He had seen his mother's body. He had felt the terrible stillness in the air. He had touched her face, brushed her hair back from her forehead, searched in vain for a pulse in her neck. Gone, this time she was truly gone. Taken from him by that monster, Cinath, as everything else he valued had been taken. His city, his freedom, his family—father, mother, and the brother he had sworn to defend.

Now he was here, in the realm of the *te-alvar's* vision.

Zevaron's pulse raced. His breath turned thick and heavy in his throat. In the marrow of his bones, he knew he was approaching a fate that would either destroy him or else serve him as no earthly power could.

Before long, he lost all sense of direction. Eriu, seemingly unaffected, kept on at an even pace. They passed more rock formations, some bearing an uncanny resemblance to the stone-drake. Lights glittered on the surfaces and the next moment went black. When Zevaron glanced back, however, it seemed they had altered their positions or disappeared entirely. There was no wall, no dividing line behind him, only more stones and more mist. This place must go on for miles in every direction.

Eriu's hoofbeats echoed eerily in the fog. Ahead, the currents of light-upon-light churned like storm-whipped waves.

Dampness chilled his skin and penetrated his lungs. Behind his breastbone, all life had left the *te-alvar.* He sensed nothing from it, as if that flare of heat had never existed. As if he had imagined it. Perhaps the gem had already achieved its purpose, and no further urging—or warning—was needed. He had crossed ocean and steppe, endured fire and frost, to arrive at this very place.

After some period of time—long or short, Zevaron couldn't tell—he began to feel warmer. The movement of the mists took on a soothing quality, like placid surf on a beach. He could almost feel himself back in Denariya while still on the crew of the *Wave Dancer*, with Chalil laughing at his side.

For all the horror and uncertainty that began his years on the pirate ship, he had known good times as well, the easy comradeship of the crew, the chance to explore exotic lands, the exhilaration of the passage through the treacherous Firelands Straits, and the air rich with spices or laced with salt-tang and ice. Most of all, he'd relished the sense of freedom, of waves as far as his eyes could see and a nimble ship to carry him wherever he wished. There was nothing to fear in that endless gray-green expanse, just as there was nothing to fear in these gently curling mists.

Fog caressed his cheek, temperate and benign.

Eriu's hoofbeats were slower now. Tension gathered in the black horse's body. One small, inwardly curved ear pricked back at him.

What was there to fear, for man or beast, in this landscape of soft mist and elegant stone shapes? The formations were so beautiful and intricate, like crystallized dreams. If he touched one, it would ring like a bell, he was sure of it. No enemy had emerged from the undulating grayness, nor ever would. He was safe here. The mist had a voice, and it sang to him of peace. No human voice could create such celestial harmony. He strained to hear the words.

With a squeal, Eriu came to a halt. He arched his neck and rooted his feet to the stony ground. Every muscle went taut, braced against any urging to continue.

Zevaron felt puzzled but not alarmed. After all, the horse might well be frightened of this transcendently glorious realm. Eriu was a dumb beast, unable to appreciate the delicate shadings of light and temperature, of movement, of song.

A fine quivering shook the horse's body. His sweat rankled the senses, sour with fear. Zevaron patted the animal's neck, but the horse did not relax or show any willingness to go forward.

Zevaron frowned as he noticed the white hairs in the horse's mane. He had thought the beast pure black, but there again, along the sloping shoulder a trick of the light gave the hide a cast like pewter instead of ebony. At first, he felt alarmed, but that quickly faded as the mist sang on.

What need had he for a mount of blood and bone? the mist seemed to be asking. Surely it would be cruel to force the animal onward. He could not remember what had prompted him to bring a horse in the first place, a dumb and unreliable creature.

Zevaron looped the reins over the pommel, took his sword, and slid to the ground. Steady and firm, the rock welcomed his weight. Now he saw that the frosting of white on the horse's body had been no illusion. The lower legs and hooves were the color of ice.

The horse shuffled uneasily, flaring rime-coated nostrils. It swung its head from side to side, gulping air, searching—

With a start, Zevaron saw the horse's eyes, once dark but now as pale as marble. Blood ran sluggishly from the sockets down the sides of the tapering muzzle. Scenting him, the beast snorted and threw its head up. No longer rooted to the spot, it wheeled and broke into a ragged trot. Within a pace or two, it achieved a full-out gallop. Whiteness swallowed it up.

Go, then, Zevaron thought without a trace of regret. Why had he ever thought the black horse courageous or intelligent? It was a nag, a broken-down hack, nothing more. The mist whispered promises of a surer mount that awaited him ahead.

His feet, obedient to the prompting of the mists, carried him onward. The ground became smoother, and the rock formations more dreamlike and fantastical. At times, he felt as if he were passing beneath the arched ribs of an immense skeleton, but not of any creature he knew, not even the leviathans of the oceanic deeps. These ribs were impossibly thin, soaring gloriously overhead, and they glittered. From afar, his ears caught a subtle resonance, perhaps from the vibration of winds between the ribs. The thrumming sound penetrated so deeply, he felt his bones soften in response.

I must go carefully here, he thought, although his pulse did not speed up in readiness for battle or flight, nor did his palms grow damp. His body refused to acknowledge any possibility of danger. That in itself—and the quiescence of the *te-alvar*—made him uneasy. This place had an odd, soporific effect. It might be affecting his thoughts as well.

The warmth must surely be unnatural, he thought, even as his muscles relaxed under its influence. But what was natural here? This entire region was in no way as it ought to be, a tumble of icy rock or perhaps a crater from the impact of the comet.

The spires and arches were far too fragile to have survived such a blow, nor could they be the result of it. No, this place and everything in it must be either the result of supernatural forces, or else illusions created in his mind. Either way, he dared not trust his senses.

Something flitted at the corner of his vision, gray on gray, white against white. He tried to follow the movement, but whatever it was had vanished. He was not alone. The back of his neck tingled as if he were being watched. Being *stalked.* He considered calling out, *"Who's there?"* to draw out whatever it was. Or simply to hear the sound of his own voice.

He drew his sword. It left the scabbard with a whisper. The mists retreated as he went on, holding the blade in front of him like a shield. One step became two and then ten. Beads of moisture condensed on the steel. The contours of the sword distorted in his sight, now flat and broad, then impossibly elongated. When he caught sight of another flicker, he was ready. He pivoted, then lunged. Vapors frothed as if storm-lashed as they gave way before him.

Then he spied a moving form, a deer of some sort. Its body shone like moonlight through clouds, and the branched, backward-swept antlers sparkled as if encrusted with crystalline shards. The beast paused, one cloven-hoofed foreleg raised, and looked at him.

He thought, *Surely this is a paragon of stags,* and then he saw its eyes. The orbs were round and

opaque, unmarked by pupils, yet piercing in thei
gaze. Zevaron's courage faltered at the sight o
them.

The next moment, the stag—if indeed it was ;
stag—bounded away. The fog swallowed it up. Ze
varon was once more alone, his sword trembling ir
his hand, his mouth dry.

Forcing himself to breathe slowly and evenly, he
studied his surroundings. Although he turned in ;
complete circle, he could discern no difference from
one direction to the next.

Which way to go?

Perhaps it did not matter, as long as he kept moving. He had been guided to this place by a power
beyond his own, a destiny ignited by the fall of Meklavar, fueled by the death of his mother, and sealed
by the sight of the stone-drake. That power would
not desert him now, not if he himself held fast.

A destiny, yes, hummed the churning vapors. The
rainbow light assured him that he was answerable
to no one and nothing except that destiny.

The mist finally thinned, and the air grew even
warmer and humid as well. He started sweating. As
he emerged into a clear space, pain lanced through
his chest. The air was so still, it took an effort to
draw it into his lungs. It felt like trying to inhale
glass. For a moment, he could not breathe, could
only stare at the scene before him. A pavilion had
been set up on polished rock. Its framework, a fili-
gree of gleaming silver, supported a canopy so
sheer as to be transparent in places, and yet he
could not make out its interior. The fabric rippled,

although there was no breeze. Silver threads depicted stylized beasts and trees, all seemingly edged in frost.

Perceiving no threat, Zevaron advanced a step and then another. The pain subsided and a feeling of well-being seeped into him. His throat was no longer dry, and his body felt light and rested, his mind alert. Power sang in his blood. He was master of himself and of his fate. He felt no impulse to lay down his sword, and that in itself reassured him.

The front panels of the pavilion fluttered and drew apart. Inside, three steps led to a dais, all of silver-veined marble. There a woman lounged on piles of snowy cushions. As if noticing Zevaron for the first time, she sat up. Her skin was so pale, only a hint of rosy blush distinguished it from the cushions. Her hair fell like colorless silk to her waist, drawn away from her face and secured with clasps shaped like snowflakes.

Zevaron had seen beautiful women before, honey-gold and copper-dark, even the cream and porcelain loveliness of Lycian. This woman put them all to shame, from the flawless lines of her cheek and brow to the slope of her neck, the shape of her generous, wide-set breasts where they pressed against her gossamer robe, the hint of tapering waist, sweetly rounded hips, and between them, thighs such as he had seen only in dreams.

He tore his gaze away. His heart was pounding, but not with battle-readiness. The woman smiled at that, and he felt her knowing gaze upon him like a rush of heat.

I have not come here to goggle at a half-naked woman.

Steeling himself, he lifted his sword and met her eyes.

"You have no need of weapons here, Zevaron san'Khored." Her voice was like the first melting of the snow in spring, her Meklavaran without accent.

"I will judge that for myself."

"So stern! So warlike! What danger confronts you here?" As she spoke, the air filled with a delicate fragrance, a trace of musk only strong enough to make him crave more. "Surely, you have nothing to fear from such as I. Come, sit beside me."

Zevaron remained where he was, sword at the ready. The woman continued to regard him with a faintly amused expression. She raised one hand to her throat. A diamond, or perhaps a very pale blue topaz, glittered there, and the movement accentuated her curves. He saw that her nipples were erect, as if begging for his touch.

In a softer voice, she repeated, "What have you to fear? From anything here? From *me?*"

He rankled at the accusation that he might be afraid, but to deny it would be to admit it was possible. Well, he need not explain himself to her or to anyone. "You know my name, but you have not spoken yours." *And this place reeks of magic!*

She rose with languid grace and came toward him. Her bare feet touched tip-toe as she descended each step. Her gown flowed behind her in gentle folds that gave rise to curls of mist. Her skin glimmered as if moon-touched, and her perfume took on a spicy undertone. Then she was standing in front of him, and she was no longer smiling.

"What do you think I am?"

"I asked *you*."

She shrugged delicately. She was right—whatever she was, she posed no threat to him. He could break her with one hand, crush her against him, cover that pale pink mouth with his own.

He jerked back, remembering in that moment another pair of lips, chapped by ice-edged wind, and muscular arms, not these overly thin, soft limbs. Skin like sun-kissed honey, eyes black and almond-shaped, at times bold or tender, instead of colorless orbs that revealed nothing of the soul behind them, if indeed such a creature had a soul.

He thought of Shannivar's obsidian-dark eyes, how secrets had glinted behind them—perhaps all the feelings she did not need to say aloud. He was struck, as he had been so many times, at her quickness and her strength. Her courage. Her honor. If he stood at the threshold of the hell Denariyans spoke of, he would hear her call him and return to the land of the living. He remembered how he had once lain in her arms, had breathed the mingled smells of cedar and wood-smoke, had felt the slowly fading pleasure in the pit of his belly.

The mists pulsed and the pale woman shone like the rising moon. He inhaled her perfume and it sent his senses reeling. *Your destiny calls you,* she seemed to be saying. *Loose yourself from the chains of the past.*

And there was something more, something that

had come of that night together, but he could not think what. It did not matter. These notions were illusions born of the weakness of his own flesh, a weakness that would soon be purged.

The ice-woman's eyes gleamed. He felt drawn into a sea of ever-changing radiance, of warmth and lassitude, of forgetfulness—

Then another woman's face rose to his mind. His heart shuddered at the sight, pressing against the stone of his chest. Black hair woven into seven braids, eyes dark with tenderness, a voice soft as thunder, calling his name . . .

"Zevaron, my son . . ." With those words came a stirring behind his breastbone.

Pain lanced through him, sudden, searing. His heart turned molten. He felt poised on an incendiary edge, where a whisper might push him one way or the other. He did not know what he might do to be free of it, except hold fast while the white mists set him back on his proper path.

He waited while the last twinges of discomfort faded. What cause had he to feel regret or guilt or loyalty? Such emotions had no place in this kingdom of kaleidoscopic glory. The light was not white but every color imaginable, every texture, every temperature, every taste. The old distinctions—*so dry and artificial!*—no longer had any power over him. He could feel anything and everything, be anyone, endure forever! He could rule the puny kingdoms of men, from the vast reaches of ocean to the unending depths of the sky. Let the nag-riders howl! He would crush them under his feet.

"Call me anything you like," the ice-woman murmured, as if the words were love-play, "and I will give you whatever you desire."

"I think you are a manifestation of Fire and Ice or else its servant." Zevaron struggled to get the words out.

She tilted her head, considering. "Does it then follow that we must be enemies?"

"It does. We must. Of course, we must." Even as he spoke, his voice sounded hollow and without conviction. Did he really believe that? Did such distinctions apply to a man of his stature, called by his destiny? Surely all the powers of the world, natural and otherwise, must serve his cause.

Now she turned so that her body was in profile, her gaze low and sidelong under thick, white lashes. He felt her awareness of him like the whisper of silk over his skin. "Tell me then, brave Zevaron, have I ever harmed you? Used you ill? Spoken unjustly about you? Insulted your honor? No? Betrayed a promise, then? Taken what is rightfully yours?"

He stood immobile, unable to summon a denial because there was none. Whatever this creature was—woman, spirit, monster—she was innocent of these things.

She faced him again. "Have I ever harmed someone you love?"

Someone I love . . .

Tsorreh.

His breath locked in his throat.

She waited, giving him time to gather his

thoughts. All the while, those pale, earnest eyes searched his face. "But someone else has harmed one you loved. So is *he* not your true enemy?"

"I will not listen to your lies!"

"Have I spoken one word of untruth? Have I tried to distract you or trick you?" Her voice did not alter from that soft, persuasive tone.

She moved so that the sword was centered on her body. With both slender-fingered hands, she positioned the tip between her breasts. "If you truly believe me to be your enemy, then you had best do away with me straightaway. If your purpose in coming here, to this Kingdom of the Mists, is to conquer whatever you find, then do it now! I will not protest. I consent freely to *whatever* you desire."

All it would take was a push. She'd fall, and he'd use his weight to drive the sword point home. It would slide over her breastbone and slice through the muscles between her ribs and then into her heart. She must have known this when she placed it just so. He could imagine the faint catch of steel against bone, the smooth glide through flesh. The blade was sharp. Would she bleed red blood or snowy meltwater? Would she sigh as the light left her eyes, eyes that now shone like moonlight? Would he feel a surge of pleasure at her death? The next moment, he was utterly appalled that he could think such a thing. But the disgust faded as soon as she began speaking again.

"Lay down your burden," she murmured. "Be free of your pain. Don't you see? That's all I want for you. That's why I'm here."

"To die for me?"

"To serve you. If this is what you truly desire. Whatever you desire . . ."

Gelon, burning. And Cinath, his face streaked with his life's blood, his eyes rolling up in his skull, his voice shrieking in agony too crushing for words. For every moment Tsorreh had lain in that filthy, lightless cell, he would dole out a century of suffering. For every whimper of pain or despair or humiliation, a thousand years of terror. For her death, an eternity of damnation.

The Gelon on the slave ship, the one who lied, who told him Tsorreh was dead — his back a tapestry of bone-deep lacerations, a dozen whips slashing down again. And again! Lines of bloody flesh overlap one another until his entire back from nape to heels turns into a single oozing, pulpy mass. Splinters from the wooden desk rise up like jagged needles to pierce his chest, his belly, rip them all to shreds. And his voice, screaming, gibbering, begging for mercy.

The same mercy he had shown. The same mercy Cinath had shown.

Each thought, each image pulsated through Zevaron to the pounding rhythm of his heart. His belly quivered, as if he were on the verge of sexual release. He craved this revenge more than he'd ever wanted anything.

Blood courses through the streets of Aidon. The riverbanks are slick and the water stinks of it. The skies turn black with smoke, the flames so hot and fierce, the sound drowns out the cries of the dying.

And not just Aidon, but Verenzza and Roramenth, Borrenth Springs, where the false scholars spin their lies, Sidon and a hundred other cities, until all that is left of them is cinders falling over the salted earth.

All the hills and valleys of that accursed country, the rivers and plains and mountains, all blacken into a continent of whitened ash, pure and cleansed, ash and ice. The burned-out, frost-blasted relics of past atrocities waited now, expectant, for the world to be reshaped and born anew.

Fire swept the horizon beyond those borders, incinerating everything in its path, cracking stone, vaporizing forest and river alike. The Firelands volcanoes erupted in an extravagance of celebration, spewing forth billows of ash and rivers of molten rock that turned the seas into steam for hundreds of miles around. Ice, pure and cleansing, glassed over the skeletal remains of the creatures that had once blemished the ocean bottoms. Snow whipped across the glassy surface, and then each flake became an ember. Ice burned, and water, and air.

He remembered vowing, *Gelon shall burn.* A fierce, wild joy filled him, as if the exultant fires and ice-storms in his vision had taken root there. The world would become the pyre of his vengeance.

Aye, indeed. Gelon shall burn.

His whole body was shaking now. His belly turned to water and then to steel. The visions were so sweet. So alluring. So compelling. A sense of peace washed over him. It was all so clear now, what he truly wanted, what he had to do, and the destiny that had brought him here.

Yet the woman before him might be an obstacle to that destiny, not an ally. A minor one, true, but an inconvenience. She had not denied his accusation that she was either an incarnation of Fire and Ice or else its agent. She had only asked what *he* thought she was. A pretty toy? A seductress? A demon with a human form? Would she turn on him the instant he relaxed his guard? Or pretend to obey him while plotting his downfall? How could he trust anything she said? And yet, if she swore rightly to serve him, she might have the power he needed. Yes, this was a place of immensely powerful magic, of uncanny forces, but was it enough to bring down Gelon? What could one frail-looking woman do against Cinath's armies?

She had stayed very still while the fever of vengeance raged through him, crested, and partially subsided. He had no idea how much of what he felt had been revealed in his expression, nor did he care. Either she would submit to him and bring him what he must have, or he would destroy her and her master alike.

"You are correct," she said. "I cannot defeat your enemies for you. The power I serve is not yet fully present in the material world. Even this—" she gestured about her with one graceful hand, "—is illusion, as you yourself suspected."

"You're useless to me, then." Zevaron stepped back, withdrawing the sword. He'd wasted enough time. Just as he turned to go, not caring whether he was heading in the correct direction so long as it took him out of her sight, the woman spoke again.

"I said *I alone* could not defeat your enemy. But there are those who can, and I can provide what will bring them under your command."

He swung back to face her. "What do you mean?"

"Not what. *Who.* Did you not choose to come here, to the northern steppe, instead of journeying to weak, ineffectual Isarre in the hope of an alliance?"

She must mean the Azkhantian riders, the only force in the known world able to hold the Gelon at bay—and not once or twice, but again and again over the centuries. Even Cinath at his worst had been unable to break their defenses. Having seen how the nomads rode and fought, even in play, Zevaron understood why.

"They will not make a treaty with me." He could not keep an edge of bitterness out of his voice. He had asked and they had rejected him.

"Not of their own choice," she agreed.

Why should they have any choice in the matter? Their filthy, insignificant lives were nothing compared to the glory of his cause!

"What if I gave you the means to compel their cooperation—their loyalty unto death?" she continued. "What if you were to ride to Gelon with the tribes of Azkhantia at your command, *all* of them, not just a few hotheads?" She paused, her chin lifted, eyes half-closed as if in exultation. Every trace of color had drained from her skin. Her lips shone like alabaster.

The clans had never banded together, that much he knew, and even if they did, they would never follow an outlander. Superstitious, ignorant nag-riders!

Compel, the woman had said. *Loyalty*, she'd said, and *unto death*.

Like the waves of a storm-driven tempest, a vision engulfed him. He looked down on the steppe as if from an immense height. From one horizon to the other he saw a mass of horsemen, so many and so densely arrayed that the coats of their horses blended into a single mottled carpet. Here and there, standards carried aloft marked the different clans, thousands upon tens of thousands of seasoned warriors, the like of which the world had never seen. The dust of their passing rose up to cloak the sun. Their swords numbered more than the blades of grass over which they galloped. Their arrows rained down so thickly, they turned day to darkness.

His to command.

Chapter 28

THE ice-woman met Zevaron's gaze, unflinching. "Such a thing cannot be done overnight, you know. There must be preparations—*you* must be prepared. Even then, progress will be slow at first. You must gain mastery over one clan, then another, and so forth. The larger your following, the easier the conquests will become."

Zevaron narrowed his eyes. "What will you get out of it? Why would you do this for me?"

"Who else?" She looked up at him and he saw no guile in her expression. No deceit, but no other human feeling, either. That was just as well, for feelings could not be trusted, any more than memories could. They made a man weak, gullible.

"The steppe riders will not answer my call," she went on, "nor that of any other creature here. I could not take them from you even if I wished. They will be yours alone." She wet her pale lips with her tongue. "You need not take my word on such a short acquaintance. We have much to discuss, you and I. I say to you again, you have nothing to fear from me. I will tell you only the truth, and even a fool can see that I have no weapons to harm you." She smiled again. "You, on the other hand, can strike me down on a whim. You can change your mind, no matter what has gone before, if that is what you truly wish."

"I will go wherever I wish."

"I have no power to hold you. Or to compel you."

She had used the same word, *compel*, that she had applied to the subjugation of the Azkhantian riders.

"Have you anything to lose by learning more?" she asked. "And do you have anything to gain by leaving now?"

He waited so long that she lowered her outstretched hand with a sigh, perhaps of resignation. Mist began to invade the clear space. The way before him was closing. In moments, the pavilion and everything in it would be shrouded, lost to view. Lost, too, would be whatever this woman offered him. He had nothing to lose and everything to gain, and he could renege at any time. She did not lie.

I can give you whatever you desire.

Gelon in flames. Gelon in ruins. The Azkhantian horde at his back, trampling the bones of the oppressors into dust. *Rivers of blood. Pillars of flame. Oceans of ice.* The unmaking of the world and the birth of a new dominion.

Something shuddered within his breast. It might have been the heart that was no longer his.

She held out her hand, the hand that he could have sworn was empty. On her palm lay a pearl the size of a plum. The shifting lights ignited pastel rainbows on its surface. Patterns moved, so that he could see into the very heart of the pearl, to the mote of quiescent magic there. He knew, without any need for speech, that she meant him to swallow it. Was this poison or some magic-infused trick designed to ensnare him? His face hardened. He had been right to suspect her!

Her eyes were as guileless as before. "I would take this myself to prove that it holds no harm, but I am not made of the same mortal flesh as you."

Zevaron snatched the pearl from her. Its surface was smooth and warm. A fragrance rose up from it, like the smell of new snow or an icy stream cascading over rocks. "What does it do?"

"I cannot tell you its name, for there is no word for it in human speech. It contains a—glimpse, a taste—of the future, and it is for you alone."

"Will it show me things that might happen?"

"Or perhaps what you yourself will bring about, simply by accepting the vision."

He looked again at the pearl, tested its weight. If this woman, this emissary of Fire and Ice, meant to kill him, why had she not done so? He still believed she had spoken truly when she said she had no power to harm him.

Before he could change his mind, he slipped the pearl into his mouth. It softened and liquefied, passing almost instantly into the tissues of his throat. He swallowed reflexively, but it was already absorbed.

Before him, the mists eddied in the same rhythmic patterns as ever. But the woman and the dais were gone.

He felt himself sway, as if he were mounted on an unnaturally tall horse or perhaps one of the shaggy two-humped camels. This steed, however, was bigger and wider. He could not make out its exact form, only the suggestion of immense power, the stony hide and the stinging vapor of its breath. From behind came a rumbling sound, not from a single source but hundreds, tens of hundreds, dull and overlapping, so many that the ground must surely crack under their combined tread.

Ahead, the light grew steadier and he knew he had come to the end of the Kingdom of the Mists. He lifted one hand, gesturing for the army to halt. They would wait for his summons. He must go on alone. This first conquest, the hardest one, would be a test. The men who lived in these barren lands must obey *him*, follow *him*, not his monstrous army. Otherwise, they would fight out of fear instead of loyalty. And loyalty—the fanatic devotion that surpassed all other allegiances—was the only way to subdue the steppe warriors and bind them to his purpose.

As if his thoughts had the power to alter time and space, he found himself on foot, nearing the outskirts of an encampment. It was a poor sort of place, the herded beasts thin, the *jorts* in need of repair, the men with sunken cheeks and glassy eyes. Here on the farthest reaches of habitable land, these families scrabbled out a meager living under conditions even harsher than those the Snow Bear people endured.

Yes, he could see now how it would be: his approach, their consternation . . . then would come the challenge . . . the duel with the chieftain, too soon ended. It was a pity to waste the man's life, for he was the only one of the clan with any courage. Cold and near-starvation and seasons of fear had beaten the spirit of the others. Yet Zevaron had no choice but to kill him. Only the ruthlessness of his victory would give him the obedience he required.

He left the body in a pool of blood, already hardening on the bare, half-frozen earth. He hardly noticed the cries of those left behind as he led the surviving men and women south. They took all the horses capable of travel, having stripped the camp of its paltry stores of food. They would journey too fast to hunt or allow the animals to graze. Poor as they were, these horses would not last long, but their flesh would feed the riders. It would be enough, and then there would be another encampment, and another, with fresh horses and better food. And yet another conquest to swell the ranks of his army.

With each victory, he would sweep over the foolish resistance with greater ease. Before long, no clan would dare to stand against him.

The steppe was wide. Even though it was sparsely populated, by the time he reached the borders of Gelon, he would be a power such as the earth had never known. *Rivers of blood. Pillars of flame. Oceans of ice.*

And always, a vast expanse of mist and light, of bitter frost and unquenchable fire, would follow him, no longer fixed to the northern mountains but liberated by his will. In its wake would come an army of monstrous creatures, ready to do his bidding. The nag-riders were but the vanguard. Against the army of Fire and Ice, the army that answered to his will alone, nothing human could stand.

Nothing could stop him now.

Gelon will burn.

PART VI:

Shannivar's War

Chapter 29

SHANNIVAR watched Zevaron and Eriu approach the wall of light, etched like silhouettes against the churning brightness. Before she could draw another breath, they were gone. The wall reformed behind them as if they no longer existed. Currents of palest gray erased all traces of their passage.

Lights glistered on the mist-damp surfaces of the nearest rock formations, which looked like massive beasts struggling to pull themselves free of a frozen bog. She found herself watching them for any flicker of animation or shudder of breath. They seemed closer. Any moment now, she thought, a whip-lean skull would lift, turning toward her. Jaws would gape wide to reveal teeth like flint daggers.

Over the sudden hammering of her heart, Shannivar reminded herself that she was a warrior and daughter of a race of warriors, beloved of the Sky People. What had she to fear from rock and vapor? She would master the fear that seeped like ice wa-

ter along her veins. She would hold fast, no matter
what came.

My lifeline, he'd said. *My safe harbor.*

Nothing came, only the slow *drip-drip-drip* of
moisture and the ever-shifting ebb and surge of the
lights behind the wall. Wind lashed her cheeks. Her
throat ached, and her muscles felt brittle with cold.

She had let Zevaron go, given him over to Tabilit
or whatever god he looked to. The colorless light
had swallowed him up. She must wait, and she'd
had no idea it would be so difficult. Was that to be
her fate? Waiting. Watching. Sitting by the cookfire.
Tending her *jort.* Dying day by slow day. If she
could have summoned tears, she would have wept.
She drew in a shuddering breath. The cold seared
her lungs. Some noxious vapor had gotten into her
lungs, curling through her belly and sapping her resolve, putting cowardly thoughts into her mind.
What was the use of waiting? Try as she might,
Shannivar could not put the questions to rest. What
was the use of anything?

Zevaron had abandoned her. He'd never loved
her, never intended to return to her. She was alone
in a desolate, shattered place.

Radu came to stand at Shannivar's shoulder. The
mare blew out through frost-rimmed nostrils. Her
breath was warm against Shannivar's cheek. *Silly
two-legs, you're not alone. I'm here.* Faithful, gentle
Radu, who smelled of wind and snow and saddle
leather and healthy horse. Weather and life. Home.

Stroking the caramel-colored mane, Shannivar
murmured, "Poor Radu." The mare's plight roused

her, for Radu had never been bold and this journey had taxed her hard. She should never have asked so much of the aging horse. Radu needed food and rest, neither of which she would find here.

Yes, the mists sang to her, she should leave this place, give up her pointless vigil, retreat to the camp, slink off to the south . . .

Leave, reverberated in Shannivar's mind. *Leave now, before it's too late.*

She swung up on the dun mare's back, shifted her weight, and nudged Radu with one knee. She might as well have been riding a camel, for all the response she got. She squeezed her legs against Radu's sides, and still the mare refused to move. She touched Radu with her heels. This time, Radu hunched her back and flattened her ears. Shannivar frowned. Never before had Radu disobeyed her. Wringing her tail, every muscle radiating distress, the mare swung her head around. One ear flicked sideways.

Clearly, Radu sensed something that Shannivar did not. There must be a reason for this untoward stubbornness. Radu's breed were called Tabilit's Dancers. Did the goddess whisper in Radu's ears, words only a horse could understand?

As Shannivar spoke the name of the goddess in her mind, the sense of hopelessness lightened. She dismounted and stroked the mare's neck, the hide rough with winter coat. "I wish you could talk. Tell me what's going on."

Radu lifted her head, turning back to the wall of white. She pricked her ears as if she heard something beyond human senses.

There's more to come, Shannivar thought. The story, and her role in it, was not yet over. Or perhaps her own quest was about to begin in earnest.

Heartened anew, she waited while the wind grew stronger, tearing away the layer of warmth around the mare's body. She pulled the ear flaps of her felt cap tighter as the exposed skin of her cheeks and nose went numb with cold. She began pacing to keep the blood flowing through her legs. The mare's focus did not waver.

Without warning, a stain appeared on the glowing surface of the wall, a blemish that quickly grew larger. Currents of luminance clashed and surged around it.

Radu gave a sharp whinny. Her ears flattened against her neck and white rimmed her eyes.

Something moved in the splotch of darkness. Something was emerging. *Zevaron?*

Shannivar took a step toward the wall. The air sizzled as if rent by invisible lightning. She tasted burnt metal and blood.

Then the shadow parted and a horse galloped through it, wearing neither saddle nor bridle. At first sight, it seemed more ice-demon than flesh. Vapors like exhalations of storm-whipped snow whirled about its form. Head down, knees about to buckle, the horse came to a shivering halt. Steam rose from the bare back, where the spine stood out like a string of beads and the hip bones jutted sharply.

Shannivar hardly recognized Eriu, he was so altered. This was not the sleek, powerful steed she knew so well. His body was no longer jet-dark, but frost white, even his hooves. Ice crusted his flaring nostrils. Blood streamed from eyes opaque as whitened marbles. Blind eyes.

He lifted his head, swinging his muzzle back and forth, gulping air, searching—

"Eriu!" The cry came from her heart.

The horse's inwardly curved ears swiveled forward. He nickered and stumbled toward her. Choking back a sob, she threw her arms around his neck. He halted, trembling hard.

They had ridden into the wall of light only a few hours ago. What, in all the living earth or under the endless sky, had happened to him? She drew back, gazing with pity and horror at the blood dripping from Eriu's maimed eyes and the dead-white hide. She wanted to wail aloud. She could not imagine what might have wrought such devastation on so strong a horse, nor did she want to.

Sweet Mother! Where was Zevaron? Dead? Or altered almost beyond recognition, even as Eriu was? Heart-sick, Shannivar buried her face in the frost-bleached mane. This was her fault. Eriu had served her in love and loyalty, had borne Zevaron into the unknown terrors of the wall because she had asked it of him. How could she have let this happen to an innocent creature who trusted her?

And Zevaron—was he still alive? Or was his death, too, her failing?

Eriu was calmer now, comforted by her closeness, her touch, her familiar scent. His trembling had almost ceased. Radu sidled closer, resting her chin on his rump so that they stood head-to-tail as they had so many times in pasture. Eriu leaned into her strength, or perhaps they each sustained the other. She would be his eyes, and he her courage.

And I—I will be the strong arm that draws the bow. I will be the keen eye that sends the arrow to its target. I will be the hunter that brings down the deer. Zevaron might be lost, vanquished, lulled by the same mists, overcome by the same unnatural evil that had smashed the very bones of Tabilit's living earth and mutilated Eriu. But she, Shannivar, she would not falter, she who had brought him this far. She would find him, rescue him if need be, and defend him against whatever demons he had encountered. She stepped away from the two horses.

She did not plan her next move, for she dared not give shape to hesitation or doubt. The horses would wait for a time, until hunger drove them to seek forage; if she did not return, their instincts would lead them back to the other horses at the campsite.

Before her courage wavered, she hurried toward the wall of shifting light. The whirlpools of brightness sickened her. Although each step was harder than the one before, she pushed herself into a run. She dared not hesitate.

She slipped on an icy patch and scrambled on loose gravel but kept going. The shock of each stride rattled her skull. The air turned to scorching ice in her lungs. It fought her, pushing back. Something clenched her throat. She tasted bile, a poison-bitter sickness. Her heart stuttered. Sobbing with frustration, she struggled for each breath, but she kept on.

Run!

The wall of light loomed ahead, larger than it had previously appeared. Perhaps a visual trick or magical guarding spell made it seem so. Ribbons of shadow raced across its surface, changing intensity with riotous speed, from the reflective brilliance of sun on snow, through shades of silver and pewter, to utter transparency. Between one gasping breath and the next, she glimpsed shadows moving within, hints of figures that could not be human.

Run!

The rocky ground was no longer as smooth as it had looked from a distance. She tripped and came down hard on her hands and knees. Her teeth snapped together from the impact. Her vision went gray. Her palms stung where the jagged rock bit deep. She gathered her feet under her, managed to stand up, and found she could not move. She pushed hard, straining her leg muscles. Something huge and dense pressed down on her. Struggle as she might, she could not advance even a tiny distance.

She turned her body, settled into a wrestler's stance, and inched one foot toward the wall of light. Her boot glided over the rough rock until it reached the farthest point of her advance. There it stopped, as if glued to the ground. She drew back and aimed a kick with all her power. Her foot shot through empty air. She staggered and then recovered. Pivoting, she lashed out with the other foot. This time, she was thrown back as if by an immense, invisible hand. Even though she wore thick boots, her feet stung where they had collided with the barrier. She tried a few more times with no greater success. Finally she gave up trying to batter her way through, lest she break the bones in her feet.

Cursing aloud to keep from weeping, she twisted this way and that. Advancing slowly made no difference. She could move backward or sideways, but not forward. Unwilling to admit defeat, she summoned the strength for yet another sally and another, only to fail each time. With each effort, her energy waned. Her muscles felt thick and sluggish, and her heart labored. Each breath became more difficult.

She glared at the wall as if it were a personal adversary. Brightness mocked her. A thought took shape in her mind. This glowing barrier was more than an inanimate structure, a trick of shiny minerals. Not only was it a thing of incomprehensible magic, but it was alive and aware. Whatever lay beyond it had taken—*chosen?*—Zevaron.

Eriu had not escaped. He had been expelled, thrown out. And neither she nor any other human would be permitted entry.

Raised to be a warrior of her people, and with abiding faith in Tabilit's mercy, Shannivar had never feared her own death. Everything that she valued had come to her through change, and through change she would one day lose everything. All except honor.

She would not give up. She would find a way through the wall of light or around it, although she did not know how. She had been training for this quest her entire life, and she would not turn back now. Wordlessly, she cried out to Tabilit, to Onjhol, to the sky hidden behind the blanketing mists. A sound like keening, yet so raw it hardly seemed human, filled her ears. Cradling herself, she rocked to its rhythm. It caught her up in savage jaws, blanketed out all other sensation. She let it take her, engulf her, drench her.

Something was carrying her, moving her through space or perhaps time. The pain from her fall had vanished, and she no longer felt the cold. She lifted her head, blinking to clear her vision. The mist still surrounded her, but the ground underfoot was not the rough, fractured rock but soft and fertile earth.

Am I dead?

Shannivar clambered to her feet. Her body felt whole and well, her legs steady beneath her. The horses had vanished, along with the barrier of light. She was alone.

Or was she? The skin along her spine tingled, alerting her to another presence, though she felt no sense of menace, the way she did from the disquieting currents of brightness and shadow. This mist felt cool and gentle on her skin, yet charged with energy. It thinned, or perhaps some other power sharpened her vision, for she could now see for some distance in every direction. As if from afar, she spied a horse and rider moving in a stately manner toward her. At first, they were only a wavering apparition. Then details came into focus: the horse's shining hide, its proud arched neck and flowing tail, the inwardly curving ears that marked the Azkhantian breed.

The rider was a woman, sitting tall on the horse's bare back, guiding her mount without bit or rein. In one hand she held a bow that glittered with an iridescent sheen, and in the other hand, an arrowcase. For an instant, Shannivar thought she might be Grandmother or even Mirrimal. But Grandmother had never been as majestic as the rider now approaching.

A hush like dawn stilled Shannivar's heart. A feeling swept over her—awe perhaps, or something she had no words for. She could make out every shimmering strand of the horse's mane, every line of cannon and fetlock, the sloping shoulders, deep chest, fluid gait. Never had she seen such a perfect horse. The beast regarded her with calm, intelligent eyes as it came to a halt. The warmth of its breath flowed into her, sending new vigor through her blood. Heartened, she dared to raise her eyes to the rider.

The woman wavered in Shannivar's sight, as if she were many women at once. A tribe of women, a nation of women, they were as strong and enduring as the sky, as the steppe itself. Behind them and through them, Shannivar sensed generations of men as well. She wondered how any one being could contain such a multitude. Or perhaps, there was something of Tabilit in every person. And then she knew.

"Mother of Horses." Shannivar would have prostrated herself, except that some instinct held her

upright. Though only human, she, too, was a woman, and one woman did not kneel to another.

Tabilit's eyes were golden, her smile as warm as the summer sun. Her long-skirted riding jacket bore the emblem of the Tree of Life. The design shifted, the leaves unfurling, coloring, falling, budding with the seasons. Birds nestled in its branches and beasts sheltered at its roots. When Tabilit spoke, spring rains laughed in her voice. "You are not dead, my daughter. Nor am I a dream, although I often come to my people in that way. As you have guessed, this is not my true form, but it is the only one that you may look upon."

The horse pawed the ground uneasily, and Tabilit's smile faded. "We have but a little time. You must act quickly, before the way closes."

"What must I do to free Zevaron from the clutches of Olash-giyn-Olash?"

"Listen well, Daughter of the Golden Eagle!" Tabilit sounded impatient now. The silver horse shifted beneath her, neck arched, hooves dancing over the earth. "A storm is coming, such as my people have never before encountered. Unchecked, it will sweep all before it, leaving only ashes in its wake. Alone, my people cannot stand against it.

"The outlander has his own destiny. You have yours. I have chosen you as my champion." Tabilit guided the horse forward. She held out the bow and arrow-case.

Shannivar stared at the weapons, uncomprehending. She had dreamed of glory, but only as a girl dreams. In truth, she was flesh, not legend. How could she, even armed with Tabilit's own bow, stand against a power mighty enough to smash mountains, to turn animals against their nature, to unmake the very fabric of the world?

"Take them! Take them now or all is lost!" Tabilit urged.

Shannivar reached out. The bow was smooth and supple, almost alive, the arrow-case perfectly balanced.

She thought, *I will wait for Zevaron, and together we will stand against the ancient foe, he with his Meklavaran magic and me with Tabilit's gifts.*

"Still you fail to understand, human child," Tabilit said. "This man—it is *he* who will lead the Shadow of Shadows, *he* who will enslave my people and turn them into instruments of destruction, *he* whom you must defeat."

Shannivar shook her head in wordless denial. It was not possible!

"I know what is in his heart," Tabilit went on. "He thinks to master the primal forces of chaos, to harness them to bring down his enemy. He thinks the magic of his ancestors will protect him. But no man, living now or in ages past, can turn such evil into an instrument of good. Instead, it will use his own strength to rule him—his valor, his love of justice, his desire to avenge those he loved."

Tabilit's voice rang out like an iron bell, like a thousand thousand mourners wailing. "One by one, the horse clans will fall under his control. Like a swarm of locusts, they will sweep across the steppe, consuming every living thing in their path. Stone-drakes and ice trolls and creatures even more ter- rible, things without a name, will crush anyone who resists. He will drive toward Gelon and set it all afire. By that time, the man you love will be utterly devoured. The annihilation of Gelon and the ruin of its cities will not satisfy his lust for vengeance or ease his pain. Empty of everything but hatred, he will destroy men, beasts, fields, rivers, even the free wide ocean, until land and water lie in utter ruin."

"What—What must I do?"

"You, my daughter, must rally the clans. Do not let them fall under the Shadow of Shadows. Strengthen them and give them the will to fight! They must hold fast!"

"But how—"

"You will know what to do."

Shannivar opened her mouth to protest, but no breath came. She had thought her worst fears had already come to pass—Zevaron lost to her, trapped behind the barrier of poisoned light. She could ac- cept that he might never return. That he might al- ready be dead. It had never occurred to her that he might be enslaved by the ancient enemy of his own people.

Tabilit's form began to dim, as if blown away. "Now ride, ride with my blessing!"

Chapter 30

"DON'T go!" Shannivar cried.

But the mist was already lifting, vanishing like dew in sunlight, and with it, the fading lineaments of Tabilit's shape. A chill bit into the air, as if the warmth of a moment ago had been but a pause in a winter gale. The earth hardened once more into rough stone. In a moment, Shannivar thought, she would be able to make out the barrier of light.

The bow in her hands hummed. She ran her fingers over the smooth, almost opalescent wood. Her chest ached, as if her heart had bruised itself against the inside of her ribs. She had been offered all the glory she could dream of, a quest worthy of Saramark herself, but at a price she had not expected. If she had known, would she have chosen a life of placid insignificance? That option had never been hers. She would take up the bow as Tabilit bade her, would string it, set an arrow to it, test it. As she herself would soon be tested. *I am an arrow in Tabilit's bow.*

What then was Zevaron?

All her life, she had believed that people made their own destinies. She could not believe that any adversary, no matter how powerful, could alter a person's essential nature. No matter what Tabilit said, Shannivar could not bring herself to accept that Zevaron would become a pawn of evil. She had seen the banners flying high above the ancient battlefield, had felt Zevaron's resolve as steadfast as his ancestor's. Once, Khored had used the shield of many crystals to defeat an enemy composed of chaos itself, Fire and Ice, Shadow of Shadows. Zevaron would do no less. She was sure of it.

She would use the bow, she would defend the steppe, she would hold fast. But she would not surrender Zevaron to such a fate, to become a mindless servant of evil.

The wall of shifting light hid a power mightier than any human opponent. It had turned reindeer into cannibals, given life to the stone-drake, terrified the *ildu'amar*, and reached into the heavens to bring the white star crashing down. It might seize Zevaron and try to break his will, coerce him into obedience. If what lay beyond the barrier held him captive, then she would find him and free him. But she would never believe that he had willingly given himself to it.

Despite the plummeting temperature, Shannivar felt new energy fill her like a rush of flame. Her doubts melted, leaving her mind clear and her pulse steady.

A horse whinnied somewhere in the distance.

She turned away from the wall of light. A short walk took her back to where she had left the horses. Radu whickered and swished her tail as Shannivar drew near. And Eriu—

The frost had fallen away from him, leaving only a trace on his lower legs, mane, and tail. His body was once more glossy black. He lifted his head, ears alert, as she came to stand beside him. And his eyes were dark and clear.

With a stamp and a squeal, Eriu arched his neck and swerved away. Not in fear, not shying away from her, but in the sheer joy of his own renewed power. He was still thin, but now charged with vitality. He was once again a warrior's steed, to carry her into battle, even a battle neither of them could yet imagine.

Shannivar held out one hand, and he came to her. Her heart lifted. He was her wings, her song. Together they would do such deeds that would never be forgotten.

On the Azkhantian steppe, the Moon of Wolves had given birth to the Moon of Melting Snow. Shannivar daughter of Ardellis rode through the newly sprouted feathergrass, still barely a hint of green in the half-frozen mud.

This time, she did not laugh.

This time, she rode to war.

New novels of DARKOVER®
by Marion Zimmer Bradley & Deborah J. Ross

"[*The Alton Gift*] is a must for fans of the series, and reads as if Deborah has been channeling Marion's spirit."
—*Center City Weekly Press*

The Clingfire Trilogy

"Ross has fleshed out Bradley's encyclopedic vision of the Darkovian Dark Ages..."
—*Publishers Weekly* for *The Fall of Neskaya*

To Order Call: 1-800-788-6262
www.dawbooks.com

DARKOVER®

Marion Zimmer Bradley's Classic Series

Now Collected in New Omnibus Editions!

Heritage and Exile   978-0-7564-0065-1
The Heritage of Hastur & Sharra's Exile

The Ages of Chaos   978-0-7564-0072-9
Stormqueen! & Hawkmistress!

Saga of the Renunciates   978-0-7564-0092-9
The Shattered Chain, Thendara House
& City of Sorcery

The Forbidden Circle   978-0-7564-0094-1
The Spell Sword & The Forbidden Tower

A World Divided   978-0-7564-0167-2
The Bloody Sun, The Winds of Darkover
& Star of Danger

Darkover: First Contact   978-0-7564-0224-2
Darkover Landfall & Two to Conquer

To Save a World   978-0-7564-0250-1
The World Wreckers & The Planet Savers

To Order Call: 1-800-788-6262
www.dawbooks.com

Kari Sperring

Living with Ghosts

978-0-7564-0675-2

Finalist for the Crawford Award for First Novel

A Tiptree Award Honor Book

Locus Recommended First Novel

"This is an enthralling fantasy that contains horror elements interwoven into the story line. This reviewer predicts Kari Sperring will have quite a future as a renowned fantasist."
—*Midwest Book Review*

"A satisfying blend of well-developed characters and intriguing worldbuilding. The richly realized Renaissance style city is a perfect backdrop for the blend of ghostly magic and intrigue. The characters are wonderfully flawed, complex and multi-dimensional. Highly recommended!"
—*Patricia Bray, author of The Sword of Change Trilogy*

And now available:

The Grass King's Concubine

978-0-7564-0755-1

To Order Call: 1-800-788-6262
www.dawbooks.com

DAW 206

Sherwood Smith
Inda

"A powerful beginning to a very promising series by a writer who is making her bid to be a major fantasist. By the time I finished, I was so captured by this book that it lingered for days afterward. I had lived inside these characters, inside this world, and I was unwilling to let go of it. That, I think, is the mark of a major work of fiction…you owe it to yourself to read *Inda*." —Orson Scott Card

INDA
978-0-7564-0422-2

THE FOX
978-0-7564-0483-3

KING'S SHIELD
978-0-7564-0500-7

TREASON'S SHORE
978-0-7564-0634-9

To Order Call: 1-800-788-6262
www.dawbooks.com

DAW 110